SANTA'S SUBPOENA

REBECCA ZANETTI

RAZ INK LLC

Copyright © 2021 by Rebecca Zanetti

All rights reserved.

No part of this book may be reproduced in any form or by any electronic or
mechanical means, including information storage and retrieval systems, without
written permission from the author, except for the use of brief quotations in a
book review.

This is a work of **fiction**. Names, **characters**, places and incidents either are
products of the author's imagination or are used fictitiously. Any resemblance to
actual events or locales or persons, living or dead, is entirely coincidental.

❀ Created with Vellum

This one is for Chelli Younker, my very good friend and the person I'd see actually crashing through a kitchen window and rolling up to fight if a friend needed help.

ACKNOWLEDGMENTS

Thank you to everyone who helped to make this book a reality!

Thank you to Tony, Gabe, and Karlina for being a wonderful family;

Thank you to FB Rebels Laurie Rich, Dali Tza, Elizabeth Lynn, Jan Fore, and Cindy Wosch for their help in figuring out the right Christmas presents for this book;

Thank you to Craig Zanetti, Esq. for the help with criminal law and procedure. Any mistakes about the law are mine and mine alone;

Thank you to Asha Hossain of Asha Hossain Designs, LLC for the fantastic cover;

Thank you to Debra Stewart of Dragonfly Media Ink for the wonderful edits;

Thank you to Liz Berry, Jillian Stein, Asa Maria Bradley, and Boone Brux for the advice with the concepts for this new series;

Thank you to my incredibly hard working agent, Caitlin Blasdell;

Thank you to Sara and Gwen from Fresh Fiction, and Cissy and crew from WriterSpace for helping get the word out about this new series;

Thank you to my fantastic assistant, Anissa Beatty, for all of the excellent work and for being such a great leader for Rebecca's Rebels (my FB street team);

Thank you to Rebels Heather Frost, Kimberly Frost, Karen Clementi, and Karen Fisher for being proof-reading angels;

Thank you to my constant support system: Gail and Jim English, Kathy and Herbie Zanetti, Debbie and Travis Smith, Stephanie and Don West, and Jessica and Jonah Namson.

CHAPTER 1

*S*anta looked like he'd been dragged behind a truck.

The last situation I thought I'd find in my law office on a Thursday morning was a dejected and bloody Santa Claus flanked by two snow-covered senior citizens. Gripping my hot latte, I quickly shut the door before anybody else arrived at my firm.

Thelma, sitting to the left of Santa, turned and stared at me, her cloudy blue eyes wide and panicked. "Anna. Thank goodness you're here."

That was a matter of opinion. Squaring my shoulders, I strode around my desk, dropped my laptop bag on the floor, slid the latte onto my ceramic coaster, and shrugged out of my new long black winter coat. Then I smoothed down my green skirt and sat, shifting my legs so my black boots with the chunky heels rested near the laptop bag. I tried to exude some sense of control while gauging what kind of a threat *Bloody Santa* might pose.

Snow still covered Thelma's white hair and bright blue scarf, which somehow went well with her lime green snow jacket. Santa wore his usual outfit along with blood and dirt, which added a

1

terrifying element. Next to him sat Georgiana Lambertini, Thelma's housemate and whom I hoped would be the most logical of the three.

I'd met both women during a legal case earlier that summer, and besides their accidentally drugging me once, I liked them. They loved me.

Georgiana smiled, making all of her wrinkles jiggle on her broad face. In her bright yellow knitted hat she appeared cheerful, while a wide black coat covered her expansive bulk. "You look so pretty today."

"Thank you," I said, waiting for the next sentence that hopefully would explain this situation. Although, the suit did fit me well. With my curly brown hair, plain grayish-green eyes, and average height, it was like I hadn't inherited any genes from either the Italian or Irish sides of my family. I dressed in a lot of jewel colors, in other words. "What's going on?" I asked.

"We need help, Anna," Georgiana said.

"Right." I looked at Santa. He had to be in his early sixties. His red coat was ripped and bruises covered his left cheekbone. The fluffy white parts of his outfit were dirty, and his hat flopped sadly to the side, covered in gravel and what hopefully was slushy mud. His eyes were blue, his beard stark white and real, and his belly round. "How did you all get into my office?" I asked.

We'd opened the Bunne & Albertini Law Office only a couple months previous, and my partner, Clark Bunne, thought I might bring too much trouble to his life. It was true. But who didn't need a little bit of trouble? Besides, things had been fairly calm all autumn. There was no way he had let in the trio without at least texting me first. "Georgiana?" I prodded.

She blushed. "I've been practicing breaking locks, and the ones on this building aren't real strong." She leaned toward me, her brown eyes refracting light in the way only those who've had cataract surgery can manage. "You really do need a better security system, Anna."

"Apparently," I agreed, my gaze drawn to the blood on Santa's belly, fighting to stay calm when I couldn't quite figure out the scale of danger here. "What happened?"

He sighed and drew a wicked and bloody knife from a hidden pocket in his red coat to slap on my desk. The handle was thick wood, the blade serrated, and the blood dripped onto my desk. "Lawrence is dead."

This stopped being amusing.

The skin prickled between my shoulder blades. I kept my expression neutral and my voice calm. "Georgiana? Please take Thelma into the bigger conference room so I can speak with Santa." My brain reeled. "In fact, I'm starving. Do you two mind heading down to Smiley's Diner and getting us a table? Order me the special if I'm a little late." I had to get them out of there and away from that weapon.

Thelma rolled her eyes. "Bernie didn't kill Lawrence, for goodness' sake. That's why we're here."

I eyed the bloody knife on my desk. The blood was crusty but still a little mushy toward the tip. Sliding back, I angled my chair slightly toward my laptop bag in case I needed to grab the gun I kept with me at all times. I wasn't sure I could shoot Santa, but I could probably scare him into sitting still while the ladies made an escape. "All right." I pierced dejected Santa with a glare. "Who are you?"

He hitched up his belly, but his chest remained sunken. "I'm Bernie McLintock. You know? Like the movie?"

This guy was no John Wayne. "Sure. Bernie? You have two seconds to tell me why you have a bloody knife in my office before I call the police." I didn't like that he sat between the two women. If I went at him, it'd have to be over my desk and straight on, and I couldn't guarantee to protect the ladies.

"I don't know what happened," Bernie said, his eyes filling with tears and his nose turning red. "After working the crowds all day, a bunch of us Santas usually meet up at the Clumsy Penguin over on Lilac Lake? We have a back room where we play poker, and that's what we did all last night. The pot lasted until six this morning, which is pretty good for a bunch of old dudes."

There was a private poker room in the Clumsy Penguin? Why didn't I know that? "What then?" I asked.

Bernie put his hands on his belly, which rounded out the torn red coat perfectly. "Well, I was on a winning streak, and most of the guys filtered out, leaving only me and Lawrence. He won the last pot, so I had to clean up. I did so, walked outside, and found his body on the steps with this knife sticking out of his back. He was still wearing his new Santa uniform, too. It was handmade with real fur. I mean, like real fur. So beautiful."

I gulped down bile. "How do you know he was dead?"

"I was in the service, missy," Bernie snapped. "I yanked out the knife, turned him over, and tried to save his life. It was too late. He was gone."

"Why keep the knife?" My gaze strayed to it once again.

Bernie shrugged. "At first, I wasn't sure if the murderer was still around. Then, well, my fingerprints were on it, and well, you know."

I didn't. Not really. "Bernie," I said evenly, "why didn't you call the police?"

A slight crimson finally wound through the too pale skin on his weathered face. "Well, I might've threatened to kill Lawrence a week or so ago. Loudly and in front of friends."

"Of course you did," I murmured. "Why?"

Bernie shrugged. "Just a simple difference of opinion about how a Santa should act. It was nothing, really. A movie is going to be filmed in town next week, and it's a horror flick with Santa as a crazed lunatic, and Lawrence was actually going to play Santa! What a betrayal. Plus, the holidays are stressful and we both took it out on each other. That's all there is to say about it."

Right. I'd have to delve into that more. "Who is Lawrence? I take it he's another Santa?"

Bernie gulped. "Yeah. We've known each other our whole lives, both having grown up in Bourn. He's a year older than me, and we've worked as Santas during our retirement years." He wiped tears from his weathered cheeks. "Even before that, really. We like to give back to the surrounding communities, and it's a good way to make extra income."

I'd learned early on that clients rarely gave the whole story, and considering the two ladies were flanking him protectively, he wasn't going to say anything that would put them off. I studied his ruddy complexion, noting again the bluish tinges on his left cheekbone. Fresh ones. "What about the bruises on your face?" I asked.

Bernie groaned. "We might've gotten into it a little last night, but it was before we played poker, and then it was done."

That wasn't good. "Tell me what was said," I suggested.

He scratched his bearded jaw. "I don't remember. We'd already been drinking, and he made a crack about my suit looking old, and I went back at him regarding the movie. Then he said that my 'ho-ho-ho' was tinny." Bernie's eyes widened. "Can you believe that? I have a great Santa chuckle, and he went right for the soul with that insult. So I hit him."

"How many times?" This wasn't looking good for Bernie, but that blood was drying, and I had to get things moving along.

"Once," Bernie said. "Lawrence wrestled in his youth, so he punched me back and then took us both to the floor."

I tried really hard not to wince. "So your DNA is all over him?" When Bernie nodded, I considered what else the police would ask. "How many people saw this fight?"

"About three," Bernie said. "Our friend Doc Springfield pulled us apart, and then we stood up, knocked back another shot of Jack, and decided to play poker. It wasn't as big of a deal as it sounds. Well, except for the DNA and I guess my finding the body. Poor Lawrence. He didn't deserve to die like that."

The man seemed a little scattered, but that made sense since he'd found a body just an hour before. I paused. "Where have you been for the last hour?"

"I sat there for a while, just kind of in shock. Then I got cold and called my friends." He reached out and took Thelma's hand. "I remembered that they were in trouble last summer and found a hotshot lawyer to get them out of it, so I figured they'd lead me to you. I couldn't remember your name. I'm sorry."

I looked at the women. "Did either of you touch the knife or body?"

They both shook their heads. So I tugged out three notepads from my bottom drawer and pens, sliding them across the desk. "All three of you need to write down exactly what happened, and Bernie, I need names and phone numbers for any witnesses."

They all dutifully filled out their notes, Thelma humming Christmas songs quietly as she did so.

"Did either of you know Lawrence?" I asked them.

"Not really," Thelma said. "We saw him at a couple of events, but he usually had a chick with him already."

Okay. That was as good as it was going to get for the morning. I took a deep breath and looked at all three of them. "All right. We need to call the police now."

Thelma's eyes widened. "Are you sure?"

"Yes, I'm sure." When nobody disagreed, I picked up my cell phone and dialed a number I knew well.

"I'm in the middle of something right now, Anna," Detective Pierce said curtly, the sound of moving bodies around him. "I can't talk but will give you a call later if you like. I'm sure it's life or death, like usual." He didn't sound like he was kidding.

I sighed. "Could your current business have something to do with a dead Santa stabbed in the back?"

Pierce knew when to draw out a moment, and he did so, no doubt trying to rein in his inherent crankiness. "Do I want to know how you've come by that information?"

"Yeah. I have the murder weapon on my desk," I said, focusing on the knife. "Want to talk to me now?"

CHAPTER 2

I managed to harangue my clients to the police department with the knife safely encased in a Ziplock bag in my laptop satchel. We were ushered to the larger interrogation room and all sat, with Bernie and Georgiana accepting mugs of coffee from a fresh-faced uniformed officer. She had to be in her early twenties but seemed younger.

We waited with the door closed. I put the knife on the table, and the blood had mushed against the inside of the plastic.

Finally, Detective Pierce opened the door and stopped short upon catching sight of Thelma and Georgiana. He sighed.

Oops. I'd forgotten Thelma had propositioned him late summer during a case.

She fluttered her thick mascara-laden eyelashes. "Why, Detective Pierce. How lovely to see your hotness again."

Pierce forced a smile. In either his late thirties or early forties, the detective had darker blond hair, stunning green eyes, and a swimmer's physique. He also lacked any semblance of an appreciation for the ridiculous. He surveyed the room. "Everyone move away from the knife."

Nobody moved.

His nostrils flared, and he walked to take the remaining chair across from us. Then he gingerly drew the bag toward him and out of our reach. "Were your rights read to you?"

"Yes," I said as he pulled a phone from his back pocket to place on the table to record the interview. "The rights were read and we're here voluntarily to help you solve this crime."

Thelma leaned toward him, her eyes sparkling. "I'm here voluntarily in any way you want." Georgiana shoved an elbow into her ribs, and Thelma sucked in air, sitting back. "Not nice," she muttered.

Bernie sighed, looking even more forlorn and sad under the buzzing fluorescent lights. While the entrance to the police station had been decorated for the holidays, the interrogation room, understandably, had not. "This sucks."

The door opened again and the young officer poked her head in. "Now?" Her blonde hair was back in a ponytail, and although she was new, she had an air about her that promised competence.

"Yeah," Pierce said, his gaze on me.

The officer smiled. "Ladies, would you please come with me? I'll get you settled in another room, and Detective Pierce will speak to you in a little while."

Bernie reached for Georgiana's hand, looking lost and scared. "They can stay."

"No, they can't," Pierce said. "Go, ladies. We won't be too long."

I nodded at the women, and they slowly stood, Georgiana releasing Bernie's hand. It figured Pierce would want to speak to them alone to make sure all the stories matched, and since I represented all of them, I'd be present. When the door closed behind them, Pierce sat back and looked at Bernie. "Start at the beginning."

Bernie looked sideways at me.

I nodded. "We're on the record as being here voluntarily, so just tell the detective what happened."

Bernie scrubbed both gnarled hands down his face and shuddered, telling Pierce the same series of events that he'd told me.

Pierce watched him without expression, but his eyes held more than a hint of intimidation. "Why did you threaten to kill the deceased last week?"

Ah, crap. Pierce was already hot on Bernie's case.

Bernie swallowed, his white beard moving against his collar. "It's like this. There are only a few of us authentic Santas left who do this with purity, and Lawrence was one of those guys, as am I. I heard that he was going to be in that movie they're filming in town, and he wasn't going to charge anything. He just wanted the glory. That's the opposite of what we do, man. The Kringle Club is better than that."

Pierce lifted one dark blond eyebrow and pulled a notebook from his jacket pocket. "The Kringle Club?"

"Yeah." Bernie sighed. "We formed an LLC about twenty years ago, which made it so we didn't need to compete for the good jobs around here, Silverville, and Spokane. The businesses contract with the LLC, and all money goes into the account. We work the same amount of hours, so it doesn't matter where, and then we split the kitty at the end of the season."

Why hadn't Bernie told me that? I had to work on my questioning skills.

"Huh." Pierce opened his notebook and a shiny silver pen rolled out. He caught it and tapped on the paper. "Give me the names for the members of the Kringle Club."

Bernie scratched his jaw beneath the white beard. "We had ten of us when we first created the group, and now we're down to five who have survived the last few years. Well, I guess four now." His gaze turned far away for a moment. "Who knew that getting old would be the goal?" He named five men, including Lawrence. I recognized two of them; Donald McLerrison, who was a farmer outside of town, and Rodney Springfield, who was a doctor that had patched me up more than once. Springfield really did look like Santa. The final man, Jocko Terezzi, was new to me. I'd have to look him up.

"Do any of these men have a reason to kill Lawrence besides the fact that he was going to work for free and not make money for your group?" Pierce asked.

Bernie shook his head. "No."

I sat back. "As a motive, that's weak, Pierce. Come on."

Pierce lifted his green gaze to me. "Agreed." Then he focused back on Bernie. "How about we discuss the fact that Lawrence has been sleeping with your ex-wife and took his portion of this year's kitty and bought her an engagement ring?"

A boulder dropped into my stomach, and I partially turned to look at Bernie, whose ears had started to turn red. I'd never understood why clients hid material facts from their own lawyers. He'd obviously wanted to keep that fact from Thelma and Georgiana, but I needed all of the facts to keep his butt out of jail. "Detective Pierce? I'd like a moment with my client."

Pierce snorted. "Yeah. You take one. I have Florence, Bernie's ex-wife and Lawrence's current fiancée in the other room right now, and I have no doubt she'll have plenty to say." He snatched the phone and knife off the table and stood, heading for the door. "I'll log this into evidence so we can get prints and DNA off it. Let's hope we find more than your client's on here or on the body." He opened the door and slipped gracefully through.

Bernie turned toward me. "I guess I should've mentioned that, huh?"

* * *

I WALKED OUTSIDE WITH BERNIE, the snow falling gently down to add to the foot already accumulated on the flowers around the justice building. Flashbulbs instantly went off, blinding us.

"Did you kill Santa?" Jolene O'Sullivan asked, stepping closer to Bernie.

I shoved my body between the two of them as her photographer, a medium-sized guy with a goatee that belonged in the nineties, kept snapping pictures. "We have no comment right now."

Jolene smiled her catlike grin. "Come on. Doesn't Santa want to defend himself?"

Why was Bernie still in the darn Santa suit? I should've had him change into anything else before we walked outside, but I hadn't thought the press would have the story so quickly. "Come on, Jolene," I muttered, not wanting to deal with the *Timber City Gazette* yet. Well, ever.

She angled her blonde head around me. "Santa? You want to get the truth on the record, don't you? What if all the kids think Santa is a murderer?"

Irritation prickled my Irish-Italian temper. Jolene had been a witch in high school who'd dated the guy I was currently dating, had slept with my sister's date on prom night, and more recently had tried to make my life even more difficult than it already was—and it looked like she wasn't stopping in her efforts now. "Like I said, no comment."

I grasped Bernie's arm and tugged him to Thelma's older Buick, where the ladies were already waiting. "Go home and don't talk to the press." I opened the back door and all but shoved him in. Then I marched back to Jolene. "Watch yourself. Libel is a good area of practice these days."

She smiled, her blue eyes glittering. "How's Aiden? Does he miss me?"

I wasn't sure how Aiden was doing right now, considering he was undercover somewhere outside of Idaho. "Nobody ever misses you," I retorted.

She tucked her notebook in a black Coach bag. "Don't tell me he's already gotten bored with you? It was bound to happen. That's not a man who'll settle down. Ever." She leaned in, the shade of her lipstick a little too red for her skin tone. "Have fun with him while you can, but when he's out the door, don't pine. It's not a good look on you."

I calculated the battery charge I'd get if I punched her in the nose and then decided it wasn't worth the hassle. "Have fun chasing ambulances today, Jolene." With that, I turned and walked toward the courthouse, not having time to return to my office before my morning hearings.

During the misdemeanor hearings, I managed to settle three cases and set five for trial, my mind on Jolene's words the entire time. There might be some truth to the fact that Aiden wouldn't settle down, but I wasn't sure I was ready for that, either. It was difficult building a relationship when one party was out of town so much pretending to be somebody else.

I finished the hearings and walked out into a frigidly cold day, tucking my hands in my wool coat before reaching my car. The ride back to my office was quick, and my stomach was growling by the time I walked inside to see Oliver Duck behind the reception desk. Oliver was around eighteen with short reddish hair and a wide smile. He did a great job with the scheduling and filing, and I wasn't sure what we'd do without him. He was also getting pretty good at tracking down information. "Howdy. Tell me that somebody ordered lunch."

He rolled his eyes. "Pauley ordered lunch."

I sighed and my chin dropped to my snowy coat collar. Pauley was my cousin, and I adored him, but he'd been on a kick lately to try different types of food. I should be ecstatic about this because Pauley was autistic and usually mired in routine, but lately, my stomach had been unhappy on more than one occasion. "What did he order?"

Oliver winced. "It looked green?"

Ugh. I took off my coat and gloves, wandering through the doorway to the hub of the office. Clark's office was right in front of me, and I turned since mine was at the very back. On the way, I passed vacant offices and then the conference room, where Pauley had already set out lunch.

He looked up, his brown eyes focused, his hair perfectly in place. "I purchased lunch." He rocked back and forth. "Not true. Not true. Not true." His fingers tapped on the table in a familiar three, two, three rhythm. "You purchased lunch. I ordered lunch with the firm's credit card. You bought lunch. Thank you."

I looked at the offerings, forcing a smile into place as I sat. "What do we have here?" Did I still have antacids in my desk? If not, I'd need to replenish my stock if this continued any longer.

He swept out his hand. "Salads with quinoa. It's healthy for people under stress. You are under stress. Santa was murdered and you are representing another Santa. There are two Santas and one is dead. Quinoa is good."

Well, it was healthy at least. I reached for a fork, wondering if Clark had any antacids. My stress level was rapidly rising, and it was just noon. I had several meetings later in the afternoon, not to mention a deposition right before suppertime. Hopefully this stuff wouldn't make me all gassy because that's all I needed. "Looks good, Pauley."

I took a deep breath and dug in, my mind already on the dead Santa case. It should be hitting the online news right about now.

CHAPTER 3

*M*y temples ached when I trudged from my garage to the front door of my cottage through a couple inches of snow. It had been a long day of not getting many answers about Bernie, although I did have interviews set up with the remaining Kringle Club members the next day. I looked at my too snowy porch, which had icicles hanging from the wood to the white blanketed brush. It was time to shovel, whether I liked it or not.

I didn't.

But I did love my place. I rented the small cottage that was part of a much larger estate overlooking Tamarack Lake, which was smaller than Lilac Lake but still big enough to waterski, jet ski, and sail. The main house was far enough away through fir and spruce trees that I couldn't even see it. The place was like my little slice of paradise, and with my Christmas lights twinkling merrily thanks to being set on a timer, it felt peaceful.

Although at the moment, it was too quiet.

I missed my boyfriend.

Not that the word fit Aiden Devlin, considering he was all man. But he was also an ATF agent with expertise in undercover work, and I hadn't seen him since Halloween. We'd been dating since June, more seriously since August, and he'd really only been in town for two weeks in October before having to leave again.

He called when he could, but sometimes I didn't hear from him for a couple of weeks. I had his Christmas present, a new wallet, in my purse. Was that a dumb gift? I'd bought it on impulse the other day and was now rethinking the purchase. Although, the leather was smooth and handcrafted.

I opened my door and dropped my bag inside, grasping the shovel and getting to work on the porch, walkway, and then the driveway. The manual labor perked up my heart rate and let my mind wander to my current cases.

The Santa murder was the most interesting, although I didn't have a good feeling about poor Bernie. While I believed he didn't kill Lawrence, the more I talked to him, the more the situation looked problematic.

Hopefully Detective Pierce would find the real killer fast. As an investigator, Pierce was one of the best, although he was grumpier than a raccoon shooed away from a nice can of garbage. He'd asked me out once, but work had interfered, and then Aiden had jumped right into my life, and that was that. Although I wouldn't mind fixing Pierce up with somebody nice just to see the guy smile once in a while.

I finished and set the shovel against the side of the door when my phone buzzed from my pocket. "Albertini."

"Hi, *Aingeal*," Aiden said, his barely there Irish brogue sounding unusually thick. "You staying safe?"

Merely hearing his voice heated my abdomen and made me feel all fuzzy. I sank to the porch swing, letting the cold wood cool my butt and watching the reflection of the Christmas lights wander across the snow. It was a legitimate question, based on some of my earlier cases. "Yeah. Are you?" An even more legit question, considering he was undercover with yet another drug running club. I started to gently swing in the cold night.

"Yep." Movement sounded behind him and then gunfire, which was close but not too close. It was sad I could gauge the distance of gunfire through the phone, but there you go. "I'm fine and trying to close this situation fast so we can spend the holidays together."

There's nothing I'd like better.

"It's our first Christmas. Any idea what you'd like?" His voice deepened.

I liked that the word 'first' promised more to come—if neither of us got shot and killed. "Just you home safely," I said honestly. The man hadn't even had enough time to move into the cabin he'd bought around the lake, and while I said I'd take care of it for him, he wanted to be there. Whatever. It wasn't like I'd decorate the place with antique dolls and pink curtains.

Well, probably.

Okay. He had a point.

I cleared my throat. "Um, do you have a wallet?"

"Yep. I have my grandpa's and I love it. Why?"

"No reason." Shoot. Well, maybe I could give the wallet to Oliver Duck at our office. Yeah. Good plan.

Headlights shone down my driveway, and I watched a battered SUV approach—one I didn't recognize.

"Anything interesting happening there?" Aiden asked, sounding like he'd settled back and relaxed. Was he in bed? I didn't know where he was, but it was possible he was on the East Coast, which would put him three hours ahead of me in Idaho.

"Just the usual," I said, not mentioning Santa. Not yet.

The SUV stopped, and a twenty-something man with long blond hair jumped out, grabbing a vase of roses. He hustled toward me along the freshly shoveled walk and up the steps, handing them over. Light snow had already dropped on them, making them look magical. "Tip's already covered." He winked and jogged back to his car.

I put my phone on speaker and set it on the arm of the porch swing, holding the heavy vase and tingling throughout my body. The roses were beautiful. "You shouldn't have," I murmured. It was just like Aiden to arrange for a delivery when he knew we could be on the phone. My silly heart went all pitter-patter.

"Shouldn't have what?" he asked, sounding sleepy and relaxed.

"Sent me roses. They're beautiful." I blew snow off the top of one.

Quiet came across the line for a minute. "You like tulips—not roses. I didn't send them." He didn't sound as relaxed all of a sudden.

I stiffened. He was right—roses weren't my thing, but these were beautiful. "You didn't?"

"No."

Oh. Well, this was awkward. I pushed the flowers around, looking for a card, but there wasn't one. I bit my lip. "No card."

He sighed, and the sound held an edge. "You received roses without a card?"

"Yeah." I looked around the darkened property at the snow-covered trees. Snow fell lightly, adding to the heavy accumulation on their branches, but the wind was calm and the night felt peaceful. Even so, I shivered. So I stood and moved inside the cottage, kicking my boots off on a thick rug before securely locking the door. My tree glittered with colorful lights from the corner of the room, failing for once to provide a sense of peace.

"Who delivered them?" Aiden asked, his tone alert.

I should've paid better attention to the blond guy. "Don't know," I admitted. "The guy came in a plain SUV with no logo. I'll call the local florists tomorrow and see what I can find out. For now, I'm not going to worry about it."

"Liar," Aiden said gently. "The card was probably dropped by the delivery guy. This isn't Jareth Davey. It's not his MO."

I sat the flowers on my table near the kitchen. Jareth Davey had briefly kidnapped me as a child, gotten off on a technicality, and then sent me two cards a year: one on the anniversary of the

June day he'd kidnapped me and one right around Christmas, which was coming up way too fast. "I'm fine, Aiden."

The gunfire sounded closer over the phone line.

He groaned. "I've gotta go. Call me if you have a nightmare, and I'll answer if I can."

"'Night," I said, hanging up and staring at the innocuous flowers. "I'm not going to have a nightmare tonight."

The flowers didn't answer.

* * *

THE NIGHTMARE HIT AFTER several hours of peaceful sleep, and somehow, I wasn't ready for it. *I was ten years old again, skipping rocks at the river when a man grabbed me from behind. I—*

The ringing of the phone jerked me wide awake, and I sat up, gasping for breath. Hoping I wasn't having a heart attack, I fumbled for the phone on my bedside table and yanked it to my ear. "Hello," I ground out, reaching over and flipping on the antique milk glass lamp next to me.

"Hi," Aiden said, sounding exhausted. "You okay?"

How did he know? I tried to calm my racing heart rate. "Yeah. You?"

"Yeah." Covers rustled as it sounded like he slipped into a bed. "It's about nightmare time, so I thought I'd call. I'm sorry if I woke you out of a good sleep."

I settled back down, looking at the picture of the two of us next to the lamp. It was taken around Halloween, outside of my cottage, with the nearest trees full of red and gold leaves and the ones behind them thick with pinecones. My sister had caught us holding hands, and the scene was natural and right. Aiden looked tall and broad next to me, his unreal blue eyes piercing through the day. I loved that picture. "The nightmare had just started."

"Did it start in the cabin or at the river this time?" he asked, prodding me to talk about it like he always did when I got scared. It did help.

"I was at the river skipping rocks with Lacey, and Jareth grabbed me," I said. Lacey was both my cousin and my best friend, and right now, she was a cop in a big city. After Jareth had picked me up, he tossed me into a four-wheeler and drove up the mountain to a cabin, stating we were now married. Before he could hurt me, a sixteen-year-old Aiden had plowed into the building, beat the crap out of Jareth, and saved me.

He'd been my hero ever since, even though we'd lost touch for about twelve years.

Now he was home. Well, usually. When he wasn't gone pretending to be somebody else. "I'm okay now," I said, partially meaning it. "I'll figure out who sent the flowers and we'll go from there." Chills still swept my body, so I snuggled down in the covers, leaving the soft light on to illuminate my feminine bedroom.

Aiden was quiet for a couple of moments. "This schedule, with my job, isn't really working for us, is it?"

It pretty much sucked, but I couldn't ask him to give up his job. He'd worked hard to get where he was, and he did a lot of good, frankly. "We can make anything work." I didn't like his tone of voice. The idea of Aiden moving on was always in the back of my mind, but he had purchased a cabin in town, so he seemed to want to set down roots. "You're excellent at your job, Aiden," I murmured.

"Is that really a good thing?" he asked. "I spend too much time being somebody else, lying to everyone around me, making connections that aren't real."

It was rare to find him in a philosophical mood, considering he was more of an action-oriented guy. I swallowed. "Are you thinking of making a change?"

"Not in my job," he said quietly.

Oh, crap. I couldn't deal with this right now. "Well, you're not making a change in us," I muttered. "Suck it up and deal with your job, Devlin. I can handle the long distance and weird schedule, so stop thinking that I need stability and that you should step out of the way." Sometimes I had a direct line to his brain, and I had no problem using it when necessary.

His chuckle was sexy. Plain and simple. "I hate the idea, but Nick Basanelli is a good guy, and he did ask you out." Aiden's voice was now teasing, so I didn't get pissed.

Basanelli was the current county prosecutor, my former boss, and a total hottie.

"He's practically engaged to my sister, Tessa," I said, grinning.

"Do either of them know that fact?" Aiden asked.

I chuckled. "It does not appear so, but surely deep down they know they're meant to be. Nonna Albertini has decreed it's a fact, so you know. It's only a matter of time." Which reminded me, I'd forgotten to add a couple of meetings to my weekly calendar.

A bang sounded over the line. "Shit. Gotta go, baby." He clicked off.

I lay for a moment with the phone still pressed to my ear. Then I sighed and set it on the table again, snuggling down beneath the warm covers. My eyelids closed and I began to relax, figuring the nightmare wouldn't catch me again.

A whistle pierced through the snowy night outside. The kind from fingers in a mouth and not from a referee at a game.

My eyelids jerked open and I stilled, listening. No sound except a slight wind filtered through the night. Had I heard a whistle, or had I started dreaming? As no other sounds came through the evening, I began to let my body lose the tenseness. All right. I must've been dreaming already.

Just as my eyes started to close again, another whistle had me sitting up in bed.

Heat flashed into my ears, and the blood rushed through my veins. I yanked the LadySmith nine mil from my bed table and shoved free of the bed, padding carefully through my cabin to the

21

windows by the front door that looked out to the trees and drive. Holding my breath, I moved a curtain aside to see the snow lightly falling in front of my porch. There was no other movement.

I sat on the sofa and watched for at least ten minutes, my gaze scouting the tree line and my hand sure on the gun. Nothing.

Something caught my eye...something red. I slowly stood and moved to the door, opening it and flipping on the porch light.

My walkway from porch to driveway ran along the side of the garage, and the light illuminated a perfect red heart painted on the side of the garage, drips sliding in a creepy display before freezing in place.

My stomach rolled over.

CHAPTER 4

etective Pierce smelled like lavender lotion when he strode inside my cottage, kicking snow off his boots first. He wore jeans, black boots, and a black sweatshirt that stretched across his muscled chest. His blond hair was snowy and mussed, and his green eyes were alert and pissed. "You doing okay?"

"Yes." I sat on my sofa, one leg crossed beneath me and a mug of coffee in my hands. "Did the techs find anything?" I'd called the police immediately upon seeing the graffiti heart, and as usual when it came to me, Pierce had been pulled in.

"Boot prints in the snow by the garage—they look to be around size twelve. Haven't found the spray paint cans yet," Pierce said, dropping into the adjacent chair. An even stronger smell of lavender came from him, and since his normal scent was male and ocean, I wondered whose body wash he'd used earlier that night. But it wasn't my place to ask, and right now, I had enough to worry about. "You were smart to call us," he added.

While I'd tried to solve more than one case on my own before, I wasn't a moron. "It could be nothing. The flowers and the heart might be misguided attempts of a secret admirer or something like that," I said, blowing on my coffee and not meaning a word. Knowing better.

"Uh-huh," Pierce said, drawing his notebook out. "Do you think it's Jareth Davey? I know he usually sends a Christmas card."

Davey always sent a card. "Anytime anything scary or weird happens, I think of him," I admitted. "This isn't his MO, so it's doubtful. Before you ask, I don't have any clients or even opponents who've acted inappropriately or given me concern lately." The more I thought about it, the more this seemed immature or silly. "I hope I haven't wasted your time."

"You haven't. It's smart to get ahead of things like this." Pierce looked around my quaint home. "Where's Devlin?"

I wished he were right next to me. "He's on a job," I said. "I don't know where."

Pierce's eyebrows rose. "What did he say about the heart somebody painted on your garage late at night when you were here alone?"

Geez. When he put it like that, it did sound creepy. Here I'd just almost convinced myself this wasn't a big deal. "He wasn't pleased about the flowers, but I haven't told him about the painted heart," I said. "He's working, and I need him to concentrate on not getting shot, which means his mind has to be on his mission and not on me."

I expected Pierce to argue.

"Yeah, that sounds about right," he mused, sitting back in his chair.

I couldn't deal any longer. "Why do you smell like lavender lotion or body wash?"

He stiffened. "I don't."

"Do too," I countered.

"Do not," he retorted, looking down at his notebook, a very slight red winding up his neck.

In spite of the chill in my gut, I grinned. "Timber City might be bigger than my hometown of Silverville, but there are very few secrets here, Pierce. Give it up. Who's the new *loooverrrrr?*" I drew out the last word like I would've with any friend.

He looked up, a veil dropping over his gaze. "I don't know what you're talking about, Albertini. Stick to the fact that you apparently have a new stalker, would you?"

"Sometimes you're no fun," I groused. In fact, he was *rarely* fun. Maybe whoever he was dating could get the guy to lighten up. I sobered. "It's possible Jareth Davey is finally making a move. I've tried to find him, Aiden has tried, and so has the prosecuting attorney's office. Nobody has found him."

Pierce nodded. "I'm aware. I also know he mailed you a card earlier this year at your home, which means he discovered where you live. Since we don't know what any of this means as of yet, you need to proceed as if this is a threat to you, either from Davey or from another enemy. If it turns out you just have a dorky admirer, then great. If not, then you need to be prepared."

I'd been preparing to take out Jareth Davey since the first moment I'd learned to shoot a gun after being kidnapped by him. "I am prepared." As much as possible, anyway. How could I prepare to meet up with a psychopath who starred in my nightmares? Well, most of them. "The flowers are one thing, but the heart and whistle in the middle of the night were meant to scare me. If I combine them, then it's a little more than scary. Unless... it's dorky," I murmured.

Pierce sighed, and the sound was heavy with sarcasm.

I dropped my chin. "You know, only you could make air sound sarcastic."

"Your luck doesn't lend itself to dorky," he retorted.

Fair. Sad, but fair. "Wait a minute. This isn't my fault," I countered, remembering at the last second to stand up for myself.

"Didn't say it was," he agreed. "In fact, I'd argue that none of this is your fault. But haven't you noticed how trouble follows you?" His green eyes narrowed on my face. "It's like you're one of those energy suck fields, like a black hole, that somehow attracts danger. There's probably a quantum mechanical theory out there that hasn't been discovered yet that could describe your energy field."

Had Pierce just likened me to a black hole? I snorted and then laughed, happy when he joined me. The guy had a great laugh—maybe this new romance of his would bring out more of this side of him. "You do have a way with words."

"Yeah." He lost the amusement as the techs began filing out. "Have you thought about getting a dog? Maybe a big one with a frightening bark?"

I had. More than once. "With my work schedule, it wouldn't be fair to a pet," I admitted. However, I did now have my own law firm, so I could probably do what I wanted. Killer the attack dog could attend work with me. It was something to think about, and it'd be fun to have a pet. When Aiden was out of town, it did get lonely. Not that we lived together, because technically, we did not.

"Albertini? I lost you. Where did you go?" Pierce asked.

I blinked. "Just thinking about getting a dog and how I'd make it work." And how I now had the man of my dreams, kind of had him, and wasn't sure I could keep him. Men and dogs. There was a joke in there, but right now, I wasn't seeing the humor. Did Aiden want to make a change? Our entire relationship was built on challenges, gunfights, and explosions. How could I make that work? He was sexy and dangerous and fun...but not around that much. Was that part of the appeal? Would we just fall apart as a couple if he hung around?

Pierce cleared his throat. "Again...you're gone. Did you hit your head or something?"

I forced my attention back to the moment. "Just thinking. It's late, Pierce. Give me a break."

He studied me and then his gaze slid away while his shoulders rolled. "Want to talk about it?" The words came out garbled as if it hurt his throat to say them.

I grinned. "That's a kind offer."

"You have no idea," he huffed. He tapped his pen against his other wrist as if he really wanted to get the heck out of there. "If you don't want to talk, do you want me to take you to one of your sister's homes for the rest of the night?"

"No, but thanks." If I ran to my sisters every time something went wrong, I'd never be at my place.

He moved toward the door. "Fair enough, but lock up behind me. I had officers scout the surrounding areas, even down by the lake, and nobody is around. Right now, anyway."

"Thanks." I followed him to the door and dutifully locked up after he'd left, making a mental note to buy materials the next day to fix the side of the garage. Then I moved to the sofa and watched Pierce disappear down the walkway to his car, and his headlights shone brightly into my living room as he backed out of my driveway. He turned at the main road, his tires skidding across the ice before he regained control and drove sedately away.

Then silence. Only a quiet night with the snow serenely falling to cover the footprints of everyone who'd visited my house, including the person with the can of spray paint.

I watched the snow fall for a while, keeping an eye on the tree line on the other side of my cottage. Nothing moved, and I didn't get the sense that anybody was near. Whoever had painted the heart was long gone—at least for the night.

Letting the curtains fall back into place, I turned and moved to the middle of my living room. Since I was already wearing yoga pants and a loose top, there was no need to change before I began stretching and methodically running through the defense moves Aiden had been teaching me. Oh, I always had a gun handy.

That might not be enough when Davey came at me.

But I was. I was more than enough.

Something told me that Davey would be learning that soon. I pivoted quickly with a roundhouse kick and followed up with a series of punches in the air that I tried to make faster each time.

In the far distance, I heard a whistle. Or maybe a cry from a wolf or coyote. It was high-pitched and rode the wind, the sound both mournful and a warning. Could've been anything—including a whistle from a man. I shivered but kept moving, my ears alert for any other sound.

Only the wind and ice breaking from the trees wound through the silence of the night.

I dropped and rolled, coming up into a fighting stance. "I'm ready, asshole," I whispered. Then my phone rang and I yelped, ducking beside the sofa.

Embarrassment heated my ears. Crap. So much for convincing myself I was a badass. Sighing, I pushed to my feet and tip-toed to the kitchen to grab my phone from the counter. "Albertini," I answered, acutely aware it was almost three in the morning.

"Anna, it's Saber. Aiden's been hurt," James Saber said, his voice pained. Saber was Aiden's second in command for their specialty ATF unit.

Everything stopped. Including my heart. "What? How bad?" I started running to my bedroom to get dressed. "Where are you?"

A scuffle sounded and then Aiden's voice came through. "Angel, calm down. I'm fine." His slight Irish brogue thickened with pain.

My knees turned to liquid, and I fell onto my bed, relief chasing the panic through my body. "You're fine? What is going on?"

Another scuffle and then Saber returned. "Tell him he has to go to the hospital and see if we need to get the bullets out. Seriously. If you don't talk sense into him, I'm knocking his skull in, and that'll just be one more injury to handle. Tell him. Now."

I sat up, my heart still pounding. "Aiden?" I whispered.

"I'm here," he said, sounding exhausted, as apparently Saber relinquished the phone. "It's only two bullets, and Saber can stop being a jackass. They probably went right on through."

I shook my head, bile rising in my throat. "Where are you?"

"Portland," he said. "Bust went wrong, things went to shit. I'll be home tomorrow. Well, later today."

"After we go to the hospital," Saber yelled in the background.

I gripped the phone tighter. "Please see a doctor. Come on, Aiden." It took another ten minutes, but I finally talked him into seeking medical attention, although he was pissed about both the bust and being shot. Since he kept talking, I figured the bullets hadn't hit anything important.

Even so, when we ended the call, I just sat on my bed and looked at the picture of a tugboat on my little lake that I'd snapped and blown up to hang on my wall. The nightmares stalked me when I became stressed or even too uncertain about my life, so there was no way I was going to sleep again.

I returned to the living room and practiced my kicks and punches until my arms slowed and my body thumped in exhaustion. Dawn slowly crept across the snowy world outside, and I forced myself to keep practicing until I couldn't take the pain any longer. Only then did I head for a shower so I could start my day.

I had to figure out who'd killed Santa Claus.

CHAPTER 5

*I*t was a power red high-heel day, but the snow kept coming, so I wore thick boots beneath my black pantsuit instead. I comforted myself with the fact that I could take out a few ribs with those boots if anybody attacked me. Humming, I strode into my office and past our Christmas tree to find my partner, Clark Bunne, already busy at work in his office beyond the reception area door.

He looked up, his brown eyes focusing. "Morning."

"Morning." I deposited his triple honey-thick latte with oat milk onto his desk.

His full lips tipped in a smile, and he pounced on the drink, shoving a series of manila case files out of the way. "All right. What did you do?" He kicked back, looking younger than his twenty-five or so years as he gulped down the drink.

"Nothing yet." I pulled out a leather guest chair and sank onto it, dropping my laptop bag to the floor. Then I told him about the flowers and the heart painted on my garage.

He lost the smile. "The flowers could be all right, but the graffiti heart in the middle of the night is creepy." He ran a hand over his dark bald head. Sometimes he grew his black hair out, and sometimes he shaved his head, and either way, Clark Bunne was a good looking man built like a cowboy who herded cattle. Long and lean. His skin was a dusky brown and his features ruggedly angled. His legal mind impressed me, and he had a core of solid honor that was unusual to find these days. I was fortunate he'd taken the leap to start a law firm with me, and I knew it.

I sipped my chai latte. "I agree. It doesn't feel like Jareth Davey, but I have thought he'd make a move soon."

Clark straightened his deep purple tie that looked chic and professional with his white shirt and gray suit. He managed to carry off bargain clothing and make it look expensive, which was a skill I'd never learned. "We don't have any odd cases right now where the opponents would try to scare you." He glanced at his wristwatch. "I'm meeting a client at Smiley's Diner in a few minutes to prep for a deposition. It's that timber trespass case."

"I think you're clear on that one," I said. "Your guy didn't give his neighbor permission to take down the trees, and it's easy to get an estimate for damages. Treble damages if you win, baby."

He nodded. "Yeah, I know. Getting three times the actual damages would be great right now. It's a hand holding meeting, but we're used to those." He stood and stretched his back. "Any idea who killed Santa?"

"No, and I'm letting the police figure it out," I admitted, having learned my lesson. Mostly, anyway. "I can't tell how close Pierce is to arresting our client, so I do need to talk to some other witnesses today. Then I have the Fraley deposition for their divorce this afternoon as well as a conference call with Judge Pernacki about the disputed boundary case over in Silverville."

Clark grimaced. "I wish we were big enough we didn't have to take on divorces."

"Ditto," I said. "However, she's much better off without him, so I don't mind this one. The guy is an ass, Clark. So is his lawyer. I might have to make a Motion to Compel for the discovery."

"You waiting until after the mediation?" He reached for his

jacket from the coat tree my Nana O'Shea had insisted he have from her basement. It was oak and well-maintained.

"No. I need to know all of his assets before we can agree to anything." I stood, my ears perked to the rest of the office. "Where are Pauley and Oliver?"

Clark secured his file folders in his briefcase and strode toward the door. "Pauley is taking a test at the college, and Oliver had a dentist appointment. They should both be in later today."

I liked that our office staff consisted of my cousin Pauley, who at sixteen attended the local community college, and Oliver Duck, a kid I'd represented a while back. They both worked odd hours for little pay and were tons of fun to have around. I'd let them choose their own business cards, and Oliver was the Czar of our office while Pauley was the King. "I'm thinking of getting Aiden a...keychain for Christmas? Maybe one of those that opens beer bottles."

Clark paused and turned. "What?"

"What do you think?"

"If you're going to break up with him, do it on the phone," Clark said.

I sighed. Okay. No keychain. I stood and followed him through the hallway and doorway to the reception area, where a woman waited patiently in one of the two leather chairs my Uncle Sean had given us.

I paused. "Hello. I'm sorry, we didn't hear you."

She stood, wearing a long red overcoat, black snow boots, and sparkly jewelry on both hands. Her blondish gray hair was swept back in a thick updo, her eyes were a faded green, and her skin was smooth for a woman who had to be in her mid-sixties. "Hello. I'm Florence McLintock, and I'm here to tell you that there is no way Bernie killed Lawrence. He was with me, in my bed, all night. Well, all morning. So he couldn't have done it." Her lips pursed, showing fine wrinkles above her mouth.

I sighed.

Clark patted my shoulder. "I'll be back in a couple of hours." He half-bowed to Mrs. McLintock and then made a hasty escape. "Why don't you come back and talk with me," I suggested, motioning the woman through the doorway to the hallway. "My office is all the way at the far end." She moved, and I followed, passing two conference rooms, the restrooms, one office Pauley utilized, one empty office, and then reached mine at the end with the wide windows, which was adjacent to the kitchen.

She walked inside and sat in one of my two leather guest chairs, planting her monstrous green purse next to her. "We used to be married, you know? Sometimes he makes a booty call."

I coughed up a little latte and strode around my desk to sit. Unlike Clark's organized chaos, my case files were perfectly lined up to the right of my desk with a pen next to a pad of paper. My computer was behind me on the credenza, and the windows looked out past buildings to Lilac Lake. "Mrs. McLintock, I already spoke with Bernie, and he wasn't with you that morning. So lying to me is just fine, but if you lie to the police, they could arrest you for hindering an investigation." I leaned toward her, softening my voice. "Plus, the truth always comes out, and the police will think you're lying to cover something up."

Tears filled her deep-set eyes. "Bernie couldn't kill anybody."

"I know," I said, not really knowing that fact but being willing to go on faith for now. "I'm glad you came in today because I was going to ask you to talk to me." I reached for the notepad. "How long have you and Bernie been divorced?"

She released the wide black buttons on her coat. "Let's see. We were married for seven years and have been divorced for about five now." She fluttered her hands. "He's a sweet man, but all he wants to do is play cards, watch golf on television, and then be Santa Claus once a year. Seven years of that was all I could take—especially since the dickhead cheated on me." She leaned in, her eyes widening. "Although he is very well endowed, if you know what I mean. I would've left him a good year or two before that, but the man is…gifted."

I could feel the latte coming all the way up, so I cleared my throat. I tried to clear my brain, but the image of Bernie being endowed was in there for good. "I see," I murmured, wishing with everything I had that I did not see. "You obviously have remained friends?"

She nodded. "I'm friends with all of my exes. I did forgive him for cheating, but I couldn't stay married to him." She shook her head. "I'm a free spirit, Ms. Albertini. I've tried love several times, and I just can't get it right."

I took notes. "If you don't mind my asking, how many times have you been married?"

"Oh, about five, I guess. Six if you count the ceremony jumping out of a plane with an Elvis impersonator reciting the vows— three husbands ago. I don't," she said. "That one doesn't really count. You know, I was hoping that Lawrence would be lucky number seven and that we might make a go of it." More tears gathered in her eyes and she brushed them away. "Why would anybody kill him? He was harmless." Her voice lowered. "And also very well endowed, if you know what I mean."

I held back a gag. "So you have a type."

She jolted and then laughed, the tears dissipating. "I like you."

I smiled. "I like you, too." Although I could go the rest of my life without mentally picturing a bunch of Santas with big dicks. I handed over another notebook. "Would you please write down the names, addresses, and phone numbers of your ex-husbands, as well as dates of marriages and divorces?" It was a long shot, but maybe one of them hadn't been happy that Florence was getting remarried. "Wait a sec. Does everyone know that Lawrence was going to propose to you?"

She reached for a pen. "Yes. He posted on social media when he was at Earl's Jewelry Store last week. In fact, I have the ring." She looked up, frown lines digging into her forehead. "I should return the ring so his son can have the money, shouldn't I?" She drew a box out of her pocket and pushed it across the desk. "It's the right thing to do?"

I slowly opened the lid and gasped.

She winced. "I know. It's beautiful. I do love it."

So did I. The ring was a simple diamond solitaire, and it had to be three karats, easy. The color and clarity were stunning. "Lawrence must've been well off," I said, closing the lid before I was tempted to try on the darn thing.

She gulped. "No, he wasn't. Well, he had a significant savings, but he spent it all on that ring."

I leaned away from the box. "All of it?"

She nodded. "Every bit. He proposed last night before meeting the guys for poker and their Kringle club meeting, and I think he was planning to celebrate with all of his friends since I accepted."

I tore my gaze away from the innocuous dark blue box. "Really?" Bernie hadn't mentioned that fact to me. Why did he keep hiding facts?

"Yes. We had an early dinner together, and then he left. I didn't know it'd be the last time we spoke." She sighed, clasping her hands together in her lap. "I liked him, a lot. While it wasn't the love of the century, we were compatible, and sometimes I think that's more important than the rush of romance and wild emotions. In fact, after my various romances, I can tell you it is much more crucial. You have to be able to laugh with each other and enjoy the boring times as well as the adrenaline-rush ones."

My stomach cramped. "I see." My entire relationship with Aiden was built on adrenaline and danger. We'd never even watched a movie in bed together. Was it the excitement as well as history that kept us together? It certainly wasn't new memories or day-to-day life. In fact, we weren't really together. He was in a different state, no doubt being stitched up by a doctor right now. Hopefully, anyway. I dragged my attention back to the grieving woman in my office. "Was Lawrence's son angry he spent all of his money on the ring?"

"Yes," Florence admitted. "He was furious. Hoyt Forrest doesn't like me very much. He runs the bait and tackle shop around Lilac Lake that has been there forever. The man is in his early forties and thinks, or rather thought, he could run Lawrence's life." She shook her head. "It's sad they didn't reconcile before Lawrence's death."

I would need to look into Hoyt. For now, I studied the box. "Do you want me to escort you to the bank so you can put that in a safety deposit box?"

"No." She pushed the finished list across my desk. "How about we go to the jewelry store and return it? I wouldn't mind having company on the way."

With that ring, she should have an armed guard. I guess I'd have to do. Plus, I still hadn't found a Christmas present for Aiden, and the idea was giving me a headache. Constantly. "All right. You can tell me more about what makes a successful relationship on the way." I stood and dug my purse from my laptop bag, figuring if she'd gotten it wrong so many times, maybe she had now learned how to make one work.

I could use all the help I could find.

CHAPTER 6

*E*arl's Jewelry Store was across the border in Washington state, and I spent the ride watching the icy roads and listening to Florence recall her various romances through the years. Her adventures were impressive, and she'd spent time in several different countries, including a summer in a castle in Scotland with a modern-day laird.

She finally wound down with a sad sigh, saying that Hoyt Forrest wouldn't even let her attend the funeral for Lawrence.

It seemed unnecessarily mean to me. "I'll talk to him," I promised, driving through an older part of Spokane, its brick buildings having seen better days. "I can't promise anything, but I need to discuss the case with him, anyway."

Florence patted my arm. "That would be so kind of you. Thanks."

"Is he a decent guy?" I asked, hoping it was grief and not cruelty that drove him.

"He's okay," she said quietly. "I know that Lawrence loved him very much, although they've been having problems lately because Hoyt likes to gamble."

I stiffened. "That's news. Any idea how much money he's lost?"

"No. He asked Lawrence for a loan two weeks ago, and it hurt Lawrence to refuse to help, but he just couldn't send bad money after bad money." She unhitched her seatbelt as I pulled alongside the curb, frowning at the barred windows set on either side of the metal door. "I remember when this area of Spokane didn't even need locks on the doors, although the jewelry store was always careful, you know."

"So do I," I murmured. Hoyt was looking good as a suspect for the murder, but I didn't have a feel for him yet. "Do you think Hoyt could've hurt his father for money? That he was that desperate?"

"No. I can't imagine anybody wanting to hurt Lawrence or being that desperate. It just doesn't make sense." She opened the door and snow blew inside my SUV.

I wondered how many of her jewelry items had been purchased at Earl's but didn't know of a polite way to ask. Dodging through the rapidly quickening snow, I grasped her arm and ushered her across the newly shoveled walkway to push open the door. A tinkly bell announced our arrival, and we hurried inside to see counters of sparkling gems. Christmas decorations danced across the walls in several winter scenes, and music played a muted holiday selection.

Did Aiden like jewelry? I'd never seen him wear any, but a nice gold cross seemed like him. Of course, that was seriously personal. He could probably use another leather jacket, but that was both out of my budget and not personal enough. I sighed.

Florence pulled the box from her pocket just as a man bustled through the door at the far end, his blue bowtie perfect over his neatly pressed shirt. His eyes were brown, his spectacles thick, and his gray hair thin. He smiled and laugh wrinkles extended out from his eyes.

"Florence. How good to see you." He moved around the counter and straight for her, reaching for her hands and losing the grin. "I'm so very sorry to hear about Lawrence."

Florence leaned in. "Thank you, Earl." She partially looked over her shoulder at me. "This is my friend, Anna Albertini. Anna, this is jewelry genius extraordinaire and a lifelong friend, Earl Jacobson."

Earl released her and held out a gnarled hand to me. "Anna, it's so nice to meet you. I know your grandparents from different events in Silverville and think very highly of them. Your Grandpa Albertini was about five years older than me in school, and our high schools were rivals. I went to Bourn High."

Bourn was the next valley over from Silverville, and I had many friends from the small community.

I shook his hand, being gentle with the obvious arthritis in his fingers. "It's nice to meet you, too." The place smelled like lemon cleaner and pipe tobacco that somehow melded neatly with the Christmas pine air freshener.

Florence handed over the ring box. "I can't keep this and would like to give the money to Hoyt, Earl. I'm sorry about the sale and hope you can recoup somehow." She wiped snow off her forehead, and a piece dripped down to her red jacket.

Earl took the box, his lips tightening. "I have no problem giving you a refund, but you really shouldn't give the money to that dolt, Hoyt. Lawrence wanted you to have this ring, and he gave it to you, so it's yours. A gift is a gift." He nodded emphatically. "Lawrence and I were friends for fifty years, and I knew him. If you don't want the ring, and you don't want cash, perhaps you'd like to exchange it for that nice opal set over in the estate sale area? I know how much you like opals, and these have yellow diamonds around them. So stunning."

Florence hesitated, indecision crossing her face. She bit her lip and hovered uncertainly by my side. "I do love opals—and diamonds."

Who didn't? I glanced at a row of truly stunning emerald earrings. "This is none of my business, but as a lawyer, I can assure you that a gift is a gift, and it's all yours. You're under no obligation to put the ring into Lawrence's estate." I paused. "Did he have a will?" It was a question I should've already asked, frankly. My brain had to get off Aiden Devlin and my personal life.

Florence nodded. "Yes. The reading is tomorrow at noon." She fluttered her hands together. "I've just been dreading it, so I pushed the entire situation to the back of my mind. Anna, would you come with me? I'm supposed to attend, and I really didn't think about why, unless Lawrence left me something, which would probably anger Hoyt. I don't want to make him mad or hurt him any more than he's been harmed by the loss of his father."

"Of course," I said smoothly. There was nothing I'd like better, actually. The more I knew about Lawrence, the more I could help Bernie, who I truly didn't think had killed anybody. "Although, you said that Lawrence spent all of his funds on your ring."

She nodded, and almost-melted snow flew off her gray hair. "As far as I understand, he did spend all of his savings. However, he owns the bait and tackle shop, his house, some coins, guns, and other personal items. I hope he left everything to Hoyt, but I don't know what he decided."

If Florence was invited to the reading, she had inherited something, whether she wanted it or not. I wouldn't mind protecting her from Hoyt in case he got out of hand, and the more I knew about this case, the better.

Her phone rang, and she pulled it from her monstrous purse to look at the face. Then she sighed.

I peered over her shoulder, having no problem being nosy. "What's wrong?"

"It's that Jolene O'Sullivan from the paper. She somehow got my number and won't stop calling me about Lawrence's murder and the fact that I formerly was married to Bernie, the prime suspect." Florence shoved the phone back into her bag with enough force that it clanked against a glass display case. "I told her I didn't have a comment."

"Good." I patted her arm. "That's great and keep saying that. Jolene can't be trusted, and she'll expand any story for more reads. Trust me." I had personal experience with that very situation.

"No problem." Florence tucked her bag tighter against her wool coat and moved toward the estate sale counter. "Since we're already here, it wouldn't hurt to look at some jewelry, I guess."

I turned to survey a series of large crosses in yellow and white gold that sparkled beautifully. Aiden's Grams had been Catholic, and that's how she'd raised him, but I had no idea if he practiced or even wanted a cross. He could use some cover while he worked such dangerous jobs, but it might not be my place to suggest that. Not right now, anyway.

Earl moved toward me, standing only about an inch taller than my five-foot-four. His gray pants were pressed and his loafers polished. "Those are lovely," he said. "Are you shopping for a present for your significant other?" His keys jangled as he drew them out of his pocket. "I can pull those out if you'd like to look at any."

Significant other? Was that what Aiden was to me? We were exclusive, although we'd never fully had that conversation. Aiden had pretty much said that he didn't share, and I'd said the same thing, so...

I sighed.

Earl's bushy eyebrows rose. "It's like that, huh? What about a nice watch? We have some very manly and yet elegant timepieces over here."

A watch? Aiden was usually running out of exploding buildings and wore a military type of watch. "I don't think so," I murmured. Of course, many men had fancier watches to wear when they weren't at work or were attending events—usually weddings in my expansive family. Would Aiden still be around during the next family wedding season?

I swallowed. We should probably have that talk when he was home, but I wasn't sure what to say. I wasn't looking for a commitment, but it'd be nice to have a path to a commitment if that's what we both decided.

"Well, you were drawn to the crosses. Here's a lovely one." Earl opened the cabinet to show a gorgeous and somehow still manly silver cross that would look amazing against Aiden's toned chest.

I gently took the jewelry. "It's beautiful." Okay. Yeah. "Love it. I'll take it."

"Wonderful." Earl took the necklace and set it in a blue felt box. The ring of a phone—an actual landline—twittered through the quiet store.

"Excuse me." He hustled toward a desk area behind the counter. "Earl's Jewelry Store—Spokane's longest standing jeweler," he answered. Then he paused. "Uh, yes. Please hold on for a moment." He set the receiver next to the cradle. "Ms. Albertini? It's for you."

I cocked my head. "For me?" The trip to Spokane with Florence had been spur of the moment. My throat went dry, but I moved around the counter to reach for the handset. Nobody knew where I was right now, so this didn't make sense. My hand shook, and I tightened my grip around cold polymer resin. "Hello?"

Silence met my words. A weighted, thick, heavy silence.

Irritation caught me and I straightened my shoulders. My breath quickened, but I forced myself to sound almost bored. If the caller wanted to scare me, I wasn't going to give them the satisfaction. Even so, this was creepy as heck. "Hello? Who is this?"

The click of a phone hanging up was quick and loud enough that I knew somebody had been there. My hand shook as I replaced the phone in the cradle, turning to Earl. Had somebody followed us to Spokane? I hadn't noticed anybody on the way in, but I hadn't been really watching. "What did the person sound like?"

Earl pushed his glasses farther up his nose. "It was a man with no accent that I could discern." He frowned. "Did you tell anybody you were coming here today?"

"No," I said quietly, looking through the barred windows at the rapidly increasing snowfall. "Not a soul."

CHAPTER 7

I finished up my day after having left Florence's sparkling ring at Earl's so he could catalog it before fetching the funds to repay her. I wasn't entirely sure she wouldn't spend some of the money on new jewelry after having spent time looking through the lovely sparkles. I'd purchased a silver cross for my sister Tessa and a gold bracelet with small emeralds for my sister, Donna.

The cross for Aiden sat heavily in my purse. Was that the wrong gift? I tried to ignore my trepidation and forced myself to think about the case.

Florence was still planning on giving most of the money to Lawrence's son, and I'd convinced her to wait until after the reading, just in case. Then I'd worked with clients for the rest of the day, having reported the prank call to Detective Pierce to add to my new and odd stalkerish-themed case file. He'd promised to have a friend on the Spokane force try to trace the call, but neither one of us had much hope we'd find anything but a burner phone on the other side. Somebody had followed me and I hadn't noticed. In addition, Pierce had called all the flower shops in the area but hadn't found where the roses had come from.

He had, once again, suggested I get a dog.

When we got off the phone, I turned to my computer and brought up the online version of the *Timber City Gazette*. Bernie and I had made the front page with the picture of us leaving the courthouse. The headline read: "A Killing for Christmas."

My blood heating, I read the entire article by Jolene, and yep, she made mention of me and the trouble I'd gotten into that summer after breaking into a funeral home. She more than hinted that I hadn't been charged with a crime, although the words were ambiguous enough that I probably didn't have a libel case. The woman had also chosen a picture that had me shielding Bernie, but since he was much taller than me and still wearing his Santa hat, plenty of him was visible.

I groaned.

Wishing a massive yeast infection on her, I turned off the website and returned to my case files, working through the divorce and the other timber case we had going on. At this juncture, I was at the paper filing stage, which was fine with me.

My legwork would be focused on Bernie and the Santa case for now. The sooner I helped Bernie, the sooner he could go back to his life, and Jolene could get her teeth into another story that did not include me.

I fielded calls from several of my family members after they'd seen the article, and Tessa's offer to egg Jolene's house cheered me considerably. Oh, we wouldn't do it, but sometimes it was nice to dream.

After finishing work, I drove home past houses all lit up for Christmas, along with several sparkling deer figurines decorating lawns. I ventured around my smaller lake and turned down my driveway by the trees, keeping an eye on the surrounding area.

The snow-covered black truck by my garage made my heart leap through my throat. I parked, grabbed my bag, and jumped to the snow, hurrying through the blizzard conditions to my front porch and past the solid Santa figure that my aunt had given to me. The walkway had been shoveled, but snow was already piling up. I opened my door to the delicious smell of a Vinnie's pizza combo with extra spice.

My skin sensitized, and I walked inside, dumping my bags near size thirteen boots before shutting out the storm. "Hi."

"Hi." Aiden performed a full body scan on me as he leaned back against the bar separating my living room and kitchen, a full glass of red wine in his hand. He wore faded jeans, a dark tee, and a lot of dark facial scruff that matched his unruly black hair. A white bandage showed on his muscled bicep.

My body reacted to his scan, my heart rate picking up and my anxiety ratcheting even higher. "How bad?" I whispered, fighting the very odd reaction to flee at the sight of the sexiest man I'd ever seen in real life.

"Not bad." His expression didn't reveal his thoughts. "Through-and-through on the arm and barely a scratch on the leg. Saber didn't even have to dig out a bullet and just was being a baby."

Saber was anything but a baby, but Aiden did look strong and formidable standing in my small cottage. The fact that he was standing calmed a fear I'd been carrying around all day—but it wasn't the only fear.

I cleared my throat. "Are you breaking up with me?" The words came out of nowhere, but I didn't call them back. I did, however, scramble to keep talking so he couldn't say anything. "We don't have to end things. How about we see other people and just take it casual?" I sounded like a pathetic dork, but the panic consuming me felt heated and sharp.

His pause didn't make me feel better. Finally, he spoke. "I don't share, Angel. Neither do you."

I wavered. What did that mean? "You feel...off." I still didn't move.

"I am," he said, his gaze sliding to the red roses I'd placed in the center of the table gifted to me by my Nonna Albertini.

I followed his focus. "Those flowers aren't my fault."

"No, they're not," he agreed softly, the tension from him tightening the room in the manner of an oncoming explosion.

I set my stance out of instinct, not knowing him like this. Not recognizing him. Aiden Devlin had always been a force beyond nature, while most of the time I felt like I was pretending to be a grownup. I glanced at the cheerful lights on my Christmas tree, acutely aware that I hadn't purchased many presents yet and Christmas would be here in a heartbeat. I winced and then faced him. "I think you should say the words." The ones I so didn't want to hear.

He gently placed the wine glass on the granite counter. "All right." Then he moved for me, reaching me in two long strides and cupping my face. His hands were warm and strong. "I'm sorry. What I said the other night about us, I didn't mean. It was a shitty night that turned into a horrific and even shittier day, and my philosophical side is an asshole who deserved to get shot."

The words filtered through the buzz in my head, and my knees weakened. Relief would come later. I had to get control of this infatuation I had for him, but I didn't know how. Especially with him right there holding my face. "How did they know just to shoot that side of you?" I murmured.

His lips twitched into almost a smile. "Just lucky, I guess." He leaned down and kissed me, taking his time and spiraling a lazy heat through my entire body. When he released me, I was breathless, turned on, and slightly disoriented. "We're not breaking up."

It was a statement and not a question. Considering I'd kissed him back and shown him how much I'd missed him, he probably felt secure in making the claim. I wasn't ready for happily-ever-after, but my rapidly thumping heart hoped he was in my future. Right now, I wanted to deal in the present. "We did go from zero to a thousand very quickly," I said, my body humming for him, even as I tried to force my brain to stay in the moment.

"Maybe," he allowed, watching his thumb caress my tingling

bottom lip. "Although we haven't been in the same town for more than two weeks at a time and haven't had the opportunity to settle into any routine. I'm not sure either one of us knows how to do a routine."

The man was not wrong. I sucked in a breath. "Maybe we're not routine type of people."

"Perhaps," he said. "The bad news is that my op got busted, but the good news is that we can spend Christmas together. We have a couple of weeks to see if we need a routine or if we can create one of our own. Whatever that means."

What if we couldn't? What if we didn't work if we lived in the same space for too long? I couldn't imagine life without him, and that was saying a lot for me. Playing the field had never been my thing, and there was nobody on the planet who compared to Aiden Devlin. Which meant it would suck if we broke up, and with our lives and jobs, nothing was for certain. I should do the smart thing and try to protect myself a little from heartbreak.

"You're not dating somebody else," Aiden said, brushing snow off my shoulder and apparently reading my mind. "Neither one of us has time to balance or deal with that type of situation, and I don't want it, anyway. It's you and me, and we'll figure out if we can make sense of us without a lot of drama or anybody else involved."

Now I lifted an eyebrow. I was an independent and adventurous woman, but oddly enough, I liked his bossy side. Even enjoyed the sense of feeling safe when he was in control of a situation. Yet I couldn't let him get away with too much. "I'll let you know what I decide about that," I said, unzipping my coat and dropping more snow to the tiled entryway.

"You do that." He helped me out of the snow covered wool and hung it on the peg near the door, his strong hands pulling my hair free and his warm fingers brushing against my nape.

A shiver took me and I couldn't hide it. He could undo me with just one touch, and I didn't like giving him that much power.

Although I did like that one touch. So I ducked my head and toed off my boots, holding his good arm for balance. I was young, smart, professional, and should be playing the field and having fun. But since the sexiest, most dangerous, Irish badass on the planet had found his way into my bed and my heart, why waste time on anybody else? I sighed.

His chuckle eased the rest of the tension from my body. "Come on. I brought pizza and wine. I don't want to talk about either of our cases or jobs tonight—all of that can wait until morning, considering it's Saturday tomorrow. For now, let's relax, eat too much pizza, and then sleep in." He turned and strode for the kitchen, his Glock nestled in his waistband against his lower back.

He never wore his gun on his body while at either of our homes.

Yeah. That tension and stress returned. Fast.

CHAPTER 8

*A*iden hogged the bed. Considering he was a solid two-
twenty-five of muscle packed into about six feet and four
inches of height, I guess he needed more space than I did.
Morning came, and I rolled over in my small area to face him. It
was rare that I awoke before him, so I took a few moments to
drink my fill.

Soft morning light cascaded through the blinds on the sliding
glass door to my small deck.

He lay facing me with the blankets shoved down to his waist.
His muscled chest held various scars from his time on the streets,
in the military, and then with the ATF. The scruff along his jaw
was growing out, and a multitude of bruises led down his arm and
neck to the bandage that was light against his bronze skin. His
breathing remained even, and I fought the urge to trace both his
straight nose and those ripped abs that led down beyond the
covers. He stirred and opened his long dark lashes, awakening.

Blue. His eyes were a mixture of impossible blues, sharp and
alert instantly.

I swallowed.

His gaze wandered lazily over my face and down my chest,

covered by a pink nightie I'd purchased on sale the week before. He reached and grasped my arm, rolling onto his back with a smooth motion and pulling me on top of him. Then he brushed my hair back with both hands, his body solid rock beneath me. "Mornin'." His Irish brogue came out strong.

"Hi." I could look at those blue eyes all day, and from the feel of him beneath me, *all* of him was wide awake.

Aiden liked mornings. Aiden really liked naked mornings that lasted for hours, and I knew this from personal experience. So when he didn't immediately try to remove my nightie, my body stiffened.

"You good?" he asked.

I nodded. "I'm good."

The night before, we'd talked about nothing over pizza and wine before watching an old action movie. I'd even forced thoughts about my stalker to the abyss, so I could just enjoy one normal night with him. Then we'd tumbled into bed, and he'd been asleep within minutes.

He shifted his weight, brushing an impressive erection against me. "No complaints about my job?"

I frowned, trying to concentrate on his words and not his hard body. "Well, I wouldn't mind it if you dodged the bullets next time." His hands around my face kept me in place, or I'd lean down and kiss him. What was going on in his head? I lifted my gaze from his tempting mouth to his sizzling eyes that were watching me so carefully. "Am I supposed to complain?"

His focus moved to my mouth, and I swear, my bottom lip swelled in anticipation. "I don't know," he said.

Ah. I got it. He'd dated other women before me, and they hadn't liked the distance. I shrugged, moving my breasts against his chest and enjoying the heated flare in his eyes. "If you like your job, I like your job," I whispered. "So long as we're on the same page, we can make anything work."

His thumbs caressed my cheekbones. "I don't love your job."

I grinned. "I know, but it has been fairly mundane all autumn, so perhaps the winter will be calm as well?"

"Right," he said, shaking his head. "Let's not tempt fate."

Fair enough. "I'm glad you're home," I said.

His mouth curved. "Me, too. I have to ask, why did you keep the roses?"

It was a reasonable question, and I knew he was just curious. "They were too pretty to throw out, and I thought I'd take them to the hospital on the way to a reading of a will today." I wriggled against him. "Do they bother you?"

"Not that you kept them to take to somebody in the hospital." His thumbs wound down to my jawline. "I don't like the anonymous aspect of them, but it's probably harmless."

I winced. "Apparently it was dark when you arrived last night?"

He stilled. "Yes. Why?"

I moved my hips against him, catching my breath at the feeling of him against me. "Let's talk about it after."

"No." He tightened his hold, his jaw firming. "Let's talk about it now."

"It'll ruin the mood," I warned him, really not wanting to lose the mood. Like, ever.

He paused to consider my statement. "That would be a travesty. Are we in danger right now?"

Considering his gun was on the nightstand and mine was next to me in my drawer, it was doubtful. "No more than usual," I admitted. "Probably."

"Only you," he whispered. His expression softened, his rugged face losing the guarded look. There he was. My Aiden. His hands swept down my sides and drew up the pink silk. "This is pretty. Meant to tell you that last night." Then he pulled it over my head and threw the soft material across the room. "You're prettier." His hands finally went to my breasts.

I leaned down and kissed him, going deep. Having him in my bed, facing the morning with me, felt right. And kind of dangerous.

He returned my kiss and rolled us over, looming above me and taking control in a way that stole my breath. He was big and strong and deadly, and he'd made me feel safe from the world my entire life. But not from him. That took trust, and I had jumped headfirst into this with him, sometimes wondering if I should've protected myself better.

If I could have somehow.

Yet when he kissed me, when he took me deep, there was only Aiden Devlin, and I was fine with that. Exhilarated, in fact.

He kissed me harder and then wandered down my body with his heated mouth and made me whimper. Aiden was good at this. Phenomenal, in fact. He knew how to draw out a moment, and he liked to play, keeping me on the edge. He also liked to make me scream.

Three orgasms later, from his talented mouth and fingers, he moved back up me, grabbed a condom from the drawer, and finally pushed inside me.

While I was on the pill, I didn't mind the extra protection. Right now, we were so not ready for a baby.

Then he paused, his mouth wandering across my cheekbone before those piercing blue eyes captured mine. "I missed you," he murmured, starting to move, powering deep inside me.

I caught my breath. "I missed you, too." Then I dug my nails into his arms, careful of his newest bandage.

He started to move harder and faster, and I closed my eyes just to enjoy the moment as he took me away again.

And yes, I screamed his name two more times that morning, ending our marathon extremely happy.

* * *

"I AM NOT HAPPY," Aiden snapped as I set a plate of scrambled eggs and huckleberry pancakes in front of him, his coffee steaming next to his fork.

I shrugged and sat across from him at the table, fluffing my napkin. Truth be told, my body was so satisfied that I would have to drum up energy to care that he wasn't happy. "Seriously, eat your breakfast." I poured syrup on my pancakes, my mouth watering. "It's not like I could've called you about the graffiti heart or the phone call."

He looked up, his sapphire-colored eyes glittering. "That's exactly what you should've done."

"Before or after you were busy ducking from bullets?" I took a bite and hummed at the sweet taste. My freezer was full of huckleberries, and I had enough to last until next picking season. Hopefully.

He paused in eating and watched me, the sight unnerving and a little intimidating.

Not that it stopped me from taking another bite of pancakes. I'd need to work out hard that afternoon, but I was due for a jog anyway.

"I thought we settled everything last night," he said mildly.

Now, most men, when they were mild and calm, were reassuring. Not Aiden. I'd learned quickly that the quieter he became, the calmer he appeared, the more feral he was feeling. I'd like to say that irritated me, but in truth, he intrigued the heck out of me. Even when he had an edge most people would heed.

"We did," I agreed, reaching for my coffee and trying to act natural.

"Then when there's a threat against you, if you don't need to call the police immediately, your first call is to me." He also reached for his coffee, his gaze not leaving mine. When Aiden wanted to make a point, he, well, made a point.

Sometimes I think he was more mired in our past, when he'd

rescued me from Jareth Davey, than was I. "I'm a big girl, Aiden. Why would I call you when you're on a job?" The coffee was too strong, so I set the cup down and poured more creamer, turning the liquid more of a sugary milky color. Perfect.

"Because you're mine." He took another drink.

The words hit me, and I performed a head and shoulder roll in the *oh no, you didn't* motion that would've made my sister Tessa proud. "Yours? I'm not a possession, Devlin. I'm not your freakin' gun," I snapped.

He sat back, his gaze turning thoughtful. "My gun? Why not?"

My mouth gaped open. "Excuse me?"

He partially lifted one powerful shoulder. "Well, you're a lot like my gun. Sleek, smooth, and just right for my hand."

Oh, for goodness' sake. That should not have warmed my thighs. Before I could answer, he continued, "And you're dangerous, deadly, and a straight shooter. Yep. Just like my gun."

It was possible to feel two things at the same time. I both wanted to grin and toss my coffee at his head. "You're going to have to get over this Neanderthal thing you have going on."

"No." He turned back to his pancakes.

My head full on jerked this time. "What?" It was a bit of a screech but not too bad.

His sigh was long suffering. "I get it. You're smart, independent, and full of life. But you need to get it, too." He chewed thoughtfully.

I paused, forgetting my sweetened coffee for a minute. This was unreal. "Get what?"

"Me." His eyes this morning were a gunmetal blue with more than a hint of shadow. "While there's plenty of evidence to the contrary, we're not living in a rom-com, Angel. This is real life with bullets, explosions, and a possible stalker. I'm trained and you're not. I'm a better shot and fighter than you are, although you have an impressive spirit and frightening intelligence. But I'm meaner and have no problem getting my hands bloody." For Aiden, that was a freaking speech.

I couldn't find an answer. What was the answer?

He tossed his napkin on his plate and stood. "I suggest you get rid of the idea that you have to handle danger by yourself in order to be a strong woman. You're strong just sitting there. Don't mess with me on this." He stalked around my counter to the sink.

Mess with him? *Mess with him?* Since the day he'd rescued me when I was ten years old, I'd wanted to be the center of Aiden Devlin's universe. Now finding myself there created warring factions inside me that were anything but comfortable. I liked that he wanted to protect me, but I didn't like being told what to do. In fact, I felt a need to stand up for all of womankind against his attitude, even if it did kind of turn me on. I'd never claimed to be logical. "I don't like your attitude."

"Tough." He finished washing off his plate and set it in the dishwasher.

I threw my napkin on the table, still off balance. "I think we're about to have a fight."

He turned and crossed his muscled arms, looking as formidable as the natural rock outcroppings on McInherney Hill, a hiking area around Lilac Lake. "Go for it."

Sometimes I really did want to punch him in his junk. It was immature and would probably end badly for me, but the temper from my Irish and Italian blood often took over. Now was almost one of those times.

His eyes crinkled. "You want to kick me in the balls, don't you?"

"Yes." I stood and handed my dishes to him across the counter.

"You'll regret that move, Annabella Fiona Albertini," he drawled, accepting them and rinsing them off. It was rare that he used my full name, which was a nod to both sides of my heritage. "But you do what you gotta do."

I straightened my pink sweater over black slacks above new

traction bottomed but stylish boots. "I would, but the reading of the will is in an hour, and I have to get going."

"I'm driving you," he said, shutting the dishwasher.

"The hell you are," I snapped, turning and moving for my laptop bag by the door.

His deep chuckle followed me.

CHAPTER 9

"We're not finished with this fight," I said, sliding from Aiden's truck to the icy ground in front of the stately brick Timber City Gazette building.

"Okay," he said agreeably, dark glasses shielding his eyes from the sun's glare off sparkling snow.

I pressed my lips together and slung my bag over my shoulder. We'd argued, kind of, and then Aiden had assisted me to his truck in a way that I hadn't touched the ground. Normally I didn't mind if he carried me around, but this was getting out of hand. "You're just going to wait out here?"

"No. I have some errands to run and will pick you up when you're finished." His dry tone held a hint of exasperation as if he'd possibly had enough of me for the morning.

"Really? Can I wait outside here for you, or should I duck and cover behind those snowy holly bushes over there?" I looked around. "There are a couple of good trees past the parking lot. I could climb one and toss snowballs to the ground to reveal my location."

He shoved the glasses up his head. "I don't think you were spanked enough as a kid."

My insides went squishy, and my temper heated. "My parents didn't believe in corporal punishment," I grit out.

"There's the problem," he said easily. "Go inside, Angel. Now." Yeah, he'd reached the end of his rather impressive patience.

So had I. "Do you have a cross necklace?" I snapped. Might as well find out.

His eyebrows rose. "Yeah. It's white gold and was my Grams' brother's cross. Why?"

"No reason." I slammed his truck door. Maybe I'd give the cross necklace to one of the Albertini boys and the wallet to Oliver. Yeah. Good plan. With that thought, I stepped carefully across the walkway to the front glass double door, which opened with a good shove. Florence waited inside a wide entryway with a plastic rain bonnet covering her gray hair and tied beneath her chin. Her galoshes were brown, her dress floral, and her makeup powdery.

She craned her neck to see outside. "That's one handsome man driving that big truck."

"He's being bossy," I said, shaking snow off my wool coat.

"He could boss me around any time." She tucked her black pocketbook against her hip. "Is he bossy mean or bossy protective?"

I wiped my boots off on the rough rubber mat. "Bossy protective."

She patted my arm. "Then I'd let it go, unless he sucks in bed. Then I'd ditch him, even though he looks like that. Is he good in bed?"

I made a strangled cat sound and searched wildly for the elevator bank. Well, elevator duo. I guess two elevators didn't make a bank. "We should get going."

She slid her free arm through mine and trod carefully across the tiled floor, her galoshes squeaking and leaving a couple chunks of slush behind. "It's okay not to talk about it, but I can tell

59

he's good in bed." She reached out and poked the button for the third floor.

The whisker burn on my thighs silently agreed with her statement. I ignored both and tried to concentrate.

The stately Timber City Gazette building housed the paper on the east side of the three-story building, while offices took residence on the west side. The offices for O'Malley & Jones, Esq., were located on the third floor. We rode the elevator and exited into a reception area decorated for the holidays in muted red and green, which looked lovely against the white leather furniture in the waiting room.

Considering it was Saturday, the two chairs behind the reception desk were vacant.

A gray head poked out of a room down the elegant hallway. "Mrs. McLintock?" A body in a nice gray suit followed the head, and the man paused at seeing me. "Anna." Chuck O'Malley ushered his bulk down the way, holding out a hand to first shake Florence's hand and then mine. "It's nice to see you," he said.

I smiled. "Thanks. You too."

Chuck O'Malley was an old fishing buddy of my dad's, a nice guy, and a shark as a lawyer. "Excellent. Can I take your coats?"

We both unbuttoned and hung our heavy coats on the metal branch coat rack that actually looked like a real tree in winter. Florence removed her plastic hat to shove in her coat pocket. When we'd finished, he smiled. "Please follow me, and again, I'm sorry we had to do this on a Saturday. I'm leaving town tomorrow to visit family for the holidays, and it was the only time I had since I represent the estate."

Florence followed him, her shoulders straight and her gaze on his butt. "Will your wife be accompanying you?" she murmured.

"I'm a widower," he said, stopping at a doorway to an elegant conference room and gesturing us inside.

"My, but that's a pity," Florence said, brushing closely by him as she swept inside.

I barely kept from rolling my eyes. "Thank you." I walked inside to find a thirty-something man already seated at the far end of the gleaming conference table, a half-full cup of coffee steaming the air next to him. He wore a black flannel shirt, dark jeans, and steel-rimmed glasses.

Florence pulled out a chair, and I followed suit, putting myself between her and the guy at the end of the table.

Chuck paused next to a credenza holding a coffee pot and water. "Can I get you ladies anything to drink?"

We both refused, so Chuck took the head of the table, where a dark blue case file was closed on the polished oak. "Florence McLintock and Anna Albertini, this is Hoyt Forrest."

"We've met," Hoyt said, nodding at Florence, his lips turning down. "But not you, Anna. Who are you?"

"I'm here as a friend," I said.

Chuck started. "A friend? You're not representing Florence?"

"Not exactly," I admitted. "I'm representing Bernie McLintock, and Florence invited me to the will reading." It wasn't a conflict for me to represent Florence if she asked. Well, probably. Unless she became a suspect in the murder, and then she and Bernie couldn't have the same attorney.

Hoyt's brow wrinkled beneath his dark brown hair, and he turned to face Florence more fully before eyeing me. "Wait a minute. You're representing the guy who killed my dad, possibly as an accomplice to this woman? You can't be here."

Florence looked around and dropped her bag to the floor. Then she clasped her gnarled hands on the table and lifted her chin. "Anna, I'd like to hire you as my attorney as long as you can be mine. I understand if there's a conflict, you'll have to withdraw."

I settled. Florence could seriously read a room, and she apparently understood the law fairly well. "You've got it," I said.

Chuck opened his file folder. "In that case, Miss Albertini has every right to attend this reading."

Florence cut me a look of triumph.

I grimaced, not wanting any of this to get more uncomfortable than it already had become. "Mr. Forrest, I'm very sorry for your loss." Somebody had to say it. "I know that Florence is grieving as well, and it's unfortunate we had to meet under these very sad circumstances." I couldn't imagine losing my father, and my heart hurt for the guy.

His lips tightened. "I think your client helped kill him, and I've made a report with the police to that fact."

Florence paled beneath her powdery pink blush. "That's not nice, Hoyt. I didn't kill Lawrence, and neither did Bernie."

"Bernie, your former husband?" Hoyt shot back.

"Enough." I leaned forward to partially block his view of my new client. Anger was an element of grief, so I kept my voice gentle. "Let's hear the will, and then we can go on from there." I still had doubts whether or not Florence should give the money from the ring to Hoyt.

Chuck cleared his throat and drew out a Last Will and Testament on the good thick paper used for wills. "As you know, we represented Lawrence Forrest and now represent his estate." He scanned the heavy stock paper. "The document sets aside funds for a funeral and directs us to pay any and all debts before distributing the rest of the estate." He read some more. "After that, Lawrence made several specific bequests."

I reached for a legal pad from a stack in the middle of the table and then took a pen from a holder next to the paper.

Chuck kept reading. "Lawrence left his various shotguns, all listed here, to the Kringle Club, directing them to disperse the guns as they see fit." He looked up as I made notes. "He left the fully owned Forrest Bait and Tackle Shop, including the land, building, improvements, inventory, and two bank accounts to his son, Hoyt Forrest."

Hoyt sat back, his body visibly relaxing for the first time.

Chuck flipped a page. "The residence at Twenty-Two Spruce

Lane, along with the accompanying twenty acres of forest land, is bequeathed to Florence McLintock."

Hoyt sucked in a breath.

Florence slowly slid her hands off the table. "I, well, this is unexpected."

"No shit," Hoyt snarled.

I exhaled and looked at Chuck. "Does that take care of the specific bequests?"

"No." Chuck flipped the page again. "All vehicles go to Hoyt, the lake cabin goes to Florence, and the investment accounts, now equaling approximately two million dollars, are bequeathed to Florence."

Florence gasped.

Hoyt slammed his fist on the table.

Florence jumped in her seat and turned toward him. "Hoyt, I didn't know. This is, well, we can come to some sort of...."

I put my hand on her arm. "Let's all take a day or so to think about this before you make decisions." I had a duty to represent my client and make sure she understood all of her options. If she wanted to refuse the bequests from the deceased, she had every right to do so—but I couldn't let her be hasty.

Hoyt's face turned a motley red, and he stood, looking taller than I'd surmised. Probably around six feet or so. He glared down at us. "If I can prove she murdered my father, then she gets nothing, right?"

I also stood. "That's enough."

Anger darkened his brown eyes behind the glasses, and his nostrils flared. "Is that it for the will?"

Chuck pushed his reading glasses farther up his nose. "Ah, no. One more bestowal." He cleared his throat. "A third stock portfolio, approximate value of one hundred thousand dollars, to a Ms. Sharon Smith."

Florence stiffened. "Who is Sharon Smith?"

Hoyt ducked his head. "I agree. Who the hell is she?"

Chuck closed the case file. "I'm sorry, but that's all I can tell you—except that I don't even have an address for her. Supposedly, she's going to contact us upon learning of Lawrence's death, and she has not done so to date. Other than that, the residual property, meaning anything that's left after the specific bequests, goes to Florence."

"Fucking great," Hoyt snapped. "I can't believe this. He's been my dad for nearly forty years and your fiancé for what…less than a week? When did he redo this will, anyway? I saw the old one, which had been in place for two decades. I find this very suspicious."

Chuck slid two envelopes across the table, both clearly labeled as one for Florence and the other for Hoyt. "These are for you."

Florence's hand shook as she pulled the envelope toward her to place in her purse. "I want to know who this Sharon is and right now."

"Me too," Hoyt growled.

Chuck placed his hands on the folder. "We're under instructions from the testator to keep that information confidential. There might be an explanation in the letters I've handed to you, but I have not read them, so I do not know."

Hoyt smacked the envelope against his hand. "I'm an heir under the will and demand to know who she is."

"Sorry," Chuck said.

Hoyt glared. "I'll get a lawyer and sue you for that information."

Chuck nodded. "Go ahead."

"Let's go." I assisted Florence to stand, wanting to get out of the building before Hoyt and figuring he'd want to stay and argue with Chuck for some time.

Florence stood unsteadily and then gathered herself, turning for the doorway. She looked old and frail in front of me, and a swell of protectiveness hurried my steps. She had to be about five feet tall, even in the galoshes, and she'd been hit with a surprise.

The bounty might be a *nice* surprise, but I figured she'd much rather have Lawrence than the money. We silently donned our coats and rode the elevator down to the first floor.

"Would you like to grab lunch?" I asked gently.

She looked up at me, her eyes wide in her powdery face. "No, but thank you. I need some time to digest all of this."

I reached for my gloves from my pocket. "Florence? Did Bernie know he'd be inheriting the shotguns?" I didn't know a value as of yet, but some shotguns could be quite valuable, and Bernie didn't need one more motive against him.

"I don't know." She looked befuddled.

I glanced at the envelope sticking out of her bag. "Will you let me know if there's any information in that letter that I need to know as your attorney?"

"Yes." She walked outside into the bright snowy day, scouting the almost vacant parking lot. "Your man isn't here."

That's because I hadn't texted him yet. "Do you mind dropping me off on your way home?" I noticed a bright green Buick parked two slots down that had to belong to her.

"Not at all." She patted my hand. "One thing I've learned in my long life of dating different men is that you have to make them work for it." She tried to smile, but her lips trembled. "If he's being bossy, you can't just roll over, dear. No matter how badly you might want to do so."

I tucked my arm through hers, taking some of her weight. "Amen, sister."

CHAPTER 10

A longstanding staple in Timber City, Smiley's Diner was hopping after lunch on a Saturday afternoon. Most of the booths were full of people and brightly wrapped Christmas presents, and Mariah Carey crooned *Silent Night* through invisible speakers. I meandered past the counter with its bright stools, beyond many of the comfortable leather booths to the last one at the end, which was vacant. Sighing happily, I slid onto the far bench, dropping my heavy purse to the side.

My sister delivered two baskets of fries to a table and then bustled my way, looking harried but still beautiful in her holiday green apron over her jeans and plain white T-shirt. "Hey. I'm on break in ten. How about I join you for lunch?" Tessa asked. She was the middle sister and favored the Irish side of our family with her strawberry blonde hair, sparkling green eyes, and skin that burned at midnight.

I smiled, instantly relaxing and not feeling guilty that I had taken an entire booth. "I'd love it."

"I'll order the usual." She turned on her tennis shoes and moved gracefully, in a way I'd never be able to emulate.

I pulled out a notebook from my bag and started taking notes for Bernie's case, trying to figure out who had a motive to kill Lawrence. Had Bernie known about the guns? Florence had left the list with me, so I could track down the value of each weapon. Hoyt had mentioned reading a will, one where he most likely inherited everything.

Had he killed his father, knowing Lawrence would change the will to include Florence once they were married?

So far, my list consisted of his son Hoyt, the mysterious Sharon Smith, his friend Bernie, the other living members of the Kringle Club, and his ex-fiancée, Florence. My gut told me that neither Bernie nor Florence had killed him, but I'd been wrong before. Really wrong. I also had a question mark at the bottom of the list because I'd learned that a case evolved rapidly, and more suspects usually showed up.

I dug in my purse for my phone and hit speed dial.

"Pierce," Detective Pierce muttered.

I tried to infuse cheerfulness into my voice. "Hi, Grant. I hope I'm not bothering you during the weekend."

"Right." Apparently my voice didn't melt him. "What do you want, Albertini?"

It was hard to imagine that he'd kind of asked me out once. "I might have a lead on who killed Lawrence Forrest, and if I hand it over, I need a favor."

"How about you hand it over and thus don't interfere with an active investigation?"

I tapped my pen on the paper. "Fine." Then I told him about the will, slightly omitting the part about the guns going to the Kringle Club. Then I figured I should add that fact because no doubt Pierce would get his hands on a copy of the will by dinnertime. Finally, I wound down. "If you could do a run on Sharon Smith and find out who she is, I'd really appreciate it."

"I don't work for you," Pierce said, not sounding quite as grumpy.

"I don't work for you either," I reminded him. "However, I just gave you several leads in your primary case right now, so maybe you can be a nice guy for a change?"

"Humph." He didn't sound quite so cranky. "I'm doing a run on all of Florence's ex-husbands and haven't found anything interesting."

I perked up. Sometimes Pierce was a decent guy who shared. "Where are they?"

"One is in Australia, one in Scotland, two are dead from natural causes, one is in DC, and the final one is here. Bernie. Your client." Papers rustled across the line. "I was able to speak with each one of them, and they all still love the woman, although seemed to have moved as far as possible away from her. She must have some magic in her veins."

Well, that didn't help my case any. "So no viable suspects?"

"Nope. Looks like your guy might be the one." Pierce clicked off.

I looked down at the phone in my hand. So much for Pierce's new love not making him so grumpy. "Jerk," I muttered, sliding my phone back into my bag.

The smell of cheeseburgers wafted around, and my stomach growled. Tessa returned with two baskets of burgers and fries, depositing them and reaching for sodas from the counter. She sat and let out a relieved sigh. "The shoppers are out in full force."

I pushed my papers aside and reached for the burger. "I can see that. It's crazy, right?" I took a big bite and chewed contentedly before swallowing. "Are you finished shopping?"

"No." She sipped her drink. "I know you're not. You always finish up on the way to Mom and Dad's on Christmas Eve." The woman wasn't wrong. "Did you find anything for Aiden?"

I sighed, my neck aching. If I had time and funds, I'd get a massage. Instead, I'd just have to lie on a tennis ball later that day and try to work out the knots. "No, but I have been piling up presents for everyone else in the family, including a new cross necklace for Knox, since I drew his name in the bigger family drawing." I ate more of my fries, enjoying the extra oil and crunchiness that the cooks at Smiley's had perfected through the decades. "I guess a cross wouldn't work for Aiden anyway—it's too personal?"

Tessa nodded. "Yeah. You're at more of a 'known each other forever but just started dating' phase of gift giving."

"Exactly," I agreed, reaching for the ketchup bottle to squirt in the side of my basket. "I don't know what that means. Socks and shirts are impersonal, jewelry is too much, and it's not like he needs a new Glock." I dipped my fries and ate more than I needed. "I'm at a loss."

The outside door opened, and Nick Basanelli spotted us, turning instantly to head our way. I straightened and chose at that moment not to give Tessa a heads up. Sometimes I'm an ass, but I really did want to see them together.

He reached the table, lifting his hands in the air. "Well?"

Tessa jolted and swiveled, looking up at him. "Well, what?" she asked, a snap of temper in her voice.

Interesting. Very interesting. I just watched him, chewing my fries, my eyes wide. Nick Basanelli worked as the prosecuting attorney for Timber City after being a JAG officer, football star, and before that, a wild and rebellious kid from Silverville. He had two younger brothers, a dad who'd hit them and then disappeared, and a mother who was almost a saint. I'd worked for him briefly, and he'd fired me—probably because working with me definitely hindered his extreme ambition to run for office someday. "Hi, Nick," I said, smiling.

He didn't look away from my sister. *Very* interesting. "Hi, Anna. Rumor has it you're representing Bernie McLintock for killing Santa."

I sighed. Word sure got around. "You're not charging him, are you?"

Nick finally looked my way, his tawny brown eyes showing both his Italian heritage and his extreme irritation. "Probably."

"Great." I drank more of my soda.

He put his hands on his very fit waist, which led to a spectacular ass and long legs in jeans to black boots. His jacket was a winter-green that showed off his wide torso. His skin was an Italian olive hue, his hair dark, and his features angle straight. "Tessa? Want to tell me why you stood me up?"

My sister blinked. "What in the world are you talking about?"

"We're supposed to be heading over the hill to the Silverville Elks Lodge to plan that stupid holiday party," he groused, straightening and then wincing. "Don't tell me. You didn't know that?"

"Nope," Tessa said, her green eyes sparkling. "Your grandma set you up, buddy. I'd think you'd know to look for a trap."

He wiped snow off his thick hair. "I wasn't thinking." Then he glanced at his watch. "They've been trying to get us to help plan for two months now, and we haven't made it to one meeting. I wish they'd stop playing games."

Tessa lost the amusement. "Me, too."

Nick shook his head. "I'm in trial next week and should get back to work. Sorry to have bothered you." He paused, studying her face.

A pretty blush wandered through her pale skin. "No problem." She turned back to her burger.

Nick watched her for a minute, threw up his hands, and stomped out of the restaurant.

"What was that about?" I asked.

She shrugged. "Nothing. Our grandmas keep trying to push us together, and we don't fit, as you know."

That was baloney. "Has he asked you out?"

Her shrug this time was a little more reluctant. "Kind of. He's asked me for drinks, but I'm sure it's just to appease his Grams. I'm not a pity date."

It was so weird. My sister was smart, kind, hard-working, and seriously beautiful in a young Maureen O'Hara way. Yet she thought, for some really stupid reason, that not going to college put her out of Nick's league, just because he'd attended law school. Sometimes I wanted to smack her on the nose, but since I'd seen her take down an undercover ATF officer in a bar fight a few months previous to defend me, I wasn't sure I'd win a scuffle. "Maybe he likes you."

She finished her soda. "Nick Basanelli likes his job, his ambition, and his future. I don't fit with any of those items."

I shook my head. "I don't have the energy right now to kick you, and you really need to get a grip. He'd be lucky if you accepted a date for drinks."

"Huh." She glanced at her wristwatch. "I have five more minutes. Give me the scoop on Aiden and how it feels to have him back in town."

I'd texted her that morning that he was home, but I hadn't mentioned the roses, heart, or phone call. Why worry my family when I didn't have any information to report? They had enough on their minds with the holidays. "I think it's good that he's back, but he's being a little bossy."

She sat back and stretched her neck. "You like him bossy."

"Yeah, but I shouldn't," I admitted. "I'm letting down all of womankind by not teaching him a lesson."

Her chuckle was soft. "We both know that you'd end up learning the lesson." Then she leaned toward me. "You like him, he likes you, so stop worrying about womankind. We can take care of ourselves, and you deserve to be you and to be happy. Let him protect you and allow yourself to enjoy that feeling of safety."

Such great advice, and it was too bad she couldn't listen to herself *for* herself. My eye roll appropriately conveyed my irritation with her. Then I finished my soda. "Can I borrow your car for the afternoon? I had a friend drop me off here."

She tilted her head. "What's going on?"

"Nothing. Just ignoring you and doing my part for womankind." I wasn't sure if avoiding Aiden and investigating on my own did much good for anybody else, but a girl did have her pride. Plus, I had a job to do and was more than prepared with a LadySmith in my purse.

Tessa grabbed the empty baskets and dodged around the counter, leaning down and then tossing me her keys.

I caught them one-handed, scooted from the booth, and started to rummage for my wallet.

She held up a hand. "Lunch is on me." Then she smoothed down her holiday style apron. "What should I tell Aiden when he shows up and you're not here?"

Yeah, my sister knew me. "Tell him to bite me."

"If I know Aiden, he just might," she called back.

My legs might've wobbled a bit on the way to the door, but I held my head up high.

CHAPTER 11

Since I hoped Hoyt was still off nursing his wounds, I headed to the Forrest Bait and Tackle Shop, which was around Lilac Lake, beyond the Clumsy Penguin, marina, and an out-of-business spa. Since I'd had a small hand in putting the spa out of business, I couldn't exactly complain. Hopefully somebody would buy the building and start an inexpensive massage service.

I really needed a massage. The knots on my neck had their own knots.

The lake road had been recently plowed with a nice gravel dumping to follow, and my tires spit up the gravel, no doubt scratching parts of Tessa's Nissan Rogue. Her SUV was several years old but well-kept, although sometimes I figured she'd bought it for the name. Smiling to myself, I took a wide turn and then drove into the parking area for the store.

Quaint white-painted and weathered boards made up the exterior of Forrest's Bait and Tackle Shop, which had been built across the road from a public boat ramp for the lake. While the location was a prime property these days, decades ago, it had been in the middle of nowhere.

Old Man Forrest, Lawrence's grandfather, had been a visionary. Or maybe he'd just gotten the land for cheap. Who knew?

The parking area had been plowed, and large snow berms bracketed the lot on either side. Christmas lights twinkled along the eves in a bright blue color, and dancing reindeer had been painted on the wide windows. A sign listed the holiday hours with a note that the shop would close after New Year's until spring.

How many people did their holiday shopping at a bait and tackle shop? Did Aiden fish?

I stepped out of Tessa's white Rogue and walked through the door. The smell of driftwood wafted around me, along with the muted sounds of Christmas music playing from a speaker on the glass counter to the right. The store held flannels, fishing equipment, hunting equipment, and other odds and ends, including several wildlife figurines. By the far window facing the icy lake perched a table displaying western jewelry along with baubles made of ash from the Mt. Saint Helen's eruption decades ago.

A woman emerged from a room behind the counter. "Hi. Can I help you?" She looked to be in her mid-thirties with light brown hair streaked with green, darker brown eyes, and a curvy figure.

I looked around. "I'm not sure." The place appeared to be well-stocked. How could I get a copy of their financials? Did Hoyt need money? Even if he wasn't destitute, his father had left millions of dollars to other beneficiaries. Millions Hoyt had apparently known about, whereas Florence had not. She'd thought Lawrence had spent his entire fortune on her ring—yet another reason I didn't think she'd killed him.

Did she even have the strength to kill a man with a knife? I doubted it. "I'm looking for a couple of things. First, I need a present for my boyfriend. Second, I have an uncle who's interested in buying a bait and tackle shop. He's from Minnesota and wants to move closer to family. Is there any chance you'd want to sell?" I was so full of it.

She tapped a bunch of stamped notebooks into place on the

counter. "I don't own the place, but I'm pretty sure Hoyt doesn't want to sell. I've worked for the family since I was a teenager, and they do a pretty decent business, and they get to go fishing all summer."

"Oh." I ran a finger along a red flannel. Did Aiden like flannel? "So it's a family business. That's nice."

She sobered. "Well, it was nice, but the main owner just died, so we're all pretty sad." Her eyes widened. "He was such a great guy, and he was murdered."

I turned fully to face her and let my eyebrows rise. "Murdered? Not the Santa who was killed."

She nodded. "Yeah. He was stabbed after playing poker. Can you believe it? Who would stab Santa?"

I took an extra-large black flannel off the rack, figuring I should at least buy something. "Do you have any idea who would've killed him?"

She took the shirt and twisted off part of the tag. "No. It's just crazy, right? Lawrence was the nicest guy in the world, and he spent extra time pretending to be Santa for anybody who needed holiday cheer. He was going to get married this summer, too. It's all so sad."

I reached in my bag for my wallet. "That's devastating. Do they think the fiancée is a suspect?" I opened my eyes wide and lowered my voice in the tone of a true gossip.

She leaned toward me. "No, but the fiancée's ex-husband threatened to kill Lawrence last week right here in the store." She rang up the sale and pursed her lips. "I might be a witness in a trial. Can you believe it?"

I should've looked at the price but just handed over a credit card. How much credit did I have on that card? "A witness? No. Wow. What happened?"

She looked around the store, but nobody was shopping at the moment. "It was wild. Lawrence was reorganizing the hunting knives over in the corner, and this Bernie guy comes running in, yelling something about Kringles and marriage and, this is weird, but lures."

I frowned. "Like fishing lures?"

She shrugged, running my card through the reader. "I guess. He kept yelling that they had a deal, and how dare Lawrence back out, and that he was going to regret it. I couldn't quite catch everything he was saying, but then he told Lawrence he was going to kill him if he didn't stop it."

"Stop what?" I asked. Was Bernie so furious because Lawrence was just working outside of the group, or was it the engagement that had him seeing red?

"Dunno." She handed over the receipt for me to sign. "I hope your boyfriend likes the flannel. You guys just started dating, huh?"

I signed. "Kind of. Is this a first dating kind of present?"

"Yeah." She bagged the shirt and handed it over. "It's a cool but not serious present."

I bit my lip. That didn't describe us. "Thanks." Wait a minute. She'd worked for the family for years? "I'm so sorry. Where are my manners? I'm Anna." I held out my free hand.

"Fran." She shook my hand. "It's nice to meet you."

I coughed. "Oh. I figured you were Sharon Smith." Yep. Totally fishing right then since I figured Sharon didn't work at the store. Perhaps Fran knew her.

She frowned. "No. Who's that?"

Great question and I was nowhere closer to finding out. "Dunno." I turned and headed to the door with my bag that contained the wrong Christmas present for Aiden Devlin. Maybe my dad would like it.

* * *

I CALLED Bernie from the Rogue and arranged to meet him at McQuirk's Deli by the prosecuting attorney's office for an afternoon coffee. I was hot on the case and not avoiding Aiden, and I could almost convince myself of that fact. My phone had buzzed a few times from him, and I figured I'd read his texts later. Right now, I needed to concentrate.

Yeah, I could bury my head in the sand like the best of them. Or in the snow, anyway.

McQuirk's was quiet this winter afternoon with more holiday music playing throughout. I sat at a table near the window that looked out past the silent volleyball courts to the frigid lake. Lilac Lake was much bigger than my quaint Tamarack Lake, even to the point of being connected to rivers on either side that could lead to other lakes. Today the cold had stilled her waves, giving her a steel-gray hue that made me shiver.

Bloated clouds had rolled in, fierce and gray, starting to smother the weak sun. A quick scroll through my phone showed that snow was coming. I didn't really need an app to tell me that.

My phone buzzed again, this time with a call. "Hi. I'm fine," I answered.

"Where are you?" Aiden asked mildly.

"I'm working but am safe. Armed and everything," I said, blowing on my peppermint mocha. "I'll need a ride home a little later, but if you're not around, I'll find somebody."

"You know, Angel, when I drop you off somewhere, I like you to be there when I return to fetch you." He still sounded calm, which might be a bad thing. "I'm gonna ask you again. Where are you?"

I was feeling fairly safe since he obviously hadn't pinged my GPS. He'd have to go through official ATF channels to do it, and my gut told me he wanted to avoid that at the moment, especially since his bust had gone south. Not that we'd talked about it yet, so I was just guessing. "I'm meeting a client, and I think you should stop being so bossy."

"I'm not being bossy. You have a stalker, probably, and I'm

being safe. What'd be very nice is if you wanted to be safe as well."

Not. So. Mild.

I breathed out. "I am safe. I've taken every precaution, I'm armed, and I don't like you making me feel like I'm helpless or can't take care of myself." The words rushed out of me.

Silence ticked for a minute. "I don't want you to feel helpless," he finally said quietly. "I'm sorry if I've been holding on too tight. It's just, knowing you might be in danger...not that I have any right to talk, considering my job."

I swallowed. "We're still finding our way, Aiden." If he got any sweeter, I'd just roll over like a puppy. "I should've told you I had plans." Yeah, I'd acted a mite immature. It was a character flaw that I should probably work on in my spare time. "I'm at McQuirk's meeting a client and then will take Tessa's rig back to her at the diner. How about we meet there in an hour?"

"Sounds good. I'll see you then." He ended the call.

I slipped my phone back into my purse. The guy never said goodbye. Was it a thing with him? I forgot all about it as Bernie walked in from the parking lot side, shaking snow off his gray hair in the entryway. He spotted me, waved, and then moved for the counter.

When he joined me at the table, he held what smelled like a pumpkin spiced latte. "It's good to see you." He sat.

I took another sip of my rich brew. "Did you know that the Kringle Club was going to inherit all of Lawrence's guns?"

Bernie's eyebrows rose. "No. Wow. He had some great shotguns—worth quite a bit."

I reached in my purse and handed over the list. "Give me an estimate for each, would you?" There were fifteen shotguns or rifles on the list.

"Sure." He tugged a pen from his front pocket and started making notes.

"Did you know that Lawrence had proposed to Florence?" I asked, watching him carefully.

He paused and looked up, his eyes pained behind his glasses. "No. Did she accept?"

"Yes."

"I knew that he'd purchased a ring but not that he'd actually popped the question." Bernie grimaced. "Lawrence and Florence. They sound dumb together." Then he jolted and crossed himself. "May Lawrence rest in peace."

The guy seemed like he was telling the truth. "Did you know that Florence inherited millions from Lawrence?" I asked.

Bernie straightened, making his blue bowtie peek over the top of his zippered down jacket. "No. Millions? Lawrence had millions?" He scratched a dark spot on his worn skin by his nose. "I had no idea. He didn't act rich."

I cocked my head, sipping quietly. "Why wouldn't Lawrence leave his estate to his son?"

"They didn't get along," Bernie said. "Lawrence got into the whiskey one night, probably late last summer, and spilled that Hoyt has a gambling problem. The guy spends all his time at the casinos on the reservations around here when he's not headed to Vegas. It caused problems between them. Bad ones."

Interesting. Did Hoyt owe people money? I made a mental note to call Detective Pierce with the new info. "Tell me about you threatening Lawrence."

Tears gathered in Bernie's cataract-riddled eyes. "I was so mad. Earl told me that Lawrence had purchased the ring, and I just lost it. Oh, I was irritated about the movie and Lawrence wanting to be in it, but that normally wouldn't have set me off. What kind of a guy proposes to his best friend's ex-wife? What was he thinking?" Bernie's entire sunken chest moved when he exhaled. "I know what he was thinking. Flo is amazing. Who wouldn't want to marry her?" He finished scribbling on the paper. "The hard part is keeping her. She gets bored easy and moves on. I got angry and made a mistake. A big one."

I kind of felt sorry for the guy. "What happened?"

"I cheated on her. Just once and just one night where I had way too much to drink. I don't even remember it." He wiped his eyes. "Biggest mistake of my life."

"I'm sorry," I said, not knowing why. "Tell me about you threatening him."

The story he related was exactly what Fran had told me earlier. "I was just mad about the ring. That's all," Bernie said.

"Okay." I cocked my head. "What was it about lures?"

He sighed. "Is there anything you don't find out?"

"Yeah," I said quietly. "But the prosecution finds out everything. How about you finally level with me?"

His shoulders hunched. "Fine. Lawrence and I were going to open a second bait and tackle shop in Montana, and I already had lures ordered, and then he goes and falls in love with the love of my life. I couldn't go into business with a guy married to Flo."

Yet another motive. The guy was killing me. He looked so sad, I reached out and patted his hand. "One last question. Do you know a Sharon Smith?"

He blinked. "Um, yeah. Why?"

My breath quickened. "Who is she?"

He turned a beet red. Like a bruised beet that somebody had stepped on several times. "She's the woman from the one-night stand. When I cheated on Florence and ruined my whole life."

CHAPTER 12

*D*arkness had prematurely descended in the form of silver-bellied clouds and falling snow by the time Aiden picked me up from Smiley's Diner. While Sharon Smith had helped to ruin Bernie's life, he didn't really know her and had no clue how to find her.

That was now my job. At least I had a direction to take the case.

I ran through the pummeling flakes and jumped into Aiden's truck, keeping the bag with his shirt against my side. "Hi." Warmth instantly surrounded me when I shut the door.

"Hi." He ducked his head, looked in the mirror, and pulled out onto Main Street, the windshield wipers swishing rhythmically. He'd ditched his coat, which lay on the console between us. A simple tee hugged his broad chest. "How did it go with your client?"

The innocuous question relaxed me as nothing else could have. Yeah, we were tripping and falling while we found our way together, but things were okay now. I secured my seatbelt and brushed snow off my jeans. "I'm not sure." For a while, I thought I was perhaps finding good information for Bernie's defense, but then maybe not. I hadn't put the pieces together yet, but my instincts were humming and strong. "What about you? How were your errands?"

"Good." He turned at a stoplight, heading west. "I think I found an office for my team."

I stilled. "An office here?" Aiden ran a Special Response Team for the ATF, and most of the elite teams were based out of big cities. Only Aiden's team was recently allowed to relocate closer to a satellite office in Spokane, but his office had been blown up during the summer, and then they'd been off on undercover ops since. "As in here in Timber City and not in Spokane?"

"Yeah." He ducked his head and turned toward Lilac Lake Road. "Since we're not going in-house with the Spokane office, there doesn't seem to be a reason we can't locate here. So long as we're allowed to relocate."

My skin buzzed. "Is there a chance you'll be called back to LA?"

He turned down the lake road, spitting up gravel. "Yes. Our last case didn't go well, so the juice we had riding from the arrests last summer is drying up."

So did the spit in my mouth. Was he going to have to leave again? Maybe not if they signed a lease. "Where's the possible new office?"

He pulled into an unplowed lot fronting what used to be the spa. The wide windows hung like dark squares in the one-story brick building. "The place is pretty convenient and has exits at key locations, including out to the lake, in case we ever need to hunt by boat." His gaze swept me. "Or escape via boat."

I punched him in the arm, and my knuckles instantly protested. "Funny." Ignoring my dream for a cheap massage, I let hope flitter through me. If the ATF signed a lease, they'd have to stay for the duration. "What are you thinking? Ten or twelve year lease?"

He chuckled, and the low sound wound right through my skin

to warm me. "I can get six months, tops. We'll have to reevaluate from there."

It was better than nothing. A heck of a lot better. I reached out and held his hand, feeling slightly like a dork but too happy to care. Aiden had great hands. Large, strong, and always warm. There were callouses on the pads of his fingers, making them slightly rough. Definitely masculine.

"What are you thinking?" he asked as fat flakes fell lightly on the front window.

"About Christmas and presents," I lied. "You're hard to buy for."

He cut the engine and let the snow envelop us in our own little world. "I have your present."

I perked up. "Really?"

"Yep." He settled back, overwhelming the seat.

"Are you going to give me a hint?" I softened my voice as the silence pounded in and turned to face him, drawing one leg up beneath me and releasing the seatbelt.

"Nope." A smile flirted with his full mouth. In profile, he was solid angles and rugged Irish features.

Curiosity, like always, rode me hard. But I also knew that Aiden wouldn't tell me if he didn't want to, so there was very little chance I could pry out information from him. How could I get access to his credit card records?

"I paid cash," he murmured lazily, still watching the snow dance on the building.

I sucked in air. His ability to read my mind was sometimes frightening. "Whatever."

His smile widened. In a smooth motion, he twisted, grasped my hips, and lifted me over the console to land on his lap. The seat was already all the way back, but he pressed a lever, and the steering wheel rose, giving me more room. "Now we're gonna talk about you not being where I expected to pick you up."

I rested my back against his door and kicked out my feet over the console, wriggling a little to get comfortable on his lap.

His slight groan bubbled humor through me.

"I might've acted a little recklessly," I said, wondering if it were true. Wondering if I'd do the same thing again in the same situation. "I don't take well to being bossed around."

"I've noticed," he said. He tucked me closer and cupped my face in his wide palm.

I sighed, leaning into his touch. "I might've irritated you, but I wasn't stupid or reckless. I was in safe places and fully armed." Then I chuckled. "You know those movies where the heroine runs into the dark forest after the killer? I always root for the killer. If she's that dumb, he deserves a win."

Aiden laughed, his chest moving nicely against me. "Fair enough. I know you're not stupid or reckless, and I'm sure you were aware and smart. Yet everyone needs somebody to watch their backs." His voice lowered. "And I do adore your back."

His phone buzzed. We made some intricate maneuvers so he could drag it out from his jacket, which was beneath my ankles. Finally, he lifted it to his ear. "Devlin."

He changed. Went from playful and relaxed to alert and intense...in a heartbeat. "Got it. I'll be there." He ended the call, deftly lifted me back to my seat, and started the truck. "I have a meeting."

"No kidding." I quickly buckled my belt as he flipped on the windshield wipers. "What's going on?"

He pulled out of the lot, turning the truck back toward town. "Our covers were blown in Portland, and Saber may have a line on how that happened. We're working out of my cabin for now." He exited the lake road and drove down the cheery middle of town, the holiday lights flashing across his lethal face. "I may be late tonight."

I hunkered down in my seat and tried not to beam at his

assumption that he'd be staying over. We were totally figuring out this dating thing.

Now. What to get him for Christmas?

* * *

I HAD Aiden drop me off at my oldest sister's home. Donna lived in a cute craftsman-style house in an older part of Timber City that she'd picked up for a dream price because of her job as a realtor. I found both Donna and my mom wrapping Christmas presents for the Elk's Christmas children's drive, and I dove right in. While I didn't have the precise expertise of either of them, I was more than capable of 'putting a finger here' as they tied intricate bows.

"How's your Santa case going?" Donna asked absently, measuring the exact size of a green ribbon.

I shrugged, admiring her white pants outfit. Donna was what could fondly be described as a clotheshorse, and I often found myself shopping for free in her closet. She was a few inches taller than me, and our coloring was different, but I still made some good finds. Unlike Tessa, Donna took after the Italian side of our family with her thick dark hair, stunning brown eyes, and dusky skin color.

I, on the other hand, had brown curly hair, gray-green eyes, and skin that burned. I didn't look like anybody in our family. Not really.

Donna frowned at the ribbon. "Is that even?"

Our mom tilted her head to the side and studied the ribbon as if the cure to cancer lived in the cut. "No. Just a bit more." She sat back when Donna cut and then smiled. "That's it."

The ribbon had looked fine to me. I grinned at our mom. She wore black pants, a green sweater, and diamond earrings. She looked like an older version of Tessa with even more of an Irish complexion, and she had a slight brogue when her temper blew, which was rare. Our mother was special. Probably the strongest person I'd ever met. She was soft spoken, humorous, and managed the world with shrewd humility. She also didn't ask for anything but respect and kindness, which were what every good mother deserved in this life.

Her green eyes sparkled when she focused on me. "I heard Aiden is back in town."

"Yep," I said. "Speaking of which, do you think Dad would like a new flannel for Christmas?"

"He does love his flannels," my mom said agreeably. "What are you going to give to Aiden?"

"I don't know," I admitted. "I'm lost. Any ideas?"

She pursed her lips. "No clue." Then she deftly snipped more wrapping paper to cover a puzzle of frogs dancing on a cloud. "Please tell me you're finished with the Santa murder case."

"Not yet." I put my finger in the middle of the wrapping paper before asking, "Do you know a Sharon Smith?"

"No," Mom answered, trapping my finger. "I do know Florence, however. She was devastated when Bernie cheated on her."

So everybody knew about the breakup. "Do you know any of the details?"

She swept her hand in the air. "Of course not. I heard the basics and ignored the rest. Gossip never does anybody good."

Gossip could actually do a lawyer a lot of good. But my mom didn't just sound classy—she was classy. The woman truly disliked gossip. However, I had other sources, including my grandparents. While they were still classy, they also liked to keep their thumbs pressed on the pulse of the world around them.

I tugged my finger free and looked at Donna. "Do you know Hoyt Forrest?"

"Sure. I sold him his lake cabin," she said, reaching for a box of what looked like Legos that would make cars. "Heard he lost it to the bank though."

That would track with what I'd heard about his gambling addiction.

"It was too bad," Donna continued. "His girlfriend loved the place and was already planning where to put the water skis on the wall for decorations."

I paused in reaching for a set of books that had fur coming out of puppy ears. "Girlfriend?"

Donna frowned. "Yeah. Her name was, what was it? Something cute. Um, Lucy. Yeah, that's it. Lucy Gardiner."

I had never heard of her, but Timber City was growing, so that wasn't unusual these days. "Do you remember anything about her?" Was she still dating Hoyt? I needed to find her.

Donna reached for sparkly white paper. "Let's see. What did she say?" She cut expertly along the line on the back side. "I think she said something about saving for more decorations and working at Buck's Candy Store and Ice Creamery over on Oakwood? The only reason I remember that is because she brought me some butterscotch candies, and I thought that was sweet."

My pulse jumped. All right. More leads to follow. The girlfriend would know how deep Hoyt was with gambling debts as well as the status of his relationship with his father.

It made me sick to think that a son would kill his own dad, but if Hoyt had been desperate and if he'd known that Lawrence was going to leave the bulk of his estate to Florence, who knew?

My mom glanced at her watch. "Oh. I have to go. I'm meeting your father for dinner over the hill."

I loved that they still had date night. My dad was a badass miner and a tough guy, but he was putty in my mom's hands. "Do you have time to give me a ride home first?" I asked.

"Of course." She reached for her jacket. "We can brainstorm a present for Aiden on the way. How about an engagement ring? Men wear those, right?"

Donna shot me a sympathetic look but didn't put herself in the line of fire.

I wished I'd just asked to borrow a car. "No, mom. They don't."

"Well," she said cheerfully, sliding her arm through mine. "We could always change that. Right?"

CHAPTER 13

$\mathcal{I}$ stared into my freezer, not feeling all that inspired. Cooking relaxed me, so I often had dinners prepped far in advance, but lasagna or Irish stew just weren't doing it for me, even though it was well past dinnertime. So I shut the dinged white metallic door and returned to my kitchen table, where I'd spread out my notes on Bernie's case. My phone buzzed, and I lifted it absently to my ear. "Anna Albertini."

"Anna, oh my. We have a situation," Thelma said, her voice shrill.

I set down my pen and stood, already heading for my boots. "Define situation."

"Bernie has been drinking all day down at Dunphey's bar and was just yelling about taking down the bastard who'd killed Lawrence. Said it was his son, Hoyt, and he's going to take matters into his own hands." Thelma sniffed. "The bartender called me, and then Bernie came on the line. I think he might do it, even though he's toasted."

I shrugged into my jacket, grabbed my purse, and scrambled for my keys in the bowl by the door. The bag hung heavily on my arm with the gun inside it. It was nearly ten at night, but I'd be careful. "I'm on my way."

"We'd go get him, but Georgiana and I might've gotten into the brownies after dinner. Cataracts, you know."

I hustled through my small laundry room to the garage door and my stomach rolled over. I'd accidentally ingested their marijuana brownies before and had ended up killing a pot of hydrangeas as the chocolate had come back up. The bad reaction had also included paranoid delusions, so I hadn't gone near their baked goods since. "That's okay. I'll pick him up. Is he armed?"

She was silent for a second. "He didn't say anything, but most of us are armed, sweetie. You drive very carefully and don't hurry. I got him to wait for you."

I hit the garage door button and jumped into my SUV, missing my summer car, which was a Fiat. The older beauty wasn't good on the snow, but she could drive fast. "How did you do that?" I backed out into the rapidly falling snow.

"I promised him a threesome with Georgiana and me."

I hit the brakes and skidded backward down my driveway. "What?"

She sighed. "We're not going to really do it. I mean, *I'm* too much for a man his age—the two of us would give him a coronary. But I had to say something."

I shook my head like a dog squirted in the nose with water and then slowly released the brakes. "Who's bartending?"

"I didn't ask, but he had a real nice voice. Deep and dark." She cleared her throat. "Maybe you should pick me up on the way."

Not in a million years. "I should get right there," I said instead, winding around a chunk of thick ice in the middle of the quiet country road. "I'll call you when I have him."

"Bring him here. He shouldn't be alone right now," she said.

I winced. The woman was probably correct, but I wasn't sure that was a good idea. On many levels. "I'll call you." I dropped the phone into my purse and used both hands on the wheel. The wind whipped more flakes across the window and I tensed my shoulders, leaning forward to see through the darkness

Dunphey's bar was for drinkers. Not millennials, not young people looking to hook up, but for drinkers. The bar took up the corner of Oakwood and Acorn in downtown Timber City. It was made of worn clapboard wood siding, the chairs and stools were 70's-style leather, and the smell of smoke and burned pizza hung heavily in the air. The bar had sat there as a place to drown sorrows and destroy livers for at least ninety years. The town had basically grown up around Dunphey's through the decades.

I parked on the curb and kicked snow out of my way to shove open the heavy maple door. Once inside, I paused, letting my eyes adjust to the darkness. The tavern was shaped in a square with the bar, stools, and booze to the right, tables and chairs to the left, and a vacant dance floor straight ahead where nobody had ever danced. More tables had encroached across the linoleum dance floor to the far stage holding several ready-to-use wooden kegs, so now there was nowhere to dance anyway.

Muted country music mixed with rock hinted in the far background.

A familiar face behind the bar caught my attention and I hustled over, shimmying my hips between two maroon-colored leather bar stools. Both unused. Most of the patrons either sat at the far ends of the bar or at tables against the walls. "Rory," I said, half-leaning over to hug my cousin. "Didn't know you were home."

Rory hugged me back, one-armed, muscles strong against my shoulders. Then he returned to drying a shot glass with a torn towel that had seen better days. "Don't tell me you're here for the drunk guy."

Not a great description, considering it fit everyone in there except for the two of us. I stood back and studied my cousin. He was the fifth of six brothers, and nobody quite knew what he did for a living. His hair was a darker brown, his features Italian, and his eyes the blue of a stormy lake. He traveled a lot for his job. When he was home he could be found helping with search and rescue, fighting fires, or apparently tending bar. "What are you doing here?"

"Joe Dunphey's wife went into labor and I said I'd cover the bar," Rory said easily, moving on to the next glass.

Well, sure. That pretty much summed up normality for Rory. "How's life in the merchant marines?" I asked, playing our usual game.

He grinned, revealing the Albertini charm. All of the men in our family had it. "Funny. I'm a traveling salesman selling pottery. The good kind that won't crack if you put hot tea in it. I should sell you some."

Right. Sure, he was. I looked for Bernie and saw him alone in a far corner, slouched against the wall, his eyes closed. "Is he wearing his Santa outfit?" I gasped.

Rory chuckled. "Only the coat over jeans. I think the hat is shoved in his back pocket."

Unbelievable. Either way, he wasn't going anywhere at the moment, and I was fine letting him sleep it off. I perched on a stool and flopped my purse on the bar with a loud clunk.

Rory's eyebrow rose. "What are you packing?"

"My LadySmith," I said, looking at the alcohol bottles behind him on wooden shelves. "Got any wine?"

"Not that you'd want to drink." He reached under the bar and drew out a cold, brown bottle of Huckleberry Shanty from Wallace Brewing, which was located just beyond Silverville. Taking off the cap, he slid it across the bar to me. No beer mugs or coasters at Dunphey's.

"Thanks." I took a deep drink, letting the sweet brew relax me. "You going to the family barbecue tomorrow?"

"Wouldn't miss it," he said easily, positioning the now some-what clean glasses to the shelf behind him. "Quint is debuting his new love. Hope she's up to handling the family."

I nodded. "She is. I've met her and really like her. Heather is sweetly thoughtful and she adores him." Their romance had started fast and wild, and I thought it'd last. "My bet is engagement by February." I leaned toward him. "Any gossip?"

"Yep. Bosco is seeing a woman named Marlie but doesn't seem to know he is, and my bet is they'll be married by July." He grinned.

Oh, good gossip. I hopped happily. "What about you? What ever happened to you and Serenity?" They'd dated for two years and had seemed close to making it permanent, and then nothing.

Rory's movements didn't slow, but a light tension poured from him. "We had a misunderstanding, and I've given her until after Christmas—maybe until New Year's—to deal with it."

I twirled the beer bottle in my hands. "Then what?"

"Then I'm dealing with it," he said, his smile one of danger.

Interesting. "Well, if you need a lawyer, which it sounds like you might, give me a call."

"Legal counsel is the last thing either of us will need when I'm finished," he said smoothly.

I didn't want to know more than that. "Any word on who killed Santa?" Perhaps he had his ear to the ground working at Dunphey's.

He poured tequila into a glass and tipped it back like it was water. "Rumor has it the ex-wife inherited a shitload of money, and considering she was seen canoodling with her ex at the Elk's Christmas party last weekend, things aren't looking good for drunk-ass Santa over there." He eyed the bottle like he wanted another drink.

I paused. That was good gossip and yet another thing Bernie hadn't told me about. I slid off the stool. It was after midnight and had been a long day. A *way* too long of a day. "I should probably take my client somewhere...else."

Rory reached under the bar again and handed over a buck

knife. "Took this off him earlier before he could lose one of his fingers. He's not armed otherwise."

I slipped the knife into my bag. "Thanks."

"Yep."

The door opened, and Hoyt Forrest stomped inside, scattering snow. Two friends flanked him, and his gaze searched the entire bar, landing on Bernie.

I sighed.

Rory planted one hand on the bar and bounded gracefully over, landing sure-footed by my side. "Guns at waist and left leg," he said beneath his breath.

I set my stance. "Someday you're gonna have to tell me what you really do for a living," I muttered.

"Huh," he returned, already moving for the men. "Take your weapons back out to your rigs." Without breaking eye contact, he nodded to the sign by the door. "No weapons in Dunphey's. You gents know that."

Hoyt measured Rory, apparently decided to use his brain, and exited as quickly as he'd arrived.

Rory lazily returned to the bar, leaning back on his elbows against it, right next to me. Waiting.

Hoyt returned with his buddies—sans the weapons this time. The buddies moved for the bar and Hoyt moved for Bernie.

I stepped forward.

"Want me to handle it?" Rory asked casually.

"No." I wanted to sit both men down and figure this out. "I've got it."

Rory, as my cousin, was just as overprotective as the rest of them. Having been kidnapped as a child had somehow set me up with a vulnerability that my family couldn't let go of—or maybe the vulnerability was theirs. Either way, he cleared his throat. "Hoyt? Anna is going to sit with you and Bernie over there. Don't make me kill you." He jumped back over the bar and thus missed

Hoyt's faltering and big swallow. Like big enough that his entire Adam's apple moved wildly.

I'd never considered Rory all that scary, but I guess he'd never threatened to kill me, either. He sounded legit. "You know Hoyt?"

"Sure. I buy my bait and tackle at his store," Rory said, moving down the bar to fetch beers for the newcomers.

That was something to delve into at a later date. I hitched my bag over my arm and tried to pick up my feet when they briefly stuck to the floor on the way back to Bernie, who'd already sat up to watch us approach.

Hoyt puffed out his chest. "Rumor has it you want to kill me."

Bernie's eyes were so bloodshot they looked swollen. He tried to sit up straighter, but his chest ended up sinking in more with his shoulders hunched. "You set me up, you fucker. I know it was you."

Hoyt's chin lifted. "You're crazy, old man."

I edged closer to Bernie. "Set up? What do you mean?"

"He knows," Bernie slurred. "It was a normal poker game and then it wasn't. I know what you did." He coughed, the sound phlegm-filled.

Now I took a step back. There wasn't time in my schedule to get sick right now. Although it was probably the whiskey and smoke attacking Bernie's lungs.

"I didn't do anything," Hoyt snapped, snow still dotting the shoulders of his down jacket. "You and your ex-wife set my father up and then killed him. Thought you'd get rich and take that Vegas trip you'd always wanted, right? You won't. I'm telling you, I'm taking you down. Santa or not." He leaned in, his expression ugly. "We both know what happened to the coffers last year, don't we?"

Bernie bounded to his feet, surprisingly quick. "That wasn't me. Your gambling debts have ruined everything. How is Gutter, anyway?"

I could swear that Hoyt paled. "When I'm done with you and that gold-digging bitch—"

Bernie threw a half-empty bowl of nuts at Hoyt's face and then lunged over the table, knocking the nearest chair into my leg. I went down, scrambling for my gun as the two men collided.

Gasping, I stood, my hand shaking.

But it was already over.

Rory had Bernie by the scruff of the neck and Hoyt by the wrist, which had been twisted in a way that made Hoyt remain on his knees with a snot-bubble poking out of his nose.

I blinked and shoved my gun back where it belonged. Yeah. Someday I was going to find out what cousin Rory did when he wasn't at home.

But not tonight.

CHAPTER 14

I glanced over at the passed out senior citizen snoring in my passenger seat as I drove away from the bar, my headlights cutting through the snow. Bernie's coat smelled like mothballs and mold, and when he farted, I nearly tossed him out into the snowstorm. Instead, I shoved him in the arm. "Bernie. Where do you live?"

He snorted loudly and jerked, opening his eyes. "What? Uh? Where am I?" He tried to sit up and farted again.

I flipped the wipers to a faster speed. "In my car. Where do you live?" I slowed down for a stoplight.

"Oh." He wiped his hands down his face. "Um, on Nineteenth Street. Just take a right at the next light."

If Timber City had a bad part of town, Nineteenth Street would meander right through it. The homes were run-down, the vehicles rusted out, and the meth busts a part of life. There were also hard-working people just trying to work out some financial problems, and I had no doubt many of them would love to leave Nineteenth Street.

I drove farther away from the lake, from the main part of town, and along mature trees nobody seemed to tend. The snow clung to their arching bows, giving them a romantic look that contrasted starkly with the crumbling homes on either side of us. The streetlights were new and boldly illustrated the run-down and depressing neighborhood. "Where?"

"Two blocks down. First white apartment complex." He dug his hat out of his pocket and sat it on his head. The white ball at the tip drooped sadly to his shoulder.

I drove around a dirty chunk of ice that looked like it'd fallen off a large truck. "What was Hoyt talking about? That something happened to the coffers?"

Bernie watched the darkened homes flow by outside. "Money went missing from the Kringle fund. I figured Lawrence took it to help Hoyt, but I don't know." He sighed, the sound weary, and his breath a mellow whiskey scent. "Maybe it's our fault. We've played poker for money for decades, and I remember the first time Lawrence brought Hoyt to a game. The guy was just a kid."

That was sad. I pulled to the curb next to an unshoveled side-walk in front of an older apartment building with a floodlight casting a wide net across the snow. The paint was more gray than white after age, and the metal railing on the steps leading from sidewalk to walkway hung haphazardly to the icy ground.

"Bernie? What did you mean that Hoyt set you up?"

He turned toward me in the quiet car, even his white whiskers looking limp. "Don't you get it? I got really drunk at a game, somehow ended up in bed with some woman named Sharon Smith, and then she's in Lawrence's will? The same Lawrence who just proposed to my ex-wife? Obviously, it was a setup."

I swallowed and weighed the stench of the man in my car versus the freezing air outside. It was several hours past my bedtime, and I had trouble concentrating. I could maybe crack my window. "I caught that, but if that is the case, you had an even bigger motive for killing Lawrence."

Bernie coughed, shaking the dirty white fur down his red coat.

"Sorry," he gasped, his eyes widening. "I need to let up on the cigars."

"It wouldn't hurt," I agreed. "Did you have any idea that night with Sharon was a setup before the reading of Lawrence's will?"

"No," he said, reaching for his door handle.

"Who's Gutter?" I asked, taking advantage of his lowered inhibitions.

He paused in shuffling out of the SUV. "Bucky Gutenfold. Guy's a loan shark over in Spokane. They call him Gutter not because of his last name but because he likes to leave people in gutters if they don't pay him."

I grimaced. Hopefully I'd never meet Gutter. "I take it Hoyt owed him money?"

"That was the rumor, but he should be able to pay Gutter off now that he has that inheritance, even though Florence got a bunch of it. From what I heard, Hoyt got enough to get clear. Well, probably." Bernie snaked out of the car, planted his boots on the snow, and instantly went down.

I sighed and stepped out of the vehicle, holding onto the freezing metal of the hood to make my way over the icy ground to the other side. The wind pierced through my jacket and straight past my muscles, freezing whatever that stuff was inside my bones. My hands hurt, and my legs shook, but I kept going until I could reach him.

Bernie just lay in the snow, the car door open next to him, looking up at the thick clouds and dark night. Snow fell all over him, but he didn't wipe it off his face. Instead, he just emitted a deep-throated hiccup.

I reached him, shut the door, and planted my hands beneath his shoulders. "Get up. You'll freeze to death out here."

"Who cares?" he mumbled, his scuffed black boots kicking against a clump of dirty ice that looked like it had dropped from nowhere. "I'll just stay here and freeze. I'm Santa. That's how Santa is supposed to go."

Oh, for goodness' sake. "You're not going anywhere." I tried to pull him up, but my boots slid on the ice, and I landed on my butt with a hard *oof*. Pain ticked up my spine, attacking each vertebra systematically to my neck. I released him. That was it. Just plain and simply it. "What about the threesome with Thelma and Georgiana?"

He rolled over onto his stomach, settled his elbows in the snow, and shoved himself up to his knees. "I'd forgotten about that."

I couldn't believe I'd been reduced to pimping out my friends. Clamping my freezing hand on the top of the iced over front tire, I pushed myself to my feet. My head hurt, my ass ached, and my temper was trying to warm my chilled body. "If you don't go inside right now, I'll tell them you decided you couldn't handle them both." Now I was just making crap up.

He scrambled to stand, slipping and falling several times until finally making it, holding the door handle for balance. "Let's go there now."

I looked over his dirty and snowy form. "You can't visit two ladies looking like that."

He brushed ice off his nose. "That's a good point." Then he swayed and caught himself with his other hand flat against my window. Snow slid down into his sleeve. He shook it out and fell on his butt, right onto the ice he'd been kicking. He howled.

I picked carefully toward him and slung my arm through his. "Come on. We'll get there together." With that, I pulled.

He stood, wavered, and then centered himself. We slid together toward the broken railing.

An engine gunned down the road. We both turned to see a lifted red truck, dented and rusted, zoom down the street way too fast for the icy conditions.

"Damn kids," he muttered, shaking his head and losing his hat. "Think they're selling meth, too."

I leaned over to fetch his hat just as a pattering ripped through the snowy night. Yelping, I grabbed his shoulders and yanked him down, knowing that sound. Knowing it all too well. He landed on top of me, his fur smothering me.

Bullets pinged the snow and ice all around us, impacting the metal railing and cracking it in several pieces. The shards flew toward us, and a piece cut into my forehead. I screamed and twisted my head, trying to breathe beneath the fur.

The truck careened down the street and took a corner too fast, hitting a tree and then punching forward.

I shoved Bernie off me and scrambled back to my car, yanking my purse through his door and pulling my gun free. Panic heated my breath and spiraled through the frigid air. Then I crouched with my shoulders to the vehicle, my heart racing. Were they coming back? How many had been in the truck? I thought maybe two people, but I wasn't sure. "Get over here," I hissed.

He rolled my way, leaving a Santa-sized indent in the scattered snow. Then he sat up, his expression dazed. Finally, he looked down at his chest. "Whoa. I got shot." His eyelids fluttered shut, and he passed out, his head clunking soundly on my car.

Crap. I scraped my boots along the ice, using my shoulders on the car for balance. "Bernie?" I shouted, fighting the snow to get to him. Panic heated me, blurring my vision. "You're okay. Tell me you're okay." My lungs burned and my throat hurt. Holding my gun in my right hand, I leaned down and felt for his pulse. Weak. My hands were starting to go numb, but I reached for my phone and punched in 9-1-1, my senses reeling. I reported the shooting, crying and coughing, giving our location.

The red truck barreled around the same corner and clipped a different tree before spinning onto Nineteenth Street. I dropped the phone in the snow and then knelt to peer over the hood of the car.

The driver's window was open. A ski mask was pulled over the driver's face, and black swimming goggles concealed his eyes. His left hand controlled the steering wheel while his right crossed over, gun in hand. I lifted my gun, and it felt like it weighed a hundred pounds. My fingers slipping, I squeezed the trigger, aiming for his face. My bullets hit the side of the truck. Then I ducked down, trying to shield Bernie with my body. He coughed, and blood gurgled through his lips, sliding along my neck.

Bullets impacted my SUV and a window shattered. Something hissed. I tried to protect both of our heads, my hands clamped against his snow-covered hair.

The truck burst down Nineteenth Street, jerking a right on Albert Avenue.

Sirens trilled in the distance.

"Bernie?" I couldn't feel my hands, but I leaned down, trying to see if he was breathing. His blood darkened the already red Santa coat, seeping into the white fur. "It's okay. You're going to be okay." While my body had frozen, my head spun, and my heart rammed wildly against my ribcage. Fear fuzzed the moment while snow billowed all around us. "Bernie?" I leaned down and placed my hands over the blood, trying to find the wound. "Hold on. Just hold on." Where were they?

Red and blue spun through the billowing snow as police cars slid to rapid stops. I recognized Bud Orlov the second he leaped out of his car. Bud was a solid bear of a man with blond hair, black eyes, and seriously wide shoulders. He'd provided cover for me before, and I'd gotten him shot.

He was the first to reach me, his gun in his hands. He was wisely wearing gloves. "Shooter?"

My nose ran, and I wiped it on my sleeve, getting ice on my face. "Red truck, lifted, no plates. I think just one shooter, wearing a mask. No plates," I repeated. "I didn't see plates." Were there plates? I'd looked, right? "Yeah. No plates."

The ambulance screeched to a stop and slid several feet, nudging a patrol car. Then the paramedics were out and taking care of Bernie.

Bud holstered his weapon and set his hand beneath my elbow, lifting me to my feet. "You hurt?"

I looked down at the snow, ice, and blood covering me. There was a fair amount of dirty gravel as well. "I don't think so?" The world morphed in and out, narrowing from the edges. I gulped, and Bud's face wavered before splitting into two distinct parts.

I'm pretty sure he caught me before I hit the ground.

CHAPTER 15

J had just finished giving Detective Pierce my report when Aiden burst into the examination room. His gaze swept me head to toe. His expression was ATF agent hard, meaning he had no expression, but those blue eyes sizzled. "You hurt?"

I gingerly touched the bandage on my head. "No. Maybe a slight concussion, and I'm freezing." I'd huddled beneath several warm blankets, and I'd checked out okay for frostbite, but I couldn't get warm.

Aiden turned to Pierce. "Suspects?"

"Not yet," Pierce said, still leaning against the wall.

Aiden's temper swelled through the room, heating every inch. "Any idea if Anna was the target?"

Pierce cut me a look, his green eyes as pissed as Aiden's. "Not yet. I'd say it's fifty-fifty between Anna and Bernie, considering he's caught up in a murder investigation right now, and she's, well, Anna."

I frowned but didn't have the energy to berate him for the comment. I still couldn't feel my feet, although the heated slippers the nurse had put on me would soon help, I was sure.

Dr. Springfield walked inside the room, scanning through a tablet in his hands. He'd let his white beard grow for the holidays, while his hair had always been a little shaggy. He looked me over. "Your MRI came back fine. You might have a small concussion, but the rest of you checks out. Keep an eye on it, and if you get dizzy or nauseated, come back in."

I clutched the heated blanket with my still shaking hands. "How is Bernie?"

Springfield set the tablet aside and walked toward me, looking more like Santa than anybody I'd ever seen. "Bernie is out of surgery and is going to be okay. The bullet went through the upper part of his shoulder, and we had to stitch him up. His blood had too much alcohol in it, so we had to be careful." Sorrow filled his eyes. "Let me take a quick look at the stitches." He dragged on blue gloves and gently removed my bandage. "Ah. That's a nice job. The new doctor is working out well." He replaced the bandage.

I swallowed. "You're in the Kringle Club. I've been meaning to speak with you."

He patted my shoulder, his touch light. "How about we speak when you aren't in a hospital bed?"

Aiden and Pierce nodded in unison, short quick lifts of their chins. Tough guy nods.

I could feel Aiden's tension from across the room, and my heartbeat quickened in response. My legs shifted restlessly beneath the blankets. He looked perfectly calm to anybody who didn't know him.

I knew him well. He was three steps away from losing his temper, and if there had been somebody around to hit, he would've already put them flat on the ground.

I wished the shooter was present because I'd love to see Aiden kick his ass.

Pierce ruffled his hair with his hand. "You're sure you didn't hit the shooter when you fired?"

"I'm not sure." My eyelids started to feel heavy. "I think I just hit the truck, but I can't guarantee it."

Pierce looked at Aiden. "We have all hospitals, doctor offices, and vets in the area on alert just in case."

Aiden didn't twitch.

A ruckus sounded outside in the hall. "Oh my. Bernie? Where's my Bernie?" Florence ran into the room, her hair in curlers, a man's overcoat covering what looked like a long flannel nightgown. "Anna. Oh, my." Her boots slipped on the now wet floor, and Aiden caught her arm before she could fall. She centered herself and walked carefully toward me, a thick white night-time lotion over her pasty face. "Are you okay?"

I nodded. It took me a moment to figure out what was off with her face. She didn't have any eyebrows. Oh. She must draw them on. She was good at it because I hadn't even noticed the other day. "I am, and Bernie is out of surgery and will be fine." My voice was still hoarse.

She dropped into the one guest chair, and some of the dried white lotion on her face flaked off. "I was so scared." Her voice shook, and she looked older than she had the other day. "Who shot at you? Was it Hoyt?"

"I don't know," I admitted. "The man wore a ski mask."

Pierce zeroed in on her. "Do you have any reason to believe Hoyt would shoot at Bernie?"

Florence's hands fluttered together on the olive-drab overcoat. "Nothing concrete. It's just that Hoyt was so angry after the reading of the will, and he said he thinks Bernie and I killed Lawrence." Tears filled her eyes, turning the lotion right beneath her lower lashes to paste.

"Did you?" Pierce asked

Florence's body jerked. "No. Of course not."

It took me a second to remember that I represented her, but my brain was still fuzzy.

Pierce angled his body so he could better see her expression. "Who do you think killed Lawrence?"

Florence turned to look at him, her shoulders shaking. "You already interviewed me, Detective Pierce. I'm going to tell you right now, just like I did then, that I can't imagine anybody wanting Lawrence dead. He was a kind man."

Pierce scratched his chin. "Was he? You know he left a substantial sum in his will to Sharon Smith, right?"

"Yes," Florence said, pivoting to face me. "But we don't know who she is or how Lawrence knew her."

I hadn't had a chance to speak with Florence yet about Sharon, and apparently neither had Bernie. "Pierce? That's enough."

Pierce was a decent man and a phenomenal detective. "Sharon Smith is the woman who slept with Bernie McLintock when you were married to him. She is the reason your marriage broke up." He watched her carefully.

I wouldn't have thought it possible, but Florence paled even further. She frowned, and more of the white lotion flaked off. "What?" Her voice shook.

"Pierce," I snapped, putting as much bite into my voice as my exhaustion would allow. "Leave my client alone. Now."

He apparently had gotten what he'd wanted, so he nodded and then exited the room.

Florence's eyes filled with more tears. "I don't understand."

Neither did I, but I was going to figure it out. No matter what.

Aiden sighed from over by the doorway.

* * *

I AWOKE FROM A DEAD SLEEP, my skin prickling and my breath stilling. Quiet pounded through my cottage. Heat seeped into me from the hard male body hogging my bed. I breathed out, forcing my lungs to start working again. Aiden slept quietly on his stomach, his head turned the other way, one arm beneath his pillow.

My head hurt.

Holding my breath again, I slowly lifted the covers and slid out, my feet touching the cold floor. I was wearing one of Aiden's T-shirts that reached almost to my knees, but my legs were bare and the world cold.

Even so, I padded quietly out of the bedroom and shut the door, wandering to my sofa to stare at the Christmas lights twinkling on my tree. I liked to leave them on at night and most of the day, wondering why we didn't have sparkling lights all year long. I sat and reached for the hand-knitted blanket that my Nana had given me last year. It was white and green with Celtic knots strewn throughout, and I snuggled deep into it, holding the soft material up to my neck.

Tears filled my eyes and I batted them away.

It was late morning outside, and I tried to match my mood to a sleepy wintery day.

My blood snapped and cracked through my veins, my heart racing and little beads of sweat popping onto my forehead. It wasn't my first panic attack, and it wouldn't be my last. Even so, each time I wondered if I was having a heart attack. My chest did hurt. And my left arm ached. Of course, my right arm hurt as well. I'd tightened so hard that all of my muscles ached.

My head thrummed and I tried to breathe. My lungs compressed, not filling at the bottom. Only barely filling at the top. The panic strengthened, and I gasped, my fingers curling into the throw blanket.

"Angel," Aiden said drowsily from behind me.

I yelped and then stopped breathing completely, my arms floundering.

He said something sharp in Gaelic and rounded the sofa, lifting me and sitting back down. "I've got you." He wore only boxer briefs, and his skin was both scarred and warm. Heated, even. He cradled me on his lap, pulling the blanket up to my chin. "You're safe. Now shut your eyes."

I did what he said, letting him take my weight.

"Good. Now I want you to slowly breathe in, not worrying about your lungs. They'll fill. You can breathe." He spoke softly, his breath brushing my hair. "Now, Anna."

I opened my mouth and tried to take a breath.

"Good. Now through your nose," he said quietly.

I closed my mouth, and my heartbeat pounded through my ears. Then I breathed in through my nose, and my lungs filled. All the way.

"Hold for a second and then let it out of your mouth." His grip remained firm but not constraining.

I did so, following his instructions for several moments. My heart rate slowed down and the buzzing dissipated. I swallowed, my face against his chest, embarrassment heating my cheeks. "I'm sorry."

His chest contracted. He took a moment and then shifted his weight, placing a knuckle under my chin and lifting my face so I could meet his gaze. "Sorry for what?"

I floundered. Heat still burned my earlobes. "I, well, I don't know."

He smoothed my hair back from my face, his touch gentle. "Why do you have to be so tough all the time?"

It was probably a question I should ponder with my shrink, Cousin Wanda. "I don't," I said, my voice weak.

"Yeah, you do." In the semi-darkness, his eyes were an animalistic blue. Deep and sharp. But his voice was soft and his body comforting around me. "You were just shot at and had to return fire. The guy with you took one. Yet you act like it's a normal day and you don't need anything. That you don't need anybody."

I'd just proven otherwise. "I need you."

Surprise lifted his brows.

I shifted uncomfortably for a minute, my panties on his bare legs. "I needed you before when we were young, and you had to leave." Before he could answer, I held up a hand. "I know that wasn't your fault." He'd been eighteen. I'd been twelve and thought the world bowed to him, and he'd gotten in trouble and had to leave town. We'd been friends, and I'd missed him. More than I'd realized.

"Are you afraid I'm leaving again?" he whispered.

I was. I hadn't realized it until just that second, but the idea terrified me. My world was complete when he was with me. When he wasn't, I was off. Was this how everyone felt when they really cared about somebody? I didn't know. This was new. "I guess I am," I admitted. "It's possible your job will take you somewhere else for good." I could move as well, but then I'd be leaving my entire family. For Aiden, I'd do it. That scared the hell out of me, too.

"But you're okay with my leaving periodically for undercover ops?" he asked, his expression intense.

"Yeah." I played with the sharp edge of his clavicle. "As long as you're coming back to me." I watched my fingers on his skin. "I'm not good at this."

He kissed my nose. "You really aren't."

His words caught me off-guard and a chuckle burst out of my chest. "I think you're supposed to lie about that."

"No lies between us." He kicked his legs out to the coffee table, holding me securely. "Did you have panic attacks while I was gone?"

"No."

"Anna?" His voice went Aiden firm.

I looked him in the eye. "I haven't had one in months. The shooting tonight triggered one." It was the truth.

He relaxed around me. "Don't hide this from me again."

I barely kept from rolling my eyes, feeling like myself again. "Bossy Aiden is back."

"You like me bossy." His gaze moved to the silent and sparkling tree.

Was that a public fact, or what?

CHAPTER 16

*a*s darkness took over outside, I finished rapidly loading my fridge with goodies my mother had shoved in my hands when we'd escaped the Sunday family barbecue over in Silverville. "You're a rat-fink bastard, Aiden Devlin," I said, slamming my fridge for emphasis and turning to face him.

He paused in hanging up his jacket. "Try again."

"No." I put both hands on my hips, more than ready to go a round or two. "How could you tell my mother that I had a panic attack earlier today?" It was unthinkable. A betrayal of the highest order. I'd already kicked off my boots, but my jeans were loose and my sweater roomy. I could take him if I had to, and apparently I did. He had a lesson to learn. "Devlin?"

He shut the closet door and turned around, leaning against it. "I didn't tell her about you being shot at."

It was a good thing the stitches could be lost in my hairline with a lot of careful styling because we'd managed the entire barbecue without anybody noticing I'd been hurt. Well, except for the black eye and bruised cheekbone. But makeup had hidden most of that damage. "Yet you're still a Judas."

He crossed his arms. "Anna." His reasonable tone was going to get him smacked.

I lowered my chin. "You waited. You waited until after our nice dinner and after everyone finished focusing on Quint and Heather." Cousin Quint was pretty much in serious love. "You waited until my mom was packaging up leftovers. You waited until you had her alone and her attention."

"Yep."

I blinked and threw up my hands. "You b—"

"Call me a bastard again, and we're going to have a problem," he said mildly.

"We *already* have a problem," I said, not mildly. Not quietly, either. "Because of you, do you know what I have to do this coming week?" Now I gestured wildly. "See Cousin Wanda."

He didn't so much as blink.

"You did this on purpose," I said slowly, finally catching up.

Again, no movement.

"You bas—"

"I wouldn't." His arms uncrossed. Why that was threatening and a little sexy, I'll never understand. "You like seeing Cousin Wanda. She's your shrink."

I glowered. "You don't get to dictate when I see her."

Then he moved. Right at me, steady pace, firm gait. When I took two steps back, putting my butt against the counter, he kept coming. Right until we stood toe-to-toe. Then he planted both hands on either side of me and leaned down. "When you awaken having nightmares, stop breathing, and nearly give me a heart attack until you start breathing again, I do dictate when you see your shrink. Especially if you're not smart enough to make your own appointment."

His body was against mine. He had me slightly leaned back, and I couldn't move. Not an inch.

I swallowed.

He lowered his head, his nose nearly touching mine. "Got it?"

"Got it," I agreed quickly. Instinctively. I hadn't realized I'd scared him. He'd been so calm and reassuring. "You're being bossy again."

"You like me bossy." He placed a hard kiss on my lips and stepped back, giving me room.

I really had to do something about that rumor.

He glanced at the fridge. "Did your mom give us some of the pecan pie?"

"You know she did." It was his favorite, so she always pretty much baked him his own when she made one. She had always liked Aiden, considering he'd saved my life, and he was Irish to boot. She didn't like that his job was dangerous, but since mine kept turning out to be a little dangerous as well, she appreciated that he carried a gun and could take care of bad guys. "You know she has a secret dream that you'll knock me up so I quit my job and raise little Irish babies without being shot at once in a while."

"It's not a secret dream," he murmured, reaching to open the fridge.

Probably not. My mom wasn't exactly discreet. "I'm not ready for little Irish babies." I also probably wouldn't be quitting my job.

"Amen to that." He snatched the pie out of the fridge and opened the door to the side of my hip, grasping two spoons. "Hungry?"

"No." I'd eaten plenty at the barbecue, and I hadn't gone running in a while. It was too cold outside, and I didn't have funds for a gym membership. Yeah, I was making excuses. Even so, I wasn't hungry. "You can't be hungry."

"It's pie." He shut the door and crossed to the table, setting down the pie pan.

"Use a plate."

"It's my pie."

I exhaled slowly, unable to find an argument for that.

He took a big bite, his eyes closing in appreciation. When they opened again, the blue struck me like it always did. "Why don't you want to see your shrink?"

I wasn't in the mood for philosophical Aiden. Nor did I want to delve into my complicated psyche right then. My phone buzzed, and I snatched for it like a lifeline. "Anna Albertini."

"Hey. It's Pierce. I have a hit on a florist on the South Hill over in Spokane. Guy called in the order, used a prepaid credit card, and paid double for the delivery all the way to Idaho." Papers rustled over the phone line. "The woman who took the call didn't remember anything special about the voice, except that he was calm and insistent and an adult. No cracking voice or anything like that. He was careful, and I'll dump the line, but my guess is he used a burner."

I watched Aiden keep eating the pie, while he watched me on the phone. "I hope you get fat," I lip-synced to him.

He grinned, the shadows not quite leaving his eyes.

Pierce continued, "No hit on the paint for the heart on your garage. We canvassed most of Timber City, but he could've bought that anywhere."

"Thanks for trying," I said. "Anything on the red truck or the shooter?"

"Nothing. I have techs going through traffic cam footage right now, and I'm pulling Hoyt Forrest in tomorrow morning. Is Devlin with you tonight, or do you want a uniform at your door?" Pierce was a good guy, and he didn't want me dead. It was nice of him to offer.

"Devlin is here, and I'm armed." I had fired back, after all.

More papers crinkled. "All right. Call me if you recall anything else."

I tried to remember if the guy had looked like Hoyt's size, but I just couldn't tell. "Thanks, Pierce. I appreciate it."

"Just doing my job. Try not to get fired upon or stalked tonight. I need a night off." He ended the call.

* * *

I WANDERED into my office on Monday morning after an early appointment with Cousin Wanda, whose office was just down the hall from ours. It had been a rough morning of delving deep and working on my trust and abandonment issues, which were crazy because my life was great, and my family always present. But the danger, being shot at, did bring back childhood fears of being vulnerable.

As did falling for Aiden Devlin.

Oliver Duck sat behind the reception desk with his business card holder proudly in front of him. I definitely shouldn't have let the kids order their own business cards, but I guess being a czar or a king made up for the meager pay we could afford right now. "Hi, Oliver."

He looked up from an appointment book, his red hair growing out to his ears. He smiled, his freckles popping. Then he cocked his head. "You look like you went ten rounds with a Rottweiler."

"I feel like it," I admitted, toeing off my snow boots to place on a rubber mat in the corner. I dug my pumps out of my bag and slipped them on my feet. "It was a rough morning." Next time I saw Cousin Wanda, I wanted it to be after hours so I could at least enjoy a beer, or five, while we talked. She was usually okay with that.

Oliver winced. "You might not be finished with your rough morning."

I straightened in my black slacks and red sweater. "I'm not in court until this afternoon." Or was I due this morning? Had I missed something on my calendar?

"No, but you have a visitor back in the smaller conference room. She was making me nervous out here, so I took her there. I'm sorry." He flushed a deep claret and his ears looked almost purple.

"It's all right," I said, not wanting his lobes to explode. "Whoever is here, I can handle it."

He nearly chewed through his bottom lip. "It's Jolene O'Sullivan."

Time and matter screeched to a sudden and complete stop. "Nope." I tiptoed over to the corner, removed my shoes, and slipped into my boots. I still was wearing my coat, so that was convenient. "Give it five minutes and tell her I called you, saying I had a meeting with a client and won't be in until much later." I had no compunction about lying. If I had a nemesis, it was Jolene O'Sullivan. "I'll see you later." Totally ignoring his panicked expression, I hightailed it out of there.

Oliver could handle her. She didn't have any questions for him, and he didn't know anything about my current cases, anyway.

I ran into Clark at the stairwell. "Hey."

"Hey," he said, pausing at the top. Snow covered the shoulders of his leather jacket and melted on his dark bald head. "Where are you going?"

"Meeting with a client," I said breezily, walking down several steps.

He partially turned. "We usually have our office meeting Monday morning. I wanted the scoop on the Santa case." He rubbed a bruise he'd gotten at the family barbecue on his bicep. He and Uncle Sean had been playing pool, and a ball had skipped. Uncle Sean was a mountain of a man, played great golf, and was a menace at the pool table. Clark kept trying to teach him. I admired that, but he was bruised every week. I'm sure he was looking forward to golf season even more than was Uncle Sean. "Anything new?"

I couldn't set him up. "No, and Jolene O'Sullivan is in our small conference room."

Clark reared back. "Why?"

"I don't know. Probably the Santa case? Or my getting shot at?"

Although I hadn't told my family, I had fully informed Clark, just in case.

He pivoted on his hiking boot and strode down the stairs to reach me. "I don't have anything pressing right now in the office. How about we have our meeting over coffee?" Taking my arm, he hustled us down the stairs to the sparkling, snowy, and unshoveled sidewalk outside of our office building.

My heart soared. I loved that I wasn't the only coward in our firm. "I would be delighted, Clark Bunne."

We shuffled down the street toward Smiley's Diner, which was only one building down beyond Duke's Jewelry store. I glanced in Duke's window past the painted snowy scene. "Any idea what I could get Aiden for Christmas?"

"What did you get me?" Clark asked, following my gaze.

I kept my arm in his, considering his balance was excellent and the tread on his boots top-notch. One thing about Clark, he believed in good footwear. "I'm not going to tell you. Speaking of which, are you coming to the family Christmas party next Thursday?"

"Yes to the family party and no to Christmas morning. I'm headed over to Seattle to see my sister." He opened the door to Smiley's Diner, and heat and the smell of cinnamon rolls wafted out. "Any idea what Sean got me? I'm worried it's the first year's tuition for welding school or something like that."

I stepped inside and inhaled deeply. My stomach growled. "That's a good worry." Uncle Sean had pretty much taken Clark into the family, and Sean didn't like lawyers. Oh, he thought I was going through a phase, but he wanted to set Clark on the right path, any path but law, as soon as possible. "What did you get him?"

"A golf laser rangefinder with flag acquisition, pulse vibration, and fast focus system," Clark said easily. "He says he can eyeball distance, and he's way too stubborn to buy a rangefinder, but if I give him one, he'll feel obligated to use it. Let me tell you, he needs it, and I'd like to win the Miner's Tournament next spring."

Now that was an excellent gift. I'd gotten Clark a new putter that he'd been eyeing at the golf course. Uncle Sean told me about it. "What did you get me?"

"A bulletproof vest," Clark said dryly, sliding into a booth.

I wasn't entirely sure he was joking.

CHAPTER 17

*A*fter sharing a cinnamon roll with Clark, then having coffee, then sharing another cinnamon roll, I pulled out a notebook and started to scratch some thoughts on paper. Clark rearranged his morning meetings to visit the offices of clients and left me, while I hoped the coffee in our conference room had gone ice-cold for Jolene.

Tessa finished serving a table of retired guys all arguing about the next election and popped my way, topping off my coffee. "Who are you hiding from?"

I looked up, my eyes focusing. "Jolene."

Tess nodded. "Good choice. I'm meeting Bosco for lunch later if you want to meet up." Bosco was the youngest brother to Quint and Rory, and he worked in the Navy but got to come home sometimes. He was stationed out of Fairchild Air Force Base, which was east of Spokane.

"I'll try." I pushed my notes away. "Could I borrow your car again this morning?"

She tucked a tip into her holiday-themed apron. "What's wrong with your car?"

"It's in the shop," I said easily. It was. Getting bullet holes taken out and the carburetor fixed. "Aiden dropped me off at work earlier."

"Why don't you two just move in together?"

I shrugged. "We're still finding our way, and I like having my own place. He dominates whatever space he's in, and right now, I like my cottage to still be mine." Was that the next step? I wasn't ready for a next step. I was still tripping over this one.

"Huh. Any ideas for Christmas?" she asked.

"Maybe a golf laser rangefinder?" I pondered. There was nothing wrong with copying presents, but I didn't think Aiden liked to golf as much as did Uncle Sean.

"No. Too impersonal for a first Christmas present," Tessa mused, tapping her finger on her bottom lip.

I sighed. She was correct. "Are you getting Nick anything?"

Her neck straightened. "No. We're not dating."

Yeah, I needed to get on that. As a potential matchmaker, I was really falling down on the job. I glanced at my watch. An earlier call to the hospital had confirmed that Bernie would be released at ten, and I'd already called Florence, Thelma, and Georgiana and told them all that I'd pick him up. A worse storm was supposedly coming in, and I thought it would have arrived by now, but only light flakes wafted down outside. "When do you need your car back?"

"When you're done with it," Tessa said breezily. "I'll have Bosco pick me up here. We're going to Margo's Thai at noon if you want to join us. I think Donna is going to try to finish with her showings by then and meet us. I guess she's seeing Aiden about a new lease first? That's exciting."

"I know." I grinned. "It's the old spa." Good memories. I'd talked Tessa into getting a treatment that had turned out to be a Brazilian, and she was probably still planning her revenge. Still, it had been hilarious. And we'd taken down a drug operation, so there was that.

I scooted from the booth, handed her money for the bill, and accepted her keys. "Thanks, T."

She'd already bustled down to take care of a mom trying to manage three toddlers in one booth.

I watched the smallest one try to shove part of a napkin up his nose. Nope. Definitely not ready for little Irish babies, even if they did all look like Aiden. Walking outside, I took stock of my surroundings, looking for any threats. My guess was that the red truck shooter had been aiming for Bernie, considering there was something definitely up with that Kringle Club, but it never hurt to be careful.

The snow gently fell, and I dodged around to the back of the building to find Tessa's Rogue. After scraping off the windows with the ultra-scraper from her back seat, I plopped my butt into the driver's seat and pulled out, heading toward the hospital. Her snow tires gripped the streets perfectly, and I arrived in time to find Bernie waiting in a wheelchair, arguing with the nurse pushing him. His face cleared when he saw me.

I took his bag of clothes. "You ready?"

"Yes." He tried to stand and the nurse shook her head. "I can walk."

"Policy." She was around fifty with braided gray hair and no-nonsense efficiency. She rolled him out to the car, which I'd parked right by the entrance. She helped load him, and then we were off.

He sighed. "The bullet ruined my Santa suit. Do you know how to sew?"

"Not really," I admitted, turning left toward his area of town. "Would it be possible to buy a new Santa suit?"

His bushy eyebrows danced. "It would. Would you take me shopping tomorrow? There's a great store in Spokane, over by Earl's."

Hmm. I thought about it. I wouldn't mind talking to Earl again about that engagement ring without Florence there. "Sure. I have hearings in the morning but could pick you up around two in the afternoon. For now, talk to me. Tell me about the night you and Sharon hooked up." I wasn't sure elderly Santas really hooked up, but I wanted to keep the conversation as neutral as possible.

He sighed. "I told you. Went to poker, got toasted, and woke up in bed with Sharon."

I took another turn, careful of the icy road. "Do you remember, um, well, the night?"

"No. I was naked and she was, too. She said we, well, you know."

My ears pricked. "But you don't remember it?"

"No." He slunk down in the passenger seat. "I felt terrible and told Florence right when I got home, begging for forgiveness." His hands shook as he patted down the hospital scrubs somebody had given him. "She isn't the forgiving type. I really screwed up."

It sounded like he might not have. "What if you didn't?"

He shook his head. "Even if I didn't, I wasn't a good husband. During that time, I was playing poker a lot. Way too much. I lost a bundle, and she was right to leave me. The Sharon night was just the final straw, you know? I was such a dope."

"She still cares for you," I said.

He turned toward me, hope alighting on his weathered face. "Do you really think so?"

"Yeah. She came to the hospital when you were shot and was in a panic."

His shoulders went back. "I don't know. It's too much to hope for. Maybe it's a good thing I didn't have that threesome with Thelma and Georgiana."

I gurgled.

We reached the curb in front of his apartment, and we both just sat in the vehicle, no doubt running through what had happened the last time we'd been there. Fresh snow had blanketed the bloody sidewalk, but a hint of red could still be seen at the edges of fresh ice. I took a deep breath and opened my door, stepping into the day.

An instant and raw cold pierced my jacket and burned my nose. I hurried around the other side of the SUV to open Bernie's door and take his bag of stinky Santa clothes. In silent agreement, we hustled as fast as possible across the treacherous ground, up the stairs next to the destroyed railing, and right into the front door of the building.

We both let loose sighs of relief at not being shot.

A rough set of stairs sat to the right of the entryway across from a door, while another door was straight ahead.

"That's me." Bernie pointed ahead of us and lumbered toward his door, fumbling in his bag for a key to unlock it. We moved inside a one bedroom apartment with hand-me-down furniture and dust covering the cold surfaces. "Florence got the house in the divorce, and I haven't entertained very much." He looked around as if seeing the dismal place for the first time. "I guess I've been a little down."

I stepped inside, rubbing my arms to increase circulation. "Does your heat work?"

"Yeah." He shut the door and moved for the thermostat near the utilitarian kitchen, which wasn't much separate from the living room. There was no place for a table, so I figured he ate on the sofa watching the older television, which had been placed on a dinged-up blue dresser. "That should help."

I set his bag down, the coffee and cinnamon rolls making themselves known in my stomach. "Do you mind if I use your restroom?" Hopefully it'd be cleaner than the rest of the place.

"Sure." He gestured down the one narrow hallway. "Only have the one. I'll see if I can scrounge up coffee."

"I've already had too much today, but thanks." My boots sank into the rust-colored carpet, leaving a little snow, but no way was I taking them off. The carpet was as dusty as the furniture, so who knew if it had ever been vacuumed. Bernie really had been down lately. It took me a second, but I realized he hadn't even put up a tree. It seemed like a shame that a guy who played Santa all the time didn't even have a tree.

I reached the first door, which had been covered at one time or another with at least ten different types of paint and had an oddly pretty plastic doorknob that looked like crystal. I pushed it open and stepped into a dated bathroom with a large green toilet and matching sink. The tile around the exposed shower was a 50's style pink. The bathroom was okay, and I used it quickly, washing my hands and stepping outside.

The door across the hallway was open, and a massive painting of Florence in a garden hung over the bed. Taking a closer look, I determined it was actually a photograph and not a painting.

"I sent it to one of those places on the internet, and they did something fancy with it to make it look like a painting," Bernie said at my elbow.

I looked at the scattered pictures of the two of them across his dresser, and they all appeared to have been dusted. He'd really loved her. "I'm sorry, Bernie," I said, turning back toward the living room.

"Me, too." He sighed heavily and followed me.

A sharp rap on the door had us both jumping.

We turned and looked at each other, our eyes wide.

"Bernie McLintock? This is the Timber City Police. Open up."

My heart settled back where it should be upon recognizing Grant Pierce's voice. I looked at Bernie. "This probably isn't good."

Bernie appeared to be done. Just plain done. "Okay." Pushing his white hair back with one gnarled hand, he moved in front of me and opened the door to Pierce and two uniformed officers.

Pierce lifted an eyebrow at me. "Bernie McLintock, you're under arrest for the murder of Lawrence Forrest." He handed the arrest warrant to me. "DNA came back—your client's on the knife as well as the body, including beneath the vic's fingernails."

Bernie turned around to be handcuffed.

"Pierce, come on. Somebody tried to kill him. Obviously he's a victim," I protested.

Pierce shrugged as the uniform set the cuffs in place. "Or he's involved in something, and his criminal friends don't want him to talk. Have him talk to us, and we'll see what we can do."

"He was shot last night. Be careful with him," I said, tucking the warrant in my bag.

Bernie's chest moved with a sigh. "Would you call Florence for me? She'll bail me out. She's done it before when I got that DUI."

"Sure. Don't say anything, and I'll find you after court." I tried not to wince that he'd just asked his possible co-conspirator to bail him out in front of the investigating detective. I truly didn't think either one of them had anything to do with Lawrence's death. "If Florence gets you out before I'm done, leave me a message, and we'll meet up later. Don't worry, Bernie. We'll figure it out."

Pierce gave me a look screaming that I couldn't promise that.

I lifted my chin. "If you're half as good of a detective as you think, you'll figure out who really killed Lawrence."

Pierce stepped aside to allow the officer to take Bernie out. "Just do your job, counselor, and I'll do mine." The scent of lavender body wash hinted from him.

"Nice body wash," I said, stepping out of the apartment and locking it up.

"Smartass," he muttered, following the officers.

I walked behind him, keeping an eye out for the red truck. Only cold snow and quiet, rundown houses met my gaze. "I'll catch up with you later to talk about this case. You have the wrong guy."

"Uh-huh." Pierce followed me around my car and opened the front door. "Anything new on your case?"

"No. No flowers, phone calls, or painted messages," I said. "Maybe the person gave up."

Pierce waited until I'd snapped my seatbelt in place. "That's unlikely. Keep an eye on your six, and if you want an officer around, I could make that happen for a short period of time."

"I'm armed and set," I said. "But thanks."

Pierce nodded. "I have feelers out for Jareth Davey but haven't had any more luck than Aiden or Basanelli. I'll keep on it, though."

"Thanks." That Christmas card could be coming any day, which was another reason I was having panic attacks. "I'm off to court. See you later."

He shut my door and moved toward the blue and white parked behind me. Bernie looked forlorn in the back seat.

Sighing, I yanked out my phone to call Florence. Hopefully she would bail him out.

Again.

CHAPTER 18

J sat in the far rear corner of misdemeanor court, where the salmon-colored bench was thick with padding, the overhead light burned out, and the heater vent blasting warmth across my legs. The docket was behind today, and several hearings took place up ahead while I rifled through the file folders Oliver had delivered to me. I'd given him cash to get himself lunch at the deli next door as a thank you for handling Jolene for me that morning.

Several people dotted the benches through this smaller courtroom, and I recognized a couple of clients up ahead. Today I had three status conferences on upcoming trials: a timber trespass case, a car wreck over a bridge case, and a minor in possession case. Nothing crucial and we were just checking in and setting trial dates. Judge Williams presided up above, and today a bright red blouse showed above the top of her robe. I couldn't see her shoes but would definitely take a gander before I left.

She had some amazing shoes.

A bailiff stood by a door, his beard impressive. Now there was a guy who'd be able to play Santa in a few decades.

A man I didn't recognize stood at the prosecuting attorney's table. From the back, he seemed to be around my age. Maybe mid-twenties, blond hair, nice suit. Right now, he faced the judge and listed a series of offenses for an underaged defendant who'd apparently been caught with marijuana in Idaho. It was legal in Washington state but not in Idaho.

I sat up to watch, surprised he was pursuing the case.

From the back, the defendant looked like a kid. He wore a black suit with his blond head down, and he stared at the table. Next to him stood a mid-sized man in a power gray suit which was probably Armani. His hair was steel gray, his manner relaxed, and his posture confident. Right behind them sat a couple, the woman with a blonde bob and the man also in a suit, his dark hair groomed.

The prosecutor argued for a ridiculous bond, the smooth attorney I didn't recognize argued back twice as well and then pretty much threw somebody named Violet under the bus. Violet must've been the defendant's friend, and she had been the person actually in possession of the pot. The judge set the case for trial and moved quickly on.

The judge called the next case, and the defendant's name had me perking up. Violet Maseretti. Aha. The girlfriend of the pot kid.

A girl of about fifteen or so shuffled to the center aisle, looked around, and then inched her way through the gate to where her boyfriend had been. She was thin with long black hair, and from what I could see, her eyes matched her name. For court, she wore clean jeans and a blue sweater that might be a size or two too big, with no coat. She pulled nervously on the edge of the sweater as she waited.

The prosecutor ran through the litany again, this time adding the fact that Timmy Stevens alleged that Violet had supplied the pot.

I angled my head to better see the judge.

Judge Williams' expression didn't change when she focused on the defendant. "You can have your own attorney."

The girl looked around again, seeming like a fish flopping on a dock. "Yes, um, your Honor." Her shaking voice was soft.

The judge ticked her head.

Violet shuffled her feet. "Um, I saw the forms, and I tried to fill them out, but they were complicated. I guess. I don't know." She pulled on the sweater again.

The prosecutor sighed, the sound annoyed. "Why don't we just plea this down? I'll offer a misdemeanor with two months in jail and a thousand dollar fine."

The kid squawked. "A thousand dollars?" It was telling she didn't object to the jail time.

The prosecutor looked her over, tapping a finger on the file folder. "All right. Five hundred."

The girl audibly gulped. "Um, well, we had the pot, yeah. But I didn't take any. Timmy had it. But I guess, well, okay."

"Whoa." I shoved from my warm corner to the aisle, dropping a file folder. Grumbling, I reached over to pick it up, settled my hair, and hustled with the contents falling out to the front table. Not only didn't I like the optics of all of these men against one girl, I didn't like the law being used unfairly. "Um, no. Not in a million years."

Judge Williams lifted a dark eyebrow. "Ms. Albertini. I didn't see you back there."

"That's where the heater is." I slapped my pile on the table and tried to regain my balance.

The prosecutor turned toward me. "We just had an agreement to a plea."

My neck went up and my chin went down. "Well gee, buddy. That's just great. Pick on the kid without the hotshot lawyer from Spokane." He had to be, considering I didn't know him. While I had complete faith that the judge wouldn't have allowed the plea and would've helped Violet find a lawyer, I was here right now, and the kid didn't seem to have anybody else. "Your Honor, I'd like to be assigned to the case."

The prosecutor snapped his lips together.

"Great. Anna Albertini, please meet Brad Boxer, the new assistant prosecuting attorney." The judge brought down the gavel. "Consider yourself assigned to the case, Ms. Albertini. Come back in a week if this hasn't settled, and we'll go from there." Her voice more than hinted that we should settle this. I totally agreed.

Brad Boxer leaned over. "Brad." He had light brown eyes and a very straight nose. In another world, I'd consider him good looking. Right now, I considered him to be an ass.

"Anna." I took his hand and shook.

He smiled, full of assurance and grabbed his files. "I'm finished today, Judge. May I be excused?"

"Yes," Judge Williams said, handing case files over to her clerk. "Ms. Albertini, since you're here, let's take care of your status conferences."

Violet looked from the judge to me, her deep blue eyes full of confusion. "What just happened?" She was pale and dark circles hovered on her high cheekbones.

"We'll talk in a few minutes." I gave her my best encouraging smile. "Do you mind sitting in the courtroom and waiting for me for about thirty minutes?" It shouldn't take longer than that to do everything I needed to get done for the day.

She gulped. "No. That's cool." She looked toward the benches. "Where did you say that heater was?"

* * *

I SAT across the table from Violet at Smiley's Diner and removed my coat, wondering if she had one. "You hungry?"

Her eyes were huge, and her fingers nervous as she settled into the booth, reaching for a napkin to start shredding. "No."

Right. Tessa bopped up, tilting her head toward Violet. I introduced them. "Are you a vegetarian or anything, Violet?" I asked.

She swallowed and paused as if considering if she was supposed to be a vegetarian. "Um, no?"

I'd take that as a no. "Two specials, extra fries, two sodas," I said to Tessa.

"You've got it." Tessa took off.

Violet continued shredding the napkin. "I can't afford a fancy lawyer." She spoke to the table, her shoulders bowed.

"Good thing I'm not fancy," I said, reaching for my water glass. "How about you tell me whatever happened with Timmy and the pot?" When she looked up, I made sure to keep my voice level and my gaze serious. "I'm your lawyer, so you can tell me anything, and I can't say a word to anybody. So please just give me the truth? It's easier for me to help you if you do."

She sighed. "Okay. So, Timmy and I started kind of hanging out last month. Nothing serious. Just met up after school to study, and that was it. Last Tuesday, he brought pot that he'd gotten from his brother, and he wanted to smoke it. I didn't want to because I'm allergic to most smoke, and we argued, and Mr. Jorgenson caught us. He's the vice-principal, and he said that he had to call in the violation because it's the law. So we got notices to appear and I came to court."

I nodded to keep her talking.

Her lips turned down. "I can't believe his lawyer said I brought the pot. I don't even have a car to go over to Washington, much less money to waste on drugs." She shook her head. "Boys suck."

Tessa set down the baskets of burgers and fries, reaching for the sodas on the counter and plopping them in front of us. "Eat up." Then she took off again.

Violet stared at the burger and she breathed deep.

Acting casual, I reached for mine and took a bite, waiting for her to do the same. We ate in silence, and I could tell she tried to go slow, but the girl was hungry. When we'd finished the burgers and fries, I ordered both of us apple pie with ice cream.

She winced. "Do all lawyers buy their clients lunch?"

"All the good ones do," I lied.

She rolled her eyes.

I grinned. There she was. I waited until the pie arrived to dig deeper into her story. "Where are your parents?"

She stiffened but didn't stop eating. "Never had a dad, and my mom died three years ago from a bee sting." She shook her head. "Can you believe it? A stupid bee sting." Her shoulders hunched. "Not that we were that close, but she was my mom. She might've had a small drug problem." Violet's eyes blazed when she looked up. "Yet another reason I'd never do freakin' pot."

I ate my ice cream for a while. "Where do you live now?"

"Over off Nineteenth Street with my great-aunt," Violet said, not seeming to hold back any longer. "I tried foster care for a bit, but then she said she'd take me, and we do okay. She's old and everything, but we kind of take care of each other." She finished her pie and set down the spoon. "I just need to graduate and then figure out college. Everything will be okay." It was as if it was a mantra she'd said more than once. More than once a day. "If I don't go to jail," she muttered.

"You're not going to jail," I said. While an attorney should never promise a client anything, there was no way this kid was going to jail.

The door opened, the bell above it jangled, and Detective Pierce strode inside, headed to the counter. He paid for a to-go bag, turned, and saw me. His eyebrows shot up and he loped our way, apparently not noticing the few female sighs in his wake. "Hey. Didn't know you were here."

Violet looked up and blinked.

Yeah, Pierce was good-looking in a surfer-dude-with-a-gun type of way. I introduced them. "What's up?"

"The red truck used by the shooter fits the description of one stolen out of Missoula three days ago. Just had a sighting of a vehicle on fire around the lake road and was going to check it out. Want to come and identify it?" He reached into his bag and drew out a fry, taking a quick bite.

I glanced at Violet. "I was going to take Violet home. Do you have to be anywhere?"

"Nope," she said, her puppy-like gaze on Pierce. "I'm on Christmas break. What truck are we identifying?"

"I'll tell you on the way," I said, scooting out of the booth. I didn't have her entire story yet, and I wasn't sure how much help she needed. Witnessing a burning truck and helping the police with a case might be good for her peace of mind, since she'd probably only seen the other side of the law when she'd gotten arrested and charged. Plus, this was the most animated I'd seen her.

She hedged by the end of the table, obviously at a loss with the amount of food we'd consumed and probable payment.

I tossed my debit card at Tessa, who was behind the counter. She knew my PIN number. In fact, we had the same one. "Just take it off the card, and I'll get it when I bring back your Rogue," I said, breezing by.

"You've got it." She turned toward the register.

Before we reached the door, I handed my wool coat to Violet. "Here. Put this on."

She leaned back. "I am not taking your coat."

Her sweater was clean but old and worn. I pushed the coat into her hands. "I'm hot. Hot flashes."

She accepted the wool. "Oh. Well, okay. I didn't know you were that old."

Pierce snorted and opened the door.

"Anna!" Tessa called.

I turned in time to catch her ski-jacket before it hit me in the face. "Thanks."

"Bring that back with the car," she said, grasping a full tray to balance over her shoulder.

Violet watched her. "Your sister is cool."

"Yep," I agreed, sliding my arms into her down jacket. "She definitely is. Now, let's go see if the right truck is burning."

CHAPTER 19

*W*hoever had torched it had used enough accelerant that the truck burned bright, even with the snow pummeling it into submission. Pierce, Violet, and I stood across the road, the wind and Lilac Lake at our backs, watching the fire. The truck had been dumped at a pullover spot nestled against the forest. Thick, black smoke spiraled high into the wafting flakes.

"That's the truck," I said, squinting to see bullet holes in the driver's side door. "I aimed too low." Although I was glad I hadn't killed anybody. Even so, that meant the guy was still out there.

Violet tucked her hands into the borrowed coat, which was at least two sizes too big for her. "Whose truck?"

"Dunno," I said, watching the uniformed police officers cordon off the area. "It was on Nineteenth Street the other night. Since you live close to there, have you seen it before?"

"No." She watched the front tire blow and then hiss steam. "I've never seen it before. It looks like it was a nice truck."

Yeah, I figured that would've been a long shot.

She sneezed.

"Bless you," I said, reaching for the keys in my pocket. The lake breeze was starting to numb my face. "Let's get out of here. Pierce, let me know if you find anything in the truck when it's done burning."

Pierce, hands in pockets, nodded. "Gut feeling, your client is in trouble. If you don't know that just from being shot at, you need to dig deeper into his story. You're missing something." With that, he turned and walked across the gravel-topped icy road to speak with a uniformed officer.

Oh, he was definitely trying to tell me something. I made a mental note to track down Bernie again, sliding into the car and starting the heat immediately. "Let's get you home."

Violet lived three blocks away from Nineteenth Street, and these apartment complexes were even more run-down if that was possible. I soon drove up to a three-story building with curb parking only. The top level had been painted a gray that was now peeling to a dingy white color, and the bottom a dark green that was more of a weary beige. Concrete stairs and black iron railings showed the only way to the upper apartments. The walkway, entrance, and roof hadn't been shoveled all winter if I had to guess.

"Thanks for the ride." Violet hopped out, removed my coat from her thin body, and put it on the seat. "I'll call your office."

Um, no. I opened my door and stepped down, sliding instantly and catching myself on the door frame. "I'll walk you in."

She shut her door and shook her head. "That's okay. I don't want to wake up my great-aunt."

I pretended I didn't hear her and clomped around the front of the Rogue, one hand on the hot hood. Reaching her, I smiled. "Shall we kick our way?" Without waiting for her to argue, I kicked a path across the snow with my boots, sending cold flakes up inside my pant legs. Darn it.

She followed me, her steps slow.

"Which apartment?" I asked, looking up at the stairs.

"Second floor." Now she sounded more like a surly teenager.

I could work with that. The railing shook in my hand, and I

tried not to lean too heavily on it, but the stairs were iced over. It was a miracle nobody had broken their neck falling down the angled cement. From a couple of dents in the wall, I guessed maybe somebody had. Landing on the second floor, there was one door to the right, toward the street, and another to the left, which revealed an empty lot that had garbage poking up through the snow. "Right or left?"

She brushed by me to the right, fumbling for her key in her pocket. Her face was red from the cold and her nose swollen. The door clicked open, and she moved inside, turning instantly. "So, um, thanks for the ride."

A dog yipped and bounded down the stairs from above, clumps of ice in his fur. Blood dotted the way from an injury on his paw.

She ducked down. "Oh, Bowser. What did you do?" Her voice crooning, she moved aside and pulled him in. "He's cold."

I reached out and tugged free a couple of notices that had been taped to the door. Notices to vacate—one yellow and one red. My instincts were humming, and a light sorrow was trying to fill me, but I remained calm and soothing. "I'd like to see your aunt."

Violet looked over her shoulder into the apartment. "She's not here, I guess."

Bowser whined.

Right. I had once been a teenager—not too long ago. "I'll wait." I stepped into her, and predictably, she stepped back. She was a sweet girl, and I'd figured she would.

The apartment was clean but threadbare. The only furniture in the room was a ripped floral sofa with a worn knitted afghan and a coffee table with more dents than an unmarked soup can. Chipped blue laminate made up the counters, and there was one cracked plate in the sink. The smell of smoke and possibly mold wafted through the room.

And it was freezing. Not just cold, but icicle cold. A blanket covered the only window, but ice curled over the bottom of it.

Even in the chill, Violet blushed. "I can have my aunt call you." She just wasn't going to give this up, was she?

Bowser limped to the kitchen and scratched at the cupboard beneath the sink.

I moved past one small bathroom with a stained sink, blue toilet, and shower stall to the bedroom, which held a bed and a partially melted plastic laundry basket of teen clothes. Pictures lined the one dresser. One was with a younger Violet and a woman who looked like her, which stood next to a wedding picture of a young couple taken at least sixty years ago. Must've been the great-aunt. "Your aunt isn't here, is she?"

Violet looked at the pictures. "No."

Unopened mail was stacked neatly next to the pictures, and even from my position, I could see several envelopes from the government. "Social security checks?"

"Yeah." Violet looked at them. "You're my lawyer and can't tell on me, right?"

"That's correct." Pretty much, anyway. If I thought she was in danger, I had a duty to report it. My stomach cramped.

She swallowed. "Aunt Mays died three months ago, and the church took care of her burial. She went to one on the other side of Spokane. I told everyone I was going to live with my aunt and uncle in Billings, but I don't have family." She sighed. "I didn't know what to do with the social security checks. It's illegal to cash them, but I couldn't send them back because I think she got money for having me, and I didn't want anybody to know she was gone."

My heart broke for her. I reached out to flip on the light.

"No power," she confirmed. "I have a job but it doesn't pay a lot. I'm kinda out of money until my next paycheck."

Somebody pounded on the outside door, and we both jumped.

"Violet? Open the door. I know you're in there," a man bellowed.

"Who is that?" I whispered.

She paled even more but patted my shoulder. "It's just the manager. Stay here, and I'll handle him." She walked down the ugly faded blue shag carpet and opened the door. "I'm getting the rent, Crackle. I told you I would."

I hurried after her. She shouldn't have to worry about rent.

"I told you how you could work off that rent." Crackle's voice came in loud and clear. "Either you let me in and do what you need to do, or I'm callin' the fuckin' state on you. I know your aunt ain't here. So it's my dick or the foster care. I'll make it good for you."

Fire roared through my head. My eyes widened, and I grabbed the door and yanked it open, shoving Violet behind me with my hip.

Crackle was around forty with thick arms and a beer gut that lost to gravity over his dirty pants. His curly hair was greasy, his beard crusted with food, and his eyes beady. He was a cockroach of a man. "Who the fuck are you, bitch?"

I reared up. "I'm her lawyer and the bitch who's going to call the police and report you for trying to extort sex from a minor." My ears rang as my temper spiraled into the ozone layer. I clutched my purse closer to my side in case I needed the gun. Shooting this asshole would be a gift to society.

"Bullshit." He clocked me on the side of the head, and I flew back, smashing onto the coffee table and rolling to the ground. Pain blew through my head and my vision blurred. My ribs screamed.

He laughed and pushed Violet out of the way. "I guess it'll be the three of us."

I was smart, and often I was cool-headed. But when I hit the floor, I lost my fucking mind. Rolling up, I ducked my head and rushed forward, hitting him so hard in the gut that we both flew through the doorway. My skull might've exploded from the impact. His back and shoulders hit the wall on the opposite side and he yelled, both of us going down. He swung out, and I crab-walked back, scrambling for the gun in my purse.

The dog bounded out of the apartment and bit Crackle's pant leg, growling and snarling.

Crackle kicked the dog and the animal rolled over, smashing into the railing of the fake balcony and emitting a doggy cry of pain.

Panic and fury swirled through me as I took advantage of his distraction and forced myself to stand, finally clamping onto my gun. My hand shook so wildly I had to use both, pointing the barrel at his head and trying to regain my breath, my entire body hurting.

His eyes bugged out, and his face turned an ugly red as he pushed a beefy hand on the wall and stood. "You won't hurt me."

I set my stance. "You've got that wrong, dickhead."

Violet hovered in the doorway, her face pale, terrified tears on her bottom lids.

I kept my gaze on Crackle. "Violet? Call 9-1-1."

She hesitated.

Crackle smiled, showing crooked teeth.

"Violet?" I asked, lowering my aim to center mass. If I shot this guy, I only had one chance to keep him from coming at me.

"I can't," she whispered. "If I call them, they'll take me away. I don't want to go to foster care. I'm sorry. Not again."

I swallowed, my mind reeling. "Okay. Get your stuff. Every-thing you need since you won't be coming back. Now."

She turned and ran back into the apartment.

"Maybe I'll call the police," Crackle said, taking a tenuous step toward me.

"Go ahead," I agreed. "I'd love to tell them all about your attempt to sexually assault a minor. I'd also press charges for battery against me as well as animal cruelty for hitting the dog. My bruises alone will look very pretty to a jury."

The ugly red stain across his pocked skin made his wide face even scarier. Or maybe it was the promise of death in his blood-shot and dead looking eyes. "This isn't the end of anything."

What did that even mean?

Violet ran out of the apartment with the melted laundry basket in her hands. She'd piled the pictures and an older wooden jewelry box onto the clothes, and she had a backpack over her arm and the old afghan over her shoulder.

"Car," I said as my hands finally stopped shaking. My lungs still weren't working properly, and my body hurt, but one thing at a time.

"Come on, Bowser," she whispered, edging past me to the stairs.

Crackle held up a hand. "The dog is mine."

Bowser stood and limped to the stairs, hustling by Crackle before he could get grabbed.

"He was June's, and she left you," Violet yelled back, running too fast down the ice-crusted steps with the dog on her heels.

Crackle glared at me. "I'm coming for you."

I sucked in frigid air. "Get in line." Then I backed away, keeping the barrel pointed at him. After taking three icy steps backward and not falling on my butt, I turned and rushed down the rest, running for the car. We peeled out on icy and rough gravel, careening out of there.

Violet had shoved her belongings in the back seat along with the dog, who panted loudly. "What are we going to do now?"

Such a great question. Now that we were safe from Crackle, I had to figure something out. But first, I had to know the details. My stomach hurt as much as the various new bruises on my body. "Violet? You can tell me anything. I have to know, did Crackle—"

"No," she sighed, reaching above her shoulder to pull down the seatbelt and attach it at her waist. "I managed to avoid the creep, and the locks on the door were installed by my aunt before she passed, so he doesn't have a key. He's never touched me."

But he would have. I hated Crackle with everything I had.

She shivered. "I know we should've turned him in, but I just couldn't."

"Oh, don't worry," I said grimly. "We'll get you figured out, and then we'll press charges against him. Nobody said we have to do it today." There was no way I was letting Crackle get away with terrorizing her. Who knew what other victims were out there? "We'll take care of that jerk," I promised.

Violet swallowed. "So, what now?"

Through my rear-view mirror, I looked at the soft eyes of the quiet dog. "Now we start with a vet for Bowser to make sure he's okay and then we'll go from there." Truth be told, I didn't know what I needed to do quite yet, but one step at a time.

I could swear that dog smiled.

CHAPTER 20

*I*t was well after midnight when Aiden woke me, sliding into bed behind me and spooning his big and muscled body around me.

"Hi," I whispered.

"Hi," he whispered back, his minty breath brushing my hair. "Busy day?"

I stretched against him, holding back a wince as my fresh bruises protested. "Yeah."

"It's only been hours since I saw you, but we've managed to pick up a kid and a dog?" He brushed his hand down my arm and held my hand, tangling his fingers with mine.

Everything inside me settled and calmed for the first time that day. After visiting the veterinarian, who'd declared Bowser malnourished and bruised but otherwise healthy, and shopping for necessities for both dog and teenager, we'd had dinner and then crashed. Violet slept on my sofa, and Bowser had snored next to her on the floor. "It's a long story," I admitted.

"Usually is," he murmured. "Want to tell me about it?"

I did, but there was a fairly decent chance Aiden would go kill

Crackle, and I just didn't have the energy to block the way with my body right now. "How about tomorrow?"

"Humph," he said.

So long as he didn't see the bruises, we could have a peaceful night. "How about you tell me what's going on with you and your case? I don't have the details." I was tired, but it felt good to be talking to him with his big body right next to me. We had a lot to figure out with our relationship and our lives, but when we were holding hands and snuggling, I felt like everything would work out. Life was weird when your untouchable hero-crush became... touchable. "Forget my job for now. What's up with yours?"

"It's interesting," he said, stretching a little bit. "Saber and I were undercover with a drug operation in Portland, using our former covers as members of the MC, figuring we'd be okay. Turns out we weren't, but I haven't figured out how we got caught. Doesn't make sense."

"What happened?" I asked drowsily.

Aiden was quiet for a moment, no doubt filtering out the information he couldn't share. "Head guy called us in and tried to shoot us for being cops. It was fairly simple."

"Yeah, but you got shot," I said, losing some of my sleepiness.

Aiden shrugged, nearly dislodging me. "Eh. Guy was a moron. We took him and his three guys down, called for backup, and arrested the entire operation. We have enough to make the charges stick, but I'm headed over to Portland tomorrow to interview the main guy."

"To find out how your cover was exposed?"

"Yeah. He also has lines on several other operations, so he has some leverage to make a deal. Although any deal will include prison time for him, no matter what." Aiden's voice thickened and his body relaxed even more. "They were running opioids smuggled in from the southern border. The fentanyl kind that kills people."

I tightened my hold on his hand, which was near my hip, his

arm heavy over my waist—right below my still aching ribcage.

"Then I'm glad you shut them down."

"Me, too." He nuzzled my neck.

I shivered.

"Tell me you're not trying to figure out how to keep a teen and a dog. Please," he murmured.

I grinned. "With our lives? No." Then I sobered. "But I don't know what to do with them. She doesn't want to go into foster care, and even if I talked her into it, she wouldn't get to keep the dog. The dog isn't really hers, although they seem to have adopted each other." It wouldn't be fair to tear them apart.

"We can't keep them," he whispered.

I knew that. I really did. "There are some really good foster homes, but she's just adamant." If Violet ran away, she'd get hurt. Enough had happened to her in her young life, and I wanted to help.

"We'll figure it out tomorrow." His breathing evened out, and that fast, he was asleep.

Yeah, I admired that ability. Was even kind of jealous. It took me forever to get to sleep, but with Aiden warming me, I finally nodded off.

The nightmares got me early in the morning. Full on, Jareth Davey, coming at me with red roses and spray paint. Crackle laughed in the background, throwing knives made of ice at me while I ducked. I awoke, gasping, still warm in Aiden's arms.

Nightmares sucked.

Morning light, weak from the weight of winter, filtered through the blinds covering my sliding glass door. I slid out of bed, leaving Aiden sleeping, and used the bathroom before tugging on yoga pants, a sweatshirt, heavy socks, and a ponytail holder. A bruise covered my right cheekbone in painful purple, red, and yellow striations. The yellow was a good sign that it was healing quickly. It was unfortunate I knew that fact. Then I padded out into the living room, remembering at the last second that I had company.

Huh.

The dog looked up, stretched to his feet, and padded right over to the door. Smart dog. I tiptoed around the sleeping girl on my sofa and let Bowser out, watching him take care of business quickly in the snow and run back inside. More snow lightly fell, almost lazily. He moved for the food and water I'd given him the night before and then returned to flop by the sofa, going right back to sleep.

Violet didn't even stir. When was the last time she'd felt safe enough to sleep like that?

My heart hurt for her. I grasped my phone from the kitchen counter and moved into my laundry room, shutting the door quietly. A washer and dryer took up one wall next to a sink, while the opposite wall held a board I used to diagram legal cases. There was a ton of room beneath the board, and I thought the owners had intended to install cupboards but didn't. I opened the door to the garage and tugged out my yoga mat, placing it on the floor.

Then I stretched before moving into several different poses, allowing my mind to wander. I enjoyed yoga but wasn't very good at it. Even so, I went through the poses and mulled everything over. Through the Santa case, through Violet's case, through Aiden's case. One thought after the next, just letting them flow.

My phone buzzed and I sat, reaching for it to see the screen. Happiness bubbled through me. "Are you back in town?" I asked.

My cousin Bosco chuckled. "Yeah. I wanted to get your scoop on this Heather."

Seriously. Everyone thought women could gossip, but the Albertini boys were in a world of their own—especially when it came to one of their brothers. Bosco was the youngest of six, and Quint was the second oldest. Although considering Bosco was a tough guy in the Navy, it was hard to imagine him as a little brother. "Heather is awesome, and I think she's perfect for Quint. The second you meet her, you'll love her," I said.

Bosco was quiet for a second. "That's good news, then. Hey. I'm watching Fabio for Knox, and if I get called into work, do you mind taking him?" Knox was another older brother and Fabio his adorable mutt.

I thought about the teenager and dog already in my living room. "No problem. Just let me know, and I'll figure it out." I actually loved dog-sitting for all of my cousins and was usually the first in line when somebody needed a place for their pooch. "I don't suppose you know someone who'd like to take in a cute teenager and her own dog?"

"You're not a teenager, and you don't have a dog."

I sighed. "Not me, dumbass. I have a young friend, and she's alone in the world, and I'm trying to figure out a good place for her."

"Like a foster home?" Bosco asked, the sound of coffee percolating in the background.

"Yes, but one that we know," I said. "She's hesitant."

Fabio barked in the background.

"Knock it off," Bosco called to the dog, and the dog stopped barking. "Well, I don't know, but what about Mom and Dad?"

"Huh?" I extended my left leg and leaned over, grimacing as pain flared through my abdomen from hitting a coffee table thanks to good old Crackle.

Bosco drank noisily. "Ugh. I need a new coffeemaker." He sighed. "Mom and Dad were foster parents years ago, and I know our mother needs something to do other than try to matchmake us all and get grandbabies. I swear, I'd like to ground her from hanging out with Nonna. They're *obsessed*."

I perked up. "I'd completely forgotten that they used to take in foster kids."

"Sure. Through the years, they've taken in kids."

There had always been so many kids at the Albertini houses

that it had seemed normal to have a bunch of extra people at family gatherings. "Do you think they'd want to take in a teenaged girl?"

"Dunno, but why not? I mean, if they want to take in another kid. They might not want to at this point," Bosco said. "Dad won't retire from the mine, and Mom is pretty busy overall with her antique shop, but she might also like having a girl around for a change. Or not. I don't know, Anna Banana."

Fair enough. I'd call after I finished with Bos. "Are you home for good?" He normally worked out of Fairchild, on the other side of Spokane, but lately he'd been traveling quite a bit.

"Not sure. I was only gone a couple of weeks, and I return to find out that Quint is in *luv.*" Bosco snorted.

"Well, Heather is a zillion times better for Quint than who he was dating. Can you believe it? He slept with my nemesis," I said.

Bosco's chuckle was all Albertini. "You have a nemesis?"

"Yeah. Jolene O'Sullivan. You remember her, I'm sure. She's now a reporter with the *Timber City Gazette.*" I settled in and gossiped my heart out with Bosco, enjoying his easy laugh the entire time. Finally, I wound down. "I should go get breakfast ready for a teen and a dog."

"All right. Catch you later." Bosco hung up.

My doorbell rang.

I stretched to my feet and opened the laundry room door to see Violet sitting up sleepily on the sofa. "Sorry about that," I said. "It's early for UPS." Although, after a quick glance at my phone, it was nine in the morning. The sound of my shower running in the master bath caught my attention as I bustled for the door and opened it.

My spine tingled as I saw the dozen red roses.

"Delivery for Anna Albertini." The delivery lady looked to be in her mid-sixties, and she'd left her van running in the driveway.

I took the flowers. "Wait a sec." There wasn't a card. "Who sent these?" A quick glance to the side of my garage confirmed that the same heart was there with no additional markings.

"I don't know," the woman said, pushing her black knit hat farther back on her gray hair. She wore a down jacket, dark jeans, and rubber-soled black boots. "I just deliver the flowers, and that one doesn't have a card."

I gently grasped her arm and drew her inside. "I need to know who these are from. What florist sent these?"

The woman pushed her glasses back up her nose. "Honey? Are you okay?" She looked at my face with a sympathetic wince.

"Yes," I said. "Long story. Again, what florist?"

"Bev and Bern's, over on Sixth." She dug a cell phone from her pocket and pressed it to her ear. "Hey, Bev? It's Mary. Just delivered those roses to Albertini, and she's a little insistent that we know who sent them. There's no card." Mary looked at Anna, nodded, and then sighed. "Gotcha. Thanks." She shoved the phone away.

I sighed. "Don't tell me. The flowers were purchased over the internet with a credit card number and no real name." Another prepaid card.

"Well, the name was Aiden Devlin," Mary said. "At least, that's what was typed into the online form. They have to type something, or it won't go through. But I can't guarantee these are really from a guy named Aiden Devlin."

"I can guarantee they're not," Aiden said, striding out of my bedroom, his hair wet and his eyes a piercing blue.

Mary swallowed. "Wow."

Yeah, he got that a lot. In his faded jeans and dark tee, he looked like a bad-boy from a television show. Except he was real, and right now he was emanating an angry tension that heated the entire room.

I handed the flowers back to Mary. "Deliver these to the hospital, would you?"

"Sure." With one last and fairly long look at Aiden, head to toe, she turned and carefully picked her way back down my walkway.

I shut the door, my head ringing. "My new admirer is persistent." Or my old one. Were the flowers from Jareth Davey? I turned to see Aiden silently looking at me. "Right?"

His chin slowly lowered. "What the fuck happened to your face?"

Violet gasped and dragged the dog onto the sofa.

Aiden read the room. His shoulders instantly relaxed and he calmed, although his eyes freaking blazed. "Sorry about the rough language." He turned all his formidable charm on the teenager. "I'm Aiden."

"Violet," she whispered.

He moved toward the kitchen. "The guy who swears has to make breakfast. How about pancakes, bacon, and scrambled eggs with too much cheese?"

Violet slowly grinned. "Sounds great."

"Good." He looked toward me. "You can tell me what happened as I cook."

Ah, crap.

CHAPTER 21

*I*n my office, I stacked case files neatly on the right side of my desk, angling my head to look down the hallway. Violet and Bowser were in the normally vacant office to the left, while my cousin Pauley worked in the office across the hall from them. He'd taken one look at Violet and the animal, shut his door and hadn't been seen since.

Pauley was a sixteen-year-old autistic genius and sometimes just didn't want to deal with people.

The firm's other employee, our receptionist and sometimes accountant, Oliver Duck, had made three trips to Violet's temporary office in the last hour. Oliver was eighteen, dorky, and a sweetheart. He'd brought Violet coffee, more markers so she could work on the filing he'd found, and then water.

As he made his way to the office again, this time with a handful of colorful pens, I motioned him to keep walking in my direction.

He paused and then did so, moving inside my office.

"Door?" I asked.

He switched all of the pens to one hand and shut the door. His red hair had been combed back, and his freckles were standing at attention. "What's up, boss?"

I'd never been great with subtlety. Since I wasn't in court, I'd worn jeans with a white sweater under a navy-blue blazer, and I felt like a grownup, which wasn't ever fun. "She's pretty but underage, and you're eighteen." Although Violet was probably more mature and definitely had a stronger edge, the numbers were the numbers.

He shuffled his feet. "I was just bringing her pens."

"Friendship only for the next two years," I said.

Oliver nodded, his ears turning crimson. "Totally agree. Is she going to work here, too?"

Clark and I couldn't afford to hire another teenager—or anybody for that matter. "No. She's just here until we figure out a good place for her to live," I said, having already left a message on my aunt's cell phone. If Aunt Yara couldn't take Violet, I'd figure something else out.

Oliver looked at my aching cheekbone. "I should've asked. How'd you get this shiner?"

It was a sad fact that my having a bruised face didn't faze him in the slightest. "Got into a brawl with a guy named Crackle."

Oliver's eyebrow rose. "Gut feeling is that you should never fight physically with a guy named Crackle." He leaned to the side, studying my face. "The yellowing is good—shows it'll heal fast."

"That's what I thought."

Oliver winced. "Has Aiden killed him?"

"What makes you think I haven't killed him?" I reached for my half full mug of coffee.

"You would've led with that fact," Oliver said wisely.

He wasn't wrong. I sipped. "Aiden wasn't happy, but he realized that he's an ATF agent and can't just go kill people. However, I have a plan to turn Crackle in as soon as I take care of a couple of things."

"Like Violet?"

Yeah, Oliver was no dummy. "Yes. Like Violet."

The blue in Oliver's eyes stood out against his pale skin once his blush retreated. "If this law thing doesn't work out, maybe you could start a business where you find strays places to live—like you did for me."

I grinned. Oliver had been arrested for trespass on a farmer's land, and it turned out both the farmer and Oliver were alone in life and could use help, and now Oliver lived on the farm. What he didn't know was that the farmer had recently changed his will to leave Oliver millions someday, hopefully in the far, far future. It was odd how life turned out. "I'm glad things have worked out for you."

"I owe you," Oliver said, turning as voices could be heard. "Sounds like your client is here." He opened the door and hustled down the hallway, skipping Violet's office as he did so.

Then he led Bernie and Florence back. They were holding hands and giggling as they sat on my two guest chairs.

I sighed.

Bernie frowned, his comb-over neater than usual. Today he wore pressed brown slacks beneath a blue vest. "What happened to your face?" His chest puffed up like he was a Silverback ready to rumble.

I waved a hand in the air. "You should see the other moron." Then I took in Florence's flushed face. She looked lovely today in a pale green pantsuit with a pink silk scarf knotted at her neck. "Please tell me you two haven't been all over town holding hands," I said.

Bernie's bushy eyebrows rose to his hairline. "Of course we have. We found each other again." He leaned toward her, happiness in his faded eyes. "We're taking it slow. Well, kind of."

Florence released his hand. "We thought you'd be happy for us."

I sat back, not wanting to squelch their happiness. "Bernie is the main suspect in a murder involving your ex-fiancé, the man who left you millions as an inheritance. You can see that this might look bad to the prosecuting attorney's office, not to mention a jury someday?"

Florence fluttered her hands together in her lap, flashing several sparkly rings. "I hadn't thought of that." She settled. "Have you found out any information about this Sharon Smith?"

"Not yet," I admitted. "I'll speak with the detective later today, and if he doesn't have any information, I may call in a private detective."

"Oh, I already have," Florence said, leaning forward, her eyes sparkling. "I can check with them, or you can, I guess." She dug through her handbag, pulling out her wallet, lipstick, and a brush before snagging a business card to hand over. "There you go. I have several because I said I'd hand them out all over town."

"Great." I took the card. While I normally used my great-uncles, several times removed, it was always good to know another private detective. Until I looked at the card. The front was pink with lime green squiggles, and the words 'Hawk Investigations' in electric blue in a fancy font. It looked like it had been printed on an older dot printer. The number at the bottom looked familiar.

My stomach sank. "Please tell me—"

"Yes," Florence said in a rush. "Can you believe it? Thelma and Georgiana have started a detective agency. I think you inspired them."

"Me?" I asked weakly.

She nodded vigorously. "Yes. You've solved so many cases together. They figured they should start a business."

I looked at Bernie, who was shifting uneasily in his chair. His expression said, 'no way,' while his mouth opened up and said, "It's a great idea, right?"

I pressed my lips together. Apparently Bernie didn't want to upset the détente he had going on with the love of his life, and I guess I couldn't blame him for that. Even so, the thought of those two ladies on the loose hiding in shrubbery taking pictures made me reach for the antacids I'd discovered in my top drawer.

Bernie held out his hand, and I dropped two tablets onto his palm.

We both chewed and swallowed in unison. Then I tried to retake control of the situation. "Bernie, I need to ask you more details about your night with Sharon Smith, and we can do that privately if you wish." The skin between my shoulder blades itched at my even bringing up the subject.

Florence stiffened and straightened her back.

Bernie sighed and rubbed both gnarled hands up his face. "Sure." He slumped in his chair, his white hair now standing on end. "We had a poker night, and we had too much to drink. I vaguely remember Sharon coming inside, and I think we even dealt her in?" His head bowed. "The next thing I remember was waking up at her place in her bed."

Florence pressed her lips so tightly together they turned white.

I frowned. "Have you been able to recollect anything else since this has been on your mind so much? Do you remember having sex with her?"

Bernie jolted. "Geez, Anna. Come on."

Florence slowly turned to face him. "Do you?"

His chest concaved when he exhaled heavily. "No. But we were naked that morning, and she said we did, so I believed her. Plus, I had a raging headache, one of the worst I've ever had, and I needed to get out of there." His voice lowered. "I needed to confess to you, and that was the only thing on my mind."

Florence's gaze met mine. "You think?"

I shrugged. "Totally possible."

Bernie looked from her to me. "What are you two talking about?"

I tried to find the right words when I truly had no clue what had happened. "What if Lawrence set you up completely and not just by introducing you to Sharon? Do you have any idea how long he'd held a torch for Florence?"

"No," Bernie said, looking at Florence.

She blushed prettily. "Truthfully, I played the field a bit before Bernie and I settled down, and I did go on a few dates with Lawrence. But no romantic sparks ignited until Bernie and I split and Lawrence was there for me. He was a shoulder to cry on that turned into more."

Hope and a flare of anger lit Bernie's cloudy eyes. "You agree with me that I didn't break my wedding vows and was set up?"

"Maybe?" I said. "Have you ever gotten so drunk you lost time like that?"

"No," he burst out, an alarming red staining his wrinkled face. "Never. Sure, I get toasted sometimes, but I've never woken up not knowing how the heck I got there. Do you think I was drugged?" Without waiting for an answer, he slammed his hands on his thighs. "That bastard. I wish I could kill him—that he wasn't already dead."

Well, crap. "That's a heck of a motive to kill him," I said quietly.

"But I didn't know," Bernie protested. "I had no clue it was a setup or that I didn't really have relations."

I reached for a legal pad. Would a jury believe that he hadn't known? "Who was there playing poker that night?"

"It was a big poker night—we hold it annually to benefit the CASA organization in town. There were several tables, and I could try to track down the guest list, but no guarantees." Bernie leaned forward and tapped his finger on my desk. "I played at two different tables, and I mostly remember who played at those. It was me, Lawrence, his son Hoyt, Donald McLerrison, Earl Jacobson, Doc Springfield, Jocko Terezzi...." His voice trailed off. "That's only seven. I need one more person—we played four at a table."

"What about Micky Sala?" Florence asked, tilting her head.

Bernie's eyes cleared. "That's right. It was Micky." His chin lowered. "Mick had prostate cancer and only lived a couple of months beyond that. He was a good Kringle. Yes, he was."

I examined the list. "I've met Hoyt, Earl, and the doctor." Although I'd need to speak to them each about this. "But I haven't met Jocko Terezzi. Who is he?"

"He's a good guy and a great Santa," Bernie said, which seemed to be his barometer for judging most friends. "He owns the Irish gift store on the other side of Spokane. They have lots of china and jewelry, and he really does a good business during the holidays, which makes it even more impressive that he takes time to be an authentic Santa." Bernie smiled, revealing smooth dentures. "He also gets the best whiskey from his ex-brother-in-law, but he doesn't sell that." Bernie added the last hastily.

"He's divorced?" I asked.

"No," Florence said. "He was married to a nice Irish gal for forty years. She died, what? Maybe two years ago? Time flies, doesn't it? Saoirse had fast-acting Alzheimer's, and she went quickly." She blinked away a tear.

Saoirse? Now that was an Irish name. "So they sold items from her homeland?" I asked.

Florence nodded. "Yes. Jocko always said he took the girl out of Ireland but wanted to bring as much of it home to her as possible." Her lips trembled. "She was a good friend. I miss her."

"I'm sorry," I said, knowing the words were inadequate but feeling for her. "Is there any chance any of these men know Sharon Smith?"

Bernie shrugged. "I don't know. That was the first time I'd ever seen her, and to be honest, I haven't seen her since." He shook his head. "I got out of that apartment as fast as I could, and then I went home, trying to figure out how to save my marriage." His voice broke. "I failed."

"Oh, Bernie." Florence reached out and patted his hand.

"Where was the apartment?" I asked.

Bernie squinted as if trying to remember. "It was one of those in the brick buildings on the Idaho-Washington border? It's a pretty big complex." He rattled off an address and apartment number.

I knew the the place. Aiden had been undercover with a motorcycle club that had owned apartments closer to the freeway, down the same arterial road. "I'll figure this out, Bernie." My stomach still hurt. Right now, Bernie had a good motive since he was still in love with Florence. If I proved that he'd been set up and had his marriage destroyed by Lawrence, then he had a phenomenal motive. "If this was a set up, is there anybody else out there who wanted to hurt you? Anybody who wanted you divorced?"

"Not that I can think of," Bernie said. "I mean, Thelma has always thought I was cute, but she likes Florence a lot."

Florence turned quickly toward him. "Thelma thinks you're cute?"

"Yeah," he said.

"Humph." Florence reached for her purse. "To think I paid their retainer for this case."

Bernie smiled again, turning his hand over to hold hers. "Don't be mad at her. She never made a move, and she won't. Besides, I am cute."

Florence giggled. Actually giggled. "Well, I guess that's true." Then she lost the smile and focused on me. "You're going to keep him out of jail, right?"

I was going to do my best, but he wasn't making it easy. "I'll try. Are we still on for shopping today?" I needed Bernie to smooth the way with Jocko.

"Sure. I'll be back around two," Bernie said. "What about you?"

"Right now, I have to find Sharon Smith." The only good news I had at the moment was that the woman's name really was Sharon Smith, considering she'd been named in Lawrence's Last Will and Testament. It was a start, anyway.

I just had to find her before Thelma and Georgiana did.

CHAPTER 22

*T*he box arrived just after Violet, Oliver, and I finished eating pizza in her temporary office. Clark was in court, and Pauley had gone to his class at the college, while Bowser had grudgingly eaten his dog food in his new plastic bowl decorated with doggie bones, looking imploringly toward the pizza on the desk after every few bites.

I was cleaning up the mess when Oliver brought back a red foil-wrapped box decorated with a shiny silver ribbon that left sparkles in a trail all the way down the hallway.

"Present for you," he said, putting it on the desk.

I finished shoving the pizza box into the garbage bag and straightened, looking at the box. "Who's it from?"

"Dunno," Oliver said, scratching his head. "It was right outside the door. Must've been delivered while we were eating pizza."

I crept closer, leaning over to look at the ribbon. "There's no card."

"It's very pretty paper," Violet said, her voice hushed. "Do you have a secret admirer?" Her face grew animated, making her eyes nearly glow. "Or is this from Aiden? Does he give you surprises like this?"

"No," I said, frowning. "Aiden is more of an 'I'll grill you a steak' kind of guy." Although, I was dying to know what he'd already bought for Christmas. Knowing us, it was a new gun for me. Maybe one with a pink slide. I leaned in even closer, turning my head to listen.

Oliver took three steps back, putting himself in the hall. "Is it ticking?"

Violet gasped.

I couldn't hear ticking. "I don't think so." A shiny metal clip on the ribbon caught my eye, and I gingerly reached out to capture it. "Earl's Jewelry?" Oh. "I know Earl."

Oliver didn't move. "Well enough to have him sending you a big box?"

"No," I admitted.

Oliver's freckles stood out on his pale face. "That box is the right size for a head. Do you think it's a head?"

I looked sideways at him. "Nobody sent me a head." Probably. So far, I'd only received red roses and a painted heart from my weird admirer. Even so, I reached for my cellphone on the desk, had Siri conduct a search, and made a call.

"Earl's Jewelry Store—Spokane's longest standing store," Earl answered almost instantly, sounding like he was stacking boxes at the same time.

"Hi, Earl. It's Anna Albertini."

"Oh, Anna. How nice to hear from you. Are you happy with the cross necklace?"

I blinked. Oh yeah. "I am." But Aiden had a cross already. Then I mulled over the pretties in his store. "You know what? I think I might want to buy one of those watches you showed to me."

Earl's small gasp sounded delighted. "That's excellent. Even if a man uses a day watch, every man requires one for special occasions. I have so many from which to choose."

I frowned. "Okay. I'll take the silver and black one to the far left in that case you showed me." I finally relaxed. That was a good present. "For now, did you send jewelry my direction?"

Earl was quiet for a minute, no doubt ringing up sales in his head. "No. Why?"

"Because I'm looking at a box that would fit a head. The wrapping paper is red with a really pretty and glittery silver ribbon with a metal plate having your store name." I motioned for Violet to get out of the room. She grabbed her belongings and the dog's collar, heading out to stand by Oliver.

"Huh," Earl said. "I've never had red paper—it's only green for me. But I did have silver ribbons last year, and I had to get rid of most of them after customers complained that they left stripper-like glitter all over the place. Can you believe that? That someone would take pretty glitter and say it came from dancing boobs."

I edged away from the box until I stood in the doorway and took a quick glance down the hallway. Yep. Glitter had created quite the trail. "Okay. I'll be in to pick up the watch tomorrow, and I was hoping you'd have a few minutes to chat about Bernie McLintock."

"Sure," Earl said. "I'll be here all day. Let me know if there's a head in the box." He ended the call.

"There's no head in that box," I muttered, slipping the phone into the back pocket of my jeans.

Oliver hovered behind me. "Should we call the police?"

"Probably," I agreed, moving for my office, grasping scissors, and heading back to the spare office. "But my new secret admirer has been careful, and I'm sure there won't be prints on this thing. I don't hear ticking, and nothing is leaking." Even so, I edged them both out of the way. "How about you two wait outside of the building?"

"Not a chance," Oliver said, his wide-eyed gaze on the box.

Violet slowly nodded, her focus completely on the present.

This was getting out of hand. Taking a deep breath, I stepped closer to the red and silver package.

The dog barked.

Violet shrieked, Oliver yelped, and I jumped three feet. My heart pounding, I turned to see the dog flop flat, putting his nose on his paws, yawning.

"Not cool," I snapped.

He yawned bigger.

Violet giggled nervously.

I gently snipped the ribbon, making sure not to disturb it too much. Then I sliced through the plain red paper to see a normal brown shipping box taped at the top. Holding my breath, I cut the tape away and gently lifted the flaps.

"What is it?" Oliver whispered, pressing closer.

I looked down. "Two wrapped presents." They were both wrapped in silver paper, expertly ribboned with a narrow green and sparkly ribbon. I pulled them both out.

Violet stepped inside. "Jewelry?"

"Maybe?" I cut open the first wrapping paper to reveal a black felt jewelry box. The snap was easy to open, and I flipped it up, revealing a stunning gold and garnet bracelet.

"Wow," Violet breathed. "That's beautiful." She angled closer. "No card?"

I doubled-checked the inside of the bigger box. "No. Nothing."

"Maybe the other box has matching earrings," she said.

"Maybe." This was so weird. My admirer was spending some serious money on this campaign. Did Jareth Davey have money? Or was this somebody new and creepy? I wasn't sure and I didn't like it. With efficient movements and more confidence this time, I cut the other paper and pushed it off the box.

It was another black felt box. Probably earrings or a necklace.

I opened it to reveal a finger on cotton batting. A real, bloated, bloody finger.

Violet shrieked. Oliver grabbed her arm and yanked her back and away from the packages.

My stomach turned over, and I scrambled into the hallway with the kids, trying not to throw up.

Oliver leaned against the far wall, gagging. "Well, at least it wasn't a head."

* * *

DETECTIVE PIERCE FINISHED with his questions after the techs had bagged the evidence, smelling like lavender and looking as pissed off as usual. "Why the hell did you open that box?"

"You've already asked me that three times," I snapped back, not having a good answer. Except I'd wanted to know what was in it and was fairly certain it wasn't a bomb. "Any clue whose finger that is?"

"Nope. We don't have any reports of a person losing a finger or of anybody missing a digit in the morgue." He stood from my guest chair and loped toward the doorway, looking long and lean in jeans and button-down with green tie. No doubt he had a sports coat somewhere, but he'd been the first to arrive when I'd called, so he'd obviously been away from his office. "Any chance you want to take a vacation from this mess while I figure it out?"

I sighed. "The mess would still be here when I got back."

He turned, his green eyes veiled. "That's the truth. All right. I'll send over a uniform to watch the office during the day, but I can't get you any cover at night. The flu is going around, and we're understaffed."

I had held it together as long as I could and needed him to leave. "I appreciate the uniform here at work." It eased my mind since Clark, Oliver, and Pauley could be caught in the middle of whatever this was. "Any word on Jareth Davey?"

"I've got nothing," Pierce admitted. "We know he was here earlier in the summer, so I'm trying to track him from that point. Devlin has better resources and must be doing the same thing." He put his notebook in his back pocket and looked down at the silver glitter on his shoes. "Have Devlin call me if he gets a hit. We should coordinate." With that, Pierce turned and walked down the hallway, kicking up glitter as he went.

My cell phone buzzed, and I paused before answering. Just in case. Then I glanced at the screen and scrambled. "Hi, Aunt Yara," I said breathlessly.

"Hi, sweetie. Sorry about the delay in getting back to you— business at the antique store has been crazy. The holiday rush is on," my aunt said, Christmas music in the background. "What's up?"

Taking a deep breath, I told her all about Violet and her situation. "I need her to find a safe place where she'll stay, and since you used to foster kids, I thought of you. I know it's a long shot, but..." I held my breath.

Aunt Yara hummed quietly. "A sixteen-year-old girl? Well, that'd be interesting. If she needs a place to live, then she needs a place to live. I'm swamped tonight with special shopping hours. Why don't you bring her over for dinner tomorrow night, and we can meet each other?" The music decreased in volume through the phone. "We might as well see if we're compatible before calling in favors with the state, right?"

Relief buzzed through me so quickly I sagged. "She has a dog."

"We have ten acres, so a dog is fine. But Anna, don't get your hopes up because if Violet doesn't want to be here, she won't stay. I won't force her. I learned that through the years."

"I understand," I said. "We'll see you for dinner."

"I'll make my taco bar," Yara said. "Be here by seven and bring dessert, would you? Oh. Gotta go. Bye." She clicked off.

I sat back and tried to calm myself. The image of that finger, a pinkie as it turned out, wouldn't leave my mind.

Violet appeared in the doorway. "Are you okay?"

No. "Yeah, I'm fine. How about you?" I'd been trying to help her and now had probably just terrorized the girl.

Her black hair bobbed around her shoulders as she walked

inside and took one of the guest chairs. "I've never seen a cut off finger, but really, I'm fine. You're amazing. I can't believe how cool you were."

Cool? I'd nearly puked. Twice. "I'm sorry you had to see that." She waved her hand. "Seriously. I'm fine." Then she cleared her throat. "We haven't had a chance to really talk, and I wanted to say thank you. For taking me and for breakfast today. That was fun. This morning with Aiden, I mean." A light pink infused her cheeks.

I grinned. "I know. He's something else, right?"

She nodded vigorously. "I, um, wanted to ask you. How do you get a guy like that?"

I opened my mouth and then shut it. Okay. That was quite the question, and my heart warmed for her. Man, I hope she and Yara liked each other. It'd be such a great place for Violet to be safe and loved. "A guy like that might be lucky enough to get you—if he treats you right and realizes how amazing you are every day." Hadn't anybody ever given her that kind of assurance? I wasn't used to mentoring kids since I still felt like one sometimes, so I had to struggle for the right words. This felt important, and I didn't want to screw it up. "You can only be you in this life, and that's a good thing because you're awesome."

She rolled her eyes, but a pleased smile hinted on her lips. "Whatever."

"It's true. You just be you. Be strong and smart and make good decisions. The right guy will like you for all that you are."

"I'll finish those file folders now." She chuckled and stood. "Aiden must really like you if getting a cut off finger in a box is a regular workday for you."

I smiled. "You're not wrong."

Her worn tennis shoes scattered glitter as she left.

I took a deep breath, my ears heating. The world narrowed around me. Ah, a panic attack. Made sense. My vision blurred. Why was it when I felt safe, the panic attacks always hit?

165

Confirming that the hallway was empty for now, I quietly pushed my chair back, squatted, turned, and planted my butt beneath my desk, hugged my legs to my chest, and closed my eyes.

I have no idea how long I sat there.

A sound caught my attention, and I opened my eyes to see black motorcycle boots and jeans. Then Aiden crouched, having to bend sideways to see me, his eyes many colors of blue. "How bad?"

I shivered.

He sighed. "That bad."

CHAPTER 23

*T*here are times in your life that you know you're surrounded by good people. Hopefully.

"I'll be right back." Aiden disappeared for about a minute and then returned, his motorcycle boots loud on the wood, and this time appearing with even more silver glitter across the tips. He sat, tossing up sparkles. "I sent the kids on errands and locked the door, although there's a uniformed officer right outside. Pierce must've sent someone over." Then Aiden reached for me, plucking me out from under my desk and onto his lap. "Just breathe."

I snuggled against his chest. "I'm better now."

"I thought we were getting the panic attacks under control," he murmured, his chin on the top of my head.

"Me, too."

He shifted his weight and put his back to the wall behind my desk, his head touching the windowsill. "The roses and heart were bothering you, and the finger probably just pushed you over the edge."

I shuddered. "It was so grotesque."

"Butchered fingers usually are."

167

I snorted. My mind wandered and then returned. "The kids didn't know—"

"No. They had no clue you were hunkered beneath your desk," he said softly. "I, on the other hand, would've appreciated a phone call when that became necessary. Pierce gave me a heads up about what had happened, so I headed over here."

I blinked. "I can't count on you to rescue me all the time, you know."

"Why not?"

Because I didn't want him to think I was a weak woman who couldn't handle things.

He leaned back and tipped my face up with one knuckle. "Don't be dumb."

I stilled. "Dumb?"

"Yeah. I think you're smart and I know you're capable. But nobody is immune to a panic attack, and if this helps—" he tightened his hold around me "—then you need to call. We're in this together, remember?" The play of muscle beneath his shirt felt strong and powerful while his voice remained soft and gentle.

"I know," I said, and I did. "Before the other night, it's just been so long since I had an attack. I just haven't been prepared. Sometimes jumping beneath the desk is the best and quickest move." The glitter wafted up, and I sneezed. Twice.

"Bless you," he said. "You're not shaking any longer."

"Nope." I relaxed. "When is it my turn to rescue you?"

His smile was slow and too sexy for my peace of mind. "You rescue me every day. Just by being you."

Now that was so sweet I could barely think…and nicely in line with the advice I'd given Violet.

"Plus, you have rescued me. Gun and all, remember?" he asked.

I nodded. We weren't keeping score, but if we were, he was totally ahead in the rescuing department. But I could live with that—he was a modern day protector, after all. "I think I can get up now. Where did you send Oliver and Violet, anyway?"

"I told them I needed holiday decorations for the new office and gave them a credit card." He frowned. "But I didn't give them a budget."

"They're smart kids and won't overspend." I brightened. "Hey. You rented the former spa to use as your office?"

He kissed the top of my nose. "Yeah. Well, to be more exact, I bought the building and then rented the office for our ATF team. It's all legit and I disclosed all details."

My heart warmed. "You bought the building?" He wanted to stay in town.

"Yeah. I need to diversify my portfolio."

He had a portfolio? I had a savings account with less than twenty dollars in it. "Huh," I said. "That sounds very responsible."

"That's me." His phone vibrated against me, and he dug it out of his front pocket. "Devlin."

I breathed in through my nose and out through my mouth, forcing my body to relax now that the panic attack had abated. Even so, when he stiffened, I stilled.

"Yeah. Got it. Thanks." He clicked off.

"What?" I asked.

He looked down at me, measuring. "So I didn't have to drive down there, I had two of the guys from the Portland gang moved up here temporarily so we could interview them and see how we were burned. We have them housed at the Airway Heights Corrections Center in Washington, and Saber brought them over here for interrogation. Pierce is letting us use their station."

"That's good." I moved to get off his lap, but he kept me nicely in place. "How long do you have them?"

"Just two days, and then they go back to Oregon for trial."

"Oh. You should go, then."

He stood in one smooth motion, still holding me. Then he set me on my desk. "I don't think I should leave you."

I looked up, feeling better. Feeling almost solid again. "I'm good. When the kids get back, we'll keep the door locked, and while I was planning to venture into Spokane with Bernie, I'll put that off until tomorrow."

"What time?"

"Doesn't matter." I ran my hands up his arms. "I'll be fine. Now go do your work." I couldn't keep him from his job any longer.

He glanced at his watch. "Either I'm with you, or a uniformed officer is with you until we figure out who just sent the finger."

I was more interested in the owner of said finger. "It's good that Pierce has assigned an officer to us during the day, especially since the kids have been around." I wasn't a moron and would take backup any chance I got.

Aiden nodded. "Agreed. Speaking of Pierce, I have a call into him but haven't heard back yet. Are we sure the finger was real?"

"The crime scene guy said it was real, but that's all he'd say." I tried to banish thoughts of cut off fingers. "I can't see how it was a joke."

"It's no joke," Aiden said grimly.

I hopped off the desk, feeling a little light-headed like usual after a panic attack, but my breathing had normalized, and I could think again. "I'll go to the station and see if Pierce knows anything. There was no way I was getting any work done this afternoon. A bloody stump of a finger did that to a gal. I reached over and rolled the chair closer to my desk.

"I'm headed that way to interview a prisoner and will drive you." Aiden looked me over. "Your plan is a good one, but there's one problem. You have glitter all over your ass."

* * *

A TALL BLONDE with killer legs nearly knocked me over as I tried to enter Pierce's office. Her hair was up in a fancy do, her makeup flawless, and her heels Prada. The suit she wore was a green linen skirt with matching jacket, and she smelled like lavender. She stormed out, and even her high heels kicked up irritation as she swept by me, heading for the stairs to the main floor.

I gulped, pausing, and then poked my head in his door. "You okay?"

Pierce sat behind his desk, his jaw tight, his tie looking like he'd yanked it to the side. "Yeah. What's up?"

I looked down the empty hallway, steeled my shoulders, and moved inside to gingerly sit in one of his guest chairs. "Should you go after her?"

"No. That was a breakup." He didn't sound horribly upset, but he didn't sound happy, either.

"Why?" I figured we were kind of friends.

He looked at the papers, case files, and empty coffee cups on his desk. "My job. Like usual."

I swallowed.

Then he cocked his head to the side. "How do you handle Devlin's job? He's not even in town very often."

I shrugged. "Well, he handles mine, and I figure we can deal with situations as they arise." I tried to dig deeper. "I guess I'd rather have him in my life and not my town than in my town and not my life." It was as philosophical as I got.

"Humph," Pierce said, picking glitter off his arm. "We all look like we've been to a strip club."

That was more than an opening, and it looked like he didn't want to discuss the end of his relationship with the sexy blonde. "Any news on the finger?"

"Just that it's a finger that was removed postmortem," he said. "The prints, or rather print, was all cut up and destroyed, maybe with a droplet of acid, so that's no help."

Shoot. I figured maybe a print would lead us to the owner of the finger. "Well, somebody has to show up, right?" Postmortem? At least the person hadn't lost a finger while alive. "From what I saw, the finger didn't look too decayed." The reality of that fact had a lump of granite dropping into my stomach. "Which means that the person hadn't been dead very long before having the finger removed."

Pierce's gaze narrowed. "Yep."

"So we have a dead body out there without a finger." I shuddered, wishing I didn't have to follow that train of thought. "The finger looked male?" Although it had been swollen and apparently desecrated, so I couldn't be sure.

"Running DNA now, and we'll know later today or tomorrow. Called in a couple of favors," Pierce admitted. "For now, we need to keep somebody on you."

I had no problem with that. "I left the uniformed officer at the office for Clark, Violet, and the boys since I'm here."

Pierce reached for a pen to tap on the desk. "That's fine, but again, I don't think I can spare anybody at night. The flu is still kicking us in the teeth, and I'm down several officers."

"That's okay. I'm armed and so is Aiden." I was grateful Aiden was back in town. I needed to take Violet over the hill to Silverville and get her out of the line of fire. Just one more night and she'd be safe and away from me. Hopefully she and Aunt Yara would like each other. I couldn't imagine anybody not liking either one of them.

Pierce's phone rang, and he lifted it to his ear. "Pierce." He pushed several notebooks out of the way and pulled a case file off the bottom of a pile. "Yeah. I have that right here. I'm thinking the witnesses—"

I stood, waved, and exited his office.

He didn't look up. One thing about Pierce, when he was on a case, he was a bloodhound. The lavender-scented blonde apparently hadn't understood that fact.

My phone dinged and I scrambled in my purse for it. "Anna Albertini," I answered.

"Hi Anna, it's Florence," Florence said quietly. "I finally read Lawrence's letter, the one the lawyer gave to me?"

My heart rate sped up, and I leaned against the wall, ignoring the hustle around me. "Yes? What did it say?"

"Nothing much. Well, he said that he loved me and was so proud that I had chosen him out of all his friends. That he'd done whatever he had to do to make that happen because it was true love for us." She sighed. "He didn't confess to anything, but I did end up choosing him, and if he set Bernie up, that could be what he was talking about. Or maybe not. Maybe he was just saying that sending me flowers and courting me was what he had to do. I just don't know."

"It's okay," I hastened to say. "You don't have to know."

She sniffed. "They were good friends, though. For years— going way back. I feel badly I came between them, although if Lawrence tricked Bernie in such a horrible manner, he wasn't who I thought he was. I'm just confused."

I couldn't blame her. "We'll figure it out, I promise. For now, is there any chance I could get you to fire Thelma and Georgiana? I love those two, and I don't want to see them get hurt."

"They'll be fine," she said. "You can't count them out just because they're old. We have a lot to contribute, you know."

I grimaced. Those two courted trouble even stronger than I did, but I wasn't going to insult her. "All right. I'll be in touch."

"Thanks, Anna. Good day to you," Florence said, sounding more cheerful.

"You, too." I hung up. How was I going to put an end to Hawk Investigations?

Sighing, I tapped the back of my head against the wall several times in a move I'd seen Aiden do more than once. Glitter wafted down to shine on the wooden floor.

CHAPTER 24

I hovered in the hallway for a second and then figured why not? Smiling at a couple of officers and passing several offices, I headed to the far end of the floor where the interrogation rooms were located. Aiden hadn't exactly said I wasn't welcome to watch. The light over the second room was on, so I dodged around the corner to the observation room, silently entering and shutting the door before walking toward the two-way mirror.

Aiden sat with his back to me, facing a monstrous man with a bulbous nose, the vibe tense in the room. Silver glitter sparkled in the back of Aiden's dark hair, and I winced. Saber sat next to him, kicked back in his chair, his brown hair longer than it had been last time I'd seen him. They both wore ATF jackets and guns strapped to their thighs, looking tough and broad.

It was weird to see Aiden on the cop side of the table. Any other time I'd watched him in interrogation, he'd been the one being interrogated. Interesting.

Even though the atmosphere looked tense, he appeared to be relaxed. At least from behind.

"Either you want to deal, or you don't," he was saying, his voice level and calm.

I stepped closer to the window for a better view of the prisoner in the orange jumpsuit. His swollen and red nose went with the rest of him. Wide chest, big belly, arms that had gone to fat. He had to be in his mid-forties, and his bloodshot eyes showed he'd spent several of those decades experimenting with leaving this reality. If he was selling drugs, he'd been sampling them first.

"I've got nothin' for you. Like I said," he muttered, his shoulders twitching along with his upper lip.

"Looks like you're coming down pretty hard," Aiden murmured. "That's unfortunate. I can't promise you drugs, but I can promise you less prison time if you work with us. Or not. At this point, I'm about done, Sorenson."

Saber slid his boots closer to his chair, losing the chill look. "Me, too. It's lunchtime, and I'm hungry. Either tell us how our cover was blown, or we're leaving. My gut feeling is that you don't owe anybody anything, so either take care of yourself or not."

Aiden nodded. "This is getting boring."

Sorenson's beady eyes looked from Saber to Aiden. If I had to guess, his spirit animal was one of those huge rats you find in alleys in New York City right after they put all the garbage out for the night in Times Square. "I want immunity."

Aiden burst out laughing. "Shit. I don't care that much about how we were busted, asshole. It's more curiosity at this point, and immunity is off the table. Completely and forever." He shoved his chair back. "Let's go eat, Saber. We're done here."

"No. Wait." Panic slithered over Sorenson's blotchy skin. "Just wait a minute."

Saber stood. "This is a waste of time."

"Wait." Sorenson waved a hand, his nails too long and a dented yellow. "Fine. I'll tell you. You'll talk to the federal prosecutor for me?"

Saber sat back down.

Aiden nodded; pieces of silver glitter fell down his back. "Yeah. We'll talk to her, and it'll help with whatever deal you get. If you go to trial, we'll let the judge know you cooperated. Your future is all in your control. For now."

Sorenson sighed. "Fine. I don't have a lot." He wiped the corner of his mouth, his shakes getting stronger. "It was just a note."

Aiden was quiet for a moment until Sorenson started squirming even more.

"A note." Aiden sounded bored. "Not enough. Let's go."

"Wait," Sorenson snapped, his eyes bugging out. "Honest. It was a note saying you two were undercover ATF officers, left on my bike outside of Sally's Bar. That's all. Simple."

Aiden glanced at Saber. "Don't we have the footage from the cameras outside of Sally's?"

Saber nodded. "Just had it gathered but haven't had time to go through it."

"I saw the guy," Sorenson admitted. "Was coming out, kind of drunk, and saw him leave the note. I chased him but, like I said, I was kinda drunk. Then curious. So I read the note."

"What did he look like?" Aiden asked.

Sorenson shrugged, and his belly jiggled. "Like a guy. Maybe in his forties, big nose, glasses, brown hair. Nothing special about him."

Aiden looked over his shoulder, right at me.

Huh. I hadn't realized he'd known I was there, but again, it was Aiden.

He dug his phone from his back pocket and returned his attention to Sorenson. "I'm going to show you ten pictures, and you're going to tell me if any of the guys look like the one who burned us. Got it?"

Sorenson shrugged again. "Whatever."

Aiden held out his phone and scrolled through, pausing several times and then continuing. Finally, he pulled back. "Anybody?"

"Yeah," Sorenson said, his eyes gleaming. "I definitely saw the guy in those pictures, and now, I kinda think I have more to bargain with, you know?"

"No," Aiden said quietly, which was always a bad sign. Was Sorenson smart enough to realize that fact? "You actually have less. We can go through the footage from Sally's, or you can tell me what you know. You have five seconds."

Sorenson picked at a scab on his neck.

"Four," Aiden said.

Sorenson's gaze darted around the room.

"Three."

"Um," Sorenson muttered.

"Two." Aiden pushed his chair back.

Sorenson swallowed. "Fine. It was the second guy. He's the one, I'm pretty sure. I mean, all of those guys on your phone look alike, but I think it was the second guy. He had a really big nose."

Aiden scrolled through his pictures again. "This guy?"

"Yeah. That's definitely him. I mean, he looks younger in the picture, but that was a nose you don't forget, right?" Sorenson smiled, showing stained teeth. "I've been helpful."

"Yeah." Aiden stood, and even through the distance, I could feel a heated swell of anger from him. "Thanks." He glanced at Saber. "You got this?"

Saber stretched to his feet. "Yeah. I'll see you at the new office in an hour or so?"

"Sounds good." Aiden crossed out of the room, leaving a light trail of silver in his wake.

I met him in the hallway. "You good?"

He grasped my arm and drew me down the hallway and stairways to the main reception area, leading me off to the side and away from the desk. "No. I am not good." He clicked a button and a picture appeared on his phone. "This is who burned us."

Everything inside me quieted and then went cold. The picture was from a New Hampshire driver's license, taken about eight years ago. It was Jareth Davey—big nose and sharp eyes. His hair had thinned and held more gray since I'd last seen him. Since he'd kidnapped me. "Oh, God," I whispered.

* * *

IT WAS hard to believe it was only after lunchtime, after the day I'd had. Finding the finger had blown reality out of the way, and I shivered, putting my hands out to the heat blasting from the car vents. Then to know that Jareth Davey had somehow followed Aiden from Lilac City to his undercover op in Portland made me want to throw up.

We'd been underestimating the nutjob, and even though I'd been preparing for a fight, I had still buried my head and hoped he wouldn't come back after me.

"This isn't cool," Bernie grumbled from the back seat of the police vehicle. "If we get in a wreck, I'm locked back here."

I looked over at Officer Bud Orlov, who was driving over the icy roads with relaxed competency. "I told you we could take Aiden's truck," I said. Again.

Bud ducked his head to see the thick white clouds above us. "No."

I shook my head, turned, and sent Bernie an apologetic look through the thick metal mesh that separated us. "Sorry about this." Until we figured out where Jareth Davey had landed, I had police protection whether I wanted it or not. I did want it. A lot. Right now, Oliver had gone home, and Violet had gone to work at a local burger joint, so they were safe at the moment. "You don't have any jurisdiction in Washington state," I reminded Bud.

"Don't care. I want my car," Bud retorted. The solid man had absolutely no sense of humor that I had ever been able to find.

For a second back in the summer, I'd thought he was interested in my older sister, Donna. Then I found out he was married. "How's the wife?" I asked.

He turned down the heater, his gaze on the road outside.

I sighed. "Come on, Bud. I didn't mean to get you shot or choked out last summer. I'm sorry. Really, really, really sorry." It did seem that Bud held a grudge.

"Not your fault," he said, flipping on his blinker and switching lanes on I-90, crossing the Idaho-Washington border.

"So. Wife?" I asked, more than a little curious. Who would marry no-nonsense Bud?

He sighed, the sound aggravated. "She's fine. We're still trying to figure things out, and I guess are still separated? I don't know. She has her life, and I have mine, and they don't seem to meet in the middle."

I perked up. That was more than I'd ever heard from him. "What's her life?"

He shook his head.

Fine. So much for girl talk with Bud. We drove in silence for the rest of the way until arriving at the cutest Irish shop imaginable. It was at the far north end of Spokane, and I'd actually never been there. My Gaelic blood quickened happily as I took in the Celtic knot across the door and the lovely, and somehow Irish, Christmas scene that had been painted perfectly across the front glass windows.

I hopped out of the car and quickly opened the back door to spring Bernie free. "I can't believe I've never been here," I said. Although, most of my Irish decorations came from my Nana O'Shea and her relatives across the pond. The one-story building stood alone with a ski shack building on one side and a two-story men's suit warehouse on the other.

Bernie smoothed back his gray hair and tugged his coat into place. "Jocko does a good business that really picks up around St. Patrick's Day as well as Christmas."

Bud crossed the street, looked both ways down the shoveled but still icy sidewalk, and motioned us inside. "We're out in the open."

I was evading a stalker, and now also worrying about being

shot. So I hurried through the doorway, smiling when the bell above the door jangled out a tinkly and happy sound. Blinking lights and Irish Santas decorated the space, along with spun angel hair and the smell of cookies. I immediately caught sight of a Celtic heart-shaped ceramic tray for jewelry that my mother would love. Humming, I grasped it and looked for more. A scarf caught my eye—green, silk, and Celtic. Perfect for my Nana.

By the time we reached the counter across the shop, my hands were full.

A tall teenager with a nose ring waited behind the counter. "You did well," she murmured.

"I know," I said happily. "Also, is Jocko around?"

"Sure." She angled her head toward an open doorway behind her. "Jocko? You have people here." Then she started ringing up my many purchases.

Shuffling sounded behind the door, and Jocko came into view. "Bernie," he said, hustling around the counter to take Bernie's hand. "I'm so sorry about Lawrence. I should've called, but business has been nuts."

Bernie shook and introduced us, making a point of asking Jocko to talk to me because I was his lawyer.

Jocko kind of matched his name. He was short and wide with a nose that had been broken a few times. His face was square, his eyes brown, and his voice husky. His hair was a grayish-white mix and his face weathered with smile lines out from his eyes. I'd bet almost anything he'd boxed at some point in his life, and not just because he had cauliflower ears. "Hi." His handshake was gentle.

"Hi." I introduced Bud.

Jocko frowned. "Why do you have an armed guard?"

"Long story," I admitted. "Do you mind if we chat for a moment?"

Jocko motioned me back behind the counter. "Sure. Let's go to my office."

Bernie rocked back on his heels. "I'm going to run next door and see what they have in the way of Santa suits. You keep the cop with you." Without waiting for a response, he chugged right back through the store.

Jocko paused and watched him go. "I don't care what anybody says, and I don't care about our pasts. Regardless of his youth, Bernie didn't have one reason to stick a knife into Lawrence's back. Not one."

I gulped. Actually, Bernie had a couple of reasons. "Your pasts?" I asked, following him through a neatly arranged storage room holding everything from Celtic crosses to Irish literature to an office at the very back.

He slipped around a worn leather chair to sit behind his old fake wooden desk. "Well, yeah. Isn't that why he was arrested?"

CHAPTER 25

I sat at the edge of the seat, trying not to sneeze from the dust. While the storage area had been pristine, the office didn't look like it had been cleaned, really cleaned, in quite some time. The carpet was a short-cropped red weave that had turned pink in some areas. "Why don't you start at the beginning?" I asked, tossing aside my line of questions for a moment.

He looked up at Bud, who filled out the doorway, leaning against the jam. "I'd like to speak privately."

"No," Bud said.

I sighed. "Bud. I'm fine here. Go find your wife something nice for Christmas, would you?"

Jocko perked up. "I just got in a new shipment of white gold jewelry. Have Bree show you the necklaces. They're lovely."

Muttering something I couldn't decipher, Bud turned and stomped back into the main area of the store.

Jocko seemed to relax when Bud left. "Why do you need an Idaho cop covering your back?"

"Long story but nothing to do with Bernie," I said. Well, probably. Somebody had shot at us the other day, and I still thought they were aiming for Bernie and not for me. "So. Tell me about this past."

Jocko reached for a mug half-full with coffee and took a deep drink. "The statute of limitations has expired on any crimes we might've committed."

I set my purse on the floor, finding a somewhat clean area, my breath stopping. That statement had not been what I had been expecting. Not at all. A warning itch flared between my shoulder blades. "I'm not with the prosecuting attorney's office. I represent Bernie and am trying to help him."

"I understand," Jocko said. "Just wanted you to know that you have no leverage over me."

I frowned. Why would I need leverage? "All right."

He took another gulp and then grimaced. "Coffee sucks cold, but I never seem to get time to drink it hot." He put the lime green mug on the desk. "Did Bernie tell you how the Kringle Club got started?"

I sat back. "Not how but why."

Jocko's smile revealed a gap between his bottom front teeth that I hadn't noticed before. "The how is the fun part. Bernie, Lawrence, Earl, Donny, Micky, and I were hard rock miners back in the sixties. The rest of the guys joined the Kringle Club later once we'd retired from mining and were just doing the Santa gig, including Doc Springfield. He has no clue how we originally made the money."

I had several relatives who were hard rock miners. It was a tough job that had the potential to pay very well if one struck a vein. Or ten. "So you worked together?"

"Yes. We made enough money that we each started our own businesses. This shop for me, the jewelry store for Earl, the bait and tackle shop for Lawrence, the leather goods shop for Micky, and the insurance agency for Bernie." Jocko flicked a feather off the side of his desk. "Oh. Duke Wells was also one of us, and he opened Duke's Jewelry in Timber City, but he didn't want to be a Kringle later on. Good guy, though."

Duke's Jewelry was right next to my office, and Duke had always seemed like a nice older man.

I studied Jocko, the facts clicking into place for me. "Mining pays well."

"Yep."

But he'd mentioned crimes. "You mined where you weren't supposed to mine, now didn't you, Jocko?" I asked quietly.

He lifted one shoulder. "We found silver, sold silver, and started our lives."

Well, he was probably correct that the statute of limitations had run out years ago. "Who did you steal from?" I had mining in my blood, and I wasn't going to mince words with him.

"Nobody big," he admitted. "We mainly went deep in abandoned mines."

That was still trespassing and stealing from the owners of those mineral rights. "Did you steal from anybody who'd be mad about it?"

"After all this time?" He snorted. "No. Of course, not. In fact, most people never found out. Flo is one of the few who did, and we paid her a fee, so we're all good."

I perked up, my ears near flicking in place. "Florence McLintock?" Wait a minute. I thought she'd already had five or so husbands before settling down with Bernie, which was years ago. Yeah. If they were married for seven and now had been divorced for five, that was close to the timeline. "She's originally from Silverville?"

"She's from Bourn, which is a couple of canyons over toward Montana, as you probably know," Jocko said. "We all palled around in our twenties, and she was the goal. Man, she was hot. We all liked her, but she had her eye set on getting out of Idaho. Married some banker from California who had a vacation place on Lilac Lake. That's how she met him, I guess."

I sat back, my instincts humming. "I hadn't realized you all knew each other way back when."

"Sure. Flo pretty much broke all of our hearts when she took off for California, but I found my Saoirse, and she was my soul mate. I miss her every day since she passed on. Flo eventually returned home, and when she hooked up with Bernie, I was happy for them both." Jocko checked his gold wristwatch over his hairy wrist. "Was sad at their split, then happy again when she and Lawrence seemed to have found love." He shook his head. "Life is weird, right?"

So weird. "Do you know Sharon Smith?"

"Nope," Lawrence said, his eyes somber. "I remember meeting her at the CASA charity poker night because she sat at our table and was dealt in. Lawrence knew her and introduced her around, but my eye was on the cards, you know? She was pretty. Redheaded, tall, stacked. Maybe ten years younger than us. Never heard about her again, but we all knew not to bring up her name because of what happened. I figured she'd been visiting from out of town and didn't want to know more than that."

I wanted to make notes but instinctively knew it'd put Jocko on guard. "Did you see her leave with Bernie?"

"No. I lost all of my chips by eleven and headed home by myself. It's no fun hanging around when you can't play." Jocko reached for the coffee again, took another swig, and then grimaced. "Ugh."

"Who was left playing at that time?"

His lips pursed as he apparently tried to remember. "Let's see. Earl lost before I did, and we walked out together to our cars. That left Lawrence, Bernie, Mick, and that Sharon. The other table had cleared out, and I lost. So that was it, I think."

"Was Bernie drunk?"

Jocko shrugged. "No more than usual. He was still playing well and was in control. I was shocked when I found out he'd gone home with that woman. He loved Florence so much and seemed happy."

I swallowed. "What if Lawrence set up Bernie? What if he drugged Bernie and only made it look like Bernie had cheated on Florence?"

Jocko's bushy eyebrows rose. "Honestly? That's crazy. Lawrence wouldn't do that."

"What if he did?" I pressed.

Jocko ticked his head, his gaze sharp. "Well, I guess I'd say that there are women in this life worth killing for—especially in a situation like that."

My throat went dry. "Really?"

"Yeah. And Miss Albertini? Florence McLintock is definitely one of those women."

* * *

MY HEAD still rang with Jocko's last statement when Bernie, Bud, and I walked into Earl's Jewelry Store. Earl was over at the far display case, cajoling a twenty-something man into buying an emerald ring to match a necklace.

Bernie hopped happily next to me. He'd been downright gleeful after finding a new Santa suit with real white fur that smelled like magic. His words, not mine.

Earl rang up the purchase and motioned us toward the cash register, where he was already putting in my info. "Card?"

I reluctantly handed over my credit card, which still felt warm after using it to buy my Irish bounty.

He ran the card, handed me the slip to sign, and then gave me a bag with the watch box already inside. "There you go. Your uncle or whomever will love that."

"My boyfriend," I said, slipping my hand through the strong handles so the bag could hang from my wrist.

Earl frowned. "What about the cross you purchased already? How many boyfriends do you have?"

"Just one, and he already has a cross. I'm going to give the one I bought here to another family member."

Earl looked at the bag. "That watch is not a boyfriend gift. That's a buddy gift." He grasped my arm and drew me toward the watch case. "You want yellow or white gold for a significant other. Not a fun black and white buddy-type watch."

I sighed, the bag feeling like it weighed twenty pounds. My wrist ached. "How about a silk tie with leprechauns on it?" I had just the one, newly packaged from Jocko. "Is that a significant other gift?"

Earl, Bernie, and Bud all answered at once. "No."

Wonderful. Just wonderful. "Earl? Could we have a couple of moments to talk?" I asked.

"Sure." He looked at Bud. "Yell at me if anybody comes in. In the meantime, why don't you shop? You look like a guy who has a significant other. Emeralds are big this year."

Bud sighed.

I followed Earl into his office, which was the exact opposite of Jocko's. The place was sparkling clean, modern, and quite lovely. Once I got him past the fact that I knew about his earlier illegal actives, he opened right up and corroborated everything Jocko had said.

He shook his head. "I have to tell you, I was stunned when Bernie cheated on Florence. He'd been in love with her since he turned eighteen, and I would've bet my entire store that he would've remained faithful."

"What if Lawrence drugged him and set up the entire situation?" I asked.

Earl's mouth opened and then closed, making him look like a guppy. Then he exhaled. "I don't know. I mean, in our youth, Bernie had quite the temper. He was often the tough guy in our group. Would he kill?" He shook his head. "I just can't imagine it. Wow. That's a lot."

Not only was it a lot so far, but the witnesses for my client seemed to think he might've killed Lawrence. Earl, also, had just met Sharon Smith that night and had no idea how or why she'd ended up in Lawrence's will—and he didn't want to know any more than that.

"Thank you for speaking with me," I said, quite dejected.

"You bet. What was the issue with my wrapping paper and boxes the other day on the phone?" he asked.

The thought of the finger made me gag. "You don't want to know." I stood and then returned to the retail part of the store where I waited for Bud to purchase a stunning sapphire necklace. He'd been a good sport all afternoon, so I didn't give him a hard time or ask any questions. Then Bernie decided to buy Florence opal earrings, and Earl was all but humming happily by the time we left and piled into Bud's car, heading through the now lightly falling snow back to Idaho. Darkness had roared in, and Bud had to use his headlights.

"Do you mind if we take a quick detour?" I asked, hoping Bud was still in a decent mood as I rattled off the address.

"It's after dinnertime," he muttered but took the offramp near the border and drove the several miles to the quaint brick apartment building. There were only twelve apartments, and we went to each one, finding somebody home, freezing our butts off in the rapidly strengthening storm. Not a soul knew Sharon Smith. Even the few folks who'd been there more than a few years didn't know her. One guy thought the far apartment had been owned by a business or a guy who had poker parties where his wife couldn't find out. But he didn't know any names. We finally reached the last apartment, the one where Bernie said he'd awoken that day.

A forty-something woman who worked in Washington at the nearest Apple's Restaurant had lived there for two years, and she had no idea who'd rented the apartment before her.

We thanked her and left, having the name of the rental company now in my notes. "We'll find out who rented that apartment, Bernie," I promised as we headed back to the car.

"I know," he said, not nearly as happy as he'd been earlier. "I just can't imagine that Lawrence would set me up, but the poker parties at that apartment does indicate that Hoyt or his dad might've rented that place. He does like to gamble."

It was looking more and more like that was what had happened.

Bud stiffened, looking around the quiet parking lot.

"What?" I asked, my nose freezing.

"Duck!" He dove over me, smashing me into the snow.

Bullets pinged all around us.

CHAPTER 26

*B*ud tackled me to the snowy ground behind his official vehicle, while Bernie full on dove for the trees, tossing up snow. "Stay down," Bud yelled.

Snow slid up beneath my shirt and I turned my head, coughing out more of it. Ice chilled my entire body and I scrambled to my knees, keeping cover by the car. Crying and shaking, I pulled my gun from my purse.

Bud already had his unholstered. He pivoted, leaning up and firing over the hood.

Residents emerged onto their decorated balconies, and Bud bellowed for them to get inside and take cover. Everyone seemed to obey.

I edged around the rear of the car, not too far, and looked for the target across the snowy street to the tree filled forest on the other side. "Where is he?" I whispered.

The shooter fired again, hitting the tree in front of Bernie.

"Stay down, Bernie," I yelled, levering up and firing several times at the guy in unison with Bud.

The shooting stopped, and the guy ducked behind a spruce dropping huge chunks of ice to the ground.

"Get down," Bud snapped.

I sucked in air, keeping my body low, trying to see the shooter. It was too dark. The wind increased in force, scattering snow and ice. My entire body was cold, but adrenaline was keeping me from shaking too much.

The sound of an engine ripped through the quiet night.

"Damn it." Bud angled around the car and kept low, running across the street.

I straightened, my aim at the darkened forest, ready to provide cover for him if necessary.

He reached the tree line and disappeared from sight.

"Bernie?" I called out, ducking and edging toward my client.

He crawled out from beneath some snow-covered holly bushes, ice and snow clinging to his wool jacket. "You okay?" he asked, reaching his feet and running toward me.

"Yes." I grabbed his arm and pulled him down behind the car. The wind speared through my jacket right to my spine, freezing me head to toe. My teeth started to chatter, and my knees had gone numb from kneeling to shoot. "You sure you're all right?"

He patted himself down and then coughed several times. "Yeah. I wasn't hit." He looked over the car at the silent forest on the other side of the road. "Now we know. The shooter was definitely aiming for me and not for you."

I gulped and nodded, the cold slithering beneath my skin to attack every bone. I shivered. "You're right. I couldn't make out the features of the shooter."

"Me either, but it had to be Hoyt," Bernie said, gasping for air, his breath puffing out. He leaned over and spat into the snow. "Man, it's cold."

My hands shook so hard I put my gun back into my purse. "Let's get in the car. Bud will yell if he finds anything."

"I didn't," Bud said, appearing by the trunk.

I gasped and lost my breath, my ears ringing. Where had he come from?

"Sorry. Didn't mean to startle you." He opened the back door for Bernie. "Inside."

I stood and tried to brush snow off my body, but it was clinging with icy clumps. "Did you see anything?"

"Taillights of a truck down a logging road," Bud said, snow covering his uniform to his thighs from his run through the forest. "That's it. Only saw the shape of a truck and no plate. Nothing."

Bernie lumbered into the backseat, and Bud shut the door before opening mine.

I stomped my boots somewhat free of ice and sat, waiting until he'd shut my door to put my purse on the wet floor.

He started the engine, and forceful heat washed over me. My hands and feet felt dead, and they instantly started to warm up with painful tingles. I winced and rode out the agony.

Bud called in details about the shooting, and sirens already sounded toward I-90. Apparently the apartment residents had called for help as well.

I pressed my head back on the headrest and tried to warm up, but a hard ball of ice remained at my core.

Within minutes, detectives and uniformed officers appeared, followed by crime tech analysts. Thank goodness we were in Idaho and not Washington, considering I'd had a concealed weapon that I had fired several times.

Detective Pierce was one of the first to arrive, and after having taken our statements, went door to door to interview people from the apartments.

From what I could make out, nobody had seen the shooter or could think of any odd trucks or happenings during the last few days.

Finally, Pierce strode to the car, where Bud, Bernie, and I waited out of the billowing snow.

He leaned down to look through Bud's window. "Owner of the complex is a guy named Joe Jonsson from JJ Realty, and he said that the apartment in question, the one you asked about, was rented to another corporation for about three years before the current resident moved in." Snow covered his head and landed on his thick eyelashes.

I leaned closer to Bud to see Pierce. "What corporation?"

"Forrest Land Development," Pierce said quietly. "A very quick glance at the Secretary of State's office confirmed that Lawrence was the sole member of the LLC. Only a couple of neighbors were here long enough to have seen anything, and apparently, Lawrence used the apartment for extra storage. The closest neighbor, just two doors down, also reported that there were often loud poker parties in the apartment."

"Hoyt," I murmured. "The man does have a gambling problem."

Pierce knocked on the back window, and Bud dutifully rolled it down. "Mr. McLintock, who wants you dead?" Pierce asked.

Bernie reared up. "I think it's obvious, don't you? It's Hoyt. It has to be. He thinks I killed his dad."

"Did you?" Pierce asked mildly.

"No," Bernie bellowed, his face turning crimson. "I did not kill that bastard. Even if I had known all of this, I would've just hit him in the face, boycotted his business, and probably tried to get him kicked out of the Kringle Club." He said the last as if it were the worst thing that could happen to a guy.

I bit my lip, not having had a chance to discuss the illegal origins of the club with Bernie yet. It's not like I could bring up the subject with Bud in the vehicle.

A gust of wind knocked snow off Pierce's head. "What about Florence?"

Bernie looked at Pierce like he'd lost his sanity. "She loves me."

"Uh-huh," Pierce said, shoving his hands in his pockets.

I rolled my eyes. "I don't see Florence running through a blizzard and shooting at people, Grant. Come on."

He leaned toward Bud's window again. "Doesn't mean she didn't hire somebody."

My phone buzzed, and I lifted it to my ear. "Albertini."

"Anna, it's Thelma," Thelma whispered. "We have a line on Sharon Smith but need a ride. If you give us a ride tomorrow morning, we'll cut you in on the action."

I stilled, noting that both Bud and Pierce had zero-laser focused on me. "Sounds good. I'd love to go shopping tomorrow with you. I'll call you first thing." I ended the call, trying to be calm.

Pierce angled his head to see the jewelry box falling out of the bag on the floor. "You look like you shopped today."

"I did." Grateful for the distraction, I grasped the box and opened it to reveal the black and silver watch. "What do you think?"

"For your dad?" Pierce asked, straightening.

I looked back down at the timepiece. "No. For Aiden."

Pierce snorted. "That's a nice gift for your dad, somebody you've been married to for twenty years, or somebody you're about to dump. Tell Devlin 'good riddance.'" He turned and strode away, walking over to a couple of crime techs.

I sighed. Well, I thought Donna had drawn either Vince or Bosco's name in the family lottery, and maybe she'd buy the watch from me. As for the goofy tie, that was going to Detective Grant Pierce.

What in the world was I going to get for Aiden?

* * *

DOG AND TEEN were snoozing peacefully in my living room with the Christmas tree lights sparkling all around them because I'd pushed off dinner with Aunt Yara until the next night, considering I hadn't even picked Violet up from work until after nine, borrowing Tessa's Rogue again. I'd just told my aunt that work had interfered, which was mostly true. There was no reason to tell her about my being shot at. Again. Especially since the shooter had been aiming for Bernie and not for me.

So I'd been staring at the ceiling from my bed for several hours when I heard Aiden come in the front door. Something clumped —probably his boots. It was interesting how easily I identified his footsteps, considering we hadn't been in the same place very often the last six months.

He moved inside the bedroom and quietly shut the door, just a shadow against the wall.

I levered up on an elbow. "Hi."

"Hi." He tugged his shirt over his head, dropped it on the floor, and unbuttoned his jeans.

My libido woke right up to match the rest of me.

"Get naked," he whispered, his Irish brogue stronger than usual.

I sat all the way up. "No. You get me naked."

His flash of a grin warmed my entire body. "That I can do." Then he was on my bed, over the covers, over me. Full on, shoving me back, his mouth on mine.

Aiden Devlin could kiss. This, I already knew. Add in his slightly cold but firm lips, more than slightly hot tongue, and he melted the worries of the day completely away for a moment.

I kissed him back, lighting on fire. He was hot, dangerous, and for the moment, all mine. I tunneled my hands through his damp hair, digging in, desire ripping through me faster than was probably healthy. He tasted a little like Scotch, and even that warmed me. Finally, my lungs protested the lack of oxygen, so I tore my mouth away. "We have to be quiet," I panted.

"I'm not the screamer." He rolled to the side and shoved the bedcovers out of his way in a totally cool and smooth motion.

I grinned because that was true. "Someday I'm gonna change that."

"Not today," he whispered, flat over me again and then rolling until I was on top of him. Quick movements had my tank top and shorts flying through the room, followed by my new cute black panties that he hadn't even gotten a chance to see.

I pushed against his chest to a seated position, all of him warming all of me. He caressed my ribcage and up to my breasts, knowing exactly how much pressure to add. Then he added more, and I gasped.

He chuckled, manacled me around the neck, and drew me back down to kiss him.

For Aiden, this was playful. I enjoyed the moment, knowing any second he'd roll again.

Yep. He rolled again, and I was under him, enjoying all of that lean and hard muscle. His talented fingers found me, and I rocketed into orgasm so quickly it surprised us both. "Guess you missed me," he murmured, his lips against mine.

"Guess so." I was more than ready for him, wanting to keep reality far away for now.

"Missed you, too." He slowly pushed inside me, the muscles in his arms bulging nicely as he kept his weight from suffocating me. "You good?" he whispered after one final push.

"Yeah," I said, tracing his biceps with my hands, trying to stay in the moment and not worry about the future. This was here, and this was now, and we were together in every way possible. A warning clinked in the back of my brain that he would be gone again, and I hadn't let go of his frustration over the phone line when he was reconsidering us, but I shoved that bitchy voice away. If pain was coming, I was going to take the good and ride it out.

Plus, who knew. Maybe the good would stay.

My mouth opened, but I didn't say the words. I wasn't ready to say the words, or maybe I was just a coward, but who cared? I dug my nails into his arms and wrapped my legs around his waist.

He ducked his head, kissed my nose, and then started to move —also not saying the words.

I shut my eyes to just feel, and he took me away, changing his angle to hit all the right spots. I went over, crying out, and he kissed me fast, swallowing the sound.

Then he kept pounding.

Two climaxes later for me, one for Aiden, and we lay in the bed with his arm banded around my waist and my back to his front. It was the one place I felt truly safe these days, and I relaxed into his warmth. "Should we talk?" I asked sleepily.

"Tomorrow," he said, his voice lazy. "So long as nobody has shot at you, let's relax."

Holy crap. He hadn't heard about the shooting at the border? I winced and then planted my hand over his on my abdomen. "About that...."

CHAPTER 27

*a*fter arguing with Aiden over coffee, we both reached the conclusion that I just couldn't hang out at my cottage and wait for my stalker to show up. Even though Pierce had to pull my protective detail because the flu had hit the department even harder the day before, I had to live my life and do my job.

Plus, I was armed and I knew how to shoot.

He had to go to work and figure out how Jareth Davey had followed him to Portland. It was a fact we still hadn't really discussed, and I had to go save a couple of senior citizens from probably getting arrested.

We'd left the dog at the cottage, and Aiden promised he'd try to make it back to let him out a couple of times during the day. No promises, though.

The blizzard of the day before had mellowed to a softly falling snow, although the roads were still treacherous. I dropped Violet at her job before driving across town to the Sunnydale Retirement Home subdivision, still in Tessa's Rogue. She said she wasn't planning on going anywhere, but I still needed to check on the repairs to my SUV later that afternoon. I made a quick call to Bernie, sternly advising him to check into a hotel and stay low until we found out who kept trying to kill him.

He assured me that he was now packing heat and not to worry.

I needed more antacids.

Then I turned into the retirement village and looked around, trying to find the spirit of the season inside me. At least it was all around me. Christmas had definitely landed hard on the small one-story homes and duplexes, with an astounding number of lit Santas, presents, and deer all decorating front lawns and sparkling lights of all colors hanging from eves. Even during the morning hours.

I wasn't surprised to see a cadre of green elves lit with blue lights decorating Thelma and Georgian's half of a duplex. When I knocked on their door, I was even less surprised to find them both ready to go, both wearing trench coats, black sunglasses, and Fedoras. Thelma's was a bright pink and Georgiana's a muted tan.

Thelma looked me up and down, her eyes large behind her thick glasses. "That's what you're wearing?"

I looked down at my wool jacket over my red sweater, black jeans, and gray snow boots. "Yeah. Why?"

"It's too conspicuous," she whispered, her pink hat sliding to the side of her tightly curled white hair.

"Uh-huh," I said. "Why do you two need a driver?" Not that I minded, but I did want to know what I was dealing with for the morning.

Georgiana nudged Thelma out the door with her extra bulk, her gray hair in a braid. "Thelma can't drive on ice, and my back has been aching, so I've self-medicated with the good stuff from over the border. We figured I shouldn't drive, but if you think it's okay, then I can drive."

"No," I said hastily, making sure the steps were covered in de-icer before getting out of their way. "I don't mind driving. How did you find Sharon Smith, anyway?"

Thelma tucked a jumbo electric-pink purse against her chest

and maneuvered carefully down the stairs and along the walkway to the car.

Georgiana followed her, carrying a black handbag neatly over her shoulder.

Both bags appeared roomy enough to contain a gun or two.

I sighed and followed them, waiting until we were all seated, belted, and moving through the neighborhood with the heat blasting merrily at us. "All right. Now please tell me what is going on?"

"Head toward Montana," Georgiana said next to me, staring out the window at all the twinkling lights.

I glanced in the rearview mirror at Thelma, who looked like a wrinkled and shrunken gumshoe from the fifties. "I don't have all day to go to Montana," I admitted. "I have a stalker, and I'm trying to stay close to the authorities and town."

Thelma calmly withdrew a .45 with a shiny and large silver barrel. "Well, why didn't you say so? Hawk Investigations can handle stalkers, right G?"

Georgiana nodded. "That's one of our many specialties."

I bit my lip, not wanting to dissuade or insult them but also not wanting to see them get hurt. Plus, it did seem that they'd found a line on Sharon Smith when none of the authorities had been able to do so. "Okay. So how about you at Hawk Investigations clue me in, considering we seem to be working together right now?" I drove south toward I-90. "Are we really going all the way to Montana?"

Thelma pushed against her seatbelt as much as her wiry body could, leaning forward. "We are. There's a snowmobile poker run in Montana right now, and rumor has it Sharon Smith will be there. If we hurry up, we should be able to catch her at the 10,000 Silver Dollar Bar for the third stop of the day."

Georgianna partially turned around. "It's the 50,000 Silver Dollar Bar now."

"Don't care," Thelma sniffed. "It'll always be ten-k to me."

I nodded, having spent plenty of time at the restaurant and bar in Haugen, Montana. It was named so because it had that many silver dollars in it. "I haven't done a poker run in too long," I murmured. It was a fun snowmobile ride where riders earned a card at each stop, and whoever had the best hand at the end of the ride won the prize. "That's at least an hour and a half drive in these conditions, probably more. How sure are you two that there's a poker ride on a Wednesday and that Sharon will be there?"

Georgiana set her purse on the floor with a loud thunk.

Hopefully she hadn't loaded her gun.

She looked at me. "It's the Elk's Charity Ride for the old folk's home, and it's today. Sharon will be there because we have the signup sheet, and her name is on it. Well, one of her names."

I drove onto the onramp to I-90, headed east. The interstate was nicely plowed, and my tires kicked up de-icer as I sped up. "Do you two know her?"

"No," Thelma said. "However, my friend Eunice from Silverville does know her, and that's how we unraveled this mystery." She squinted through the glasses, catching my eye in the rearview mirror. "Should I get a pipe? I feel like all detectives, the good ones, should have a pipe."

I switched lanes. "I think the trench coat is enough, to be honest."

She looked down at her lighter-beige coat. "You're probably right, although this isn't very warm. They should make wool detective trench coats."

"What's Sharon's other name?" I asked.

Georgiana seemed to ponder the question for a moment. "We really can't divulge privileged information, Anna. You understand."

I sighed. "None of your information is privileged. You're not a priest, medical provider, or lawyer."

Thelma reached out and almost patted my shoulder, just

waving in the air since she couldn't reach me. "We took an oath, you know."

I flipped the windshield wipers to a faster speed. "I did not know that."

* * *

THE 50,000 SILVER Dollar Bar was hopping at lunchtime on a Wednesday, and a trickle of snowmobiles had started arriving outside. I sat with Thelma and Georgiana to the far side of the bar, happily eating a club sandwich. I'd always loved the atmosphere of the place, and the food was incredible. Both ladies had hung their trench coats over their chairs and put their hats on the free chair at the table. "If we have time, let's hit the gift shop on the way out," I said, finishing my fries.

Thelma wiped her hands on a napkin. "What did you buy Aiden?"

"I'm still working on that," I admitted. "Any ideas?"

Georgiana paused in eating her burger. "Gun?"

I shook my head. "I think he likes to choose his own guns. I do have a cute leprechaun tie I bought the other day."

Thelma snorted. "No, unless you're trying to ditch him. Truth be told, I have been worried about you two."

I jolted, surprised. "I thought you liked him."

"I do," she said, leaning toward me and lowering her voice. "But no man that handsome can be good in bed. They just don't have to be, and I think you probably are good."

I coughed out some of my soda. "Um, huh." Was there a way to answer that?

Thelma snatched one of Georgiana's onion rings. "I was right? That's sad."

"No." I tossed my napkin on my empty plate. My very empty plate. "You're not right. He's a god in bed and that's all I'm going to say." I felt the oddest responsibility to defend his honor, even while knowing that he'd rather I just didn't say anything to her.

Thelma brightened. "A god? Well, that's lovely." She ate the onion ring, staring at the varied bottles of alcohol stacked on glass shelves behind the bar. "Well then, how about a new leather jacket? He does look good in leather."

"I think he likes the jackets he already has right now," I said, my hopes sinking. I sucked as a girlfriend.

"Chaps?" she asked.

Georgina, normally the quiet one, nodded. "He does have a nice caboose."

I shouldn't have brought up the subject. What had I been thinking? Snowmobilers began striding inside, tearing off gloves and hats and dropping snow on the way to the bar. "All right. Let me know when you see her."

Thelma stood and moved her chair next to mine so she could see the door as well. "We don't know what she looks like."

I sighed, barely keeping from allowing my chin to drop. "You don't?"

"Nope," Thelma said agreeably. "But I know who she's with."

I perked up. "Who?"

"Should we tell her?" Thelma leaned forward and twisted her stick-thin body to better see Georgiana.

"Sure." Georgiana chewed thoughtfully on an onion ring, watching the doorway carefully.

A group of men stomped inside, and I smiled. "Hey, Bos!"

Bosco turned, spotted me, and made a beeline. In a second, he'd plucked me from the chair in a strong hug.

I chuckled and swatted at his riding jacket. "Your jacket is wet, dummy."

He set me down. "Sorry." Like most of the Albertini brothers, he was over six feet tall with light brown eyes, and his brown hair was thick and wavy. He was the youngest, like me, and we had commiserated through the years. "You're looking good, Anna Banana."

I grasped his hand, feeling lighter than I had in ages. Bos was home and was safe. I introduced him to Thelma and Georgiana, and I swear, Thelma fluttered her eyelashes and pushed her sunken boobs out under her knitted sweater.

Bosco winked at her, and that was it. I hoped he knew what he'd just done.

"Are you home for a while?" I asked. While he was stationed at Fairchild, he did a good amount of traveling. Something about refueling jets in the air.

He shrugged. "Dunno. I'm staying with Vince for a few days and then will head over to my apartment in Timber City. Rumor has it you're dating Aiden Devlin, and I'd like to have a nice dinner with him."

I rolled my eyes. "I can take care of myself."

Thelma reared up. "Jacki? Hey, Jacki."

A woman with bobbed gray hair beneath a gray knit cap turned and waved. "Hey, Thelma," she called over the crowd. "You made it."

Thelma stood, her gaze eagle-like. "Where is she?" she yelled.

I stilled. "I thought we were going to do this quietly?"

Jacki turned just as another woman walked inside, this one with red hair over a black jacket and snow pants. "Sharon is right here." She jerked her thumb toward the redhead.

Sharon frowned, turned, and spotted us. Then she pivoted and ran out the door.

"Damn it," Georgiana muttered, tossing her chair back and barreling through the crowd with Thelma right behind her.

I ran after them, aware of Bosco at my side.

We all skidded outside to see Sharon plunk a helmet on her head, jump onto a green sled, expertly start it, and zip out of the parking lot.

I spotted my cousin Rory next to his snowmobile and ran for

him, jumping on. "I'll be back." I twisted the key and grabbed the throttle.

"Hey." Rory barely shoved his helmet into my gut as I roared past him.

"Thanks," I yelled back, slamming the heavy metal onto my head and flipping up the visor to follow the redhead through the snow. Lowering my chin, I settled into the seat and twisted the throttle, going full out through two trees onto a trail.

CHAPTER 28

S haron was a decent rider on the older sled, but Rory had a new Arctic Cat, and so long as I kept it on the trail, she couldn't outrun me. She tried to take a couple of different trails, and I followed easily, my palms kept warm by the heaters built into the handles. Unfortunately, the skin on the outside of my hands was freezing.

She looked over her shoulder at me, and I gunned it, coming up to her skis. I hit a couple of rocks in the trail, and my back protested, but I kept up the speed. The wind blew mercilessly, and my breath fogged up the helmet since it was too big for me. No way was I taking it off, though.

Then she took a sharp right turn, climbing up a hill.

I slowed and then stopped, considering my options. My sled was more powerful than hers, and I could probably climb the hill. She wasn't going to make it.

She had to stop halfway up, partially turned and then sank right down into the heavy snow. Her head dropped. She was only about six yards up the hill from me, but the snow was at least at thigh level, if not more.

I cut my engine and took off my helmet. "Looks like you're stuck."

She turned off the sled and removed her helmet, turning to sit and face me. "Looks like it."

The wind whistled through the trees, and the snow lightly fell, cocooning the two of us in the wilderness. Sleds could be heard in the distance, but right now, there were just the two of us and the snowy trees. "Why did you run?" I asked.

"I know who you are and that you're representing Bernie McLintock," she said, not having to raise her voice. "Gossip travels fast from Idaho to Montana, as you know. Also, I've seen you in the paper a lot lately—usually in bar fights or ridiculous situations."

"Don't believe everything you read," I said. That darn Jolene O'Sullivan. At least she hadn't caught up to me about the Santa case yet. For now, I had a job to do, so I studied Sharon. Red hair, blue eyes, fairly smooth skin for a woman in her sixties. "Should I know you?"

"Probably not." She rested her elbows on her knees and seemed content to just sit there in the cold. "I actually go by Rona or Ronnie and not Sharon, but I have met your Grandma Albertini before. Nice lady."

"You're going to need assistance digging out the sled," I said, rather helpfully.

She sighed, her nose turning pink. At least she was wearing gloves. I shoved my hands in my pockets, wishing I'd grabbed gloves before chasing her into the wilderness.

I cleared my throat. "Did you know you inherited a bundle from Lawrence Forrest? I was at the reading of the will."

She cocked her head to the side, watching me. I had to admit, there was something impressive about her, about the way she just sat there unconcerned with anything.

I shifted my weight on the snowmobile, setting both feet on the runner and facing her. "I'm not leaving. You might as well talk to me." I thought through what I knew about her. "Here's the deal, Sharon. I've pretty much put it together that Lawrence hired you to pretend to sleep with Bernie McLintock, and you did so. It was five years ago, and any statute of limitations on fraud or anything else have run. You can't be arrested or charged with a crime." Bernie might have a civil case against her, but criminally, she was off the hook. "So talk. Either now, or I'll subpoena you to come in and speak with me. It's up to you."

She sighed.

I wasn't entirely sure I'd be able to find her again, but I kept my expression confident. Well, as confident as possible, considering the frigid wind was trying to shred the different layers of my face off. I shivered and huddled deeper into my jacket, which was not made for snowmobile riding.

"Fine." She pushed her hat farther back on her head. "Yeah, I helped Lawrence set up Bernie McLintock. Lawrence had been in love with Florence for eons, and apparently Bernie wasn't being nice to her, so I figured, why not?" She rubbed snow off her face. "Although, it really wasn't like Lawrence. I mean, I loved the man as a good friend, but he wasn't a master planner, you know?" She shrugged. "Guess that's what love does to a guy. I wouldn't know."

"Did you sleep with Bernie?" I figured I owed the guy to actually ask the question.

"No. Lawrence drugged him, and we carted his butt out to some apartment Lawrence kept for mainly business, after we put a bed in the night before. Woke up naked, lied, and figured I'd helped out Lawrence." She blinked snow out of her eyes, her voice echoing off the trees behind me. "I think he and Florence would've been happy."

I swallowed. "You know Florence?"

"No," Sharon said.

The snow was clinging to my hair, so I shoved it over my shoulders to keep my face free. "How do you know Lawrence, then?"

Sharon smiled, making her look like a snow sprite. "Until I retired, I worked for Elroy's Flies and met Lawrence at a trade show in Vegas about twenty years ago. We became friends. In fact, when I retired, I went to Montana after talking to him about it. I live in Missoula, and it's a great place to be."

"That's it?" I asked, curling my fingers into my hands, trying to banish the chill. "You were just friends, and he left you a hundred thousand dollars in his will?" Sure, it wasn't the millions he'd left Florence or even Hoyt, but it was still a boatload of money.

She chuckled, her eyes dancing. "Yeah, I know. Crazy, right? We were pen pals most of our working lives, and we became really good friends. I would've done anything to help him, and I guess I did." She brushed snow off her forehead. "He sent me a letter after Florence divorced Bernie, saying that now he had a chance and would always owe me. That he was putting me in his will, and someday he'd be able to repay me, but hopefully not for a long time." She sobered. "I can't believe Bernie killed him. So sad."

"Why haven't you contacted the lawyers? Obviously you've heard of Lawrence's death," I said, my teeth chattering.

"I called them yesterday," she said. "To be honest, I'd figured Lawrence was just talking and joking about his will. I'm shocked he left me that much money."

I swallowed. "Where were you the night he was killed?"

Her smile was rueful. "I was at a Christmas party my neighbors threw and have about twenty witnesses. We partied all night, man. I had a heck of a headache the next day."

"I'd like the names of your neighbors."

"Sure," she said, looking down the distance between us.

I tilted my head. "If Bernie didn't kill Lawrence, who do you think did?"

She gingerly stepped down, sinking up to her hips in the snow. "Nobody. Bernie's the only person in the world who would've wanted Lawrence dead, as far as I know." She kicked snow out of her way. "You going to help me get this sled out?"

The roar of engines finally pierced the silence, and I turned to see Rory and Bosco riding with Thelma and Georgiana holding on tight behind them, both wearing helmets and protective gear. I wasn't sure whose sled Rory had borrowed, but it looked like a new Polaris.

Sharon's chin dropped and she snorted. "This is your backup?"

I looked to make sure everyone was safe. "Yeah. They found you, didn't they?"

* * *

THE LADIES COULD BARELY CONTAIN themselves on the drive home from Montana, past Silverville, and through the pass. Unfortunately, my back was already aching from the ride, and my feet would not warm up. Plus, I was driving them all the way home, and then I needed to collect Violet and drive back over to Silverville. I should've thought of a way to combine the trips, but it wasn't like I could've taken Violet to hunt for a woman in a bar.

"So," I said, cutting into their excited chatter. "You never did tell me how you two found Sharon Smith."

This time, Thelma sat in the front with the heat filtering across her tightly curled hair, and Georgiana sat in the back.

Thelma hopped in place, looking like a happy chipmunk who'd found some brightly colored fabric to play with. "It's so wonderful. We canvassed Timber City and then headed over to Silverville where everybody knows everybody." She grinned. "We talked to everyone we could, including the Lady Elks. They didn't know a redhead named Sharon, but then Betty Johnsville mentioned that she had a cousin named Sharon who went by the name of Ronnie."

I sped up to pass a truck that was catapulting dark chunks of ice up from its rear tires. "So you figured out Sharon's name was Rona?"

"No," Georgiana said, leaning forward as far as the seatbelt would allow. "But we did start to ask about Ronnie's, and then we talked to Bobby Castanza, who leads the Silverville Snowmobile Club, and he mentioned a hottie named Rona, and well, we went from there. Got a description of her, talked to Bernie, and then we just had to find out when the next poker run or ride was happening."

It was late afternoon, and the sun had disappeared, so I double-checked that my headlights were on. It was decent detective work, actually. "You two did a really good job." It was true, and I appreciated it. "I'm not sure how long it would've taken to find her if you hadn't been so successful." They'd found Sharon before Pierce could, which was impressive.

Thelma preened. "It's so nice to find a calling late in life. We were getting a little bored."

Georgiana patted my shoulder, having no problem reaching me from the back seat. "We do need to find a hacker. You know? Somebody who can break into everyone's computers."

I swallowed rapidly. "That's illegal, Georgiana."

She lifted both hands. "Sure, but every detective agency has a good hacker to crack cases." She eyed me through the rearview mirror. "You have tons of relatives. Surely one of them can break into the Pentagon or something."

"Nope," I said instantly. "The Albertini's aren't good with computers. Sorry." Actually, I could name several relatives who probably could hack into a bank database or something, but none of them would do it. Probably. Either way, I wasn't getting involved with that one.

We drove in silence for the rest of the way until I dropped them off, politely refusing the tray of cookies they offered. I'd eaten their spiked bakery goods before and wasn't taking the chance. Then I drove across town and parked in front of Mac's Burgers, Violet's workplace, ducking through the snow to find her at a table across from Jolene O'Sullivan.

I blinked away fury as well as snowflakes, my boots squishing on the tiled floor to reach the booth. "Violet, how's it going?"

"Good." The girl sipped what looked like a milkshake, looking young and sweet in her yellow sweater and faded jeans. "I finished work about a half-hour ago and was just eating a really late lunch." Her deep blue eyes sparkled. "Your friend sat down, and we've been chatting."

"Great." I forced a smile and barely kept from smacking Jolene on the back of the head. "Why don't you get your stuff, and we'll take off?"

"Sure." Violet scooted from the booth. "Nice to meet you, Jolene." She took her empty glass and basket, heading around the counter.

I slid into her seat, losing all niceties. "What do you think you're doing?" I kept my voice low.

Jolene smiled, still looking like the perfect high-school cheerleader with her blonde hair and light blue eyes—until you really looked at those eyes. They held a boatload of calculation and what I imagined to be evil. Maybe not pure evil. Just the annoying kind like tree sap on a new car. "I was just talking to your young friend about how you're helping her to find a good place to live and not foster care. Do the authorities know about this?"

I could not believe Aiden had dated this witch in high school. "Have you been following me?" That was the only way she could've known about Violet.

She shrugged. "You won't talk to me about the Santa murder, and my editor wants the story. Now."

"Translation is yes, you have been following me." I wondered what she'd do if I just smacked her on the nose. Probably hit me back, and then we'd be in a fight at a burger joint and not illustrating a good example for young Violet. "Leave me alone, or I'll have you arrested for harassment." I started to scoot from the booth.

"Before or after I call the authorities about your young friend?" Jolene purred.

Yeah, I so wanted to hit her. If for no other reason than she put a dent in the sisterhood and how we should treat each other. "I have no comment on your story, Jolene."

She sat back, looking like a cat that had caught a good ball of yarn. "How's Aiden, anyway? You two finding domestic bliss, or have you discovered that there's no way that man is settling down? Ever."

Violet returned with her pack over her shoulder and a donut in her hand, Bowser trotting behind her. He must've been hidden in the back somewhere. "Do you want a pastry?"

"No thanks," I said, ushering her to the door. "We should probably get going."

"I'm not done with you, Anna," Jolene called out. "I'll be at your office first thing in the morning, and I suggest you talk to me." She left the threat unsaid.

The one against Violet.

CHAPTER 29

$\mathcal{W}$e were already on the other side of the pass, dog snoring in the backseat when my phone buzzed. I saw on the car's navigation screen that it was Aiden, so I swiped it. "Hi. You're on speaker with Violet, Bowser, and me." I peered through the windshield at snow that seemed to be blowing sideways.

"Hi, Angel," Aiden said.

Violet sighed, snuggling deeper into her seat.

I hid my sigh but tingled all over. "Hi."

"Where are you?" he asked.

"About ten minutes out from my aunt's," I said.

The sound of papers being shuffled filtered through the speakers. "What's Yara serving, anyway?"

"Her taco bar." I passed a camper going way too slow.

"Oh, man. I played football with a couple of her boys, and she made that taco bar every season. It's the best," he murmured.

"I'll bring you leftovers."

Bowser snored louder in the back seat.

Aiden cleared his throat. "I'm having Saber install a security system at your house, including outside cameras. There's a good chance we're headed out next week again, and I'd like you covered." Now he sounded all business.

I took the hit and forced a smile. "Sounds good. I don't want some crazy alarm that I accidentally set off all the time."

"No worries. Saber is the best," Aiden said. "I'll see you later tonight—might be late. Text me before you leave Silverville and are on the road." He ended the call.

Violet watched the snow ting against the front window. "He's kind of bossy, but I like him."

"Me, too," I murmured, letting Jolene's words echo in my head. Was he ever going to settle down? For that matter, was I? Yeah, I was, and I was kidding myself if I thought differently. Not that my life would change a lot. But I would like a big family wedding, kids, basketball tournaments, and the whole happily ever after scenario. Did Aiden? We'd only dated for about five months, and most of that time had been apart from each other. How much of our emotions were from the past, from when he'd saved my life?

"What's wrong?" Violet asked.

I cleared my expression. "Nothing. Just wondering what to get Aiden for Christmas." I looked at her. "By the way, what did you and Jolene talk about?" I'd waited to ask, so the subject didn't seem important or stress her out.

Violet shrugged. "Not much. She asked about my past, and I told her. She also wanted to know about your cases, and I said I didn't know much about your work." She picked at a string on the hem of her sweater. "Figured if you wanted anybody to know about the bloody finger sent to you in a box that you would tell them."

Thank goodness for untrusting teenagers. "Thank you. She's a reporter, and she would've run with that story."

Violet winced. "Shoot. She didn't tell me she was a reporter." Panic lifted her voice. "Am I in trouble? Is she going to turn me in?"

"You're fine," I said, hoping it was true. "I know you don't want to go into foster care, but there are some really good homes out there, and they want to help kids like you." I wished I could make this easy for her, but I didn't know how. "My Aunt Yara is one of those people, and I hope you two like each other. If you don't, then that's okay. But we'll have to find you somewhere to live."

She flattened her hands down her legs. "Why can't I stay with you and Aiden?"

My heart broke a little for her, and I reached out to take her hand. "Besides the fact that I need an alarm system and have somebody sending me bloody fingers?"

She cracked a smile. "That's a good point."

"I know. I promise that no matter where you end up, I'll make sure you're safe and happy, and we'll hang out." I wished I could hire her at the law firm, but we were financially tapped right now.

"No matter what?" she asked, sounding much younger than sixteen for a moment.

I squeezed her hand. "Yes." Then I pulled down a long driveway toward the river. "Uncle Buddy is my dad's younger brother, and he married Yara, who's awesome. They have six boys who were all pretty wild and now are all responsible and tough." I paused. Wait a minute. If Violet became family, she'd have six older brothers. I winced. What was I thinking?

"Wow," Violet said as we pulled up to the two-story log home with multi-colored lights hung on every eve. Several of the surrounding tall trees outside were also covered in lights, and a bundle of sparkly deer decorated the lawn.

I parked and opened the back door so Bowser could lumber out and take care of business. Then I fetched the pie I'd brought out of the trunk, leaving Violet's and Bowser's belongings for the time being.

"What if they don't like me?" Violet asked as soon as she was out of the car and huddling in front of it.

I hurried to her and put my arm over her shoulders. "Why wouldn't anybody like you? You're delightful." With that, I propelled her through the snow to the front door, opening it and all but shoving her in. "Aunt Yara?"

"She's in the kitchen." Uncle Buddy emerged from his den, wearing a nicely pressed blue flannel over dark jeans. My heart warmed and flipped over. He'd dressed up to meet Violet. The delicious smell of tacos filled the air, and my stomach growled. I moved into his arms, letting him completely enfold me in a hug. Then I stepped back and introduced them.

He shook her hand, his movements gentle.

I grinned. Uncle Buddy was a barrel of a man with a wide chest, wide trunk, and more than six feet of height. He was a miner and had the muscles to prove it. He was also the biggest teddy bear I'd ever met. Well, until somebody threatened family. Then teddy bears turn into grizzlies. Like my dad, he had thick blackish-gray hair and soft brown eyes.

Violet shuffled her feet next to me.

Uncle Buddy bent and scratched Bowser behind the ears. "Cute dog. Has smart eyes."

Violet smiled. "He's really smart."

Yara bustled out of the kitchen, wiping her hands on a towel. "Hello, you two." She moved forward and held out a hand for Violet. "Hi. I'm Yara."

Violet shook her hand, looking shy again.

Yara grinned. "Your eyes match your name. That is so cool."

My aunt was cool, for sure. While Uncle Buddy was bulky, Yara was petite with light brown hair, deep brown eyes, and a pert nose. It was surprising she'd birthed my six huge cousins. I handed over the pie. "Huckleberry. I made it last week but let it thaw all day. We just need to warm it up."

Yara drew Violet into the kitchen. "I hope you're hungry. The boys always drop in, so I make tons of food."

With that, I let my aunt take over.

* * *

217

It was after nine when I left Violet with my aunt and uncle. Within minutes of starting to eat, Yara had gotten Violet relaxed enough to talk about her life, what she wanted to do after school, and her hopes and dreams. Uncle Buddy had pretty much adopted Violet by the end of dinner, promising he'd teach her how to snowmobile next week if she wanted to learn.

Violet really wanted to learn.

My belly was happy and my heart was full when I left them. Yara had already cleaned out the guest room that had an attached bath, saying they could decorate the room that coming week however Violet wanted and that Bowser was more than welcome to sleep with her.

I drove for about five minutes and automatically turned down the driveway of my childhood home, parking outside my parent's garage. The Christmas lights were still on, as was the patio light. I ran through the storm, not surprised to find the door unlocked. I walked inside. "Mom?"

"Hey, honey." My mom walked out of her office, which was to the side of the living room. She looked younger than her age with her blondish red hair and green eyes. Tonight she'd dressed in a yoga outfit with pink socks. "Yara texted me when you left, so I figured you'd stop by. Come have some tea with me." She slipped her arm through mine and took me into the kitchen, where she already had a kettle on. "Yara is so excited to have Violet staying with them."

I sat on a chair at the wide oak table, more relieved than I'd expected to be. "I think Violet is excited, too. At least she's safe now." My aunt would take care of everything in the morning with the county and state. Sometimes it was so helpful to live in a small town. "Where's Dad?"

"He's at the Elk's tonight but should be home in about an hour," she said, pouring two mugs. Then she sat and pushed one toward me, taking hers and blowing on the steam. "What's up?"

I gingerly took a sip, letting peppermint explode on my

tongue. The kitchen was massive with hand-carved maple cabinets, granite countertops, and stainless steel appliances fit for a big family gathering. "I can't figure out what to get Aiden for Christmas."

"Hmmm." She sipped quietly, her presence calming me.

I drank my tea, my mind spinning. "I don't know what we are. What we're doing." I frowned. "Where we're going."

She sipped some more. "Do you have to know those things right now?"

I blinked. The woman wanted grandchildren almost more than anything, and she was asking me if I wanted to slow down? "You're confusing me."

She patted my hand. "Why are you feeling pressured? You've only dated for a few months."

I opened my mouth and then shut it again. Why was I feeling pressured? Aiden hadn't prodded me, and I wasn't sure what I was doing, so what was going on? "He seemed reluctant on the phone before he came home. Like he was reconsidering us dating with our current jobs." I thought we'd taken care of that issue, but apparently it had been rattling around in my head. "I'm afraid he's going to change his mind and leave for good." There. I'd said it.

She stood and fetched the kettle, pouring us both another cup. "You know what to do with fears."

I sighed, cupping the mug. "Confront them." I guess I needed to talk to Aiden about those fears, but I was afraid of what he'd say. If I gave him the out, would he take it? He'd starred in every fantasy I'd had since I was twelve, and if he walked out of my life again, it was going to hurt. "I don't know what I want. I mean, I want him, but I'm not ready for marriage or any of that, so..." I couldn't find the right words.

"You know what you want," Mom said, taking another drink. "It's okay. What is it?"

I mulled it over, feeling at home in the family kitchen with my mom so close. "I want...a chance. Just a chance that we could have forever, even if we're not ready for it now. I guess I need to know that he wants that, too. That there's a potential for us somehow to have more." Wow. I hadn't even realized that's where my emotions had gone.

My mom nodded. "That makes sense. Now you just need to talk to Aiden about it. He's been in your heart most of your life, and even if he leaves, a part of him will still be there."

I wanted more than a part of him. "That's true."

She smiled.

That suddenly, I finally figured out what to give him for Christmas. I'd need to visit my childhood room before I left. I grinned. "You're the best, mom."

"True," she said, her eyes twinkling. "So true."

The front door opened. "Hello?" Nonna Albertini called out, bustling through the living room to the kitchen and spotting us, setting a tray of Christmas cookies down. "Anna. So good to see you." She leaned over and placed a kiss on my head before moving toward the kettle. Nonna was all Italian and looked a bit like Sophia Loren but maybe taller, and I thought she was just as beautiful.

"Hello?" My Nana O'Shea then appeared, having more quietly opened the front door. She slid a platter of candy cane cookies across the table. She looked like an older version of my mom, more like Maureen O'Hara in her later days. Still stunning. "Anna. How wonderful." She accepted the cup of tea from Nonna.

My mouth gaped open. My grandmothers had a sort of détente because they loved the same people, but they weren't close and rarely did anything together. Then everything inside me went warm and gooey. "You're worried about me."

Nonna waved a hand dismissingly in the air. "Don't be silly. We heard you were here and figured you'd like some sweets."

They both sat, blowing on their tea.

I shared a smile with my mom. It was almost time to receive the Christmas card from Jareth Davey, and I was struggling with what to do with Aiden. Apparently my grandmothers had noticed. They were here to help—even just to offer quiet support.

The female power in my family was strong, and right now, it was focused on me.

I reached for the treats, making sure to take one of each. While I might be a little confused currently, I was no dummy.

CHAPTER 30

It was midnight by the time I trudged up my snowy steps, bathed in twinkling Christmas lights, and nudged open the door to my cottage. Aiden sat at my round kitchen table, case files, notepads, and coffee mugs in front of him. He looked up, and his blue eyes were veiled and his aura a pissed off hue.

I forced a smile and crossed to the kitchen counter, placing several tight-lock containers down. "We had a taco bar, Christmas cookies, candy cane cookies, and huckleberry pie," I said as cheerfully as I could.

"Thanks." He glanced at the screen on his phone. "Not hungry right now, but it smells delicious."

Dread clicked through me. He wasn't hungry? Well, it was midnight. "All right." I shifted it all to the fridge before removing my coat and boots, taking them toward the door. It was late, I was tired, and I couldn't deal with emotion right now. "Any luck with the case?"

"No," he said shortly.

I looked at him. Even at my table, he looked dangerous in a

ripped T-shirt, worn jeans, and a vibe that was hard to quantify. "That sucks."

"Yeah," he said softly. "Jareth Davey somehow followed me from here down to Portland. We've caught him on different CCTV cameras all the way. That means he was watching us, stalking you, maybe for months."

"Oh." My arms chilled, and I rubbed them.

Aiden's voice roughened. "That means that he's been watching us, and I had no clue. Not a one. I *know* when somebody is following me, and I have a sense when something is up with you. Yet I didn't feel him." He scrubbed both hands down his face, ending at that shadow on his jaw that had gone way beyond five o'clock. "There's always something up, and I feel the tension, but I didn't realize it was Davey. There's just too much to separate all the crazy."

I wished he were joking about that, but crazy seemed to follow me. "Your life would be a lot easier with a girlfriend who taught kindergarten or was an accountant or something like that," I said quietly, my anxiety ratcheting up to the bubbling level.

His grin was quick and unexpected. "Honey, if you were a kindergarten teacher, you'd end up with miniature hitmen throwing homemade clay bombs at me that somehow were poisoned with something I'm allergic to. Or as an accountant, one of your clients would end up working for the mob, and then they'd want to hire you, and I'd have to take them all out."

"Hey," I protested. "Besides this last week, I haven't been shot at for months." Even as I said the words, I realized the ridiculousness of them.

He sighed.

I tugged on my ear, feeling chilled. "The only constant in the crazy is me."

"Amen to that."

I shuffled my feet, scrunching my toes in my thick socks. "What now, Aiden?"

"Now I find him and end him," Aiden said quietly. "He's got a plan, he's probably here, and now I know it." He reached for a mug and tipped back the contents. "He's smarter than I thought with trying to get a drug runner to take me out during an op. I won't make that mistake again."

"I meant with us," I said quietly.

He studied me. "I'd like to put you somewhere safe until I handle this, but I know that's not an option for you. I'll take a leave of absence if needed to cover you, but right now, I'm working seven cases, and I'd hate to do that to my team."

My body slowly released the tension, head to toe. So he wasn't breaking up with me. At least not right now. We needed to have that talk, but it was late, my head now hurt, and I wasn't up to it. From the look of him, neither was he. "I'll be careful," I said. "I'm armed and trained."

"If you point a gun, you shoot that gun," he said softly. "Tell me you get me."

I did. If it came down to it, I could shoot Jareth Davey. "I know."

"It's different face to face, Angel." Tension swelled from him. "You're tough and sweet, and I need to know in that situation that you can follow through. This is not a guy you show mercy to—it'll never end. I'll do my best to make sure I'm between you and him, but in the off chance I'm not, I need to know that you can squeeze the trigger."

My stomach cramped. "I can, Aiden. I know I can." I yawned, finally relaxing. "I'm exhausted. Bed?"

He looked down at his files. "You go ahead. I have to get some of this organized before I meet with the team tomorrow. I'll be in shortly."

"Okay." I walked into the bedroom and got ready for bed, sliding beneath the covers and wondering if I should get him something more generic for Christmas than what I'd planned. But what? I heard the fridge open in the kitchen, and I grinned. Not hungry? Right.

I dropped off to sleep faster than I'd expected, feeling him come to bed a couple hours later. Then I slept like the dead with no nightmares, waking up early morning feeling much better. Aiden slept quietly next to me, so I gingerly slid from the bed, hit the bathroom to brush my teeth, and then wandered out to the living room, hoping there was huckleberry pie left.

My tree twinkled merrily at me, and peace filtered through the cottage. I padded to the kitchen and started my one cup coffee maker, turning to pull out the huckleberry pie.

I cut a generous piece, poured my coffee, and looked at the mess on my table. Shrugging, I moved into the living room, placing my plate on the coffee table and sipping my coffee. The warmth poured through me, and I sighed, rolling my neck to loosen the muscles. The snow fell gently outside, peacefully, and I turned to watch it.

Something red caught my eye.

I frowned, setting down my mug. Then I stood and moved toward the curtains, sliding them aside.

The world halted. Sharp and quick. A man knelt in my small front yard, in the freezing snow, with a massive red ribbon on his head. "Aiden!" I screamed.

* * *

AIDEN CAME out of the bedroom at a dead run, wearing only his boxers with a gun in his hand. His muscled chest was bare and his thick hair ruffled. "What?"

I pointed outside the window. "There's a man." I hustled to the entryway, jumping into my boots.

He reached me, stepped into his boots, and gently pulled me back. "Stay here." Then he grabbed a coat, slugged into it, zipped it over his naked torso, and opened the door.

I reached for my coat, pulled it shut, and followed him out into the snowy day, keeping to the walkway. The wind and cold pierced the bare skin on my legs, nearly sending me down. "Oh," I whispered, bile rising in my throat.

"You know him?" Aiden asked.

Numbly, I nodded. "His name is Crackle, and he's the guy who hit me and came after Violet."

Crackle knelt in the snow, a bullet hole square in his forehead, his body frozen and icicles coming off his chin. His skin was a bluish-white, already frozen, and his blank eyes stared unseeingly at the heart still painted on the side of my garage. The large red bow flopped on the side of his head, and a matching ribbon wound around his body to be tied in another bow at his waist.

Aiden stepped through the snowy lawn, crouching down and looking over the body. "He's missing his pinkie finger."

I gagged and swallowed several times to keep from throwing up. "How is he kneeling so perfectly?"

Aiden prodded Crackle's shoulder and the body didn't move. "Best guess? He was killed in this position, and the killer waited for rigor mortis to set in before moving him."

Crackle still wore the dirty shirt and jeans that I'd seen him in the day he'd hit me. "The killer? It has to be Jareth Davey," I whispered, my breath creating clouds in the frigid air.

Aiden looked over his shoulder and at my bare legs. "Go inside and call this in. I want to scout the area, even though snow has already covered any tracks that might've been left." He turned and looked toward the tree line and then the road, which hadn't been plowed yet today.

"You come put on jeans," I countered. "It's below freezing out here." It was probably around ten degrees Fahrenheit, and Aiden could get frostbite easily, even though it looked like furious steam was coming off the guy. When he didn't move, I shoved my chilled hands into my pockets. "I'm not going inside until you do."

He moved then, right at me, tossing me over a shoulder and stomping through the snow.

I rolled my eyes, happy he was coming inside. Keeping my view on his butt, I purposefully didn't look back at the frozen man in the snow. Crackle had been a jerk, but he hadn't deserved to die like that. He had deserved to be arrested and put in jail, and denying any of his victims that result had taken something away from them.

Had Jareth Davey done this? I'd learned enough during my brief tenure as a lawyer that making assumptions like that was often a mistake. But I couldn't imagine anybody else who would've done it.

We reached the cottage and walked inside, where Aiden flipped me back over and made sure my legs were steady before releasing my arms. "Call it in." Then he hustled to the bedroom.

My phone was on the counter, and I reached it, calling Pierce directly.

"Detective Pierce," he answered, a printer humming in the background. Good. He was already at work.

"Hi. It's Anna." I reported all details, and he was on the move before I'd finished. "See you soon."

Aiden emerged fully dressed and headed back out into the lightly falling snow, his gun still in his hand.

I moved into my bedroom and pulled on jeans and a white knit sweater, yanking a Smiley's Diner ball cap over my head and tucking my hair behind my ears. Then I drew on my jacket and gloves again, walking out into the frigid air as the police began arriving.

Aiden had disappeared into the woods.

Pierce arrived after the first uniformed officers, who were tying off the area with yellow crime-scene tape. "Inside," he said, gesturing with his notebook.

I turned and went right back inside, wondering if any of the men in my life knew how to ask nicely. I tore off my jacket and gloves, heading into the kitchen to make us both some coffee.

"Tell me what happened," Pierce said, glancing at the mess on my table and turning to sit on my guest chair by the fireplace. Today he wore a long-sleeved green shirt, black jeans, and black snow boots. He fumbled for a pen in his pocket, drew it out, and clicked the roller free. Then he started making notes before I even began speaking.

"Say please," I snapped, handing him his mug.

His eyebrows rose. "You're in a mood."

"There's a dead body on my lawn, and none of the people in my life have manners." I sat on the sofa and drew a leg up beneath me.

He frowned. "Where's Devlin?"

"Out scouting in the woods for the killer," I retorted. "The footprints were all gone, so I'm not too worried. But who knows. He might find something."

Pierce took more notes. "Tell me everything." Then he looked up at me. "Please."

There we go. I told him everything, including all about Violet, feeling comforted that she was now safe with my aunt and uncle. When I wound down, Pierce was just staring at me. "What?" I asked.

"How? How do these things always happen to you?" He sounded genuinely curious.

I drank more of my coffee, wishing for my huckleberry pie, but my appetite had disappeared. "I have no idea."

He tucked his notebook back into his pocket. "I don't suppose I could talk you into taking a long vacation?"

"Sure, but why? If it's Jareth Davey, he's proven he can track fairly well. If it isn't him, then we have no clue who it is, and the problem will be waiting for me when I get home," I said reasonably, keeping it together on the outside. On the inside, I could feel the mother of all panic attacks headed my way when I had a chance to breathe.

Pierce pressed his lips together, looking like an irritated surfer. "I'd suggest you find another line of work, but frankly, you'd just find more interesting ways to court trouble."

That was almost exactly what Aiden had said the night before. I glared at Pierce. "None of this is my fault." I'd been reasonable and safe for as long as I could remember.

"I know," Pierce said. "Stay here." He shook his head. "Tell me Devlin is planning on staying in town for a while, at least until we catch this guy."

"You can count on it," Aiden said, walking through the front door and brushing snow off his thick hair.

CHAPTER 31

I dropped Tessa's car off outside Smiley's Diner and then got into Bud's cop car, wanting to somehow reassure him that I wouldn't get him shot this time. Today he was even more silent than usual after having seen the dead body on my lawn. "So, I think I'll wrap up the cases I can, give the rest to Clark, and maybe take a week or so off," I said. "For the holidays, you know?"

Bud grunted.

I held my hands out to the heater. Even though I was wearing gloves, my fingers hadn't warmed up after my early trek outside that morning. "Thank you for covering me again."

He drove around my building to park in the back alley where I usually parked. "You're good job security for me." He stopped the engine.

I looked at him. "Did you just make a joke? Like a real joke?"

He rolled his eyes and opened his door. "The holidays bring out my fanciful side."

I opened my door and stepped out, slashed immediately by the maniacal wind. His fanciful side? "All right," I said doubtfully. "How's it going with the wife?" I stepped over a chunk of ice toward the private rear door to the two-story building.

"Not sure." Bud fell into step beside me, his solid bulk breaking some of the wind.

"Want to talk about it?"

"No," he said.

I slipped on the ice, and he grasped my arm, helping me to regain my balance. "Okay."

He released me. "Did you find a present for Devlin?"

"Maybe." I wasn't ready to share that yet, angling around the green dumpster toward the door.

A scratching sound caught my attention, and then electric leads shot out, attaching to Bud's chest. Electricity zipped, and he gasped, tasered.

"Bud," I cried out, trying to swat the leads off him.

He went down to the ice-covered ground, convulsing wildly.

A man grabbed my arm and yanked me toward the building, shoving me face first against the bricks. I kicked back, struggling, panicking. The barrel of a gun pressed against my temple, and I subsided.

Was it Jareth Davey? Terror rippled through me. The gun was cold and heavy against my skin. I gulped in air, trying to breathe.

"Drop Bernie McLintock as your client," the man hissed in my ear, his voice muffled by something and sounding tinny and fake. An odd smell came from him, but I couldn't identify it. What was that? Something sweet with a hint of...mint?

I blinked, trying to make sense of the words. Drool popped on my lip. "Huh?"

"Do it, or I shoot next time," the guy growled, feeling solid behind me. "Count to twenty and don't turn around, or I'll shoot your friend."

Then the gun was gone.

No way was I counting to twenty. I gasped and tried to catch my breath, pushing against the wall to turn myself around. Then I ducked to grab Bud and pull him around the dumpster and out of any possible line of fire.

He shook violently but still managed to plant both hands on the ice and shove himself to a seated position. "Call...it...in..." he gasped.

I looked down the alleyway to see our assailant rush around the building next door. Gasping for breath, I fumbled in my purse for my gun, which I placed next to my knee. Then I found my phone, where I dialed the police, giving the 'officer down' statement I'd heard on television so many times. I grasped Bud's arm. "You okay?"

"No," he snapped, rolling his neck. He pushed to stand and I did the same, levering a shoulder beneath his arm to help him.

We swayed in place, and then he started moving us both toward the door. I ducked and clasped my gun, falling into step with him, breathing out in relief when we got inside. Warmth hit us. "Sit down," I said, nudging him onto the back stairs for the building. "Take deep breaths."

"I'm fine." Even so, he sat. "I can't believe I didn't hear that guy."

Cops poured through the back door and down the hallway from the front door, all angry and on high alert. Bud turned a deep red color and shook off concern.

Pierce jogged inside, took a look at him, and then visibly relaxed. "You need to go get checked out."

Bud stood and shook his head. "I've been tasered before and am fine. Didn't see much. Guy was in a thick parka with a full face mask that covered his entire head beneath another knit blue cap. He was about six feet tall, eyes were maybe brown? He also wore ski pants, thick ones, so I can't give you an accurate body type, weight, or even age."

Pierce looked at me. "You?"

"I just saw the heavy parka, smelled something minty, and heard his voice." I related what the attacker had said, my mind sluggish now that the adrenaline had escaped my system. "He was muffled behind the mask, and I think he wore some sort of voice distorter over his mouth. He sounded robotic."

Pierce frowned. "He told you to drop Bernie?"

I nodded. "Yeah." Were all the odd happenings lately because of the Santa case? It didn't make sense. Right now, nothing made sense.

"We're hauling McLintock in again," Pierce said. "Bud, you go to the hospital and don't argue with me because it's department policy. Albertini, you might as well come with me since I'm bringing in your client. That way, at least you're covered until Bud gets the okay from the doctor."

I looked at the wounded officer. "Bud needs the rest of the day off."

"No," Bud said, a healthy color coming back into his face. "I'll get the doc's okay and then will be back to cover Anna."

My heart warmed. "That's nice of you, Bud."

His dark gaze met mine. "I wouldn't wish you on any of my brothers." Then he hobbled toward the door.

* * *

PIERCE ARGUED, but I made him stop at Duke's Jewelry, right next to my building, before he drove me to the police station. Christmas was coming up fast, and while my life was a disaster, it helped to fixate on something positive, although I wasn't completely sure about Aiden's present yet. I'd just get Duke to do what I wanted, and then I'd figure out whether or not I should give the gift to Aiden.

Soon I sat in the interrogation room when Pierce brought in Bernie McLintock, who was in full Santa uniform, complete with candy canes sticking out of his pocket. Bernie's faded eyes were concerned, and he patted my hand when he sat next to me. "I heard through the grapevine what happened, and I'm so sorry. I just don't understand it."

I took in his new outfit, impressed by the fluffy fur. "I'm okay and so is Bud."

Pierce sat across from us, looking irritated. Since it was his default setting, I didn't worry too much about it. "The uniforms brought you in from the Timber City Mall?" he asked.

Bernie nodded. "Yes. It's almost Christmas, so we spend every day at the local malls. Tomorrow we're having a blowout in the Spokane Valley Mall with all of the Kringles in one place, and the next day, on Saturday, we'll be here at our mall. Everyone loves my new suit."

I shook my head. "I thought you were going to lie low until we figured out who keeps shooting at you?"

"I'm Santa," he said quietly. "Santa doesn't hide." Then he grinned, showing he'd gotten new dentures. They looked nice.

Pierce noticed as well. "New dentures?"

"Yeah. Early Christmas present from Flo," Bernie said happily.

I kept a sigh from emerging.

"She's already spending her inheritance on you?" Pierce made a notation in his book.

Bernie lost the smile. "Geez. You sure know how to be a downer."

I nodded. That was true. "Who wants you to go to jail, Bernie?"

"I don't have any enemies," Bernie said. "Except for Hoyt Forrest. Why don't you ask him if he shot at me and then attacked Anna today?"

"He's on his way in," Pierce confirmed. "I've been trying to find him since you were shot at the other night, and apparently he's been out of town and just got back. We'll see what he has to say."

That reminded me that I still hadn't had a chance to track down Hoyt's ex-girlfriend and see what I could find out. As things were going, Bernie was still a good suspect in Lawrence's murder, although the fact that somebody wanted Bernie out of the way might work in his favor if it was the real murderer. Unless it was Hoyt trying to exact revenge for his father's death, in which case, Bernie was the only viable suspect right now. Except for Flo.

Pierce ran Bernie through a gamut of questions, and I kept alert to make sure my client didn't say anything that hurt him. Basically, Bernie didn't know more than either of us. Finally, Pierce let him go with a stern warning to stay in the local area.

I walked Bernie down the stairs to the front door. "I really wish you'd take some time off."

"After Christmas." Bernie adjusted his Santa hat on his head. "With Mick and Lawrence gone, we're down a Santa. Managed to talk Earl into joining the Kringle Club, but he hasn't been trained completely, and his 'ho-ho-ho' is a little weak."

I frowned. "You're in danger."

"So are you." He patted my arm and ambled outside.

True. Very true. I jogged back up the stairs and almost ran into Pierce in the hallway. "I'd like to watch you interview Hoyt."

"Sure." Pierce strode into his office and then emerged with a sparkling red file folder. "I did a deep background check on Sharon Smith now that you found her, had some colleagues in Montana speak with her neighbors, and confirmed her alibi for the night Lawrence was murdered." He handed over the folder.

I watched as sparkles fell lazily to the ground. "Where do you find these?" He always had a bright and sparkly folder for me when he was being nice and sharing information.

"In the storage closet. Nobody wants them, and they remind me of you." He watched as two uniformed officers placed Hoyt in an interrogation room down the hallway—the same one we'd just vacated. "You can watch, but don't leave the station while I'm in there." Without waiting for a response, he turned and walked back down the hallway to enter the interrogation room.

I hustled after him, going around the corner to the quiet viewing room and walking up to the two-way mirror.

Hoyt hadn't shaved since I'd seen him last, and his beard was fuller than I would've expected. His eyes were bloodshot, and stains dotted his plain T-shirt. He'd taken off his coat to place around his chair and looked like a walking headache.

Pierce drew out his chair. "Where have you been?"

"At a buddy's cabin outside of Whitefish," Hoyt said, his voice rough. "Ice fishin' and drinking. A lot."

Pierce waited a beat. "Where were you last night?"

"Got home around midnight and crashed," Hoyt said, flattening his hand on the table. His knuckles were scratched and looked swollen.

"What happened to your hand?" Pierce asked.

"I told you I was ice fishin'," Hoyt hissed. "It's not like normal fishing." He looked around the small room. "Why don't you go do your job and make sure the case against McLintock sticks? The bastard and his bitch killed my dad for money, and you know it. Everyone knows it. But you're so far up his lawyer's ass that you can't manage the job."

I couldn't see Pierce's face, but his shoulders tightened just enough for me to notice.

He didn't move otherwise. "Somebody has shot at McLintock twice, and earlier today somebody threatened his lawyer to drop his case. Uniformed officers found you at your place of business, where you could've easily gone afterward. The police are serving warrants on your home and the bait and tackle shop, and if they find a taser, I'm arresting you."

Hoyt smiled and the sight wasn't pleasing. "I have a taser, as do most folks around here. That's not probable cause, and you know it."

"How much do you owe in gambling debts?" Pierce asked, smoothly changing topics.

Hoyt shrugged. "Nothing now, but I'd rather have my dad than money, so don't go there."

"Any chance a loan shark took out your dad as a warning? Or to get paid?" Pierce asked.

I stood closer to the window. Huh. I hadn't thought of that.

"No." Hoyt clasped his hands on the table. "Not a chance. It was that Bernie asshole. Period."

"Speaking of whom, were you aware that your father set Bernie up by drugging him and convincing him that he'd slept with Sharon Smith, the woman your father included in his will?" Pierce asked.

Hoyt shrugged. "I knew something was up with the apartment, but I didn't pay attention. Good for Dad. We play to win, you know."

What a jerk.

Pierce took more notes. "You're going to walk me through your activities during the last week, hour by hour. Then you're going to give me a full list of anybody you owe money to as well as the amounts owed. Start at the beginning."

I pulled a chair closer to the window so I could sit. Was Hoyt the guy who'd shoved me against the building?

CHAPTER 32

I didn't learn anything of significance by watching Hoyt's interview and had a uniformed officer escort me around the park to the prosecuting attorney's office, where I used to work. Before Nick fired me. Somebody had placed a pink tree in the corner of the reception area and had half decorated it with silver bulbs. There was nobody behind the reception desk.

Nick walked out of the nearest office, my old office, reading a case file. He looked up, glanced at the tree, and sighed. "We ran out of bulbs. Just sent the receptionist to buy more."

I looked around. "Where is everyone?"

"Either in trial, depositions, or on vacation already," he said, not sounding happy about any of it. "What are you doing here?" Without waiting for an answer, he turned on his polished black shoe and headed down the hallway.

I followed him, noting his dark gray suit that he'd partnered with a yellow power tie. "Are you in trial?"

We reached his corner office at the very end of the hallway, and he stretched his long legs over several file boxes before striding around his desk, yanking his tie free as he went.

His jacket went on his chair, and his tie ended up on his desk next to three empty coffee mugs. "Yes to the trial, no to why you're here."

I stepped around the boxes and lifted a couple of notebooks off a leather guest chair before sitting and crossing my legs. "You know why I'm here?"

"Nope." He released the first two buttons on his shirt and then did the same with the ones at his cuffs, rolling up his stark white and very pressed shirt. "Don't care."

I frowned.

Nick Basanelli was something to look at, and I wouldn't mind if he and my sister got together. They'd make the most beautiful babies. His dark hair was a little ruffled from the snow, since he'd probably walked back to his office after trial. He was long and lean, and his brown eyes made women twitter from the jury box.

I angled my head to see five jewelry boxes behind him on his credenza. "How many women do you buy presents for during the holidays?" Maybe he wasn't a good fit for Tessa.

He rolled his eyes and reached for the five boxes, slapping them on his desk in front of me and opening all five. "They're on loan from Duke's. From my Grandma Basanelli."

I covered my mouth and tried really hard not to laugh. I failed. When I'd recovered, I leaned over to look at the selection, which ranged from a delicate St. Christopher medallion to a simple diamond heart. "None of those look like Tessa." Although, the emerald and sapphire necklace in the Celtic Knot kind of looked like Donna. "Your grandmother just borrowed these?"

"Yep. I'm supposed to choose and return the others by end of day tomorrow." He shook his head. "Your sister and I haven't even gone on a date."

"Do you want to date her?" I asked straight out.

He flipped the boxes closed, one at a time. "No."

My jaw nearly dropped. "Then you're nuts. She's amazing."

He finished and leaned back in his chair, making the expensive leather protest. "The Albertini women are a pain in the ass and way too much work."

Yeah, he probably had a point. Well, about the pain in the ass part—not about the too much work part. "Fine. If you don't have the balls to go out with Tessa, I'm not wasting time with you on that." Then I remembered why I'd sought him out and tried to plant a smile on my face. "However, it's the season to be charitable, and I need you to do your job."

He just watched me. "What?"

I told him about Violet and the boy with the expensive lawyer out of Spokane. Nick wouldn't like that last part. Then I wound down, hoping he'd do the right thing.

"I don't like the part about the Spokane lawyer, but it's Boxer's case, and you need to talk to him." His jaw was set.

"Who is this Boxer, anyway?"

"Smart lawyer out of Los Angeles, and I don't want to lose him over his first case," Nick said.

I sighed. We'd been through this before. "Well, he's off to a bad start by going after an innocent girl. Violet is a good kid, and now she has a chance with Yara and Buddy. Make it easy on everyone and just dismiss that case. It's stupid, anyway." I looked at the jewelry boxes. "It's Christmas, Nick."

His eyes narrowed.

I squirmed in my chair, having seen that look before when he was about to strike in the courtroom. "What?"

"I can't dismiss, but I can plea it down to a petty charge that is taken off her record the second she completes fifty hours of community service."

I brightened. "That's a good deal. For Violet and the boy?"

"Of course," Nick said smoothly.

"Can the community service be conducted in Silverville?" It'd be easy to find Violet somewhere to volunteer over there, probably at the animal shelter.

Nick smiled. "Sure."

I eyed him, my instincts pricking wide awake. "What's the catch?"

"Well, I'll have to pass a good case to Boxer to get him to agree and not quit on me, and then I'll have to do the paperwork, which I don't have time to do. So it'll cause me more than a little bit of irritation," he said.

"It's the same result that we'd get if we went to trial, probably," I muttered.

He nodded. "If that. But this is a sure thing, and it'll go away. I just need you to do one little favor for me."

I frowned. "You want me to do you a favor because you're doing your job?"

"No. I'm doing Boxer's job. Favor or not?"

"Fine." I blew out air. "What is it?"

He drew out the moment like any good trial attorney. "Talk your sister into going to the Elk's New Year's Eve Ball with me."

I blinked like I'd been sprayed with water. "You don't want to date her, remember?"

"Oh, I remember. But if I take her to the ball, and we decide to go our separate ways at the end, then I will get my grandmother off my back. It's simple."

"Why don't you just ask Tessa to go? I'm sure she'd love to get *our* grandmother off *her* back."

His eyebrows drew down. "I did, and she told me to get bent."

A chuckle burst out of me before I could stop it. "Come on, Nick."

"That's the deal, Albertini." He turned to his computer, ignoring me.

"Fine." I stood and kicked over one of his boxes while leaving his room, soon finding myself out in his reception area, where Jolene O'Sullivan stood, looking at the sad pink tree. I paused and then tried to sidle to the door.

"Already saw you," Jolene said, turning to face me. "Were you and Nick meeting about the Santa murder?"

At least she didn't have her photographer with her.

Movement sounded down the hallway. "Anna? Wait a minute. I need to put a couple of stipulations on the deal," Nick said, coming into view and halting instantly.

"What deal?" Jolene asked sweetly, her blonde hair in a ponytail.

"No comment," Nick bit out. "Get out of my office."

Yeah, I wasn't the only person who often starred on the front page of the *Timber City Gazette*, although Jolene was usually kinder to Nick. Probably because he was cute.

She batted her eyes. Like really full-on had those eyelashes fluttering. "Now, Nick. I thought we had a good working relationship." Somehow, she purred the sentence.

I'd never met anybody who could purr words until now, and she sure the heck had never talked to me like that.

"We don't," he retorted. "Now please leave."

"You need to go on the record about the Santa case," she said, losing the purr. "The public has a right to know if we have a psychotic Santa going around stabbing people in the back."

Nick moved and opened the door. "No. Comment."

She swept by him, her head up. "I'll be back."

He shut the door and faced me. "Did she hear us talking about our agreement?"

"I don't think so."

"Good. Tessa has to wear a dress to the ball and look like she's making an effort." He walked back down the hallway, disappearing from sight. "There will be pictures and proof that I tried."

I walked to sit by the pink tree and pulled out my phone, calling Tessa.

"Hey," she said. "What's up?"

"Do you love me?" I asked quietly.

She was quiet for a couple of moments. "What did you do?"

"Nothing. But I need a huge favor." I told her the entire story and could feel her temper pulsing over the line as I finished. I gulped and kicked more snow off my boots.

"Oh, he wants a date? Yeah. I'll give him a date." Her voice was almost hoarse. "But you owe me one. I drew Aunt Rachel in the Christmas lottery, and I love her, but...."

I sighed. Yeah, Aunt Rachel was tough to buy for. She was a sweetheart but didn't have hobbies or collections, and she bought what she wanted. I had an idea. "Okay. I'll trade you Aunt Rachel for Knox since I drew his name. I already bought him a cool cross."

"Deal," she said, now sounding amused. "Tell Nick he has a date and I'll dress appropriately. Do not tell him that he'll regret this stunt with every ounce of his being by the time I'm done with him." She clicked off.

"No problem," I murmured.

The door opened and Bud walked inside. "Pierce told me to pick you up here when I was done."

I stood, looking him over. His eyes were clear and his stance set. "Are you okay?"

"I'm fine. The doctor cleared me. It's not like I haven't been tasered before." Now he looked irritated. "When we find whoever did that, I'm going to have a fine discussion. For now, where do you want to go?"

"Give me just a sec," I said.

He looked at the tree. "That's depressing."

"Right? I'll be back in a minute." I wandered back to Nick's office. "Talked to Tessa, and you have a deal."

He turned to face me, his expression clearing. "Seriously? That easy?"

"She's my sister," I said. "Of course she wanted to help me out, and more importantly, she wanted to help Violet. Tessa is one of the kindest people I've ever met, and you're a moron for not just asking her out and falling in love. But that's your problem."

"Fine." Truth be told, there was a gleam in his eyes I didn't know how to interpret.

I moved around the boxes with trial notebooks until I reached the edge of his desk. "With one caveat. This is now mine." I took the necklace with the Celtic Knot. Aunt Rachel would love it.

CHAPTER 33

I walked outside Nick's office with Bud on my heels, his solid presence giving me some sense of peace, although I just couldn't figure out who'd pushed me against that brick wall. The man had felt solid, but he'd been wearing quite a bit of clothing, so who knew.

Bud looked down at me. "Where to now? How about nowhere? How about we stay at the station and do some paperwork?"

"Can't. Have to at least get Bernie off the hook before I take that vacation," I said, feeling the clock ticking down. Usually, Jareth had sent his Christmas card by now, and nothing. Well, unless the roses, heart, and dead body were gifts from him. I swallowed down panic and pushed open the door, noting that the snow had finally stopped falling, leaving the world white and sparkly. The clouds had even parted to reveal blue sky and a weak sun that increased the glitter across the snowy carpet. "How about some ice cream?"

"It's too cold," Bud said, at full alert, his gaze sweeping the parking area.

"It's never too cold for ice cream." I slipped into the passenger side of his cruiser and waited until he'd sat and started the engine.

"Let's go to Buck's Candy Store and Ice Creamery over on Oakwood."

Bud sighed but drove in that direction. "Why?"

"I need to interview a possible witness." I watched a couple of young women shovel the sidewalk fronting the justice building.

"Great," Bud said, driving slowly. We finally made it to Oakwood, and he parked right in front of the candy store. "You're buying," he muttered. "Stay in the car until I open your door." Apparently he wasn't taking any more chances.

I didn't bother arguing that nobody knew we were headed to the candy store and that the attacker earlier had waited for us outside my place of business. The guy had been tased, so I might as well humor him.

He looked around and then opened my door, keeping his body between me and the street.

I slid across the snowy sidewalk into the door and kept going, pushing it open. The smell of butterscotch instantly hit me, and I inhaled deeply, smiling because it's impossible not to smile when surrounded by butterscotch. Then I looked over at Bud and revised that thought. He was not smiling.

The candy displays, loose in glass barrels and already wrapped in bags with holiday ribbons had been placed to the left. To the right was the ice cream counter with all of the toppings in a separate case. A forty-something woman with curly black hair and light blue eyes was behind the counter, shoving scoops into the ice cream buckets. A red apron with a snowman across the top protected her white blouse and dark jeans. She looked up and smiled. "Hi. Can I help you?"

"Yes." I moved toward the counter to see if they had huckleberry ice cream. It was often seasonal, and we were way out of season. "I'm looking for Lucy Gardiner?"

Her gaze took in Bud, who was still in his uniform. "Am I in trouble?"

"No," I hastened to say. "He's here for me."

Her dark eyebrows rose. "Are you in trouble?"

"Always," Bud muttered.

I kept my smile in place. "I was hoping you'd talk to me about Hoyt Forrest."

She grasped a torn towel and started rubbing down the glass. "What has he done now?" Her voice was more resigned than anything else.

"I'm not sure," I admitted. "We're investigating his father's death, and I wanted to ask you about Hoyt since you dated for...."

"Six months." She rubbed harder and showed cut muscles in her upper arms. "Hoyt is a good guy with a demon on his back." She stopped cleaning and straightened, stretching her shoulders. "If he didn't gamble, he'd be the perfect guy. Instead, he's a nice guy who turns into an ass and steals your grandma's jewelry to pawn so he can gamble some more." She waved the towel and then tossed it toward the sink. "Of course, he's sorry, and he plans to pay you back."

I winced. "That sucks."

"Yeah. I had to dip into savings to get the jewelry from the pawn shop," she said, her eyes sparking. "But at least I got it all back. I ended things with him the next day, and since we were about to be evicted from the cutest cabin you could imagine, it was easy to part ways."

"Sorry," I said, meaning it. She seemed like a nice person. "Do you think he could've hurt his father for money? I mean, if his gambling debts got bad enough that he was in danger?"

She rubbed her chin. "No. He loved his dad and wouldn't have hurt him. Well, he would've stolen from his dad, but he wouldn't have killed him."

At this point, I wasn't sure about that. "Did you know about his father setting up Bernie McLintock with a fake lover?"

Now her brows drew down. "What?"

Guess not. "Any insight into Hoyt you can give us?" I asked.

"The usual, I guess. At the beginning, it was wonderful

between us, but he was winning poker tournaments then. It wasn't until he started losing that things went south." She eyed the ice cream toppings. "I don't know much more to tell you."

I wasn't sure what else to ask. "Did Hoyt ever exhibit any stalker-type tendencies?" It was a long shot, but maybe Hoyt was my crazy admirer.

She snorted. "That would take too much effort, I'm afraid. And if the tendencies included actually buying gifts, then no way. Not a chance. All of his money, and anybody else's he could get his hands on, went into poker games."

That figured. Once again, I hadn't found out anything to help Bernie.

"Anything else?" she asked.

"When was the last time you talked to him?" I asked.

She blushed a light pink.

So it was like that?

She shifted her feet and rolled her eyes. "I know. I really do. He's bad news, and he's bad for me, but at his core, he's a decent guy. He stayed over last night."

If there was a way to help her, I would. "Do you know where he was the night of the murder?"

"No, but there's no way he'd kill his own dad." She looked around and then seemed to settle. "I think that's it. Can I get you something to eat?"

I stepped closer. "Yeah. I'll have a double scoop with huckleberry and coffee-mocha with a waffle cone."

"Ditto," Bud said from behind me. "Mine with sprinkles on top, please."

* * *

I SPENT a couple of hours at my office managing paperwork and tried to pretend my life was normal.

"Anna!" Oliver yelled, running down to my office. "You have another box."

Bud hurried to the reception area, beating both Clark and me. He looked at the box and then bent over to read. "Anna Albertini, this firm, from Hewsom Enterprises in New York."

"Oh." Relief batted through me. "That's mine." I fetched the box, my heart still skipping beats. I'd found an early copy of *Catcher in the Rye* for Pauley for Christmas to go with the socks I bought him every year. Pierce would definitely like the tie, and I was now almost done shopping. "I'm ready to get out of here," I told Bud, realizing he'd been off the clock for almost an hour.

"Great," he said.

We headed through the door, and he covered me the entire way to the car, almost looking like he wished the attacker would return.

I had Bud drop me off at my sister's house, where Aiden said he'd pick me up after he finished work. If my stalker wanted to make a move, he'd be a moron to do it with the three Albertini sisters banded together.

Donna's neighborhood was as decorated as the retirement community but in a sedated and more color-coordinated way. Her Christmas lights were a light blue fluorescent that glowed prettily. I walked inside, instantly inhaling the scent of pork chops. "Hey." I kicked out of my boots and hung my coat in the closet before walking the long hallway to the kitchen in the back.

"Hi." Tessa sat on a bar stool swinging one foot with a glass of wine in front of her.

Donna turned around from stirring something on the stove, a ladle in her hand. "Hi. You okay?"

I nodded and put the box on the counter, quickly ripping it open. While I had ordered the present for my cousin, I probably should've double-checked it before leaving the office. Relief, pure and simple, poured through me when I took out the perfectly wrapped book. "It's for Pauley."

"The book?" Donna's brown gaze swept across me. When I nodded, she leaned over and poured red wine into another glass. "You sure you're okay?"

"Yeah." I accepted the glass and took a healthy drink. My sister always had the good stuff. My phone buzzed, and I looked down to see a text from Aiden, saying he was going to have to work really late. I figured he was trying to clear his schedule just like I was so we could regroup with this whole dead body and Jareth Davey situation—and maybe even take a vacation. It was starting to seem like it'd be a good idea. I glanced at Donna. "Do you mind if I stay here tonight?"

"Fine by me," she said. "I have a good alarm system as well as a LadySmith."

Tessa poured more wine into her glass. "I'll stay, too. We can have a slumber party and X-box marathon." She topped off my glass. "Before I forget, do you have extra wrapping paper, D?"

"You know I do," Donna said, reaching for plates. "You ask every year."

Tessa grinned.

I texted Aiden back that I'd stay with Donna that night and not to worry about me. Then my phone buzzed, and I answered the call. "Albertini."

"Hey. It's Pierce. Don't have news from the coroner yet, but considering Crackle had a hole in his head, I'm not expecting any surprises. For now, I've been tracking down Hoyt Forrest's loan sharks, and so far, he didn't owe any of them enough to have put his father in danger. I don't see that as a motive, although Hoyt might still look good for it. I have to say, Bernie is still the strongest suspect."

"I feel like Bernie didn't kill Lawrence," I said, hoping it was true. I just couldn't imagine the sweet old Santa killing anybody. "Anything else?"

"Yeah. Prints and blood came back on the knife. The only blood is Lawrence's, and the only prints are Bernie's. In addition, it's a hunting knife commonly sold everywhere, including at Forrest's Bait and Tackle. It could've been Lawrence's knife, or it could've been anybody's, to be honest."

I swallowed. "You're being awfully generous with the information." Pierce had a good gut, and he must be telling me that Bernie wasn't a killer.

"It's Christmas." Pierce clicked off.

I set my phone aside. "All right. Who wants to take me on in the new velociraptor game?"

"After dinner," Donna said, bending and taking a pan out of the oven.

Definitely after dinner.

CHAPTER 34

*M*y phone woke me from my sprawl on Donna's sofa. Tess had grabbed the guest room, and I'd planned to share the bed with one of them but had fallen asleep in front of the TV. I tugged on my ripped T-shirt and shivered in the boxer shorts I'd borrowed. Groaning, I noted it was only five in the morning. What the heck? "What?" I mumbled sleepily into the phone.

"Hey, it's Bosco. I need a favor."

"Sure." I pushed my hair out of my face and sat up, trying to get my bearings. "What's up?"

Movement sounded across the phone. "I've been called in but have Fabio here. Any chance you could come get him until Knox can grab him later today?"

"Sure." I yawned. It was nice of Bosco to watch Fabio for Knox, and I always wanted to help. "I'll drive over to collect him now."

"Thanks." Bosco ended the call.

I blinked several times. Then I wrote my sisters a note and put on jeans, boots and coat, borrowing Tessa's car. It was doubtful my stalker knew where I was, but even so, I kept an eye on my surroundings and the handle of my gun within reach. I wasn't going to change my life or hide from this jerk, but I wasn't going to be stupid, either.

I drove through town, reaching Bosco's place. He lived in an apartment in a converted turn-of-the-century house that had two other apartments in it, and I'd always felt like he'd found the perfect place for himself. I carefully viewed my surroundings, didn't see anything interesting, and ran up the stairs into the house, falling once and getting my jeans wet.

My key opened his door, and I was nearly bowled over by an energetic and massively big dog. I dropped to scratch his ears. "Hi, Fabio."

Fabio was a mutt, plain and simple. His fur was a mixture of brown, black and white, and his teeth were sharp. He was so ugly that he became adorable.

I locked the door behind myself and looked around Bosco's place. It was dusty and needed a good clean, and often I helped him out. Right now my brain was foggy, so I ditched my coat and boots, wandering to his sofa. Then I tugged off the jeans to hang over the sofa so they could dry. "How about a quick nap, and then we'll go to Donna's?" I asked Fabio. My head really hurt.

He wagged his tail happily and then lay down at the end.

I was asleep within minutes, waking sometime later when Fabio was barking at me. I opened one eye. "Fine. I'll take you out."

Somebody knocked on the door.

Sleepily, not thinking, I stumbled and opened the door. A pretty brunette stood there, her eyes wide. "Morning?" I asked.

She stepped back. "Sorry, I…."

Fabio shoved by me and nearly bulldozed the woman, panting happily. My vision cleared. Who was this?

She scratched the dog's ears. "Sorry. I heard him bark and thought he was alone." She tried to back away, but Fabio stopped her.

My brain finally cleared. "Oh. You're Marlie." I liked her

instantly. There was something sweet and smart about her. "Inside Fabio. Now."

The dog trotted happily inside.

I held out my hand to introduce myself and make sure she knew I was Bosco's cousin and not some hookup, especially since my jeans were still hanging over the sofa. Hadn't Rory said Bos was quickly and unexpectedly getting serious without knowing it?

Just then, the outside door opened and Aiden stomped inside, his anger pulsating through the atmosphere and kicking my heart rate into the 'I've been running' range.

"What the holy hell are you thinking, Angel?" he snapped, reaching me.

I sighed and nicely reminded him that I had a gun in my bag and that I was safe.

He leaned down and nicely told me that my gun had better be in my bag. "For all that's holy, you are not safe. In fact, I know you're not safe because your ass isn't at your sister's house, where it should be right now." He was going to scare Marlie off, and I couldn't let that happen.

I forced a smile. "Aiden, I am not giving up this case."

"I'm not asking you to give it up," he snarled. "What I am doing is asking you to be smart and hightailing your very nice butt across town to babysit a dog is not doing that."

I couldn't stop the eye roll I gave him, and then I reminded him that I was okay.

He ducked, the world tilted, and I was once again over his shoulder. I sighed and called for the dog to come along as we headed back into the apartment.

Fabio stepped right up into the action, following us. I slapped a hand to Aiden's back and levered up, hoping somehow to save this first meeting with Bosco's love. "Sorry about this, Marlie. It has to seem weird." Yep. The woman looked like she wanted to make a run for it.

Then, she impressed the heck out of me by running in front of

Aiden and trying to stop him. Man, she was perfect for Bosco. I laughed, so happy he'd found somebody.

Aiden tossed a blanket over me, grabbed my jeans off the sofa and my bag off the floor. Then he marched toward the hallway.

Marlie jumped in front of him again. "Should I call in a kidnapping?"

Amusement took me. I loved her. Really loved her.

"I'm thinking the Albertini family might be a little odd," Marlie muttered.

That stopped Aiden cold. He hitched me into better position. "They are. Get out now, if you can. Trust me. Run fast and run far."

I laughed and squirmed.

Marlie swallowed. "We're just friends. I mean Bosco and me. Just friends."

"Ha," Aiden said, sidestepping her easily and shutting the apartment door behind us. "That's how they get you, darlin'. I've already heard about you, which means the family has heard, and you're as good as in. I hope you like big weddings." He kept walking.

I whistled. "Fabio, come!"

The dog panted after us. My phone rang, and Aiden dug it out of my bag to hand to me. I answered, not surprised that Bosco was on the other end. Bos yelled at me because he'd heard about the dead body, and then he and Aiden exchanged some guy talk. Whatever. Aiden kept walking outside the exit and the wintery cold hit my bare legs.

Just as he was tossing me into his rig, Marlie ran out with my wallet, which must've fallen. I grinned at her. Oh, she fit in perfectly. I needed to take her to lunch and figure out more about her. "Thanks." I smiled. "Welcome to chaos, my new friend."

* * *

"I AM NOT AMUSED," Aiden said, not sounding amused in the slightest.

I shimmied into my jeans and then boots, finger combing my hair into some semblance of curly order. "I was safe." Before he could argue, I held up a hand. "Do you mind if we pop by the hospital on the way? I still haven't talked to Doc Springfield about my case, and he's the last Kringle on my list."

"Sure. Have Bud meet you there," Aiden said, gritting his teeth.

I texted Bud. The poor guy was on Anna-duty for another day? Even I could feel a little sorry for him. We reached the hospital and waited in Aiden's truck for Bud. I started. "Crap. What about Tessa's Rogue?"

"Donna said she'd drop Tessa off to get it on the way to work," Aiden said, his gaze scanning the parking lot of the hospital.

Oh. It was nice that my sister had ratted me out. I'd give her a hard time later, although I didn't want her lying to Aiden, and I didn't lie to Aiden, so I guess she hadn't had a choice.

Bud drove up.

Aiden grasped the back of my neck and dragged me in for a deep kiss, taking me under. There was a hint of passion and a bucket-load of frustration in his kiss, topped off with a slice of anger. Even so, my body warmed and my breathing quickened. He leaned back, his hand remaining at my nape. "Stay with Bud. All day. Got it?"

Numbly, I nodded. My jeans felt too tight all of a sudden. "Bye." I zipped my jacket to hide the ripped T-shirt and jumped out of the truck, smiling at Bud.

He handed over a latte, and I almost hugged him.

"Thanks," I said. "Let's go talk to the doctor."

The interview didn't take long. Doc Springfield looked more like Santa than the other men, and he had the jolly laugh to prove it. In addition, he only gambled for charity, had no clue the other members had stolen minerals as seed money, and truly didn't believe Bernie had killed Lawrence. He also couldn't imagine anybody else committing murder.

An hour later, Bud and I drove away from the hospital.

"Nice guy," Bud said.

I nodded. "Not a lot of help for my case, though."

Bud slowed down behind a logging truck. "Maybe your client is guilty. Did you ask him straight out?"

I couldn't discuss the case with Bud, but Bernie had said he hadn't killed anybody. I did believe him. But what if he'd known about Sharon? It hadn't taken Thelma and Georgiana very long to find the woman, and Bernie had the same contacts, probably. If he'd looked for her, he would've found her. But he'd said he hadn't thought about her again.

"Where to?" Bud asked.

It was Friday, but I didn't have court this week. "Just to the office. Maybe I can wrap everything else up." I angled my head to see the clouds rolling in. Good. It'd be a snowy Christmas next week if the clouds kept coming. "I need to stop by Duke's first."

"Sure." This time, Bud parked at the curb in front of the buildings, and we both jumped out.

I paused on the sidewalk. "Do you mind if I talk to Duke alone?"

Bud stilled and ducked his head to see inside the jewelry store. "Go ahead." He angled his body by the door.

"Thanks." I edged inside, seeing Duke at the cash register to the right. He was in his sixties and as wide as he was tall. His bald head gleamed under the soft lights, and silver spectacles perched on his wide nose. "Hi, Duke."

"Hi." He set a notebook to the side. "I'm finished. You want to pay in full today?"

I gulped, hoping I had enough credit left on my card. "Sure." Digging it out of my purse, I walked across the soft gray carpet to hand over. "I had a nice talk with Earl Jacobsen about how you all seeded your companies."

Duke calmly swiped my credit card. "I don't know what you're talking about."

"Yeah, you do. It's too late to be charged because too many years have gone by," I said, accepting the card when he handed it back.

He shrugged his wide shoulders, making his big belly jiggle. "Nope. Sorry."

I sighed. "Fine. Don't admit anything, but at least talk to me. You've known everybody in my case for a long time. Do you think Bernie could've killed Lawrence?" It figured they all went way back.

"Maybe," Duke said. "I was at the CASA poker party the night Bernie supposedly cheated on Florence—at the other table and not with the Kringles." He shrugged. "Heard the rumor within a week that Bernie had cheated. Florence was in here a couple of days ago saying that it might've been a setup." He pointed to the screen for me to sign.

Good. My credit card had gone through. I signed my name. "What do you think?"

"If that's true, Lawrence deserved a knife in the back," Duke said, printing out my receipt. "All of these guys were so much in love with Florence when we were young, and I guess that never went away. I mean, I liked her and all, but she didn't hold a candle to my Jennie. Still doesn't."

That was sweet. Jennie was a friend of my Nana O'Shea's, and I'd always liked her.

He shook his head and pointed to a box of what looked liked pictures. "Florence asked me to get her copies of the pictures of our younger days. I think she wants to make some sort of video for Bernie. Guess they might be getting back together." He handed over a bag with Aiden's present in it. Probably. I mean, if I gave it to him.

I accepted the bag. "So you think Bernie could've done it?"

Duke looked at me, his eyes blazing behind the glasses. "I

would have if somebody did that to me. Bernie really loved her, and it almost killed him when they split."

I wouldn't be calling Duke as a character witness for Bernie. My gaze caught on the box of pictures. Maybe I could get a feeling about all of these people and how they fit together by looking backward even further than the night Lawrence had set up Bernie. "How about I deliver those for you?"

CHAPTER 35

J was halfway through a bottle of wine, sitting on my washing machine, staring at the case board I'd created on the mounted board. A picture of Lawrence was in the middle surrounded by Bernie, Florence, Hoyt and the rest of the past and current Kringle Club members. The box of pictures sat next to me on the clothes dryer, and I picked through them, noting that Florence really was stunning in her youth. Bernie was kind of cute as well.

Aiden worked at my table in the other room, his case files scattered and his notebooks full. Saber worked with him, and they bounced ideas off each other fairly well. The rest of their team had taken the night off.

I glanced at my phone, noting it was nearly midnight. We'd met up to eat spaghetti and then had each retreated to work. It felt like Aiden was just as motivated as I was to get things settled with our work so we could concentrate on Jareth Davey or my stalker. My gut told me it was Davey because who else could it be?

I sipped my wine and looked at the board again.

What if? Jumping off the washing machine, I slid Lawrence's picture to the side and put Florence's smack dab in the middle. All of this might be about her. She was Bernie's motivation for murder, and quite possibly Hoyt's as well if he'd known his father was going to leave her so much in his will. Left without anything else to do, I took out older black and white photographs to tape beneath the current ones of everyone.

Duke Wells had a head of hair in his twenties, and Earl had long golden curls. Seriously. His hair had been gorgeous. Bernie looked the same, Lawrence's nose was much smaller, Jocko stood like a tough-guy, and Doc Springfield looked like a young Santa. He'd always had that round face, although his beard had been brown. He must've been in medical school while the others were miners.

All of the men were fairly muscled, which made sense considering they'd been hard rock miners to start.

There were many pictures of them camping, partying, or just hanging out at many of the bars that still thrived in Silverville. I wasn't surprised to find photographs of my grandparents in several of the places.

A picture of Bernie, Lawrence, and Florence caught my eye. She was between them, arms around their waists, smiling. They were both staring at her, puppy love on their faces, and she was looking at the camera. There was a crowded campground behind them, and I could almost hear the hum of people. I taped the picture on the board because, at this point, it said everything.

I sipped my wine, missing something. I didn't know what it was. All of the pictures were in front of me, and I'd even drawn one of Sharon Smith so she'd be represented. It was a stick figure, but I didn't care much because she had an alibi for the murder. I even had a picture of Lucy Gardiner on the board that I'd gotten off her Facebook page. She'd seemed nice, but she was still seeing Hoyt, and he stood to inherit quite a bit. They hadn't known that Florence would be left so much in the will.

Lucy didn't feel like a murderer to me.

Of course, nobody involved did. I had a square box on the

board for the unknown suspect, but I certainly hadn't seen any evidence in that direction. Bernie's life was fairly simple.

I hopped back on the washing machine, pulled my legs up, and just stared at the pictures again. Oh, I could take a break and wrap Christmas presents, but I was tired, and none of this was making sense.

The front door closed and soon Aiden poked his head into the room. "Solve your case?"

"No. You?"

He shrugged. "We've tracked Jareth Davey from here down to Portland and then Portland to Seattle, but then we lost him."

Seattle was only a five-hour drive from where we lived. "He's here, isn't he?" I asked, already knowing the answer. There was nobody else who would've left a dead body on my lawn. Probably.

"Yeah. I think he's here," Aiden said, his voice calm. "Which is good because now I can handle him." He looked over his shoulder. "I'm glad the dog is staying with you. Do you think Knox would let you keep him for a while? The alarm system is working now, but there's nothing better than a dog."

"Sure," I said. "Especially if I get my cases wrapped up and can hang here with Fabio for a while." I could use a vacation, actually. "What's your plan?" I kept my voice light.

"We've passed off four of our cases and are close to finishing three more," Aiden said. "My entire team is due a vacation, so if we get everything wrapped up, I'll give the gang a week off, although at the moment, they're full on trying to help us track down Jareth Davey. They don't like that he burned us any more than I do, and we're hitting it hard tomorrow even though it's Saturday."

I cocked my head, noting his eyes looked tired. Aiden never looked tired. "What does that mean?"

"It means I'm clearing my schedule so I can hunt *him*," Aiden said evenly. "If I'd have known he was stalking you all these years, I would've done so before."

Yeah, I had often wished Aiden would've kept in touch after leaving town, but my moron shrink at the time had told him to leave me alone, and he'd had to move away anyway. "How do we hunt him?" I asked, never having hunted a human before.

His lips twitched. "*We* don't."

I pushed off the appliances, landing on my feet to face him. The thing is, I understand Aiden. He hadn't had much in his life, not many people he trusted, and when he found somebody, he was all in while he was in. I'd seen it with his team, and I'd experienced it first-hand. That didn't mean he saw orange blossoms and a priest in our future, but it did mean he'd take whatever control he could and fight any threat. It's who he was and what he did.

I also knew myself. Pretty much. Jareth Davey had tried to hunt me most of my life, and so far, I hadn't found a way to turn the tables. Through the years the local authorities had tried to find him, my family had tried to find him, and nobody had succeeded. Also, we couldn't prove he was the one sending the cards to me, so even if we'd found him, there wasn't much we could have done.

Within the law, anyway.

Now I had a chance to find the bastard with Aiden. Aiden was the best at what he did, and if anybody could hunt down Jareth, it was Aiden Devlin.

Finally.

"I'm going to help," I said.

"No," he said, not unexpectedly.

Aiden was an old-fashioned guy who was also used to jumping into the line of fire before anybody else. It's why he led a specialty ATF team that would follow him into the bowels of hell. He cared about me, and he'd try to protect me, even to the point of infuriating me and leaving me out.

I walked toward him, noting the darkening of his eyes.

Yeah, I could argue with him. I could threaten, beg, or plead to be part of the hunt. Instead, I placed both my hands on his chest, looked up at those unreal blue eyes, and gave him the truth. "I *need* to be a part of this."

He blinked. Just once, but it was enough. "My team is treating this as an op, and you're terrible at obeying orders." He wasn't wrong. I opened my mouth and he shook his head. "We are not using you as bait."

Yeah, that was what I had been planning to say. "Okay. You're in charge of the op." Although, I was bait, whether or not he liked that fact. Jareth Davey was invested in me for some reason, and that hadn't changed in fourteen years. But I didn't need to put a label on it. "I feel like he's been in charge for so much of my life as I waited for those stupid cards twice a year, and I couldn't do anything about it. Couldn't find him and fight him," I said in a rush. "I don't like feeling helpless." If I could help take the control away from Jareth Davey, I needed to do so.

Aiden breathed out. "Okay. That's fair." He slid his arms around my waist. "Since my team is clearing all other cases to concentrate on the new campaign starting Monday morning, you can be a member of the team."

The new campaign was finally stopping Jareth Davey. If he'd committed that murder, we'd prove it and put him away forever.

Yeah, I adored Aiden. Putting me on his team went against every instinct in his body, but he was doing it because I needed to be there. Oh, he'd still jump in front of any bullets, but I was pretty quick there, too. I didn't mind being able to cover his back while he hunted.

I wasn't going to lose Aiden to Jareth Davey. "He's after you, too," I said softly.

"No. He's after me only as a way to get to you," Aiden said. "Don't forget that."

I stepped in and snuggled into his broad chest. Christmas was coming, our talk was coming, and right now, I just wanted to feel him. It seemed like our lives were on hold until we locked down Jareth, and I was tired of it. Finally, there was a path to ending his reign of harassing me from afar. Or maybe closer if he'd been the one to kill Crackle. "Considering Jareth followed and burned you in Portland, he's making his move," I murmured.

Aiden stiffened. "Definitely."

Okay. We were on the same page.

I leaned back to look into his face, keeping my hands on his warm body. "I haven't seen your new office yet."

"We can't move in until late next week." His hands flexed across my lower back. "We'll work either out of my cabin or here this weekend. I assume you'll be here?"

"I'm going to the mall early tomorrow afternoon where all the Kringles will be," I said, running through my case in my mind. "Bud is working and will be on my six, so I'll be safe. I just want to see them all interact and maybe question them with each other around. I'm missing something but can't figure out what it is."

Aiden's eyebrow rose. "Bud's working on a Saturday?"

"Yeah, but he's off Sunday, so I'll be here all day and can help your team if you need anything." Not that I was involved with their cases or even knew what their cases were about, but I was a heck of an organizer when it came to file folders. I also made a mean cup of coffee. "We also have the family barbecue that night, and it'd be nice to see how Violet is fitting in with Aunt Yara."

Aiden's cheek creased. "Apparently I was included in the family lottery and drew Lacey O'Shea's name. Is she even coming home for Christmas?"

My cousin was a big time cop in Detroit, and she needed to come home for good. "Right now, we don't know yet. But even if she doesn't, you can send her a present." Yeah, my mom had put in Aiden's name. She really was hoping for him to stick around. "Is it okay you're in the lottery?" Our family was so big that we drew names for everyone except immediate family.

"Sure," he said, frowning. "But I have no clue what to get her."

I brightened. "I have the perfect thing. I bought her a necklace at the Irish shop in Spokane and also splurged on matching earrings. You can give her the earrings." Lacey was my best friend, and we always exchanged gifts, even though we were both also in the family lottery.

"I'll pay you for them," he said, looking relieved.

It was a little scary how easily he fit in with my family, considering I wasn't sure he was going to stay. But now wasn't the time to worry about that. I had enough concerns. I smiled. "You look tired. Let's get some sleep."

"Don't want to sleep." His hands moved to my hips and he lifted me against him.

I wrapped both arms around his neck and clamped my thighs to his hips. "I was hoping you would say that."

Then I kissed him, forgetting all about the world.

For now.

CHAPTER 36

*T*he smell of sugar donuts and pine trees wafted through the mall as frantic shoppers scurried from store to store, emerging with bags and wrapped presents. I jumped out of the way of a middle-aged woman with a deranged gleam in her eye as she darted into the closest toy store.

Bud sighed next to me, wearing his uniform and looking nicely polished. "I should get hazard pay for covering you."

Probably true. I rolled my eyes and stood in line for donuts, buying us both a bag. He took his, looking at the cinnamon and sugar. "We could share one of these bags."

I would've answered, but my mouth was full of a miniature donut. A choir from a local elementary school belted out *Jingle Bells* from a stage near the JC Penney's and out of the main drag.

Chewing, I led him beyond a couple of elves, several decorated shops, and shoppers weighed down with bags to the fountain of a large lotus flower surrounded by a green pool of water in the center. Santas spread out in every direction, handing out candy canes and thanking people for slipping cash into their charity buckets. A raised platform showed one Santa listening to wishes. I squinted, trying to make him out.

"They all look alike." Bud wiped cinnamon on a napkin, feeling like a solid presence at my side.

I frowned. We did work together, and I had gotten him shot earlier that summer. Did that mean I should buy him a present? He was on the outs with his wife, whoever that was, so maybe he needed a friend and an invite to my family's party. "Do you have plans for Christmas?" I sat on a wooden bench, the paper of my donut bag crackling.

"Yeah." He sat next to me, his gaze sweeping the festive atmosphere. "Thanks, though."

I ate another donut, feeling my blood sugar happily spike. "There's Bernie," I said, recognizing him finally by his new coat over by Macy's. He posed for a picture with several giggling teenaged girls, his chest proudly puffed out.

Bags rustled, and Florence came up on my right, her eyes bright and her cheeks rosy. "Aren't they adorable?"

I scooted closer to Bud so she could sit on my other side. "They look like they're having fun." I tilted the donut bag her way.

She dropped her packages and took a treat. "They are. It's so cute. The mall does pay them, but they each have a bucket for their charity of choice. Bernie is giving to the Humane Society this year. We might get a puppy from them after the holidays."

"So you two are getting serious." I reached for another donut.

"Yes. I can't believe Lawrence set Bernie up like that. I guess I should have questioned him more at the time, but I was so hurt and angry that I just believed him." She shrugged, looking festive in a green sweater over white linen pants. "He believed it, so I did as well. I wish I could just smack Lawrence in the face and yell at him. How dare he do that to us."

I looked around. "Speaking of which, if he did that to Bernie, did he hurt or betray anybody else through the years?" From the sound of it, nothing held Lawrence back.

She sighed. "Not that I know of, but how would I know? This whole thing is shocking." She winced. "I don't mean to speak badly about the dead, but it wasn't as if Lawrence was a master-mind of anything, you know? His first wife, God rest her soul, was the brains behind the bait and tackle shop. Lawrence was nice to look at and had a great package and moves in bed, but I can't imagine he put together such a betrayal of Bernie. Of me, too."

I stole a napkin from Bud to wipe off my fingers. "Do you think Hoyt helped him? That Hoyt created the plan?" The apart-ment they'd used had been utilized by Hoyt to gamble, so perhaps?

She reached for another donut. "I don't know. The apple didn't fall far from the tree on that one. Hoyt doesn't seem like much of a mastermind."

That had been my observation as well. I noted the different Santas. "That's Doc Springfield over there, and Jocko Terezzi is near the gaming store. Where are the rest?"

Florence pointed to a Santa near the huckleberry treat store. "There's Donald McLerrison, and Earl is up on the main stage right now. He's doing a good job for his first gig, I think." She pointed up at the main Santa. "It's his turn to have kids give wishes and get their pictures taken." We watched as one little boy smiled, and an elf helped him to the small slide that brought him back down to cotton batting in a bin. The kid giggled the whole way.

I couldn't help but smile and noted that Bud did the same.

The choir switched to a rambunctious version of *Little Drummer Boy*.

"Donald McLerrison is the only Kringle I haven't spoken with," I said, putting my purse over my shoulder. "I'll be right back."

It took me several moments to reach my favorite farmer by Kat's Jewelry store, and he smiled widely when I appeared. "Howdy. What's your wish for Christmas?" He handed me a candy cane.

"World peace and a chance to figure out my love life." I took the treat. "Thanks. What did you get Oliver?" It was so cool that

McLerrison had all but adopted Oliver Duck and taken him in to live on the farm.

"Oh, he wanted one of those X-boxes, and I figured why not? It's not as great as working the farm, but the kid needs a break sometimes."

That was sweet. A smell caught me, and I leaned toward him. Hey. What was that?

He pulled more candy canes from his jacket. "Any luck figuring out who killed Lawrence?"

"No. Do you think Bernie could've done it?"

McLerrison shook his head, and his Santa hat flopped to the side. The white fur on his uniform had turned a light gray, but he still looked authentic. "Bernie would never kill anybody, although, for Flo, it'd probably be worth it. I can't believe Lawrence did such a horrible thing."

What the heck was that smell? It was sweet and kind of minty. I'd smelled it before. "Do you know of any other horrible things Lawrence did to other people during his life?" I asked.

"Nope," McLerrison said.

Bernie ambled over, carrying his bucket. "Do you want to relieve Earl, or should I? It's one of our turns up on the stage, and they just barricaded the picture space for a ten-minute break." His beard moved when he talked.

The same scent came from him, and my instincts started to hum. Sweet and minty. Then it hit me like a rock to the head. The man who'd shoved me against the brick wall had smelled like that. Like both of them. The man had wanted Bernie to fry. I stood a step back. "What is that smell?"

Bernie frowned beneath his beard. "Huh?"

"That smell. Kind of sweet and minty," I whispered, my legs starting to shake.

McLerrison started. "Oh. That's muscle relaxant. You'd be surprised how sore our shoulders get shaking a bell all day. Earl has it made special, and he shared with us earlier today. Gotta be honest, it does help."

I slowly turned to look at Earl up on the platform in a brand new Santa uniform with a big round ball at the end of his shiny red hat. "Have you used it before today?"

"No." Bernie followed my gaze. "I usually use Ben Gay, but Earl just got this stuff and said it was a miracle. It does feel good. Why?"

My mouth opened and closed. Why would Earl have tasered Bud and threatened me? Why would he want Bernie to go to prison? The older black and white pictures flashed through my brain. "Is Earl a strategic kind of guy?"

McLerrison snorted. "Who do you think came up with the hard rock mining plan for us all to get some money to start businesses? I heard you learned about our misspent youth."

I pivoted to gain Bud's attention. He was watching two women fight over a blouse on a sale rack. I gulped. "Way back when— before he started his jewelry store. Did Earl have a crush on Florence as well?"

We all looked up to see Earl eating a candy cane on his throne, his gaze riveted on Florence as she sat chatting with Bud.

"Yeah," Bernie said slowly. "We all were in love with Flo. I think Earl asked her out a few times, and they went on a couple dates, but she still left town."

McLerrison cocked his head. "I'd forgotten about that. Also, after you and Flo split, he asked her out again. Several times. But she decided to date Lawrence and ended up engaged. Well, until he was murdered."

The choir moved on to a rock-like version of *Silent Night*.

Bernie's mouth dropped open as he quickly caught up. "I knew Lawrence wasn't smart enough to come up with that whole plan with Sharon Smith. I knew it." He threw his bucket to the ground and coins rolled out. Kids ran from every direction, sliding on the tiled floor to gather up the money. He looked up at Earl. "You son of a bitch," he yelled, launching into action and knocking me into McLerrison.

Pain flashed along my ribcage.

McLerrison dropped his bucket to catch me, keeping us both from falling into a glass wall.

Bernie huffed toward the fountain, candy canes falling from his pockets as he went.

Bud jumped up, looking frantically around.

I pushed free of McLerrison, ran after Bernie, my feet sliding through the candy canes and my arms windmilling to keep my balance. "Bernie, stop," I yelled, trying to catch his Santa sleeve in my hand.

He shrugged me off. "I'm gonna kill you," he bellowed, looking up.

Earl stood, panic in his eyes. The beard covered most of his face, and his suit was a little too long, going past his black boots. He looked wildly around.

Bernie ran toward the stairs, and two mall security guards blocked him, both looking confused.

People scrambled around, watching him, several getting out of the way. Bernie threw his gloves down to the ground, marching toward the fountain.

Bud rushed toward him and tripped on the gloves, grabbing for Bernie's shoulder.

Bernie pivoted and shoved Bud in a surprisingly smooth motion, pushing the cop against the edge of the fountain. Almost in slow motion, Bud's arms windmilled, and he fell backward right into the pool. Water splashed up in every direction, turning the white tiles green.

"Wait," I yelled, rushing after Bernie.

Bernie jumped into the cotton batting and started roaring up the slide, using his hands and feet, his boots slipping and squeaking loudly.

Earl moved closer to the edge and pummeled Bernie with

candy canes and what looked like rubber balls, hitting him in the head and shoulders.

Bernie swore in graphic detail, ducking his head and trying harder to get up the slide.

The choir sang louder, now belting out *Santa Claus is Coming to Town*. Their teacher looked over her shoulder at the ruckus and then moved her wand faster, no doubt wanting to keep the kids focused and not watching the mess. Their voices got louder and the tempo even faster as they switched into a wild version of *God Rest Ye Merry Gentlemen.*

I clambered after Bernie, snatching his boot and pulling him down the slide. A candy cane hit me in the face and I snapped, shoving Bernie out of the way and climbing quickly. Unlike Bernie's boots, mine had plenty of traction, and I also didn't have a Santa suit holding me back.

Earl pelted red and green rubber balls at me, making me lose my grip. I slid back down and swore.

Bernie tried to catch my leg, but I kicked him away. Enough of this crap. Earl had tased Bud and scared me, and I was done with this. I climbed quickly, ducking and dodging the balls, reaching the top. Earl tried to kick me, and I grabbed his ankle, yanking hard.

He fell flat and emitted a loud and pained *oof*.

Coughing and swearing, I hitched up and crawled over him, grabbing his lapels and shaking him. "You tased my friend!"

"And he killed Lawrence," Bernie yelled from down in the cotton batting.

That, too. Sucking in air, I stood and tried to haul Earl up with me.

Bud pushed past the two security guards, running up the stairs.

Earl stood and grabbed my arms, his eyes wild behind the Santa spectacles. "I love her," he yelled.

Then he pulled a knife out of his pocket.

Time paused. Everything moved in slow motion. He stabbed toward my stomach, and I grasped his wrist, pivoting like Aiden had taught me and forcing Earl to drop the blade.

He screamed, captured me in a bear hug, and then propelled us both off the high stage.

CHAPTER 37

The fall down felt like it took an eternity, although it had to be only twelve feet. I screamed, panicked as I flew through the air. I hit first, flat on my back, and he landed on top of me. The wind whooshed out of my lungs, and pain exploded down my back. It took me a second to realize that we'd landed in the cotton batting.

He shoved off me, and I grabbed for him. The bastard punched me in the cheekbone, and I lost it, punching up at his face with all that I had, my vision cloudy.

Bud yanked him away and flipped him around to quickly cuff, shoving him toward the security guards. "Watch him." Then he turned and crouched down, leaning over me. "Hold still. What hurts?"

Everything hurt. "Not sure." I breathed deep, thankful I could fill my lungs, shutting my eyes.

Bud ran his hands down my legs, over my torso, and then my arms. "Don't any feel breaks. Start with your legs and slowly start moving."

I blinked and looked up to see not only Bud but several Santa Clauses and Florence staring down at me. The choir moved into a song about Rudolf, and the absurdity of the entire afternoon hit me. I started laughing. Hard and fast, I laughed, tears streaming down my aching face.

Florence frowned. "I think she's concussed."

"Move. Your. Body," Bud said, his voice clipped.

Doc Springfield pushed him aside and knelt next to me, his authentic beard really making him look like Santa. "Stop laughing."

I stopped laughing.

He leaned closer and looked into my eyes. "Does your head hurt?"

"Not really," I whispered. "My face hurts."

He nodded. "You're going to have a heck of a shiner. On the other side of the one that's almost gone, too. It's a pity." He gingerly probed my shoulders. "Any neck pain?"

"No." I wiggled my legs and feet and then moved to my arms and hands. I frowned. "I think I'm okay." The cotton batting had probably saved my bones from certain breaks.

"Vision clear?" he asked.

I looked up at the concerned senior citizens looking down at me. "Yeah." Slowly, I moved to sit, letting him help me. The world remained stable and not swirling around me. "My hips hurt a little, but nothing I can't handle."

His eyebrows rose. "Let's see if you can stand."

I held his hands and stood, my stance set. Then I rolled my neck and shoulders. "I'm okay." Thank goodness we'd hit the cotton and not the tile floor.

"Oh, you're going to hurt tomorrow," Doc Springfield said. "Nothing is broken, though. But you should ice anywhere it hurts, including your face, and take ibuprofen. It wouldn't be a bad idea for you to take a vacation." He kept my hand and assisted me out of the tub of cotton.

Food coloring from the fountain had turned Bud's buzz-cut hair a dark green, and even the skin on his neck looked holiday-themed. He moved for Earl and jerked the hat and beard off his head. "You don't deserve to wear these," he muttered.

"Amen to that," Jocko snapped. "You are officially out of the Kringle Club, Earl Jacobsen!"

Earl hung his head and looked at Florence. "I love you, Flo. Have my entire life. Why didn't you give me a chance?"

Her hands shook when she clasped them in front of her stomach. "You killed Lawrence. Murdered him."

Earl blinked. "He took advantage of me. It was all my idea— with Sharon Smith. Oh, Lawrence knew her and set it up, but I created the entire plan. Then he wooed you and got you to fall in love with him. He *betrayed* me."

"So you killed him?" I asked.

Earl shook his head, tears in his eyes. "It was an accident. I doubled back after we'd left the night of the poker game and just wanted to threaten him. I waved the knife to scare him, telling him that Florence was mine. He fought back, and things went south."

Right. "You stabbed him in the back," I snapped, twisting my hips. Yep. I was gonna hurt in the morning.

Earl's mouth opened and closed. "I want a lawyer."

"It's a little late for that," I said. "But you go ahead. Find yourself a lawyer." It sure as heck wasn't going to be me.

Florence moved into Bernie's embrace. "You were so brave to go after him like that."

Bernie beamed, looking like the proudest Santa on the planet. "To think the time together that we lost because of him." He hugged her close. "We'll be okay now, Florence. I promise."

Bud looked me over. "I have to take this guy in, and you're coming with me. Front seat. Right?"

"Yes." I gingerly stepped over spilled green water. I probably needed to make a statement for the record anyway.

In the background, the choir switched to *Winter Wonderland*.

* * *

I FINISHED WRAPPING all of my Christmas presents, wanting to keep my body in motion for as long as possible. As soon as I relaxed and tried to lie down, I'd stiffen up from my fall with evil Santa. I was working on the bar between my kitchen and the living room while Aiden finished working through case files on the table, still having taken it over.

My cousin had arrived earlier to get his dog, and I wondered if I should get a pet of my own.

It was after nine at night, and we'd had a nice dinner of takeout pizza with Aiden's team, whom I liked very much. They'd all left about an hour before, more than ready to work the next day, even though it was Sunday. I felt a kinship and warmth for this family Aiden had somehow put together while also pretending to be other people and being in danger the entire time.

"How are you feeling?" he asked, not looking up from his notes.

"Like I could use more ibuprofen," I admitted, reaching for the icepack for my face again. The new bruise was a deep purple, looking all the worse compared to the light yellow one on my other cheekbone. I was at least an hour away from being able to take any more medication.

He glanced up, studying my face. "I'm not taking very good care of you."

My grin felt lopsided because half of my face was frozen from the ice. "Not sure that's your job, Ace."

"That's where you're wrong," he said quietly. Then his gaze landed on my large stack of presents. "How do you keep everyone straight?"

I shrugged. "We usually just buy for our immediate family and have a drawing outside of that. Well, except for Lacey and Pauley —and friends. I don't know. I should make a list." Then I stared at him. "What about you?" The grandparents who'd taken him in while he was a teenager in Silverville had passed away. "Do you buy presents for your team?"

"No," he said. "Well, not really. Sometimes we give gag gifts, but we've been too busy the last few years."

"Do any of them have family?"

He nodded. "They all do—though nobody is married."

"What have you done for the holidays since you left Silverville?" I asked, feeling for him. With my huge family, I couldn't imagine not having anybody expecting me to be there during the holidays.

He shrugged. "Sometimes I've gone home with Saber to his family farm in Wyoming, and other times I've been with a girl-friend, or I've just worked. If I've been undercover at the time, I played whatever part I'd created."

"Sounds lonely," I murmured.

"Yeah." He looked at the colorful wrapping paper again. "I guess so, but I didn't realize it until now."

I rubbed my chest. "I signed your name to my presents," I blurted out.

He focused back on me. "Okay?"

I winced. "I didn't know if I should or not, or where we were right now, but since you're coming to the festivities, I figured you'd be covered?" Of course, with my family, that might be a declaration of something that wasn't happening with us. Yet. If ever. "I don't know. Was that a mistake?"

"No," he said, stacking the case files. "But should I pay you for half or something?"

"No," I hastened to say. This was awkward. Was it? Yeah, defi-nitely. I might've overstepped, or maybe we should have that talk, but Jareth Davey was over our shoulders right now, and I couldn't get my feet beneath me. My head and back hurt, and the ibuprofen had worn off, and I didn't want to deal with emotions right now. Plus, if I was honest with myself, I didn't know what I wanted to say yet. I sighed.

Aiden sat back and stretched, not releasing my gaze. "I'm not very good at this."

I perked up. He was taking it seriously. "At what?"

"This." He gestured to the Christmas tree and then the presents. "Being completely in somebody else's life and having somebody in mine. Being included with a huge-ass family that is involved in everything." He held up a hand. "I'm not complaining, but I am saying that it's all new, and I don't know what I'm doing." At the end, he sounded thoughtful—and surprised.

It figured Aiden usually knew what he was doing. In fact, so far, it seemed like he was doing just fine with my family. "I know they can be overwhelming, and you've handled it all perfectly," I admitted, realizing the truth of the statement. I'd seen more than one prospective suitor run for the hills after meeting my family. In fact, I wasn't entirely sure that wasn't the reason that Rory's love had dumped him. "I don't know what I'm doing, either." Sure, I'd dated before and even brought men home to meet the family, but never anybody like Aiden.

There was nobody like Aiden.

He stood. "Let's get some sleep. Tomorrow we'll meet with the team and come up with a game plan to take out Jareth Davey."

I loved that idea. We both got ready for bed, and I gingerly stretched out, wincing as my hips ached.

"You okay?" Aiden asked sleepily.

"Yeah." Thank goodness for cotton batting.

His breathing evened out and soothed me, but I couldn't sleep. My back hurt a little, and my face hurt a lot, and there was too much going through my mind to really relax. Finally, my eyelids started to close, and my body began to relax into the warmth created by him.

The first explosion had me jumping right out of the bed.

CHAPTER 38

I staggered on my feet, shoving my hair out of my face and nearly doubling over as pain slashed through my back from my earlier fall.

Aiden leaped from the bed, drawing his gun from the bed table, his phone already in his other hand. "What's going on?"

"I don't know." I yanked my weapon from my nightstand and followed him into the living room, where smoke was already billowing toward the kitchen. It looked like the front door had been blown open, and the sofa was already engulfed in flames.

An alarm blared high and loud, piercing the sound of the fire.

He grasped my arm and drew me back into the bedroom, locking the door. "Get dressed. Now."

As I hustled to draw on jeans, a sweatshirt and boots, he called in the explosion and then called his team. Afterward, he drew on jeans and his boots, his face set in brutal concentration.

The smoke puffed beneath my door and I coughed, heading toward him. The smoke burned my eyes and they teared.

"We can't wait for backup. We have to go out the sliding glass door now. Stay behind me." He nudged open the door and looked outside, both ways, before stepping onto the snowy deck.

I followed, my gun at the ready, my heart thundering so hard my teeth rattled.

He moved swiftly and gracefully, positioning his body between me and any threat. "Keep with me," he grit out. "Side of deck and then to the trees. We'll evaluate from there."

I nodded, looking out at the darkened lake, illuminated by a high moon that peaked through the clouds as they lazily dropped snow. I blinked flakes out of my eyes and edged along with him, reaching the end of the deck and the stairs. The wind blew like frigid blades against my exposed skin, and my eyes chilled.

He strode down, his gun sweeping the area.

I followed quickly, keeping to the house and then measuring the distance between the cottage and the forest.

Aiden didn't move. The moon glistened across the sparkling fresh snow, lighting the area with an ethereal glow, even though lower clouds still managed to drop snow. "We're too exposed. Keep to the cabin and the far side of the garage. Follow me."

Gulping, I nodded, the cold seeping into my bones and already aching muscles. My legs shook, but I followed him to the edge of the house. Smoke curled into the sky and fire crackled eerily. Something crashed. We moved along the garage to the front, and Aiden paused, leaning around the side to look at the driveway.

Gunfire erupted around us, pinging up snow and ice.

He pivoted and took me down to the ground, his body unforgiving muscle over me. Ice smushed up my back and the wind blew right out of my lungs. My ears rang and my body pulsed in renewed pain. "Stay down." He lifted up to a crouch, turned, and fired toward the nearest spruce trees. Snow crashed down from the boughs. A man yelled and then turned, becoming visible as he started to run toward the road. "Stay here," Aiden said, jumping up and running after the guy, firing rapidly.

The guy jerked and fell to the snow, his legs kicking up.

Aiden hit the area between the driveway and the trees, and

suddenly, everything around him exploded. He flew through the air and smashed into a tree, falling and hitting the ground hard.

"Aiden!" I screamed, leaping up and running toward him as fast as I could.

Somebody tackled me from behind and took me down. Snow blew up all around us. I landed hard, and my chin bounced off the ice beneath the snow. My gun spun out of my hand and I scrambled for it, coughing and trying to concentrate, my nails scraping the frozen ground.

The attacker flipped me around, straddling me.

I punched up as hard as I could, trying to find purchase with my boots to roll him off of me. His entire head was covered by a ski mask, and I fought him, my feet sliding on the ice and my head ringing. He tried to punch down, and I blocked by crossing my arms and taking the blow, my body shaking with the impact. I screamed and clawed for his face beneath the mask.

Ice and snow rippled up my back and my hips protested, but I didn't stop.

He tried to punch again, and I blocked, only slowing his hit this time. The impact smashed into my injured cheek, and my vision blurred. Pain flashed behind my eyes and deep into my skull.

I punched him back, hitting him in the neck.

He hit me again, and the blackness took me completely under.

My last thought was of Aiden.

Then time became blurry and dark. I came in and out of consciousness, trying to hold on but losing to the darkness every time. The floor beneath me was hard like wood, and I rolled back and forth, my body protesting. Finally, the hum of an engine caught my attention right before it was silenced.

I sat up to find myself in the back of a van. My vision was cloudy so I blinked several times, trying to see. Bile rose in my throat, and I swallowed rapidly, burning my throat on the way down to my stomach. The two outside doors opened, and the

283

man, his features still covered by a ski mask, reached in and grabbed my arm, yanking me into the stormy night.

I slid and stumbled outside, my boots sinking into the snow.

Confusion blanketed me, but the cold shot right into my ears and mouth, jerking me wide awake.

He dragged me through the snow to a log cabin set in front of the lake. I blinked several times, taking notice. We were on the southern side of Lilac Lake, not far from home. Maybe twenty minutes. He pulled me up the stairs and pushed me through the front door. I moved away from the door as warmth from an already lit fire heated the place.

I shook my head, trying to concentrate. It was freezing outside, and I needed to get the keys to the van. Or I had to take care of this guy and stay in the cabin. Even so, I slowly turned to face him, my body chilled and my muscles not working very well.

He shut the door and turned to lean back against it.

The cabin was small with a bed against the far wall, a kitchenette to the east wall, and a living area in front of a fireplace. That was it. No bathroom. The only way out was the door he was currently blocking—or maybe through the small window over the kitchen sink.

"Well?" I asked, my voice shaking.

He drew off the ski mask.

My knees wobbled but I lifted my chin. "Hi, Jareth. I've been waiting for you."

* * *

JARETH DAVEY LOOKED at me while I stared right back at him. The years hadn't been good to him. His nose was even bigger than it had been before, his skin an ugly red, and his hair thin. Very thin. But he'd been working out, and it showed in the muscles beneath his black sweater. His skin sagged at the jaw and wrinkles cut lines to the side of his narrow lips. Even so, he wasn't as big as I remembered. "You've been some trouble," he said.

His voice shot through me with a jolt of painful memory. It was the voice I still heard in my nightmares.

I shook out my hands, trying to get feeling into them. My fingers were chilled, and my nails broken from my clawing the ground. Firing nerves erupted through my extremities, and I welcomed the pain, needing to be able to move. "Why now?"

He wiped snow off his face and scalp. "I saw pictures of you dating people in the paper, and I figured you were old enough to have children now. I want children." A dresser had been placed near the door, and he opened the top drawer to toss in his ski mask.

"No," I said. "Any other questions?" My hands were almost at full feeling, but my feet weren't quite there yet.

He sighed. "You have always been such a problem for me."

"I get that a lot." I scrunched my toes in my boots to force blood back into them. "Where have you been all these years?" I had to keep him talking, but the terror racing through me wanted to run right out the door. I'd have to make it past him to the door, and then where would I run? There was a blizzard outside. "Jareth?"

He smiled, showing crooked teeth. "All over. I had to leave town, and then I just worked and lived my life, sending you cards until you were old enough to take again. I was wrong the first time. You were way too young. Everything was supposed to work out this way." His eyes were a deeper brown than I remembered, but the insane light was still there. Bright and glowing. "This is fate."

I exhaled slowly, taking control of my body and centering my breath. "Have you been following Aiden all these years?" Oddly enough, a couple of the cards from Jareth had come from places Aiden had been undercover. Not during the same timeframe, though.

"No. Didn't find him until I came home last summer, and then I was on his trail." Jareth preened, apparently wanting to show off. "Almost got the big bad agent killed, didn't I? Guess I'll have to try again. Once we're settled."

The moment was almost surreal. For so many years, I knew this was coming. Yet now that it was here, that he was in front of me, I was numb. My brain felt foggy. I shook my head to clear it, scattering snow across the uneven wooden floor. "Who helped you tonight? The guy that Aiden shot—who was that?"

Jareth shrugged. "Just a guy I hired out of Spokane. Didn't think I'd get him shot, but oh well. He needed a job and I needed somebody to help, and it's fate again. It's always fate. How can you not know that by now?"

I set my stance. It was now or never.

He drew a gun out of the top drawer and pointed it at me. It was a Colt .38, and I only knew that because I'd seen one on a television show. It was a small revolver, and the hammer was already cocked.

I looked at the gun. "Mine's bigger." I wished it wasn't buried in the snow at my cottage. Right now, I couldn't think about Aiden, although my brain kept going to the sight of him unconscious in the freezing snow. I pushed the thought away and concentrated on right now. "What's your plan here?" I subtly took a step toward him. If I tried for the window, he'd shoot me. There was only one way out of this.

"Take off your clothes."

"No." I took another step.

His face flushed and he huffed out air. "You are not listening to me." Shaking the gun, he stomped toward me, and he pointed the barrel between my eyes. "We have to do this. Now."

I couldn't breathe. Then he was in my space. Full on, the barrel just inches away. I let instinct take over.

My body dropped, hunched, and I ducked beneath the gun and smashed my head into his stomach. We crashed to the floor, and I swept out, knocking the weapon out of his hand. I punched him in the groin.

Then I slid toward the gun, kicking his hands as they clutched onto my jeans over my ankles, and grabbed it.

Crying, spitting, coughing, I scrambled back, pointing the gun at his head.

He sat up to kneel, tears flowing from his face, his hand over his balls.

I slowly stood, my hands shaking on the gun.

He looked up, his eyes vacant. "Do it. Just get it done."

CHAPTER 39

*E*verything inside me stilled and then went rock solid cold. My hands stopped shaking. For most of my life, I'd imagined what would happen in this exact situation. In every scenario, I shot him in the head.

Every. Single. One.

Nobody would blame me. He'd kidnapped me and terrorized me, and he deserved to die.

He smiled, showing one longer canine. "You can't do it. We both know you can't."

"I can," I said softly, widening my stance. "Oh, I definitely can." It was shocking I hadn't pulled the trigger yet.

He wiped snot off his face with his sleeve. "We belong together." His chin lowered. "How can you treat me like this? I wooed you. I left you gifts."

I gagged. "The flowers and the heart on my garage?"

"Yes." He sniffed loudly. "I was trying to ease you into this. Why can't you see that?"

"What about Crackle?" I asked, my voice trembling.

Jareth's eyes blazed. "He hurt you. I was following you and I saw what happened. He deserved to die. I even wrapped him for you."

My stomach lurched. This guy was nuts. "You need help."

He extended both hands to me. "No matter what, I'll never give up. I have friends, more than you know, and they'll help me."

I doubted that. "Bull," I muttered. "You don't have friends. You're not capable of it."

"Maybe not, but I have money and will hire myself some friends like I did tonight." He smiled. "You and I are meant to be. I'll come for you. No matter how old we are, you'll never be free of me."

One little squeeze. That's all it'd take on the trigger. One small squeeze and he'd be out of my life forever. I promised Aiden if I pointed a gun, I'd use it. I'd prepared for this my entire life.

Jareth lifted one knee and planted his foot on the wood. "You can't do it."

I swallowed, serene in the moment. "I can. You deserve to die. To be gone." Yet I didn't pull the trigger. "I don't deserve this. I don't deserve to have your blood staining my soul." If I didn't have to live with that, I wouldn't. "You don't get to win. Not in this." I kept the aim at his head and angled to the side, toward the door. "Give me the keys."

"I'll never stop," he said.

"You'll never win," I promised. "Now. Keys."

He reached in his back pocket. "Fine." Then he drew out the keys and threw them at me.

I backed up, trying to catch them.

He leaped toward me far faster than I would've expected, tackling me into the dresser by the door. Something popped in my shoulder, and I cried out, falling. The pain stole my breath. He elbowed me in the face, and I tried to swing the gun around, but my arm wouldn't move.

He yanked it out of my hand and head butted me.

Lights flashed behind my eyes. I dodged forward, my only

option to tackle him. We went down in a flurry of arms and legs, grunting and struggling to hurt each other. I landed on him and drove my chin into his mouth, splitting both his lips. He screamed and blood burst across my face.

The barrel of the gun pressed against the back of my hip, and I swung out to hit it away.

He grabbed my good arm with his free hand and squeezed.

I lifted a knee and smashed it into his groin, frantically trying to get away from the gun. Cold metal pressed against my side. He howled, trying to get away from my knee. I went on pure animalistic instinct, dropping my chin to his nose as hard as I could. A pop echoed and pain rippled through my head. He yowled and moved, his arm around me and his hand pressing the weapon to the back of my waist. My torso was smashed against his and I needed to get free.

The sound of the gun firing blew through the night. He'd pulled the trigger?

I stiffened.

Pain detonated in my abdomen. I cried out, my body short circuiting. Grasping for my stomach, I rolled off him and kept going until I hit the dresser. Then I shifted up so I could sit, my stomach on fire, my head ringing.

Blood covered his torso. He remained on his back, his eyes wide, his face stark white. His hand, still holding the gun, dropped to the floor. Blood gurgled out of his mouth. Taking one last wheezing breath, he went limp. His pupils dilated. Then the light, the small amount of light, wisped out of those eyes.

I panted, my hand pressed to my side. What had just happened? He'd shot me in the back, but the bullet had gone through me? His entire torso was covered in blood, so I couldn't tell where the bullet had entered. But it had definitely hit his heart.

Groaning, I planted a bloody hand on the dresser and tried to stand.

The door burst open and Aiden rushed in, followed by Saber. The window over the kitchen counter shattered, and Chelli rolled inside. She was on Aiden's team and apparently came in the smaller entrances.

Dazed, I slipped back to a seated position.

Aiden rushed for me, dropping to his knees. Blood flowed down his face from a cut above his eye, and bruises were already forming along his temple and down the side of his face. "How bad?" He grasped my sweatshirt and lifted it.

"Dunno." I was going nicely numb, and I wasn't fighting it. "He's dead. Shot us both." My voice sounded like it came from far away. Very far away.

He grasped my arms. "Angel? Hang in there. Just hold on. An ambulance is coming." Then he pressed a hand against my side, and agony ripped through my entire body. I futilely tried to slap at his hand, but he didn't move. The pain was too much. The smell of coppery blood filled my nostrils, and the room spun around me.

This time, I didn't fight the pull of unconsciousness.

* * *

I CAME to laying in a hospital bed with Santa at my side, stitching up Aiden's face. "Santa?" I whispered.

Doc Springfield looked over his shoulder. "You're awake." He pressed a bandage over Aiden's eyebrow and handed the tray off to a young nurse before moving toward me. While he wore a red shirt beneath his white lab coat, he wasn't in his Santa uniform. "How are you feeling?"

"Great," I said, the room all fuzzy and sparkly.

"That's the morphine." He checked my pupils with a bright light. "You're looking better."

I blinked as the night came back to me. "What time is it?"

"Around nine in the morning. You had a calm night. Well, after you were brought into the hospital."

Morning? Already? I tried to concentrate and remember the night before. "I was shot?"

"Yeah. The bullet scraped your side," the doctor said. "You needed fifteen stitches, but there was no other damage from the bullet. You do have a dislocated shoulder that is now back in place but will be sore, and I'm fairly certain you have a concussion." He patted my good shoulder and walked out of the room, his Santa boots squeaking on the sparkling clean floor.

Aiden pushed his chair closer and flopped back down. "How are you?"

"I like morphine," I said, looking him over. "How are you? You got blown up."

"Just bruised with no internal damage." He took my hand, his feeling warm and solid around mine. "I didn't expect him to make a move until Christmas, and I really didn't expect him to hire an accomplice or set explosions."

I gulped and searched for the terror inside me, but all I found were warm fuzzies from the morphine. "Me either," I slurred. "What happened to his accomplice? I think I remember you shooting him?" The night was a bit of a blur.

"Yeah. That's how I found out about Jareth's cabin around the lake. I called my team and then I had a nice talk with him to get the exact location," Aiden said grimly.

I winced. "Did he live afterward?"

"Yes. He made it through surgery and will be fine to give a formal statement, tell us everything in greater detail, and then go to prison." Aiden's jaw hardened.

I lifted my arm, and it fell flat back onto the bed. "I had Jareth in my sights and didn't pull the trigger." Might as well confess all.

"Okay." Aiden's neck was mottled with a purple bruise.

"He got the gun back, we struggled, and he actually fired," I murmured.

Aiden didn't twitch, but his eyes darkened to a just-after-midnight color. "He could've killed you."

"He killed himself instead," I said softly.

Detective Pierce rounded the corner, his hair ruffled and his clothing wrinkled. "Doc said you were awake."

"Yep," I said, glad I wasn't feeling much at the moment. "Here's what happened." I gave him the entire night from my perspective, not leaving anything out. By the end, he was staring at me, and Aiden was too still. I sighed. "I'm sorry. I just couldn't, or rather *didn't* want to kill him in cold blood." There was a reason people said if you aimed a gun, you should be prepared to fire that gun. But I hadn't done it. This time, anyway.

Pierce snapped his notebook closed. "That's all I need for now. The press is in the waiting area, and I gave orders for hospital security to keep them, or rather her, out of your way."

I smiled my thanks. "Do you have plans for the holidays?"

"I'm headed out tomorrow to see my sister and her family," Pierce said. "You take it easy until I get back." He shook Aiden's hand and then disappeared from view.

I smiled at Aiden. "Let's have that talk now that we've been avoiding." The morphine made me brave, and if it dulled the pain, then why not?

Violet ran into the room, panic on her face. "Are you okay? Tell me you're okay." She clutched the other side of the bed from Aiden, her eyes wide.

"I'm fine," I said.

Aunt Yara followed at a more leisurely pace. "Doc Springfield said you're going to be all right." She looked slightly calmer than Violet but her gaze still raked me head to toe.

I nodded. "What are you two doing?"

"We were driving in from Silverville to get breakfast and then do some Christmas shopping." Violet patted my good shoulder awkwardly. "The family text came through the line that you'd been shot, so we came right here instead."

"Family text?" Aiden asked, eyeing the door.

Yara patted his arm. "Too late. We saw cars arriving. You're stuck."

He leaned back and shut his eyes. His sigh was long-suffering. But he didn't let go of my hand. I took comfort in that, although I was holding his pretty tightly.

I grinned. "So, Violet. You settling in okay?"

She all but hopped in place. "Yes! In fact, I drew your name in the family lottery." She leaned in and smoothed my hair off my face. "To be honest, there was some shuffling around since I just joined the family, and I requested you during the trading process. I hope that's okay." Her brow wrinkled.

"That's great," I said, meaning it. "Seeing you happy and safe is the best gift ever."

Donna barreled through the doorway with Tessa on her heels.

I waved to my sisters. "Hey. I'm on morphine."

"Can I have some?" Aiden asked.

I chuckled. He might be a badass of a hottie, but he was funny, too.

CHAPTER 40

he manufactured Christmas tree had burned edges on every bough, and several of my ornaments were singed, but it still looked cheerful with the new sparkling lights in the corner of Aiden's cabin. He'd salvaged it for me, as much as possible, when he'd brought me to his home after I was discharged from the hospital.

It had been almost a week, and we'd moved in my furniture that had survived the explosion. The fire had taken out most of the living room and kitchen, but my piano and bedroom had been spared, as had my jewelry and the photographs in my bedroom. It looked like the owners of the estate weren't going to rebuild any time soon, and I kind of figured they wanted me out of there.

Trouble did seem to follow me.

I sighed, sitting on a thick rug by the tree. My shoulder ached but didn't require a sling, so I kept careful not to bump it.

Aiden didn't have any other living room furniture yet, so there wasn't another place to sit. I didn't mind. The tree was lovely, even if a little damaged. Kind of like all of us, really.

He finished in the kitchen and brought out two steaming mugs of Tom and Jerry's, and I hoped he'd spiked mine big time. "Merry

Christmas, Angel," he said, looking even tougher than usual with the bandage and bruises on his face. Even in his dark sweats and T-shirt, he seemed something more.

"Merry Christmas." I accepted the mug and took a deep drink, wondering about the present I had next to me. I'd just put it in a gift bag, and maybe I should've bought him a shirt instead. Or given him one of the many presents I'd purchased and then decided to give to somebody else. "Thank you for letting me stay and for housing my furniture for now. Well, the stuff that survived the fire, anyway." I should probably start looking for an apartment but would miss my view of the lake.

I could always visit Aiden and see his. He'd bought the sprawling cabin to fix up, and maybe I could help a little bit.

He sat on the rug next to me. "How much time do we have?"

I jolted and then realized he meant for the day. "We don't have to be at my parent's house until three." Then I patted his thigh. "You did a great job at the Albertini Christmas party and the O'Shea dinner last night for Christmas Eve. We just have dinner with my folks and sisters tonight, although it seems the whole family shows up again around dessert time." It was only fair to warn him.

"I've had fun," he said, sipping his drink. "It was cool to see Sean's reaction to the gift from Clark, and it was nice of him to call. What did Clark get you, anyway?"

"A stun gun," I said, grinning. "It's in my desk drawer at work."

Aiden smiled. "Smart guy." He drank more of the sweet concoction. "It was kind of you to invite Thelma and Georgiana to the dinners, although I'm not sure they weren't kidding about including your Nonna Albertini in their new detective agency."

Amusement tinged with fear bubbled through me, but my chuckle pulled the stitches in my side. "Let's worry about that another day."

"Fair enough," he agreed.

"Florence called earlier, and she and Bernie are getting remarried," I murmured. "She's still mad at Hoyt for not letting her go to the funeral, although I'm not sure she would've gone, so I don't know what she'll do with all that money."

Aiden shrugged. "I'm sure she'll find something good to do with it."

I nodded, my throat suddenly dry. "So. I guess, hmm." I handed him the bag. "Merry Christmas."

His smile was sweet. One I'd rarely seen on him. He set his mug aside and took the bag, opening it and drawing out the jewelry box. His eyebrows rose. "Interesting."

"I wasn't sure what to get you, and this just felt right," I said in a rush.

He drew out the box and then opened it to look. Realization dawned across his chiseled face as he pulled out the necklace. "Is this..."

"Yeah." I looked at the perfectly smooth river rock. "The day you saved me, I was skipping rocks with Lacey. That one was shaped just right, so I'd put it in my pocket to save for the championship toss. It was there when I was kidnapped, and it was there when I was safely home."

He looked at me, his eyes an unfathomable blue. "*Aingeal.*"

I swallowed. "I've kept it all these years for good luck. For a reminder that everyone has a hero, and you're mine." Duke had done a great job cutting a hole in the top of the dark green rock, and I'd chosen a strong black cord as the chain. "You can wear it during your undercover ops for good luck and to think of me. Maybe it'll keep you safe, too." My chest hurt it was so full.

He slid the necklace over his head, and the rock settled right over his heart. He planted a hand above it. "It's perfect. Thank you." His voice deepened, and that Irish brogue emerged full force.

Relief buzzed through me. He liked it. Good.

The sweet smile stayed on his angled face. "I have two presents for you."

Joy filtered through me. I freaking loved presents.

He reached under the tree and drew out one box, handing it over. "Here's the first."

I ripped the green wrapping paper off and opened a box to see a key. An old, weathered, scratched key. "This is, um, pretty?"

He laughed. "It's a key to this place—for now. I'm going to install a top of the line security system next week. I thought you might want to live here. I mean, with me."

My jaw almost dropped open, but I held my composure. Mostly. "You want to live together?"

"Yeah," he said. "What do you say?"

I bit my lip around a smile, happiness bursting through every nerve in my body. Living with Aiden? "I say yes." Then I looked around. Oh, the things I could do with this place.

He dug under the tree again and tugged out another box, this one with light pink wrapping paper. He handed it over.

I slowly took off the paper this time, wanting to savor the moment. The box was green felt, and I opened it to see a sparkling white-gold Claddagh ring, the two hands holding an intricate heart-shaped Celtic knot beneath a crown. The knot protected a stunning dark emerald. My part-Irish heart swelled and I gasped. "Aiden, it's beautiful."

He took the ring and slipped it onto my right ring finger with the bottom of the heart pointing up toward mine, showing I was taken.

Had I ever been this happy? I wasn't sure. I looked closer. "That emerald looks real. I mean, natural." It was darker than a man-made emerald, although you usually couldn't tell the difference.

"It is real." He bent to kiss the ring over my finger. "It's the closest I could come to your eye color with the green and gray. Sometimes, in the moonlight, this is exactly the color of your eyes."

Tears gathered in my eyes. "Aiden," I whispered, overcome. "Thank you."

He lifted his head and gently tugged me onto his lap, careful of all my hurts, his other hand over the necklace I'd given him. "Guess we're going to give this thing a real shot, huh?"

I turned and kissed him, pouring everything into it. Whether we were ready for this or not, it was here. "Yeah, a real shot, just you and me," I whispered against his mouth, finally feeling settled.

He grinned, his lips perfect against mine. "Merry Christmas, Angel."

HOLIDAY ROGUE

GET A LITTLE HOLIDAY ROMANCE NOW!

When the Albertini men fall...they fall fast and hard. Buy Bosco's romance, Holiday Rogue, wherever books are sold!

Danger and Mistletoe are a Deadly Combination

Bosco Albertini learned the hard way that focusing on his career is a lot safer than investing in love. So when he meets his sweet new neighbor, he puts her firmly in the friend zone, despite her soft hazel eyes, sharp wit, and tempting curves. It soon becomes difficult to keep her there because his brothers, his Nonna, and even his dog already adore her—and he's not far behind.

Marlie Kreuk accepts the friend zone from the too sexy soldier because, hey, when a guy puts you there, he's a moron who doesn't deserve more. But when danger comes for her and Bosco risks his spectacular body to protect her, she can't help but wish for romance. Although, he's going to have to work for it.

With danger all around, Bosco and Marlie must face their explosive attraction while defeating deadly attackers, but even that is nothing compared to handling the Albertini matchmakers during the Christmas season. Busting out of that friend zone and surviving will take all of Bosco's training, Marlie's courage, and the magic of the holidays.

Buy Bosco's romance, Holiday Rogue, wherever books are sold!

WOLF

A NEW PARANORMAL SERIES!

Read the First Chapter of Wolf.

A predator stared back at her.

Mia Stone set her face into calm lines, her hand inching toward where her weapon used to sit on her hip. Only a leather belt existed there now. She shook off the unease. Jail Bars. Many bars, evenly spaced, stood between her and the man currently meeting her gaze without expression.

She'd faced evil, she'd faced good people who'd committed evil...yet she'd never really faced someone who had no expression. She swallowed.

His gaze dropped to her throat.

An odd quiver wandered down her spine. What in the world was wrong with her? Maybe she'd been out of the game too long. Focusing, she did her job and studied him.

Near the end of a cot, he lounged against the far wall of the cell. Most prisoners automatically sat when waiting time in jail. Not this guy. He had to be, what, early thirties? At least six and half feet tall, he leaned his shoulders against the worn brick. His black hair showed possible Native American heritage, as did his

sharp features. Though his eyes were a mixture of different blues
—light to dark.

A scar ran along the right side of his jaw to disappear in thick
hair that almost reached his shoulders. Too rough to be called
handsome, there was no doubt he was compelling.

Many killers were.

Mia cut her eyes to the quilt. Pink and homemade, the bed
cover belonged in a jail cell as much as the diamond earrings she
wore belonged in the small-town sheriff's office. But she'd
promised her mother, and there wasn't time for a fight before
driving to the middle of nowhere. So she'd left her hair down to
camouflage the sparkle.

She steeled her shoulders and stepped up to the bars. "Mr.
Volk, my name is Mia."

Upon arriving at the station, she'd asked to talk to the prisoner
alone and had promised to stay in the hall. The sheriff had shut
the door separating the main office from the two cells while
shaking his head. Seeing the man in the cell, gratitude filled her
that she hadn't pushed to go inside with Volk.

She tried to appear in control. "I was hoping we could talk."

Slowly, one dark eyebrows rose. "You're a cop."

"No, I'm not." She kept her face in pleasant lines, showing
honesty.

"You reached for your weapon," he said softly.

Surprise had her stilling. "Yes. I used to be a cop. FBI actually."

Volk straightened. "That makes you sad." Intense, he studied
her.

The breath caught in her throat. She forced herself to exhale
easily. This wasn't the first subject who'd tried to get in her head.
"Are you sad, Mr. Volk?"

"My father is Mr. Volk." Two long strides and he stood much
closer on the other side of the bars. The scent of wild sage came
with him. "Call me Seth."

Courage had her lifting her chin and refusing to retreat. He

304

could easily reach through and grab her. The last time she'd messed with a psychopath, she'd lost. "Seth."

He cocked his head to the side. Slowly. "I like how you say my name."

A warning trilled in the back of her mind. "So you'll talk to me?"

"I am talking to you." Low, rough, his voice wrapped around the silence.

"Thank you." She'd learned early on that respect went a long way with killers and sociopaths. "I'm not a cop, but they've asked me to speak with you. If you're okay with that, we can talk."

His upper lip quirked, making him approachable. Almost. "I want to talk to you."

She frowned. "Why?"

"Your voice is pretty." He rubbed the stubble on his chin. "Kind of like Ingrid Bergman's in Casablanca. Soft and classy with a hint of sass."

Warmth messed with caution in her chest. Bogie embodied everything she'd ever wanted in a man. Plus, that was her favorite movie.

"But your eyes are sad. Haunted." Seth gripped the bars with large hands. "Who hurt you, Mia?"

She jerked her head to the side. Instinct told her to run. "I'm asking the questions."

His expression went blank again. "You said you wanted to talk. Talking goes both ways."

This was no stupid country hick. She stared deeper into his eyes, seeing intelligence and...what simmered in those dark depths? An emotion deep down. Anger. The guy was pissed. "Do you have a temper, Seth?"

"Yes." His knuckles whitened on the steel. "Did somebody hurt you?"

"Yes." She kept her arms loose at her sides, just in case he reached for her. "Do you harm women?"

"No." His jaw firmed. "Is the person who hurt you still alive?"

"No." She shoved emotion into a box. "Did you kill Ruby Redbird?"

"No. Why did you just lie to me?"

"I didn't."

Exhaling, he released the bars and turned his broad back to her. "Yes, you did." Faded jeans covered a hard butt and led up to a dark T-shirt. Those shoulders spread wider than a linebacker wearing pads. The flak boots on his feet were probably size fourteen, yet he moved with masculine grace. "You can go now."

Panic threatened to cut off her air. She needed to prove she could still do the job. "I shot and killed the man who wanted to hurt me." When had she lost control of the conversation?

"And?"

Seth should've been the profiler. "I believe that man had a partner. If so, he's still alive." She could do this. Reveal past pain to get to the truth.

Seth turned around. "I'm sorry."

"Doesn't matter—and most people think I'm wrong." The world centered again. "If you didn't kill Ruby, who did?"

"I don't know. But I will find out."

Now he was lying. She didn't know how she knew that fact, but she did. What she didn't know was *the lie*. Had he killed Ruby — or was he protecting the person who did? "I thought you disliked lying. That goes both ways, too."

His eyes darkened while his gaze traced every contour of her face. Nerves sprang to life as if his fingers caressed her skin.

She stepped even closer to the bars. "Have you killed before?"

"Yes." Thick boots clanked against metal as he took the final step toward her. Warmth from his massive body brushed her silk shirt. Only metal bars separated them...no air. "Besides the man you just mentioned, have you killed before?"

Her head jerked back. "No."

"Now who's lying?" he asked softly, curiosity and an odd gentleness curving his bottom lip.

She blinked twice. Something about his voice was mesmerizing. A killer who hinted at safety right before killing. His mouth caught her attention. Full, sexy, male. "I will find out who killed Ruby."

The moment stretched until her heartbeat echoed in her head.

"Mia. Step away from the cell." Seth took a large stride back from the bars.

Keys rattled outside the exit door.

Startled, Mia shuffled across the rough concrete until her shoulders rested against worn brick on the opposite wall. There was no logical reason she obeyed his command.

Yet there she stood.

His gaze remained on her, dark and thoughtful, as the door opened.

Then a metamorphosis occurred. His expression went blank with boredom and a fierce insolence. He glanced at the two men striding toward them.

"Sheriff, you'd better have a decent reason for arresting Seth this time." A tall man in sleek gray Armani led the way, his hair a perfect salt and pepper, his skin bronze from sun obviously enjoyed away from Washington state.

The sheriff sighed. His hair was *more* salt than pepper, and grooves cut lines into the sides of his mouth. During the last year, apparently he'd spent some time at the local diner if the strain on his brown uniform gave any indication. "Your client is a killer," he said shortly.

"That's slander," the tall guy said. He stopped in front of Mia. "Who the hell are you?"

Seth stepped toward the bars.

Mia had the strangest urge to waive Seth back. She focused on the man and held out her hand. "Mia Stone."

The man took her hand, gripping tightly as they shook.

"Phillip Lenessee, Mr. Volk's attorney. I do hope you didn't question my client outside of my presence, Detective Stone."

Mia slid her cop face into place, biting back a wince at the hard pressure. This wasn't the first asshole lawyer she'd dealt with. "I'm not a cop."

Lenessee released her. "If the police invited you here, then you're an agent of the police, so you're as good as a cop."

Yet she wasn't. She might not ever be a cop again. Any case. Instead of wallowing, she allowed a slightly pissed off smile to curve her lips with the unintimidating pink lipstick she'd chosen. "I've shaken a lot of men's hands, Mr. Lenessee. The ones with obvious insecurities," she dropped her gaze to the pressed pants and then traveled up to his face, "always grip too hard."

Surprise opened his mouth, which he quickly snapped shut.

Her smirk widened just enough to let him know she saw the surprise. "*You* grip too hard."

In her peripheral vision, she caught a flash of Seth's grin.

The sheriff chortled, not even trying to hide his amusement.

Yeah. No doubt the lawyer thought she'd shake off the purposeful show of strength. She hadn't been the best profiler in DC for nothing...well, until they determined she'd grown crazier than the bastards she hunted. Throwing an attorney off track was half the fun of her former job.

He leaned over her in an obvious intimidation tactic. "Perhaps you're too soft to play with the big boys."

Seth hissed out a breath. "Lenessee, get me the hell out of here." His voice rumbled low with threat and anger.

The attorney straightened to stare at Seth. "Of course. Your bail has been paid, Mr. Volk." No deference, no affection, no respect hinted in the lawyer's tone. If anything, he seemed indifferent to the point of condescension.

The sheriff exhaled loudly and unlocked the door, sliding it open.

Seth stepped out.

Lenessee stepped back.

Interesting.

Mia glanced from Seth to the lawyer. The attorney was on guard. Just how dangerous was Seth that his own lawyer feared him?

He brushed by the attorney, heading down the hallway without another word.

Lenessee turned to the sheriff. "You had no basis to arrest him, and you know it. You might want to contact the county attorneys, because there will be a civil rights violation filed by the end of the day."

"No there won't." Seth's low voice rumbled back before he shoved open the exit door and disappeared.

Lenessee inhaled, both nostrils flaring. Pivoting on Italian loafers, he strode after his client.

The sheriff raised an eyebrow. "Well?"

Mia shrugged. "I don't know. But I want to find out." Turning, she hustled away from the cells, through the small interior of the police station, and to the waiting room.

The room held several worn leather chairs around a large coffee table displaying magazines about hunting, farming, and football. A wide wall of windows looked out onto a deserted Main street.

Mia skirted the table and glanced out the window.

Seth and his attorney spoke on the sidewalk, the lawyer keeping his distance. Well, the lawyer talked, while Seth glanced around the quiet street. He stood next to a 'no parking' sign, his head nearly as tall as the sign.

His shoulders straightened, and he shifted his attention to her.

Finally, the lawyer wound down, turned on his heel, and headed for a Cadillac parked across the street.

Seth cocked his head to the side, his expression full of dare.

Mia shoved open the glass door. She should get a weapons permit if she continued to work in the state—not that she hadn't already stuck a small Glock in her ankle holster. Several steps across a rough sidewalk had her close enough to smell wild sage. Her shoulders went back.

"You're very pretty, Mia."

Not what she'd expected. She frowned. "Who killed Ruby Redbird?"

Seth slowly shook his head, wrapping a hand around her bicep. "That's a mystery you're no longer involved in." His grip was warm and unbelievably strong.

He moved into a stride.

She tried to yank free.

His hold slid smoothly to the back of her elbow, effectively putting her in a position where she had to move, much like a parent with a wayward toddler. For the briefest of moments she felt vulnerable—like a civilian and not a trained law enforcement officer. Confusion had her biting back an expletive. They'd traveled half-way down the block before she dug in her heels and turned to face him.

She swallowed, angling her head. Up close he was even bigger than he'd seemed in the station. Heat cascaded off the man. "Stop manhandling me."

"Where's your car?" No expression sat on his harsh features.

She shook her head. "None of your business."

Sighing, he glanced toward the parking lot that served the entire block and pointed to her older Toyota. "That's the only one I don't recognize. You need to take your sweet butt over there and go home, wherever that might be."

Small chunks of concrete scattered when she settled her stance. "I'm trained, Volk."

His smile was instant and almost charming. "You're half my size, darlin'. And your training won't do you any good."

Something in his tone suggested she believe him. But she'd faced killers before, and she'd solved murders before. This was her one chance to get back into the life she'd loved. "I'm not going anywhere until you tell me the truth."

He released her. Almost in slow motion, he reached out to run a thumb along her cheekbone.

Shock kept her immobile.

With a sigh, he dropped his hand. "Please leave."

"No."

Those blue eyes darkened to almost black. "Leave or you'll be as dead as Ruby."

Mia retreated a step, her heart shooting into a gallop. "Is that a threat?"

"No." A veil dropped over his eyes. "That's a fact, Mia Stone."

You can get a copy of Wolf where all books are sold!

YOU CAN RUN

Read the First Chapter of the Laurel Snow Thriller, You Can Run!

Laurel Snow swiped through the calendar on her phone while waiting for the flight to DC to board. The worn airport chairs at LAX were as uncomfortable as ever, and she tried to keep her posture straight to prevent the inevitable backache.

Christmas music played through the speakers, and an oddly shaped tree took up a corner, its sad-looking branches decorated with what might've been strung popcorn. The upcoming week was already busy, and Laurel hoped there wouldn't be a new case. She stuck in her wireless earbuds to allow an upbeat rock playlist to pound through her ears as she rearranged a couple of meetings.

The phone dinged and she answered while continuing to organize the week. "Snow."

"Hi, Agent Snow. How did the symposium go?" asked her boss, George McCromby.

"As expected," she said, swiping a lunch meeting from Thursday to Friday. "I'm not a teacher, and half the time, the audience looked confused. A young woman in the front row had serious daddy issues, and a young man behind her was facing a nervous breakdown. Other than that, one guy in the last row exhibited narcissistic tendencies."

"For Pete's sake. We just wanted you to talk about the FBI and help with recruitment. You're a good face," George muttered.

Laurel tapped her phone when the Wi-Fi struggled. "My face has nothing to do with my job. I'm not skilled at recruitment or teaching."

George sighed. "How many people have you seen today who wore red shoes?"

Yeah, she should change the computer update meeting from Tuesday to Wednesday. "Six," she said absently. "Ten if you include maroon-colored shoes."

George laughed. "How many people in the last month have worn yellow hats around you?"

"Just eight," she said.

George warmed to the subject. "Right now, where you are in the airport and without looking, who's the biggest threat?"

If she changed one more meeting, she could fit in a manicure on Friday. "Guy waiting in the adjacent area for a plane to Dallas. He's five nine, wiry, and has cauliflower ears. Moves with grace." Yes. She could fit in a manicure. "Another man to the north by the magazine rack in the bookstore is built like a logger and could throw a decent punch." Would there be time for a pedicure? Probably not.

"Why aren't you the biggest threat?" George asked.

She paused. "Because I'm currently performing parlor tricks for the deputy director of the FBI." She looked up to check her boarding time.

"I have a call on the other line. We'll talk about this when you get back." George clicked off.

Laurel didn't have anything else to say on the matter. Her phone buzzed and she glanced at the screen before answering the call. "Hi, Mom. Yes, I'm still returning home for Christmas." It had been three years, and her mother's patience had ended. "I promise. In two weeks, I'll be there."

"Laurel, I need you now," Deidre said, her voice pitched high.

Laurel froze. "What's wrong?"

"It's your uncle Carl. The sheriff wants to arrest him for murder." Panic lifted Deidre's voice even higher. "You're in the FBI. They're saying he's a serial killer. You have to come help."

Uncle Carl was odd but not a killer. "Serial killer? How many bodies have been found?"

"I don't know," Deidre cried out.

Okay. Her mother never became this flustered. "Is the Seattle FBI involved?" Laurel asked.

"I don't know. The local sheriff is the one who's harassing Carl. Please come help. Please." Her mother never asked for anything.

Laurel would have to change flights—and ask for a favor. "I'll text you my flight information, and I can rent a car at Sea-Tac." Murderers existed everywhere but Uncle Carl wasn't one of them.

"No. I'll make sure you're picked up. Just text me what time you land." Her mother didn't drive or like to be inside vehicles.

"Okay. I have to run." Laurel clicked off and dialed George's private number with her left hand while reaching in her bag for a printout of her schedule. Being ambidextrous came in handy sometimes. Though she didn't have many friends at the FBI, for some reason, George had become a mentor and was usually patient. Sometimes. Plus, she had just closed a serial killer case in Texas, and she had some juice, as George would say. For now. In her experience, juice dried up quickly.

The phone rang several times before George picked up. "I said we'd talk about it in DC."

"I need a favor," Laurel said. Her gaze caught on a younger man escorting an elderly woman through the terminal, both looking up at the flight information boards. "I don't have much information, but it appears there are at least a few suspicious

315

deaths in Genesis Valley up in Washington State. I need to investi-
gate the situation." There was something off about the guy with
the older lady. He reached into the slouchy beige-colored purse
slung over the woman's shoulder and drew out a billfold, which
he slipped into his backpack.

"Wait a minute. I'll make a call and find out what's going on,"
George said.

"Thank you." Laurel stood and strode toward the couple,
reaching them quickly. "Is everything okay?"

The woman squinted up at her, cataracts visible in her cloudy
blue eyes. "Oh my. Yes, I think so. This kind young man is
showing me to my plane."

"Is that right?" Laurel tilted her head.

The man had to be in his early twenties with sharp brown eyes
and thick blond hair. His smile showed too many teeth. "Yes. I'm
Fred. Just helping Eleanor here out. She was a little lost."

Eleanor clutched a plane ticket in one gnarled hand. Her white
hair was tightly curled and her face powdered. "I was visiting my
sister in Burbank and got confused after security in the airport."

Irritation ticked down Laurel's neck. "Return her wallet to
her."

Eleanor gasped. "What?"

Fred shoved Eleanor and turned to run.

Laurel grabbed him by the backpack, kicked him in the
popliteal fossa, and dropped him to the floor on his butt, where he
fell flat. She set the square heel of her boot on the lateral femoral
cutaneous nerve in his upper thigh. "You know, Fred? There's a
nerve right here that can make a person . . . bark like a dog." She
pressed down.

Fred yelped.

An airport police officer ran up, his hand on his harnessed
weapon.

Laurel pulled her ID out of her jacket pocket and flipped it
open. "FBI. I think this guy has a few wallets that might not be

his." She shook out the backpack. Several billfolds, bottles of pills, and necklaces bounced off the tile floor.

"Hey." Eleanor leaned down and fetched her billfold and one container of pills. "You jerk." She swatted Fred with her purse.

He ducked and pushed the bag away. "Let me up, lady."

"Make him bark like a dog again," Eleanor burst out.

"Sure." Laurel pressed down on the nerve.

Fred groaned and pushed at her foot, pain wiping the color from his face. "Stop it."

The officer stuffed all of the contraband back in the bag and then pulled Fred to his feet once Laurel moved her boot. He quickly cuffed Fred. "Thanks for this. I've got it from here." They moved away.

Laurel reached for Eleanor's ticket. "Let's see where you're supposed to be." A quick glance at the ticket showed that the woman was going to Indiana. "Your flight is over here at gate twenty-one. Let me grab my belongings and I'll take you there." She retrieved her over-sized laptop bag and rolling carry-on before returning to slide her arm through Eleanor's. "The gate is just on the other side of those restaurants."

"Excuse me?" George barked through the earbuds "Assistant Director of the FBI here with information for you."

"Please hold on another minute, sir," Laurel said, twisting through the throng while keeping Eleanor safe.

Eleanor looked up, leaning on Laurel. "How do you know my gate number? You didn't even look at the information board."

"I looked at it earlier," Laurel said, helping the elderly woman avoid three young boys dragging Disney-themed carry-ons.

Eleanor blinked. "You memorized all of the flight information with one look?"

"I'm still here," George groused.

Laurel took Eleanor up to the counter, where a handsome man in his thirties typed into the computer. "This is Eleanor, and this is her plane. She's going to sit right over here, and she needs extra time to board." Without waiting for a reply, she helped Eleanor to the nearest seat. "Here you go. You should be boarding in just a few minutes."

Eleanor patted her hand. "You're a good girl."

Laurel crouched down. "Do you have anybody meeting you at the airport?"

Eleanor nodded. "Yes. My son is meeting me right outside baggage claim. Don't you worry." She pressed both gnarled hands against Laurel's face. "You're a special one, aren't you?"

"Damn it, Snow," George bellowed through the earbuds.

Laurel winced. "I am happy to help."

Eleanor tightened her grip. "You have such lovely eyes. How lucky are you!"

Lucky? Laurel had rarely felt lucky to have heterochromia. "You're very kind."

"You're beautiful. Such stunning colors and so distinct. I've never seen such a green light in anyone's eye, and your other eye is a beautiful dark shade of blue." Eleanor squinted and leaned in closer. "You have a little green flare in the blue eye, don't you?"

Laurel smiled and removed the woman's hands from her face, careful of the arthritic bumps on her knuckles. "Yes. I have a hete-rochromia in the middle of heterochromatic eyes. It's an adventure."

Eleanor laughed. "You're a pip, you are. God speed to you."

Laurel stood. "Have a nice trip, Eleanor." She turned to head back to her gate, her mind returning to her trip to Genesis Valley. She'd have to move all of her appointments in DC to the first week in January, so her brain automatically flipped dates. If she juggled a Monday meeting that week, she would have time for a pedicure. Maybe she could skip her Wednesday lunch with the forensic accountants to discuss the recently developed tactical reasoning software. The accountants rarely escaped the computer lab, and when they did, they always talked for too long. "Sorry about that, sir. What did you find out?"

George's sigh was long suffering. "Multiple body parts, including three skulls, were found this morning by kids four-wheeling on a mountain called . . ." Papers rustled. "Snowblood Peak."

Laurel switched directions, her heart rate kicking up. "Just this morning? It's a little early to be narrowing in on a suspect." She'd spent some time snowmobiling that mountain as a child with her uncles before leaving for college at the age of eleven. "Could be an old graveyard or something like that. Might not be a case."

"I know, and this is a local case and not federal, I think."

She paused. "Actually, it depends where the bodies were found. The valley below Snowblood Peak is half owned by the federal government and half by the state. It's beautiful country."

"Huh. Well, okay. We could have jurisdiction if you feel like fighting with the state and the locals." George didn't sound encouraging.

She never felt like fighting. "Don't we have an office in Seattle?"

"Yes, but it's in flux right now. We were in the midst of creating a special unit out of there called the Pacific Northwest Violent Crimes Unit, but there was a political shakeup, a shooting, and a bunch of transfers. The office is restructuring now, and currently in place I have two agents dealing with a drug cartel." Papers shuffled across the line.

"So I'm on my own with this case, if it turns out to be anything." Which was normal for her, actually. A flight from LAX to Seattle had been scheduled to depart out of gate thirteen, and a flight from LAX to Everett had been listed as gate seventeen. "Has my flight been changed?"

More papers rustled. "Jackie?" George bellowed. "Does Snow have a new flight?"

Laurel grimaced at the sudden pain in her ear.

George returned. "You've been switched to Flight 234, leaving in ten minutes. They're holding the door open for you, but we could only get you a middle seat."

At least the gate was close to her current location, and she'd be flying into Everett, which was a quicker drive to Genesis Valley than the drive from Sea-Tac. She loped into a jog, pulling her wheeled carry-on behind her. "I only have a weekend bag and my agency-issued Glock." She hadn't brought her personal weapon.

"I'm not expecting this to be anything. I'll give you forty-eight hours to see if it's a case we want or not, and don't forget, you called in a favor," George said.

Her temples ached. "Even so, you don't want me being the face of the FBI. I don't relate well to students or prospects." At least two people had actually left during her presentation.

"Get good with people," George countered.

She reached the gate and flashed her ID to the impatient-looking gate agent. The woman kept tapping her heel. "I'm boarding. If you get any more information on the skulls, please send it to my tablet so I'm not going in blind." Her stomach cramped with instinct as well as from her knowledge of statistical probabilities. Three different skulls found on the peak?

There was a murderer close to her hometown.

Preorder Today!

You Can Run

ALSO BY & READING ORDER OF THE SERIES'

I know a lot of you like the exact reading order for a series, so here's the exact reading order as of the release of this book, although if you read most novels out of order, it's okay.

THE ANNA ALBERTINI FILES

1. Disorderly Conduct (Book 1)
2. Bailed Out (Book 2)
3. Adverse Possession (Book 3)
4. Holiday Rescue novella (Novella 3.5)
5. Santa's Subpoena (Book 4)
6. Holiday Rogue (Novella 4.5)
7. Tessa's Trust (Book 5) - TBA
8. New Anna & Aiden Book - TBA

* * *

LAUREL SNOW SERIES

1. You Can Run (Book 1)

2. You Can't Hide (Book 2) - 2022

DEEP OPS SERIES

1. Hidden (Book 1)
2. Taken Novella (Book 1.5)
3. Fallen (Book 2)
4. Shaken (in Pivot Anthology) (2.5)
5. Broken (Book 3)
6. Driven (Book 4)
7. Unforgiven (Book 5) - June 7, 2022

REDEMPTION, WY SERIES

1. Rescue Cowboy Style (Novella in the Lone Wolf Anthology)
2. Christmas story 2022 (subscribe to newsletter)
3. Novellas 2&3 in summer 2023
4. Book # 1 launch in 2024

Dark Protectors / Realm Enforcers / 1001 Dark Nights novellas

1. Fated (Dark Protectors Book 1)
2. Claimed (Dark Protectors Book 2)
3. Tempted Novella (Dark Protectors 2.5)
4. Hunted (Dark Protectors Book 3)
5. Consumed (Dark Protectors Book 4)
6. Provoked (Dark Protectors Book 5)
7. Twisted Novella (Dark Protectors 5.5)
8. Shadowed (Dark Protectors Book 6)
9. Tamed Novella (Dark Protectors 6.5)
10. Marked (Dark Protectors Book 7)
11. Wicked Ride (Realm Enforcers 1)

12. Wicked Edge (Realm Enforcers 2)
13. Wicked Burn (Realm Enforcers 3)
14. Talen Novella (Dark Protectors 7.5)
15. Wicked Kiss (Realm Enforcers 4)
16. Wicked Bite (Realm Enforcers 5)
17. Teased (Reese -1001 DN Novella)
18. Tricked (Reese-1001 DN Novella)
19. Tangled (Reese-1001 DN Novella)
20. Vampire's Faith (Dark Protectors 8) ***A great entry point for series, if you want to start here***
21. Demon's Mercy (Dark Protectors 9)
22. Vengeance (Rebels 1001 DN Novella)
23. Alpha's Promise (Dark Protectors 10)
24. Hero's Haven (Dark Protectors 11)
25. Vixen (Rebels 1001 DN Novella)
26. Guardian's Grace (Dark Protectors 12)
27. Vampire (Rebels 1001 DN Novella)
28. Rebel's Karma (Dark Protectors 13)
29. Immortal's Honor (Dark Protector 14)
30. Garrett's Destiny- 2022
31. Warrior's Hope - 2023

* * *

SIN BROTHERS/BLOOD BROTHERS spinoff

1. Forgotten Sins (Sin Brothers 1)
2. Sweet Revenge (Sin Brothers 2)
3. Blind Faith (Sin Brothers 3)
4. Total Surrender (Sin Brothers 4)
5. Deadly Silence (Blood Brothers 1)
6. Lethal Lies (Blood Brothers 2)
7. Twisted Truths (Blood Brothers 3)

* * *

SCORPIUS SYNDROME SERIES
**This is technically the right timeline, but I'd always meant for the series to start with Mercury Striking.
Scorpius Syndrome/The Brigade Novellas

- 1. Scorpius Rising
- 2. Blaze Erupting
- 3. Power Surging - TBA
- 4. Hunter Advancing - TBA

Scorpius Syndrome NOVELS
1. Mercury Striking (Scorpius Syndrome 1)
2. Shadow Falling (Scorpius Syndrome 2)
3. Justice Ascending (Scorpius Syndrome 3)
4. Storm Gathering (Scorpius Syndrome 4)
5. Winter Igniting (Scorpius Syndrome 5)
6. Knight Awakening (Scorpius Synd. 6)

* * *

MAVERICK MONTANA SERIES

1. Against the Wall
2. Under the Covers
3. Rising Assets
4. Over the Top
5. Bundle of Books 1-3

ABOUT THE AUTHOR

New York Times and *USA Today bestselling* author Rebecca Zanetti has published more than fifty romantic-suspense and dark paranormal novels, which have been translated into several languages, with millions of copies sold world-wide. Her books have received Publisher's Weekly starred reviews, won RT Reviewer Choice awards, have been featured in Entertainment Weekly, Woman's World and Women's Day Magazines, have been included in retailer's best books of the year, and have been favorably reviewed in both the Washington Post and the New York Times Book Reviews. Rebecca has ridden in a locked Chevy trunk, has asked the unfortunate delivery guy to release her from a set of handcuffs, and has discovered the best silver mine shafts in which to bury a body...all in the name of research. Honest. Find Rebecca at: www.RebeccaZanetti.com